pretty little sinner

NORTHERN REJECTS - BOOK THREE

ANNA FURY

copyright

Editing - Mountains Wanted Editing

Proofreading - BooksChecked

Cover - GetCovers & Anna Fury

Cover Photo - James Critchley Photography and DepositPhotos

❀ Created with Vellum

For every girl who ever wanted a boyfriend AND a daddy...

content notice

Pretty Little Sinner is an omegaverse romance, and as such, deals with difficult topics like generalized violence, possessiveness, physical dominance, consent and more. This book in particular also references kidnapping of adults, drugs, a car wreck resulting in trauma, human abuse and trafficking at a high level. It is intended for mature audiences due to the dark themes.

Still, this series is all about the alpharoll hero - my men are possessive, dominant, and kind. They've got hearts of gold and abs of steel.

Hit me up with questions! author@annafury.com

a quick note

This book features a deaf character named Julia. Julia is smart, loving, sassy and one of my favorite characters I've ever written! Because this is a made-up world, I took a few liberties with my storyline as it relates to Julia's hearing loss. For instance, nearly the whole pack learned sign language quickly. In real life, sign language fluency would take a long time to learn well.

Also, because sign language is "speaking", you'll notice the use of verbs like "says" or "told" when referencing her. That is not an error, it's intentional because she is speaking in ASL.

While I did have sensitivity readers read Julia's parts to give me suggestions, I'm aware it's not possible to encompass all deaf and hard of hearing peoples' experiences. My fervent hope is that I've created an amazing character who feels real.

Huge thanks to Brittany and others for taking the time to help!

what came before

When the Awaken Virus hit humanity, men became ravenous, uncontrollable beasts. They wrought destruction across the globe, causing humans to live in fear.

But then billionaire Mitchell Bancroft's alpha pack broke the news that the Awakened weren't all they seemed. There's a softer side to alphas, a side the world should know about.

This series takes place immediately after the end of The Alpha Compound Series. While there's no need to read that series to enjoy this one, it's got all the same vibes and it's hella sexy.

You can find it on Amazon.

get the freebies

WANT SPICY AUDIO AND EBOOK EPILOGUES?

Sign up for my newsletter at www.annafury.com to access the FREE bonus epilogues to every book I write.

LOVE ISN'T A BUCKET THAT'S DONE WHEN IT'S FULL.
THERE'S INFINITE SPACE IN YOUR HEART TO LOVE
SOMEONE OR SOMEONES...

LOVE IS A MULTIPLIER OF ALL THINGS

- CONNOR FROM WIDE AWAKE, BY ANNA FURY

CHAPTER ONE

I'M a big fan of the age-old adage that you don't go to bed angry. My father drilled that into my three brothers and me.

I'm a bigger fan of a saying I made up myself: always wake your mate with an extra dose of happy.

Which is why I scoot my way under the covers, pressing Julia's pale, freckled thighs out wide to slide my tongue over her clit. Her body reacts to me before she begins to wake, slick wetting that sweet pink pussy. I alpha purr for her, letting the vibration in my chest serve as her sexy alarm clock.

Julia lets out a soft moan as I suck gently on the soft skin of her inner thigh. I turn my attention back to her clit, teasing as she shoves the covers off, propping her head up on the pillow so she can watch me.

"Every morning?" she teases in ASL.

"I need to watch you fall apart at least once before breakfast," I confirm before returning my hands to her hips, my tongue seeking entry deeper into her wet heat.

Julia's spine arches, her hands coming to the back of my head. It's a possessive touch, and it lights a fire in my chest, knowing if I pulled away from her, she'd drag me back for more. She can't resist me—she never could, not since the day we met.

When my former pack fled the American Task Force, which was created to round up transitioned alphas, I found a new home here in Canada. I connected with the Canadian pack, and they needed a brilliant tech whiz who loves security. Between that and laying eyes on Jules that first day, I knew I'd never leave Bent Fork Ranch.

Delicate hips begin to quiver under my hands as I hum into my mate's skin. Dragging my nails down her thighs, I revel in the way her hips buck, my mouth sliding along her heat. I know just what she needs.

Remember our first kiss? I tease into our mate bond as her breath ramps into desperate, short pants.

Our first kiss was stolen up against the side of the lodge, my hands all over her body. I knew when I kissed her that I'd be keeping her forever. I left my pack for hers, knowing no force on this earth could part me from her. They understood, because there's no power stronger than the bond between an alpha and his omega.

A ragged scream tears from my omega's throat as bliss overtakes her, dainty thighs clamping around my head as our mate bond lights up with satisfaction. I lick her all the way through it, sending heat along our bond, letting her know how in love with her I am.

Always you, I whisper into that golden tether, smiling as I press a soft kiss to her clit. She rocks against me but shudders, wriggling out from under my hold. Our bond thrums with the heady weight of her love.

"On your back," she signs.

"You haven't even had coffee yet," I counter, my hands moving quickly as I shoot her a wink.

She slaps my chest before repeating her demand more forcefully, blue eyes sparking with mischief.

Grinning, I flop down beside her and pull her on top of me, groaning at the feel of her lithe, delicate body against mine. She's the tiniest woman I've ever met, and some days I still can't believe she fits with a male who stands two feet taller than her.

But fit me she does. God, she fits me well.

I wanna suck you off, she teases into our bond. *And I want you to tell me what you're thinking about while I do.*

That request causes me to tense slightly. It's a new game for us, a game loaded with tension and aching. Because there's a particular subject who's taking up more and more space in both of our playful daydreams.

Cassian.

He isn't technically part of our pack, but he helped us save our packmates from his psychotic former alpha, Declan. Needless to say, Cass is staying with us for now. But if Jules and I have our way, he'll never leave.

Julia slides down my much larger body, hovering pink lips just over my hard cock, a knowing smile on her face. *You're thinking about him, aren't you?* she questions into the bond, swirling her tongue around my cock as heat shoots up both thighs, settling with sharp intensity in my stomach.

My mate sucks softly, then takes me as far down her throat as she can with a happy hum. *Are you wondering if he could take you farther?* She pauses as I thrust up into her lips. *I'd love to see him try.*

I let out a groan at the idea of the powerful silver fox alpha on his knees before me, Julia watching us fuck. I want it. I've wanted it since I met him, the same way I wanted her the day I arrived at Bent Fork Ranch with Mitchell Bancroft's pack months ago from New York. We were running for our lives, but everything changed for me when I met her.

My head falls back as Julia takes me harder, faster. And I fantasize about Cass's beautiful lips, imagining them stretched around my big black cock. I want to know what it looks like for all three of us to be tangled up in this bed together. I'm desperate to sandwich Julia between us and take her in every way a woman can be taken by two dominant men.

Not men—*alphas*.

My mind wanders to the unleashing of the Awaken virus over four years ago. I was terrified in those early days, watching men contract it and become raging, violent monsters. But then I transitioned and never hurt anyone at all. I eventually stumbled on Mitchell's pack and made my way here to the western slopes of the Canadian Rockies.

I'm grateful for the virus, because if I hadn't become an alpha, I wouldn't be here right now, enjoying my favorite person in the whole fucking world.

Well, one of my two favorite people. Because the second one still hasn't joined us like this yet.

I want it so badly.

With a choked roar, I fill Julia's mouth with my seed, white-hot heat barreling along our bond as she swallows what she can. And then she looks up at me with a devilish grin. *I imagined him too, you know.*

I groan and haul her up onto my lap, parting her thighs as I thrust up into her. Her head falls forward as we let out matching gasps. I marvel at how her pale skin looks pressed to my pitch-black shade. And then I take her hard and fast with my teeth in her throat as we fantasize together about the alpha we've started teasing.

It's not simple teasing to me though. Or to her.

We want him.

And we will have him—no matter what it takes.

Half an hour later, my mate is sated and curled up in bed with a coffee while I head for my pack alpha, Stone's, office. Our whole leadership crew is gathering early—there's a lot to discuss.

Stone looks up when I come in, dark eyes sparking as he waves his radio at me. His dirty blond hair is slicked back, harkening to the days when he played for the masses on a concert stage—but that was before the virus. Technically, alphas are still illegal, although Canada isn't rounding us up anymore. The world is changing—slowly.

Stone smirks. "I called you a while ago, brother. You too busy to get down here on time?" There's no hint of malice in his words though. He just likes to give me shit, even though he's newly mated to our town's mayor. Feigning grumpiness is his permanent state of being.

"My father taught me how important it is to dote on your partner. I was doting," I joke back with a wink.

Stone snorts, but he really can't say shit. He's wrapped around his omega's finger like a pretzel. He dotes harder than any alpha I've ever met, a fact I love to tease him about. The reality is that while alphas hurt a lot of people in the beginning days of the virus, there's a lot more to our packs than that.

Most alphas love hard and mate harder. We band together like this pack has. And even though I can't travel home to visit my father and brothers in New York City, I think there's a future where that'll be possible.

I settle down at the conference table in Stone's massive office that borders the back of the expansive lodge at Bent Fork Ranch. When I look out the window, I'm treated to an incredible view of the valley our home sits in. There's still a dusting of snow on the ground, reminding me of New York, not that I miss it. I miss my human family, but the Big Apple itself? Nah.

Although, I'll admit, the idea of showing Julia around New York does give me a thrill.

Maybe someday.

A huge figure sits next to Stone, striking blue eyes focusing on the television, which is already tuned to the BBC news station. Our pack enforcer, Titan, is in charge of overall security. As our resident tech whiz, I work closely with him to keep our pack safe. I imagine he's been watching the news for a while.

"Anything yet?" I question the red-headed alpha who sits at Titan's other side.

Clay, our strategist, shakes his head. "Nothing yet, but that's not wholly unexpected. It's only midday in the UK. I'd expect our news to go live during the evening broadcast."

An uncomfortable prickle raises the hair on my nape as I look at Clay. "You think there's a chance they won't break the story about Declan's crimes?"

Clay sighs. "I'm trying to be optimistic, because we want to force Declan's hand so we can rescue his pack's omegas, but the fact we haven't seen the story go live yet troubles me."

Frowning, I steeple my fingers and open the laptop I brought with me, scanning the security program I developed. It tracks not only activity around the lodge, but the whole valley too. It's a new addition to the multitude of ways I keep a wary eye on our home. Declan has committed too many crimes for us to risk our safety.

Titan frowns over at me. "Any activity at the old mill, James?"

I scan through the log of past security events and nod, sighing as I click on the recorded video for the timestamps. What I see sends my heart up into my throat. "Nothing going out via the train line like before, but more alphas are arriving. A dozen maybe. Where the fuck is Declan bringing them in from?"

Across from me, Clay lets out a frustrated growl. "At this point, we have to assume that asshole is building an army. Our packs are evenly matched right now, which probably keeps him from being any crazier than he is."

"No omegas have arrived though?" Stone's deep voice takes on a curious lilt as I shake my head.

"All alphas."

Stone scratches at his five o'clock shadow and looks up at the ceiling, lost in thought.

The office door swings open, and I forget to breathe for a moment. Cassian appears in the doorway, an enormous figure taking up nearly the whole space. Salt-and-pepper hair is gelled back and shaved short on the sides. A matching five o'clock shadow lines his angular jaw. He's a sexy biker romance book cover if I ever saw one, down to the big rings he wears on both hands. The only thing he's missing is the black leather jacket. Shit, he's even got a Harley Davidson motorcycle parked out front right now.

He steps gracefully into the room, stalking across Stone's expansive office and settling down in the chair next to me. I work to close my mouth, because I'm sure I gaped in awe when he came in.

Fuck me, he smells good. Clean like aftershave but deep and manly and dominant. He's a pack alpha the same way Stone is. It's not natural to have two in one pack. But somehow, with Cassian, it works.

Or maybe that's just wishful thinking on my part since all I wanna do is fuck him and keep him forever.

I've always known I was bi, but I've never talked to Cass about it. I'd like to explore that conversation and ask what he thin—

"Anything happen yet?" Cass's deep voice breaks through my fantasy. I shrug against the weight of his resonant, commanding tone. Squirming in my seat, I clamp my thighs together and study my computer screen, forcing myself not to watch the way Cass's power hits the rest of our leadership group.

Stone shakes his head. "Nothing yet."

Displeasure rolls off Cass as he glances at me, pale gray eyes focused when I look up. He escaped from Declan's pack. He's well aware of what an asshole Declan is. Declan has killed and injured people, and he gets away with it every time because he's the Deputy Prime Minister's goddamn nephew—a fact I uncovered after countless hours digging through police reports and red tape. I've tapped into enough government servers at this point that if they ever figure out it was me, I'll spend several lifetimes in prison.

Cass's gray eyes pause on mine for a moment, but just when I think he's about to say something, River sails through the door with a mock salute. I grin, because her showing up usually means she's here to needle Stone about something. The plucky teen omega loves to nitpick him to pieces, and for all his bluster and bark, he loves it. He and his mate Erin dote on River and her twin like crazy. I don't think they can help it, not since Titan invited them into our pack.

River stops next to Stone, bumping him with her shoulder. "You're looking especially somber, alpha. BBC didn't break the story about Declan and the DPM's connection?"

Stone shakes his head, dark eyes glittering as River crosses her arms. "Cool. Can a couple of us go into town then?"

Cass shifts in his chair next to me, and I sense he's holding back from barking at the teenager.

Stone turns in his seat to look at her. "River, just because the BBC hasn't blown Declan sky high doesn't mean it's safe to go into town. I'd rather you didn't."

"I'm so bored," she grumbles, rolling her eyes. "It's not like me and Rogue can do anything to help. Please, please, please, please…" she continues as Stone shakes his head. But then she starts poking his shoulder and tickling his neck, until finally he swats her hands away, snapping his fangs at her fingertips.

"Don't go without Titan or Cass," Stone snaps. "If they'll take you, you can go."

"Well shit," Cass growls next to me. River bounds over, throwing her arms around Cass's big neck as he rolls his eyes, frowning as I huff out a laugh.

River is nothing if not persistent.

On cue, she starts up a needy whine, arms still around Cass's neck. "Aww, come on, alpha. We're not that bad. Please take us into town before I shrivel into a dry husk of pure boredom."

Cass's pale eyes flick to me and then over to Titan. "I'm busy until this afternoon, but I'll take you later, alright? Unless Titan can take you now?" He gives Titan a hopeful look.

Titan snorts. "Hell no."

"Thank fuck," River shouts, blushing when Titan scowls. "Cass talks more than you do." She shrugs as she winks at him, although I see the edges of his mouth curl up into a smile.

"Language, young lady!" Stone barks from the other end of the table.

"Lay down the law, Daddy Stone!" Clay laughs from his spot next to Titan. Both he and my enforcer barely restrain grins as Stone grumbles from the head of the table.

River leans over Cass's broad chest to peck him on the cheek. Shit, I want to do that. She sails out of the room as Stone massages his temples, eyes closed.

Cass clears his throat and looks at Titan. "I'm more certain by the minute that it's a bad sign we haven't seen anything on the news yet. Declan being the Deputy Prime Minister's nephew is a big fucking deal. It explains so much of why he runs rampant around here, and our police reports disappear into a hole. This story should be all over the TV. He killed two people, for God's sake."

Titan nods slowly, turning from the television to look at Cassian. "Agreed, alpha. Somehow, when the evening news rolls around, I don't think we'll see mention of Declan's connection to the DPM on it."

I let out an angry growl. It took me days to figure out that connection. But I did it because Declan has committed crime after crime, and no matter how many times we report him, nothing ever changes. Alphas have a habit of taking the law into our own hands. Declan's connection at the topmost levels of our government changes that, though, because if we come down hard on him, there's sure to be blowback.

Cass shifts in his chair, crosses his legs at the ankle and strokes his short beard, lost in thought. "So, we've got a dossier full of proof that Declan is not only connected to the DPM, but his crimes have been covered up. The BBC should be breaking that news today, but they're not. I think the question is why..."

Clay shrugs. "BBC is a British station, so it's entirely possible someone above the DPM orchestrated this, or that the DPM has a connection and pulled in a favor. I can't help but think this is politically motivated. The DPM has not been pro-alpha rights."

Clay looks over at Stone. "If they don't air the news today, I think we can assume what we've already guessed—the DPM is fine with Declan wreaking havoc here in Ayas, and has no plans to put a stop to that, despite sending out a so-called handler to keep Declan in line."

Next to me, Cass sighs and rubs his temples. "We need to revisit our plan for rescuing the omegas from his pack, given this new information. We only held off because this story was supposed to force Declan's hand and help us avoid an outright fight. I don't think that's the case now."

"Agreed," Stone murmurs, looking over at our side of the table.

"If we have to go in and get them, we should ask Isabel to share more about her time in that pack. Any piece of intel we can get will be helpful if it's coming down to a fight." Cassian sounds confident as he shares the beginnings of a new plan.

"I hate to ask her to relive any of that," Stone counters, "but if you think she'd be willing to, we should ask her."

Cass nods. "I have no doubt she will. I'll speak with her later, and we can talk after dinner."

I nibble at the edge of my lip while I consider that. Declan nearly killed the pregnant omega, leaving her for dead when he burned our pack's general store. She's barely healed from that. Plus, she gave birth just a few days ago. To say she's been through hell and back barely covers it.

My eyes drop back to my computer screen as I rack my brain for any idea of how to do the right thing and protect not only my pack, but the broader valley, from our biggest foe.

CHAPTER TWO

I HOLD back a snicker when the door to my bedroom flies open, and Luna rushes in with Cherry in tow. Luna's blond waves bounce as she drags Cherry by the hand, a wry smile on Cherry's round face. I smile at my omega packmates—they're so fucking great.

"Guess what arrived?" Luna signs. When she drops her hands, I realize she must not know how to sign what's next. Either that or she's so excited, her hands can't keep up with her mouth. That's the more likely option.

Cherry drops Luna's hand and translates as Luna barrels on, practically vibrating with joy. "I'm sorry I don't know all these signs yet, Jules, but I swear I'm working hard to pick them up fast."

I raise my hands to tell her I get it; ASL is hard as fuck to learn. I should know—I got a crash course three years ago when an accident robbed me of my hearing. I was lucky to pick it up fast and had a lot of help doing so. Not everyone has that benefit.

Cherry translates for Luna, "My girlfriend sent all my

clothes from California, and the festival gear arrived today. Wanna try it on with us?"

While I can't hear Luna's words aloud, I can just imagine how bubbly and happy her voice would be right now. Although, in my head, I picture her sounding like Taylor Swift, a little bit of throaty depth to her despite how bubbly and effervescent she is. It's a game I play with myself since losing my hearing—what famous person do my friends sound like?

"Festival gear?" I risk a glance over at Cherry, wondering how she feels about this. She's hardly been in party mode these last few months. But to my surprise, she looks happy about this news. Maybe her new gig stripping at the Moonlight is why she's into the sexy clothing.

Luna's eyes drop to the tablet in my lap. "Whatcha drawing?" She's learned those signs well. I've taken up digital art recently —it helps me channel my emotions when they feel big and over-whelming. Lately that's been more and more necessary. So many external forces are pushing and pulling our pack right now.

Not to mention the sexual tension between James, Cassian and myself.

Drawing is a good outlet. Fucking would be better, but I'm still working on that.

Smirking, I flip the tablet around. Luna takes one look and pretends to faint into Cherry's arms as she fans herself.

"That's your sexiest work yet," Cherry signs with a wink. "Gonna show it to Cass and see what he thinks?"

"I might," I respond. "Maybe that'll tip him over the edge into joining James and me."

My obsession with our current house guest is no secret. Shit, he's aware of it too. But since he's so clearly a pack alpha, I understand his resistance to joining James and me. James didn't shift when he mated me, which means he's probably our pack's healer or spirit. Cassian can't be either of those—the only designations that mate in a triad. It's not as if he can switch his designation. He is what he is. He believes that's problematic—but I don't.

The fact he's a pack alpha hasn't stopped me from knowing in my heart he's mine. The pull I feel toward him is as strong as the one I feel for James. I need them both. And I will have them, no matter what I have to do to get Cass to open his eyes.

Zipping my lips, I toss the tablet down onto the bed and look up at the omegas. "You gonna show me all this sexy gear or what?"

"Yes!" shouts Luna. Lip reading is hard as hell, but that one was obvious as she starts jumping up and down with excitement. She picks up her walkie, and moments later the twins and Sal show up.

They're all new to sign language as well, so Cherry translates as Rogue gives me a devilish grin. "I heard you all were gonna be trying on sexy lingerie. I'm here for it."

"Not lingerie," Luna corrects. "Festival wear."

When Rogue gives her a confused look, she clarifies, "Music festivals? EDM? Never heard of it?"

Rogue's face falls slightly. "River and I have been on the run since the early days of the virus. We were like, what, Riv...fourteen when I transitioned and we left home? Festivals weren't really top of mind."

Luna's face falls, and she throws herself into the big teen alpha's arms.

When she pulls away, she gives me a baleful look. "I'm sorry," she signs. "I'm an asshole."

Rogue musses her hair and rubs his cheek along hers in a friendly way. "Not your fault the virus made me an alpha," he corrects gently. "There's nowhere else I'd rather be than here with all of you. It was kismet we met Titan and he suggested Stone take us in."

Cherry follows their words with her hands since the twins

are still learning ASL too. I fucking adore that soon our entire house will be signing. It sort of feels like I'm taking over the world, and I love it.

"Okay," I sign quickly. "I need snacks if we're gonna do this. Let me run to the kitchen and see what we've got. Any requests?"

"Halo Top!"

"Cheetos!"

"Ramen!" That last one comes from River and causes me to hold back a ragged laugh. That girl is nearly as obsessed with ramen as Stone is. What a weird food to love so deeply. Truly, I think it's what bonds them together.

Giving my packmates two thumbs up, I grab my tablet, lest anyone decide to take a sneak peek. There are some half-finished pics that are so scandalous I haven't shown anyone yet —not even James. Suffice to say, the idea of two big dicks swinging around together gets me hot.

Heading down the broad staircase to the first floor, I cross the lobby to the kitchen. I make River a bowl of ramen and grab tons of other snacks, throwing them in a fabric bag that I sling over my shoulder.

I turn to grab a plate when the hair on the back of my neck stands, heat making its way through my chest. There's a moment when stabbing heat bundles in my core, and then I whip around. Cassian is right behind me, so close I could reach out and touch his chest. I'm so surprised to see him standing there, I throw my hands up, tossing the tablet and the plate and dropping the bag of snacks.

Cassian scrambles to grab the tablet, but time slows, and we watch it fall to the ground. It bounces once and spins on its corner.

Then it falls face up.

My drawing of him fucking James is clearly visible on the tablet's brightly lit screen.

Oh my fucking God. I was gonna ease him into my dirty drawings with a to-be-determined sexy plan, but now I'm mortified.

Against my better judgment, I look up at Cass, and his gray eyes are on me, his lips slightly parted. His tan cheeks are flushed pink as sharp fangs slide down from his upper lip. His pupils blow wide as he takes a step toward me, then shifts backward, seeming to think better of it.

God, I ache to put my hands on him, to slide them up his jean shirt and rip it down the front. I want to examine the tattoos that snake up both arms and across his chest. Jesus, I want to lick him so badly. I bite my lip to avoid panting with need.

I open my mouth to say something, anything, but Cass drops to one knee. I'm ashamed to admit that seeing his head down around my waist makes me want to fist his salt-and-pepper hair and shove my crotch in his face. His mouth is literally pussy-level right now. And I know what it feels like for him to put those soft lips on me. We shared a stolen afternoon once, months before I met James.

I can't help myself, so I take a step closer. Gray eyes flick up to me, then back down to my waist. His tongue peeks out to run along his bottom lip before he bites it. I desperately want to know if he's thinking about that day he found me sunbathing nude at the hot springs. He did delicious things to my body then, and I need it again.

That was all before James, but James doesn't change what I want. If anything, my desire for Cass is even worse now, because James wants it as badly as I do.

One big hand reaches for the tablet as my cheeks heat. Cass takes it and stands, his pale eyes drinking in the scene.

Is he shocked by what he sees? Turned on? Mad? Maybe he feels violated?

In this drawing, he's behind James, whose black skin is a

stark contrast to Cass's paler tone. One muscular, tattooed arm is wrapped around James's torso so he can fist my mate's cock. His teeth are buried in James's neck as James cries out in pleasure. Cass is dominating James in this pic, something James and I have fantasized about many times.

It's triple X artwork for sure, and Cass just stares.

After an eternity of time passes, during which I hold my chin high and try not to look as embarrassed as I feel, he hands the tablet to me.

Cass lifts his hands to sign a response when two figures come through the open doorway. Sal, one of the omegas we rescued from Declan's shitty pack, lights up when she sees Cass. She speaks animatedly as Cass turns back to me, signing that she came to help with the snacks.

I grin and hand her the bag of junk food. She wraps both arms around Cass and squeezes him tight as he murmurs something in her ear.

River, who came with her, grabs the ramen and a spoon and heads for the door. With Cass's back to her, she looks at me and gyrates her hips in a wild, suggestive motion. I bite back a laugh, wondering if Cass can scent how hot I am from what just happened between us.

Sal extricates herself from Cass's embrace and looks at me. She's learning ASL fast, but it's so hard, she can only do words here and there.

"I need. Talk. Cassian," she signs.

Ah.

Well, shit, girl, get in line, is what I want to say. Poor thing was tortured by her former pack, and it's a miracle our enforcer, Titan, was able to save her. It's been a big deal for her even to leave her room in the lodge. Cassian is practically her lifeline, and I refuse to stand in the way of their connection.

I give her a friendly smile and nod, then leave the kitchen, disappointment settling in my gut.

CHAPTER THREE

cassian

JULIA LEAVES, and it takes every ounce of my formidable control not to watch her go.

Sal chuckles and slaps my chest. "Oh boy, you've got it pretty bad, huh?"

"Got what?" I murmur vaguely, as if it isn't obvious to this whole pack that I want the diminutive omega just as much as she wants me.

Sal's smile falls. "I'm not gonna bother to state the obvious. But if you ever want to talk about it, I'm here for you, alpha." Her blue eyes flick to mine as I pull her in for another hug. I'm not just an alpha, I'm a pack alpha. I'm drawn to protect Sal the same way I was when we both lived with Declan.

Fucking prick.

"I'm worried about the girls we left behind at Declan's," she whispers.

"Me too," I remind her. "I won't rest until I get them out, Sal. You know that, right?"

"Of course," she whispers. "It just feels like with Declan blowing up the research trailer and burning the store and almost killing Izzy…our reasonable plans got smashed to smithereens, and now I don't know what we're going to do."

It's a painful reminder of the drama my former pack alpha Declan caused over a week ago. The only good thing to come out of it was the fact that now two of Declan's omegas are here instead of there. Six remain stuck in his pack, hostages at his mercy.

It's a relief to have two of the girls here and safe, but I think about the others twenty-four hours a day.

"If the story doesn't air, we'll have to take a more forceful approach," I share, wanting her to know what's realistically in our future.

"I know," she whispers, throwing her arms around my middle. "I'm terrified for you, because I know you'll want to lead that charge. But if there's any other possible way that's not an outright war, I know you'll think of it."

"It's on my mind constantly," I admit as I rub her back.

"Imagine what it must be like in Declan's pack without you to protect the girls," Sal says sadly, her blue eyes filled with tears. "You were literally my godsend while I was there. I think I would have lost my mind if you didn't protect me from the rest of those assholes."

Sharp pressure crushes my lungs in my chest. If I'm honest, I expected we'd need a Plan B. Initially I planned to involve Mitchell Bancroft's pack—they're larger, and their omegas have already developed powers. But the reality is he's back and forth to the States constantly as he works to secure alpha rights, something that's arguably more important than the small packs in this valley. I can't count on him to be there to help get my girls out.

Sal pats my chest again, seeing I'm lost in thought, before leaving to find the twins. Despite my worry for the omegas, my brain circuits back to Julia and her tablet. Her fresh berry scent still fills the kitchen, so I breathe her in, closing my eyes. She smells heavenly.

I've been here a week, dodging her advances and trying not to stare at James, but seeing Julia's fantasy of what it might be like for us to touch was shocking.

I've never fucked another man. It's not even that I necessarily think of myself as straight. I'm aware there's a spectrum of attraction, but I've always been more attracted to women than men. I never thought about men romantically at all until eight years ago when my wife suggested bringing my best friend into bed with us. At the time, I wasn't interested in that, and eventually she took him into our bed without me there.

That was a breach of trust, and I've been alone since then. I was happy with that until I met Julia.

Breaking out of the piss-poor memory of my ex-wife's infidelity, I shake my head to urge the sensual image of James and me away. Still, it stays with me all the way to the front of the house.

Grabbing my walkie in case the news happens to break, I head toward the pack's general store site, halfway up the valley between the lodge and the street. I need to work off my frustration at our current state of affairs. Plus, I'm hoping the twins forget about the plan to go into town by the time I get a few things done.

Stone had a roll-off dumpster delivered so we can demo the general store and start over. Declan, fucking asshole, burned it to a crisp, along with a trailer that houses a team of government researchers. They're ostensibly here to learn about alphas, but I can't shake the sense that the Canadian Alpha Research Group isn't on alphas' side. Especially given Stone didn't apply to have his pack be part of the research in the first place. That's another thing I'm relatively certain Declan had a hand in, maybe through his connection to the DPM.

The bigger question is why would he even care?

We're enmeshed in a spider web of Declan's making, and somehow the threads continue to pull tighter while we endeavor to take the high road. I should have just killed him when I lived with him. When I imagine the suffering he's visited on other packs and the humans in this valley, I want to punch myself for not taking him out when we met.

Sighing, I walk through the blackened, charred remains of the site that functions as not only a store for this pack, but travelers passing through who don't want to take the extra half hour to get to the small town of Ayas. It's not a particularly busy store, but it's a nice little reminder to regular humans that alpha packs aren't all assholes, despite what they've seen on the news for years.

When I hear an ATV, I look toward the lodge to find the pack's seer, Asher Chen, headed my direction. His dark hair waves in the chilly breeze, and there's a slight smile on his face.

He parks the ATV next to the dumpster and hops off with a big grin. "Thought I might help you out here for a bit. I can't sit there anymore and watch the BBC not break our fucking story. I'm about to go crazy. Well, crazier than I already am."

I gesture to an extra pair of gloves on the edge of the roll-off. "Happy to have the help, seer."

He blanches at his official title. "It doesn't feel right to call me that when I'm a fucking basket case. I haven't foreseen any of the shit Declan's done."

My alpha senses ping. Asher's had a tough go the last few years. He was the Awaken virus's very first victim after his father and sister accidentally created it and let it escape—not that that's public news. Pain followed him for years after that, and he's wallowing in misery at this point.

"I'm not typically a fan of telling another man to get his head out of his ass, but it's time, Ash," I growl. "You're so worried about the voices in your head that you're failing to actually look for a way through this shit. And not only are you miserable, but you're making your mate miserable."

Ash snarls at me but looks in the direction of the tiny cabin on-property, the last building before the turnoff from the highway. I moved Cherry into that cabin just yesterday because she couldn't stand to be in the main lodge any longer. Ash balls his fists, his body vibrating with tension.

"There's a lot of power in you, alpha," I reassure him. "And we need you to come into it for the good of not only yourself, but everybody else here."

"You and Stone sound like a bad song on repeat," he spits. "I'm not like other seers. I—"

"You're seeing mate bonds, aren't you?"

"Yeah, but—"

"You're a goddamn seer, Ash, and you have a mate who desperately wants you. Every time you push her away, you break her heart."

He crosses his arms, his foot tapping on the ground. "Better to have a broken heart than to be hurt by your own fucking alpha." His words are angry and bitter.

Turning to him, I step over bits of burnt wood and look him dead in the eye. "I don't believe for a second that you'd ever hurt her, and neither does she."

"Yeah, well, the things I want to do to her are dark," he snaps. "I can't control my thoughts most of the time."

"Maybe she likes dark," I counter. "Maybe what Cherry wants is for you to choke the shit out of her or run her down in the woods. Do you even know, alpha? Have you even asked? Maybe there's a darkness in her that matches the darkness in you."

Ash looks disconcerted by my frank words, but it's my opinion that Stone coddles him too much. I'm not this pack's alpha, but I can't help giving out advice. I'm older than everyone here by a solid fifteen or twenty years. I have a lot of life experience.

And what Ash needs, in my opinion, is a swift kick in the ass.

"Cherry came out to her cabin a little while ago," I offer in a kinder tone. "Why don't you ask her to take a walk with you? Head into the woods for a bit, maybe put a move or two on her. Ask for her help tackling the issue rather than letting it be between you. Remind her how much you want her."

"Oh, like you and Jules?" he snaps back. "You gonna take your own advice, alpha?"

I let out an angry laugh. "If I thought I could make her mine and not tear this pack apart, I would. But you all have something good going on here. She and James are great together."

"They *both* want you," Asher states. "It's clear as day."

"Let me ask you this then," I counter, irritated that he's deflecting his issues back onto me. "Do you see a mate bond between the three of us? Because if you do, I'll drop what I'm doing this second and go up to the lodge to take them."

Asher's mouth closes into a tight line as his eyes narrow. But he says nothing.

"That's what I thought," I snap. "So I can't fuck up the good thing they have going. James is most likely your healer or spirit. They need a mate who can fulfill the partner designation, and it's not me."

For a long moment, Asher stares at me, and I wonder if he's going to tell me I've got it wrong. That he sees a golden thread binding me to Julia and James. But he says nothing, instead stalking toward Cherry's cabin as he mutters about alpha assholes under his breath.

I watch him go, and then I get to work as disappointment settles heavy in my chest.

CHAPTER FOUR

julia

I DON'T KNOW what I thought Luna meant by festival wear, maybe some sexy tank tops and bedazzled shorts. I was woefully unprepared for see-through plastic bras and assless chaps covered in sequins. Every fucking piece of this wardrobe, if you can call it that, has fringe. We could be headed straight for Burning Man with this gear.

It's beautiful.

Luna stands in front of the fireplace in my room, attaching a fringy strap to a clip at the front of barely-there latex panties. She clips it at the back too, and a drape of fringe sways along her outer thigh. She starts dancing in the room as we all snicker and laugh.

My door opens, and Titan, our pack enforcer, comes in. His face is drawn and worried until he sees Luna, every bit of her sensual figure on display. Blue eyes narrow as his lips part. His grip on the doorknob tightens.

I want a certain silver-fox alpha to look at me with such ferocity so badly, I feel like I might die.

Titan stalks across the room as Luna scoots around a chair, dodging out of his way. He catches her easily and tosses her up over his enormous shoulder, laying a hard smack on her ass as she pretends to fight him.

Looking over at me, Rogue and the twins, he grins. "Self-defense practice in the morning, okay?" he signs. After Declan's recent attack, he's requiring all the omegas and the twins to take self-defense seriously. It's a good plan, because we'd be sitting ducks right now if someone from Declan's pack cornered us.

"Hell yes!" I respond, my eyes traveling to Luna's sparkly ass as she continues to beat his back with her tiny fists.

Titan pinches one tan ass cheek and then stalks out of the room, hauling his mate with him.

I search inward into my own mating bond, tugging softly at James. He feels worried and anxious, and I wish I could help. *I'm gonna go tease Cass a little bit; you wanna come?*

You're doing the good lord's work for us, baby girl. I can't leave the office right now, but send me sexy teasers. Imagining you touching him has me so hard, Jules.

Wish you could come too, though, I grumble. We've discussed the teasing a lot. We're both fine—excited, even—to get time with Cass alone. But I'm still anxious to have them at the same time.

Smiling, I look over at my packmates and sign to let them know I'm leaving.

The twins and Sal haven't picked up enough ASL yet to respond fully, although they're trying so hard, and I love them for it. "Tell Cass hi," River signs, grabbing Sal around the waist and pretending to hump her. Sal's dark waves fly all over as she tries to extricate herself from River's embrace.

I snort out a laugh as Rogue slaps his sister, and Sal cackles. Rogue signs, "Tell him hi, and good luck," with a suggestive wink.

I need it.

I know Cass is working on the general store site right now. James and my room is at the front of the lodge, and I totally sat in my window and watched Cass walk all the way up there. God, that man can fill out a pair of jeans.

Throwing on a thick coat, I run to the kitchen to grab a few things, then hop on an ATV and gun it for the work site. The chilly winter breeze freezes my cheeks as I revel in the feel of my strawberry blond hair waving behind me like a flag. Our valley is so beautiful, all flat along the middle with aspen and pine forests covering the hills on either side. I pass the mostly empty cabins that dot the valley floor as I head for the aspen grove our former store sits in.

When I park at the site, Cassian stands there, a suspicious look on his face.

I smile at him and grab the small cooler bag I brought with me, picking my way across the burnt debris until I stand in front of him.

Cassian is so big, I have to tilt my head way back to look up at him. Pale gray eyes are carefully neutral, although the hint of a smile tugs one side of his plush lips upward. Lips I had on my body once, long before I met James. I know what his mouth feels like between my thighs, and I'm desperate for more of the same—with James, without James, all over James.

Reaching into the bag, I pull out a bottle full of lemonade. "Thought you might be thirsty." I give him a little wink and hand him an airplane bottle of gin from my pocket. "It's gonna be a long day; might as well make it a good one."

Cassian laughs, opening the bottle I handed him.

"Bring one for yourself, little omega?" He signs, but his voice is so deep I feel it in my chest when he talks. I can't hear him, but this close, the low vibration is tangible.

Nodding, I grab another couple bottles, and he helps me make a strong-ass spiked lemonade. I watch as he takes a big sip of his, his throat bobbing when he swallows. And just like that, slick floods my panties, soaking my jeans as Cass's grip on the water bottle tightens.

He leans up against a worktable, big thighs spread wide as I follow him and step between them. I sigh. "Do you want to talk about what you saw on my tablet?"

Cassian cocks his head to the side, pale eyes not moving from mine. I roll my shoulders against the weight of his dominance; it feels so damn good on my skin.

"Is that where you wanted us to head yesterday, little one?"

He's referencing the way James and I followed him to the Omegamatic, the pack's life-sized sex toy.

"Watching you fuck it was the highlight of my day," I admit, watching the flush spread across his cheeks. "We were trying to open a door, Cass, to make it clear that we want you. Together, separately. We want you in every way we can have you."

Cass's pale eyes flash, but he takes another sip of his lemonade.

"What do you think would have happened if you hadn't run from us?" I tease back with a cheeky grin.

"The two of you are driving me mad," he returns before running one hand through his salt-and-pepper waves. "You're playing with fire, little one." He sets the lemonade down as my heart hammers in my chest.

I straighten my shoulders, meeting his intense gaze. There's something about the way he actively listens and focuses that's a huge turn on for me, like nothing else in the world is more important than whatever I have to say.

"We want you," I state. "I keep trying to show you how much, and you keep pushing us away. But I will never stop." I give him a little smile as I take a step closer. "You opened the floodgates that day in the springs. And I've thought about you every day since. I feel you, Cass." I rub at my chest. "I feel you here. So does James."

For a long moment, I think he'll push me away, but instead he brings both hands to the backs of my thighs and drags me closer.

He lifts his hands from my skin. "You can't be mine, Julia," he signs. "You belong to James and probably another alpha someday in the future. If James didn't shift when you and he mated, it's because he's meant to be this pack's healer or spirit." Cass pauses his explanation as I scowl.

"I know that," I counter. "And he knows that, and it doesn't change how we feel. We want what we want."

Cass presses my hand to his chest, his dark pupil overtaking the pale gray iris as he purrs low in his chest. The reverberation lights up my skin as I shudder.

He lifts his hands to continue, "I'm half tempted to take you. Except I know it would kill me to have you and give you up. I can't do that." He looks so fucking sad, I can practically feel my own heart being crushed in my chest. "Don't ask me to make that choice."

I hate that this is his excuse. James and I have made it clear we want him, but it's equally clear Cass doesn't see a future between us. I've settled on teasing him within an inch of his life until he breaks. I'm a hundred percent sure he'll come around to my way of thinking. It's kind of like Luna's favorite saying: "If I want something, I get it."

There was so much willful miscommunication and drama between her and Titan, and I don't want any of that. I'm a big fan of being painfully clear and obvious. Like now.

"There is no other choice," I sign gently, pressing my hips deeper between his muscular thighs. "Don't say I didn't warn you." Reaching for my coat, I unbutton it and open the halves, revealing my bare torso and bedazzled, fringed bra from Luna's collection. I don't have huge boobs like her, but what I do have looks really damn good hoisted up to my chin and covered in glitter.

Cassian's dark pupils fully overtake the steely iris as fangs descend from his beautiful lips. His gaze falls to the bra as he shifts on the edge of the table. His huge chest heaves slightly as his eyes travel back up to meet mine again.

The look on his face is pure, unbridled alpha desire. If I can shove him all the way off the edge of this cliff, I suspect I'll get the ride of my life.

I want it. Now.

"Has James seen this?" Cassian counters as I grin, watching his eyes pull back to the swaying fringe dangling off my tits.

"James and I are great communicators, Cass. He is aware of, and encouraging, everything I'm doing right now. Plus," I lean in a little closer, my lips almost brushing his as I sign, "he's gonna start teasing you a little more directly too. Better to just give in to us now and get it over with."

"You're gonna be the death of me," he retorts. "I'm on the knife's edge of losing all control here." Cass's hands move with swift, confident motions. "I don't think you know what that means."

"Show me, alpha," I retort. "I want it."

Cass brings one big hand to my chin, his thumb brushing along my lower lip as gray eyes fall to it. I wonder what he sees when he looks at me? I'm tiny and quiet, but I'm fierce and wild. I love hard. Does he see all of that? I have to believe he does.

I capture the tip of his thumb with my lips and suck gently as a flush spreads down Cass's neck and into the salt-and-pepper chest hair peeking out of his shirt. I keep my chin up, my eyes on his despite the intense heat barreling through my body.

I'm ready to sob when he pulls his thumb out, but he replaces it immediately with his middle finger, shoving it all the way into my mouth.

"Suck," he commands. It's a simple enough word, and I'm so focused on his lips that I read it with ease. I swirl my tongue around his finger and suck hard, and then I'm going wild, desperate for more as the hand on the back of my thigh moves to my ass and squeezes.

Cass's broad chest rises and falls with quick, shallow breaths. I let my lips pop off his finger and pull back, reaching for the buttons on his shirt. "I need to touch you," I sign before undoing the top bottom.

He sits up straighter, dominance rolling off him as his lips hover ever closer to mine.

I undo the buttons on his shirt fast, shoving the fabric down his huge shoulders to get a look at all that stacked chest, covered in tattoos and sexy-as-fuck chest hair. He might be in his early fifties, but he's in incredible shape. Every thick muscle is visible to my hungry eyes.

Taking a step back, I wink at him. "Got another surprise for you, Cass."

"Is that right?" he signs, licking his lips as I bring his hands to the waistband of my pants, using his fingers to slide them down a few inches. And then I lift my hands up.

"I'm wearing nothing underneath these jeans, alpha. Remember that day in the hot springs? I need your mouth on me again."

Cassian's lips fall open, and while I can't hear the groan, he pulls my hand to his chest so I can feel it.

Warring indecision is clear in the way he stares at me with unabashed desire, but he maintains some distance. My body is on fire with need, goosebumps covering my skin under the weight of his heavy perusal.

Even so, I'm shocked when he grips me hard by the throat, yanking my body to his as he takes my mouth. His sudden, violent attention sends shockwaves through my system as I shiver in his arms. Cass's warm tongue demands entry, his lips sucking at mine as he devours me like a man starved. His other hand goes to the back of my head, and I'm caught in his scorching embrace, the heat from his skin lighting me up from the inside out.

Yessss. God, yes. It's everything I want and need, everything

I've been missing without him. Wrapping both arms around his neck, I throw everything I have into a kiss I'm desperate to repeat every moment for the rest of my life. This close, he smells so fucking good—all rich, velvety spice. He is utterly masculine in every way.

His hands move from my throat to slide down around my waist and over my ass. He uses that touch to crush me to his chest, bending my upper body backward as his lips chase mine.

A growl from his chest tightens my nipples into aching, needy points as one big hand slips up my back into my hair, fisting it tight. Cass's soft tongue is everywhere, licking at mine, teasing my lower lip. His desperate exploration of my mouth stops, and I think he'll pull away, but instead he pulls my head farther back to teasingly bite his way along my jawline and down my neck.

I let out a soft cry as I claw at his chest. More, God, I need so much more.

Cass freezes and stiffens, his chest reverberating with a growl as he startles and looks away from me. He tugs my coat tight to cover my boobs. And that's when I look up to see Ash and Cherry staring wide-eyed at us both. Ash's dark eyes flick to Cass's. He frowns, grabs Cherry's hand, and heads off into the woods.

The spell is immediately broken. Cassian stands and moves away, his back to me as he runs his hands through his hair and utters a string of words I don't hear.

Fuck.

0 and 3, I mutter into my bond with James. *Your turn to tease, alpha.*

CHAPTER FIVE

I SHIFT IN MY SEAT, reaching down surreptitiously to flatten the hard-on poking my thigh. Julia's heat, that swirl of pleasure and triumph in our bond, it can only mean one thing. She was victorious in her quest to tease Cassian into giving in to us. I'm hard as fuck imagining them touching each other. Before we started teasing Cass, we talked about boundaries. It's incredibly important in a relationship like this, but the truth is, we have none when it comes to him.

We want him, and it's really that simple.

There's a knock at the door just before a dark-haired human woman strolls in, glancing around the room.

Stone smiles. "Hello, Bianca." Despite the fact that our pack didn't apply for the government's alpha research program, he's managed to be very welcoming to her team.

Bianca smiles and leans up against the back of the sofa, looking at each of us. "My sister, Leandra, will be here shortly. I thought I'd give you a heads up, although I'm sure James would notice her on the security cams." She gives me a hesitant look.

"Is there something else?" Stone questions, shifting back in his chair as he focuses fully on the beautiful researcher.

Bianca examines the floor but nods and meets his gaze. "Leandra is my older sister, and I've shared that she's an alpha. I told her the team didn't need her protection; we've got all of you. But she was very insistent after Declan burned the store and all that. Leandra's—well, to be honest, she's a *lot*."

Titan gives her a pointed look. "How much is *a lot* on a scale of zero to Luna?"

Bianca laughs aloud at that before scrunching her nose up as she considers it. "On the Luna scale, I'd put Leandra at an eleven maybe. Imagine Luna with an alpha's bravado and strength."

Titan shifts uncomfortably in his seat before looking over at Stone to grumble, "Why don't we attract more introverts?"

Titan looks over at me, pale blue eyes focused. "I'll stick around to meet Leandra. Asher's done with his patrol of the valley. Why don't you and Cass take the next shift? Clay and I will take the one after you."

Perfect. I'll head out to the store and find the big alpha. A little alone time sounds perfect.

I give Titan a mocking salute and shove my computer across the table to him. I've already taught him how to monitor the security program I built—he can keep an eye on things while Cass and I run.

Hopping on the nearest ATV, I head for the store, passing Jules on her way back. We stop next to one another, and then she climbs off her ATV and up into my arms.

"I can smell him all over you," I growl into her lips, biting the plump lower one as her cheeks turn pink.

"He kissed me, and it was so good," she whines. "But then Ash and Cherry showed up, and he backed off. He was so close, mate. He just needs a little push."

Laughing aloud, I set her back down and watch as she climbs onto her ATV again. "I'm good at pushing," I sign. "I love you, baby girl."

Jules strokes me through our bond as I preen under the attention, and then she heads toward the lodge.

When I arrive at the general store site a few minutes later, Cassian tosses a pair of gloves aside. "Jesus, it's a never-ending barrage of teasing. Is that what you're here for?"

I grin right back, because, Jesus, he's so handsome. "Titan wants us to run the valley. He and Clay will take the shift after us."

Cass blanches but recovers quickly. "You wanna run toward the front of the valley first, or the back?"

"Back to front. Think you can keep up?" I'm teasing the big alpha, but he grunts and gestures for me to get going.

Cass and I take off through the trees, heading up into the forest as we trail along the valley's edge toward the backmost section. We're looking for anything amiss. We're quiet for the first quarter hour, but I stop every now and again to check my security cameras and ensure they're not tampered with.

So far, so good.

"Do you ever miss Mitchell's pack?" Cass's question catches me off guard as we slow to an easy jog, making our way to the very back of the long, thin valley Bent Fork Ranch sits in.

I shrug as I pull up next to him, pumping my arms rhythmically. "I made a lot of friends there, and it felt like home because Mitchell created a safe place for us in New York. Those early days were so fucking perilous. When we had to run from the Task Force and ended up here, I knew I was home."

Cass is silent, but I love that he's asking about me, about my life. And I wonder if part of him wants to know me better because he feels a pull like I do.

"I'm grateful to Mitchell and Stone," I continue on. "When Mitchell first found me, I was running with a group of asshole alphas. I hated it, but there was protection there. I hadn't seen my father or brothers in years. Now, because of the work

Mitchell's doing, I might get to see my family again. It's a blessing I never thought I'd have."

Cass glances over at me as we jog. "They in New York?"

"Yeah," I laugh, "Bronxers through and through. They'll never leave. But one day, I hope I'll be able to travel home. I'd love to introduce Jules to them."

Cass grits his jaw. "I'm sure they'd be happy for you to have someone."

It's on the tip of my tongue to mention how Jules and I consider him part of the equation, but the moment doesn't feel especially right to me somehow. Instead, I push my legs a little harder, nudging him in the side. "Race you all the way to the back of the valley?"

Cass growls and pumps his arms harder, and then we're sprinting through the forest, around gigantic boulders that dot the landscape. I stop just once to check on a camera, and he stands patiently while I do it. But the moment I hop out of the tree, he takes off again, and I'm treated to a view of Cassian from the back, thick thighs and well-muscled legs obvious even through the fabric of his jeans.

Jesus, I want to climb on top of him and ride that big body, and thinking about it stiffens my cock in my pants. It pokes uncomfortably into my leg as I slow. We're nearing the back of the valley anyhow. From here, the trail leads up to a giant rock, and we can see the entire stretch of valley from there, the lodge nestled in the center of all this beauty.

Nerves bundle in my core, because as we slow, Cass's focus returns to me rather than a need to win our little race. He's silent, but his gray eyes move from my face to my neck before he pulls them back up.

I grin at him, shoving my hands into my pockets, hoping I don't appear confrontational. "You kissed Jules."

Cass stiffens, a flash of remorse crossing his handsome features before he lifts his chin as if he's going to apologize.

Taking a step closer to him, I let out a low growl, watching his pupils dilate as he matches the sultry tone. "I want you to do a whole lot more than just kiss her," I purr. His lips part, tongue peeking out as fangs descend. Good, his emotion is running high. "I want you to fuck her."

His lips curl back into a snarl. "That gets you two off? Playing with a third?"

"Playing with *you*," I correct. "Only you. We have no desire to play with anyone else." Shit, I didn't mean to come on quite this strong, and he looks shell-shocked and torn.

Might as well go full throttle at this point. Taking a step closer, I let my gaze rove down his body before I manage to drag it back up. "You gave Jules a kiss, Cassian, and I want one too."

His hand comes to my throat as he growls, getting in my space as my dick presses uncomfortably against the zipper of my jeans. He's grappling with his self-control, and I love that my suggestion has him on edge enough to put his hands on me. His fingers are rough on my skin.

"We could play out here for a few minutes, Cass," I counter. "Would you kiss me like you kissed her?"

"I've never kissed a man," he growls, his face so close to mine, I could shift forward a few inches and press my lips to his.

"Whether you have or haven't is irrelevant," I whisper, my gaze falling to his plump lower lip. "Do you *want* to?"

Cass doesn't answer, but he takes another half-step forward, his chest brushing against mine. His fingers still grip my throat tight, but he uses his thumb to angle my head to the side. When he brings his nose to the side of my neck and inhales deeply, I let out a needy growl. My whole body tenses, but Cass purrs, dragging his lips up my neck, over the bob of my throat, up my chin, where he bites, hard, before pulling away again.

I startle but push into his dominant perusal. "Is this what you did to her?"

He growls, sending heat streaking down my thighs.

"She smells so fucking good, doesn't she?"

He stiffens again and goes to take a step away. The idea of both of us is still disconcerting to him; that much is clear. I suspect, more than anything, he's worried I'll think he's trying to steal her from me.

As if that were even possible.

"Did you put your hands all over her?" I press. "Did you run them up her legs, maybe touch her sweet pussy? I know you tasted her once before. Wouldn't you like to again?"

Cass's breathing goes deep and fast, like he can't pull air quickly enough into his lungs.

"I want you to do all that and more," I reiterate. "To her, to me. Separately. All together." I pause for a beat, watching Cass's lips curl into a snarl. He takes a step closer to me as I lick my lips and stare at his mouth. When I drag my eyes back up, I smirk. "You've seen her art, I take it?"

Cass's eyes fall to where he just bit me, and I cock my head to the side to give him a good look. He reaches up, warm fingers trailing over the indents from his teeth. Pale gray eyes meet mine again.

He presses closer to me, his mouth hovering just above mine as he brushes his lips against my own. It's a soft touch, a testing of the heat between us. His warm breath mingles with mine, and I'm acutely aware of how hard his body is, how dominant he feels so close like this. I slick my tongue along his bottom lip before sucking it into my mouth, tugging on it lightly as he snarls.

I'm all in on this adventure, so I reach between us and grip his cock, stroking it roughly as he gasps and stiffens. His surprise falls into a groan as his lips part for a soft, full kiss. It's tender and teasing and exploratory.

Having his lips against mine sends my need sky high, and I

growl as I push harder into the kiss, dipping my tongue between his lips as he meets it. Cass pulls back ever so slightly, looking at me in wonder. A kiss, our first. I hope it's the first of a million. Because I will never not want more of this.

CHAPTER SIX

cassian

JAMES COCKS his head to the side and smiles, dark eyes falling to my stomach. He touches the waistband of my jeans. I can't fucking breathe through the heat that kiss produced in my core. I'm hard as granite, ready to throw him down on all fours and take until I'm sated.

I've never been with a man, but kissing James felt natural, so goddamn natural. This first one was tender, but I don't want tender. I want to dominate him. I've just never done this.

His dark fingers slide the fabric of my shirt aside before slipping up underneath it. His touch roves over the dips and valleys of my abs as I struggle against the rising pleasure. This is new, and so fucking hot, I'm a hair's breadth from exploding. My muscles tremble as I ball my fists, staring at his beautiful mouth as he looks at me. Despite the heat, my brain spins around what's happening.

I kissed another alpha.

"Cassian," James murmurs, a deep rumble that sends my dick leaping in my pants. His voice is so low, so seductive, infused with confidence and authority.

I rip my shirt open and watch his hands move up my abs to

my chest. He runs his palms up over my nipples as I huff out a groan. One hand slides up to my throat, and he grips it in his big hand, using that to pull me closer, his mouth barely brushing against mine.

My self-control disintegrates as I slant my mouth over his and take a more forceful kiss. My lips are rough as I force his mouth open with my tongue, sucking at his with his hand still around my throat. Snarling into the kiss, I drag his other hand behind his back and hold it at his waistline.

I want him caught and overpowered, so I push my bigger body hard into his, backing him up a few paces until he hits the nearest tree. James grunts as I bite at his lips, licking my way along them both, sucking and nipping at them. God, he's got the most beautiful fucking mouth.

With one hand, I grip his shirt and twist, pinning him to the tree. I bite at his tongue as he growls and uses my shirt to shove me away, dark eyes hard on mine as his chest heaves. He's teasing, offering to fight me, knowing it'll make me harder for him.

Snarling, I shove him back hard against the tree and throw myself up against him. My hips rock with his, my dick straining against my zipper. He must realize it, because he reaches down to unbutton my jeans and briefs and shoves them down my hips. James gasps when my cock falls out of my pants, bobbing against his waistline.

"Jesus, Cass, you're huge," he murmurs, cupping my balls before running his rough hand down my length.

I laugh and rock my dick through his fist, snarling as I crush our lips together again. Now that I've had a taste of him, I'm desperate for more.

I want to tease the idea of him and Julia and me all together, but this is so new. Still, they've been clear with me. So I grip his hand and help him jack me. "You think Julia would fit on this big cock?"

His lips part into a grin, and he lets go of me long enough to unzip his own jeans and shove them down to his feet. James grabs my hand and guides it between his legs, and I'm touching another man's dick for the first time. It feels familiar and not, because he's a little longer, a little thinner. His head flares a little higher than mine, and when I roll it between my fingers, he lets out a plaintive whine.

Heat streaks down my spine as I stroke his silky skin, reveling in his thickness. He's hot and smooth but hard and throbbing under my touch.

James smiles at me again. "She fits beautifully on this dick, Cass. You think she'll fit on both at the same time?"

That mental image has me groaning aloud as I stroke him, exploring the bulbous head and the veins that trail along both sides. I want to flip him face-down onto the ground and explore his body with my tongue.

"Whatever you're thinking, do it," he snaps, squeezing my dick tight as precum drips from me into his palm. He growls and uses it to jack me harder as I lean forward and moan into his lips. This is an overwhelming first experience. I'm a highly dominant lover, but this is unexplored territory. I'd like a bed and Julia to be present and space and time to learn them both slowly.

"I'm losing you," James murmurs. "What are you thinking about?"

"Being in a bed," I whisper, not wanting him to think I'm not enjoying the fuck outta this. "I want to be in a bed with you and her, to learn you by putting my lips all over you both. Kissing you has me ready to explode, James. Between her teasing me earlier and this, I give up. I give in."

His dark eyes flash with need, and it calls to me. I want him falling apart with pleasure, so I sink to both knees. "I have to taste you," I growl, teasing his dick with the barest hint of my lips.

"Jesus, you look good down there," he growls, gripping the

base of his shaft and dragging it along my lower lip. "You'll look even better sucking me off."

Another dominant growl rolls out of my chest, and James shudders, rolling his shoulders. "It feels so good when you do that."

I open my mouth and guide him between my lips, sucking softly at his tip before pulling at it gently with my teeth. James grunts and bucks, bringing his hands to the back of my head as I hollow my cheeks.

I'm sucking on another man's cock. I thought it might be uncomfortably new that first time, but if anything, it's far more natural than I imagined. Groaning, I take him deeper, working him into my throat.

A sudden scratchy pinging noise has us both jolting as I fall backward onto the ground, my face burning as James scrambles for the walkie at his waist. He winks at me as he puts a hand out to haul me up off my ass.

Stone's voice comes through the radio, "I'm sure you're nearly done with your patrol, but Leandra's here, and you should both get back."

He doesn't give us any more context, but James pauses for a moment, and I suspect he's checking in with Julia.

"Ah," he starts. "The new alpha's a flirt." He says it with another wink, teasing me, I'm sure. It takes a moment for that to sink in, and then all I can think about is getting back up to the lodge and tearing Julia away from Bianca's alpha sister.

Julia's mine, screams every emotion in my mind. She's mine, and James is mine, and what I said was true. I give up. I thought I could hold them at arm's length, but they've shredded my willpower.

I don't mean to let out the needy, anxious whine that rolls out of my throat. The moment I do, James grips my throat again, his dark eyes focused on mine. "She's only ever ours. Understood?"

Except she's not, and she probably never will be. The arrival of a new alpha simply reminds me how my designation precludes me from mating in a triad, no matter how hot it was kissing James. Already, reality is crashing in on me. I recognize this for what it is—my mind wants to preserve some of my sanity, knowing there's a time when they'll belong to someone else.

James senses my change in focus, zipping his bobbing dick back into his pants. I tuck mine away as I frown, urging myself not to fly into a rage at the idea of someone flirting with Julia.

I can't find it in me to respond to James's comment. He may feel a certain way, but alpha biology is what it is.

Growling, I take off at a sprint toward the lodge, James following me. We make it back in record time, although I'm careful to keep an eye open for anything else unusual as we pass through the valley.

When we get back, we jog around the front to find most of leadership in the RV park, along with the research team. Everyone's hovering just outside the brand-new research trailer. Except now, a tall, muscular female alpha stands next to Bianca, regaling the group with a story about some goddamn topic or another. I'm so irritated looking at her that I don't absorb a word she's sharing.

She's tall, over six feet, with short, dark, shaved hair and flashing black eyes. Even in the colder weather, she wears a short-sleeved tank, her muscles flexing and pulling under the shirt. She's in her prime physically, and I dislike her immediately.

Like any pack alpha worth his salt, though, I shove that personal feeling down. How I feel about her doesn't matter. How she fits in with everyone else is what's important.

Julia stands next to Rogue and River, an arm through Rogue's as they listen to the newcomer talk. I don't miss the way the female alpha's eyes flick to Julia every time there's a pause in her story. Stone is translating for Julia.

James pats me on the back with a huffy laugh as we join the group and introduce ourselves. When I reach out to shake her hand, Leandra smirks, eyes falling to my shirt. It's still open from playing with James. I forgot to button it back up in my haste to get here.

"Another pack alpha? That's unusual," is all she says after squeezing my hand tighter than absolutely necessary.

"Yep," Stone offers, not saying anything further on the topic. I appreciate him for not undermining my designation, despite the fact I'm not this pack's alpha.

"Noted," Leandra murmurs, pulling her attention from me and back to Julia.

Bianca slides her hand around Leandra's waist, pinching her sister on the side playfully as she looks at me. "I was just telling the rest of the pack, but Leandra has insisted on coming to keep an eye on me and the team."

Stone smiles at the newcomer. "Any questions, find myself, Clay or Cassian. We want to keep the team safe as much as you do, so let us know if something comes up."

"No offense," Leandra chirps, "but you didn't keep my sister safe before. She's just lucky she and the team weren't inside when that asshole burned it to a crisp. Speaking of which, why is he even still alive? If I had been here, I—"

"Wouldn't have done shit," James speaks up just as I open my mouth. "You don't have all the information, alpha. If you did, you'd be aware of why we've taken the path we have. Bianca can fill you in, I'm sure."

Bianca pinches her sister hard, giving her a warning look. Leandra's mouth opens again, but she zips it shut as she looks at her sister.

My eyes flick over to Stone's, and I see my own emotions mirrored there—mistrust and irritation. I find myself wondering how this new addition will change pack dynamics. Hopefully she doesn't stay too long.

I'm ready to kick her out myself.

The crowd dissipates, Leandra following Bianca and the other researchers into their trailer as I watch. Stone gives me a look that says we'll talk about it later, following the rest of leadership into the house.

James gives Julia a sensual kiss, wrapping her in his big arms as River turns to me with a look. "We can still go into town, right?"

I watch James stroke Julia's hair down her back with both of his hands before I nod at River. "Anyone who wants to go is welcome. Let's go now and then be back for dinner."

James shoots me a knowing look as the twins jog off toward the trucks. Then he, Julia and I are standing there together, and I don't know what the fuck to say.

I don't have to say anything, though, because Julia grins at me, nipping at her lower lip before crossing the small space between us. She leans in conspiratorially as she brings her hands up. "Told you, we are relentless. You stood no chance; it's okay to just give up." She shrugs as I laugh, but I can't resist pulling her into my arms and leaning way down to bury my face in her neck.

"So hot," James murmurs, and I know he's sharing the sentiment through their mate bond because Julia chuckles into my shoulder before sighing happily. For a long moment, I just breathe her in, letting her scent ground me.

"Get a room, people!" River shouts from the parking lot behind the RV park. "We have shit to do!"

I watch Rogue roll his eyes at his sister as I step away from Julia, reminding myself that I'm playing with fire.

CHAPTER SEVEN

MY BOND with Jules is awash with pleasure and excitement. I shared the highlights of what happened between Cass and me, and she's positively victorious. Truth be told, she was right when she told him he had no chance. We are determined to tear down any wall he puts up.

It's a whole lot more than simple lust. In fact, it's not lust at all. We want him physically, of course, but we want to be *with* him, and that's far more meaningful.

I pull Jules into my arms bridal style and carry her to the car as she peppers my neck with teasing kisses. River feigns a gag as Rogue grins at Cass and hops into the front seat.

We barely manage to get to the end of the ranch's long driveway before River starts chatting about Leandra. "She's just so cool, don't you think?" she gushes, barreling on before anyone can answer. "Have you ever met a female alpha?"

I translate for Julia as she smirks next to me. It's obvious she knew Leandra was flirting, and she knows it irritated Cass. If I were a betting man, I'd assume Julia is hoping his general possessiveness will kick in, and Leandra's flirting will push him irrefutably into our arms.

It's a solid plan.

"Met a few," Cass grumbles as River slaps his arm from the back seat.

"Tell me everything! Don't be so grumpy just because she flirted with Jules."

Rogue reaches back to whack his sister on the leg. "Stop needling the man, Riv. You're being rude!"

Cass shoots the teen a thankful smile as I translate for Julia, despite the awkward comment. Her smile overtakes her face as she preens.

Cass grumbles but finally relents to answering River's question. "Female alphas are rare. I met two when I was on my own, before I came to this part of Canada."

"Where were you before?" Rogue questions, interest creeping into his deep voice. I translate for Jules as I lean forward to listen. She and I have been dying to know more of his back story, but we haven't had many chances to learn it.

"Montreal," Cass continues. "I owned a little property just outside of the city, and I worked from home, so I rarely left. The virus was running rampant, so I avoided going into town and mostly kept to myself. In the end, it didn't matter. Two female alphas were on the run from a pack of males. They stumbled into my basement, and when the alphas tried to come onto my property to take them, I shot them. They decided it wasn't worth it to fight me and the females. The girls stayed with me a few months before moving on."

"Hot," River quips. "Just you and two sexy alphas. Ooh la la."

Cass laughs aloud. "It wasn't like that at all. They were looking for a pack, and they weren't interested in me. Although I contracted the virus while they were living with me. They guided me through the wildling phase right after. I wasn't too much of an asshole, but they chained me up through most of it."

Fuck. That wasn't my experience when I transitioned, but I know alphas who went crazy during that initial transition, the wildling phase. It makes me sad Cass had to go through that, but I'm thankful he had help from friends who understood.

"River helped me through mine," Rogue says softly, looking over his shoulder into the back seat where Riv sits.

Julia is thoughtful as she takes in everything Cass just shared. She turns to Rogue. "How'd she help you?"

Rogue gives her a sheepish look when he doesn't know all the signs. I translate for him as he gives me a thankful look.

"She chained me up," he shares, his voice soft as River leans her head against the back of Cass's headrest. "She made sure I couldn't hurt anyone, and she fed me. I bit her once during the madness. She's still got a scar." His eyes flick to his twin's arm.

River holds it up with a proud grin, showing us a pale scar running down her forearm. "I was really brave. He was *such* a douchenozzle."

I chuckle as I fingerspell that particular word for Julia, who lets out a throaty laugh as she tucks her strawberry blond waves behind her shoulder. Her neck is visible to me, and I ache to put my mouth on it, to suck at that soft skin and drink in her scent. My love and need for her shock me some days with their strength. She is my greatest gift, and I thank God every day for her presence in my life.

"You can stop staring at Jules like she's a piece of candy," River snarks, waggling her dark brows.

But the thing is that I *can't* stop staring at my mate. I never could. And I have no intention of even trying.

⸻

By the time we get to the small town of Ayas, River is in rare form, and the entire truck is cracking up. As we pull onto downtown's main street, I watch Cass's focus move from the road behind us to the front and either side. He's wary, and I'm not surprised. Declan has committed too many crimes for any of us to feel truly safe, and more than anyone, Cass is aware of what an asshole Declan is.

We get to town, and thankfully the main street is bustling with activity. Humans move up and down the sidewalks, and each storefront is brightly lit. It doesn't look like a town crushed under the heel of a psychotic asshole alpha. Still, I don't let my guard down. Declan has a history of showing up when we least expect him to.

Cass pulls the truck over in front of a beautiful white storefront, and Julia smiles as she looks at it.

Betty, Stone's mother, has obviously been at the new window arrangement. She's got an eye for beautiful design, and her store Tournesol's front display is no exception. Fabric mannequins stand in jagged rows in both front windows. Each one is draped in swathes of pale-colored fabrics. Splashes of color among the fabrics indicate this season's hottest colors.

Betty came home from her most recent buying trip to Paris with a slew of creative ideas, and a handsome French boyfriend named Arnaud. He's charmed the whole pack in short order, and we all adore him.

Speaking of the devil, Arnaud shows up at Tournesol's door, his angular face breaking into a grin when he sees us. I slip out of the back seat, offering my hand to Julia and River. I do a quick visual sweep of the street, but there's nothing amiss—everything seems normal right now.

Arnaud is quick to pull us each in for a hug, although he gives Cassian a friendly handshake before gesturing us into the store.

Inside, a spicy, warm scent fills my nose. Betty's burning new candles, and they smell delicious. Julia stops in place, reaching out to rub my chest as she looks at Cass and me. "I've got inventory to do so I can update the website. Let me know if anything comes up or we need to leave?"

She means with Declan, and that forces an angry growl up

out of my chest. That my mate has to spend even a minute wondering if we might need a quick escape irritates me.

"Of course," Cassian signs when I don't immediately answer.

Julia reaches out and rubs my chest protectively, and I pull her in for a tender kiss. She's been hurt in the past, and that accident stole her hearing. There's nothing less about her now that she's deaf, but I'm protective of her because of what happened. I wasn't even here then, but knowing someone could run her over and not even stop to help is a fact I cannot get over.

My emotions run high as Jules threads her arms around my neck, allowing me to pull her up into my arms. Without even thinking, I back her against Cass's chest. He freezes, but she laughs into our kiss and turns her head, giving him a peck on the cheek as she lifts her hands.

"We could be doing a whole lot more than this, alpha. Maybe later?"

Cass looks a little surprised, but he nods and helps her down out of my arms.

Julia picks her way through racks of beautiful women's clothing, hugging Betty, who stands at the cash register counting money. They sign briefly before Jules follows the twins into the back storeroom.

Cass opens his mouth to say something, but Betty waves us over with a worried expression. We quickly join her as she closes the cash register and leans against it, long arms folding over her chest.

"I'm glad you're both here. I was going to call Stone in a moment, but I'm hearing distressing news from my neighbors here on the street."

"What kind of news?" Cass's voice is a direct command, and even though Betty's not an omega, it's easy to see the way her lashes flutter at his dominance. While it hits alphas harder, humans aren't immune.

Betty points to her left. "My neighbor at the bakery shared that Declan came by her store this week to invite her to Gabriel's sermons."

"Invite her?" I press. This is terrible fucking news. The DPM sent Gabriel to handle Declan, but if anything, he's almost worse than the alpha himself. Together they're a maelstrom of religious assholery.

"She was *highly encouraged*," Betty continues with air quotes. "Declan made it seem as if she wouldn't be allowed to continue running the bakery unless she either pays him to protect it, or begins attending the sermons."

"A protection racket?" Cass questions as he looks over at me. "This is the first I've heard of it. I wonder how long this has been going on?"

Betty frowns as I reach out to rub her arm. Her dark eyes are filled with tears as she squeezes my fingers tightly. "It just happened in the last day or two, but she's decided to close up shop and leave Ayas. She says others are doing the same. It's not worth it for them to stay. Everyone remembers how he burned the Stephenses. She feels something worse is coming, and she's not willing to risk her life for her business."

"We've got to tell Stone and Erin," I murmur, my eyes meeting Cass's. He purses his lips but nods, looking back at Betty.

"You should consider leaving as well. Take Arnaud and go back to Paris for a while," he encourages.

Betty scoffs, dropping my hand. "I didn't leave Stone when he became an alpha and the world was insane. I certainly won't leave my son now. The only way I'm leaving Ayas is if the pack decides to go. We could do that, I suppose."

"It's a thought," I hedge. "But I suspect Stone and Erin would be reluctant to leave the town at Declan's mercy."

"Erin would never," Cassian counters. "She's dedicated to the people here. I'll call Stone and update him. Let's get going as soon as Julia finishes what she came for."

Betty nods and breathes in a deep breath as if she's trying to calm herself. When she looks up at Cass and me, I can see she's devastated. "Let's go now. I'm going to close up the store. Based on what my neighbor shared, I think it's best if we aren't in town until we figure out how to resolve this issue with Declan and Gabriel."

I nod, although I can see it kills Betty to think of Tournesol's doors closing.

Still, it's probably for the best. At least for the time being.

CHAPTER EIGHT

cassian

I CALL Stone to update him as James heads into the back storeroom with Julia and the twins. As I expected, Stone rages for a solid five minutes and then calls Erin into his office so I can repeat the whole thing.

She goes into mayor mode immediately, leaving Stone with me so she can call the Ayas Town Council.

"Just get home," Stone growls into the phone when I ask how he wants to proceed.

Betty calls River and Rogue up front to help her close things down, and I step out into the street to keep watch while they finish. Having learned what Betty just shared, I'm more anxious than ever to get back to Bent Fork.

An hour later, we pile back into Stone's truck to return to the ranch. When we arrive, there's more bad news to pile on top of what we learned today.

The BBC never did air any of the info from our dossier on Declan and his connection to Canada's DPM. James spent painstaking weeks pulling together every scrap of info he could find, combining that with every police report we've filed against Declan in recent months.

We need a new approach to rescuing the omegas.

I head upstairs and knock softly on a door, entering when a quiet voice greets me. Isabel sits in a chair in her room, her daughter Abigail sleeping on her shoulder. Isabel flashes me a smile and gestures to the chair opposite hers.

"You look like you need something, alpha. You want to talk about the sweet little omega who's so obsessed with you?" She's teasing me, but her smile falls at the somber look I give her.

I speak softly to avoid waking Abigail. "Izzy, honey, you've had a shitty week with Declan's attack and then giving birth. You've probably heard the BBC didn't air the information from our dossier on Declan. That means we need a backup plan to get the other omegas out."

She nods, her pale eyes filling with tears as she rubs Abigail's back absentmindedly.

I press on, knowing I'm about to ask her to relive shit she'd much rather forget. "It's probably going to come down to a fight, and we need to know everything we can about life in that pack right now. What are we up against, if we take Declan on head-to-head?"

She sucks in a ragged breath, her lower lip quivering. A muscle in her jaw clenches and unclenches as she stands and paces with the baby. "I'll do anything to help you get the girls out, but an outright attack is a terrible fucking idea. Declan might be a stupid asshole, but Gabriel's not. I don't think we'll win a fight, Cass."

Running my hands through my hair, I grimace. She's confirming what I've worried about myself. Declan already had a large pack, and James confirmed he's brought in a dozen or more alphas. Our disadvantages are growing by the minute.

I look up at her as she paces. "After dinner can you meet with Stone's leadership? We'll keep the group small, but I'd like you to share anything you're comfortable sharing—anything that could help us."

She agrees, but she's immediately lost in thought. After a quick reassuring hug—for myself and her—I head downstairs to update Stone.

At dinner, the entire pack is in a terrible mood. Leandra and the research group join us, and they manage to joke with Sal and the twins at one end of the table. Everyone else is almost silent, as if we're waiting for the other shoe to drop.

Add all of this to the scorching kisses I shared with Julia and James, and I'm ready to rip something to the ground out of sheer frustration. Every way I turn, it seems like a wall is up in front of me, and I've got very few choices for how to move forward.

Glancing to my left, I watch James stroke his dark fingers along Julia's pale cheek. It's such a tender move. It's obvious he adores her.

I've been fantasizing about Julia for eight months—since that day in the hot springs. There's a wild ferocity to her that's unmatched. She throws herself headlong into everything she does; I've always admired that about her. She can't be more than five feet tall, and she's tiny, but her energy is so big, so strong.

James is an addition to our dynamic that I didn't even know I needed—but after what we did earlier, I'd be a liar if I didn't admit to wanting far more with him.

I'm a pack alpha; I read people well. And this couple wants to be mine so badly. I jacked off four times last night imagining how good it would be between us if I took things all the way like Julia keeps suggesting. But then I remind myself that James is probably this pack's healer or spirit, and he needs an alpha partner who can fill that other designation. This pack *needs* that. The world around us is hard and getting harder by the second.

If there's a chance for every male here to come into their power, we need it.

I can't hold them back from that, no matter how much their teasing entices me.

That knowledge settles uncomfortably in my gut as I pick at my food.

After dinner, James and I head to Stone's office. Clay, Asher and Titan follow. I watch Isabel hand the baby to River, and then she follows us, anxious nerves vibrating from her in disconcerting waves.

I fucking hate asking her to do this.

Thankfully, Stone reads her as well as I do. He closes the door behind her and offers her a chair. "Isabel, we would never ask you to do this if there weren't lives on the line. Still, your mental health is important. If there are things you can't share, we get it, okay?"

She lifts her chin up high as she looks him square in the face. "There's nothing I won't do to help get those girls out. We're family."

"Go on, Izzy," I encourage her. "You said earlier you didn't think an outright war was a great idea. Can you tell us more?"

She crosses her arms and looks out a window. "Gabriel's smart and dangerous. He's expecting you to make some sort of move, and that's part of why he's encouraging Declan to continue growing the pack."

James tenses from his spot next to me. I can hear his teeth grind together as she continues.

"He keeps an eye on Mitchell Bancroft's pack—he knows they go back and forth to the States a lot. When Mitchell's omegas aren't around, Gabriel's aware. That's part of how he picks and chooses when to do things like burn the store down. Mitchell was gone for a few days."

Titan's voice is soft as he questions her. "I got the impression

Gabriel felt omegas are second-class citizens in that pack. How is it you know all this? It almost feels like a plant, honestly."

She shudders, tears filling her eyes as Titan apologizes for pressing her. I growl at him, but she continues on.

"Declan took a special interest in me, even when I was pregnant. I truly think he and Gabriel felt the omegas are so beneath them, they didn't even need to worry about conversations they had in front of me. What would I do with that information?"

"They did drop you on our doorstep," Titan reminds her, giving me a look when I snarl at him for pushing her.

"I don't think they expected me to survive the injuries," she whispers, tears finally spilling down her cheeks. "He said some things to me when they threw me into the burning store. He absolutely meant to get rid of me. It's a miracle I didn't die."

"Izzy, you can stop if you need to," Stone reminds her.

"Please keep going," I encourage instead. She's so strong, so fucking strong, and she's already telling us what she knows. "You've got this, honey," I murmur.

Isabel sobs once. "All the newer alphas are young, and Gabriel indoctrinates them fast. He tells them your pack wants to take the omegas. Gabriel wants them ready to fight you when you start a war. His hope is that they'll find mates when he brings new alphas in, and those matings will result in omega powers.

"But the reality is that he'll kill the girls before he ever lets you get ahold of them. He can't risk them coming here and finding their power with a mate in this pack."

"Jesus," Clay snaps. "What's his end game in all of this?"

"I don't know that," she continues. "And I don't know this for sure, but I suspect there will come a time when he moves the omegas elsewhere if they don't develop powers. There's chatter of packs like Declan's in other places."

I snarl at that bit of information. It's yet another red flag.

"What's Gabriel's relationship with the omegas?" Clay asks, clearly distressed by what she's shared.

Isabel shrugs. "The omegas seem to be the only topic he and Declan ever disagreed about. It's Gabriel's opinion that any nonbelievers shouldn't be part of the pack. It's part of how he riles up the younger alphas about your pack—you don't believe the message, so you're a threat to the future of alphas. Gabriel would rather move the girls quickly if they don't fit in by mating an alpha."

The room is silent for a few moments, but I cross it and pull her into my arms, whispering into her hair how strong she is. How proud I am to know her. How I'll protect her with every fiber of my being so her daughter grows up safely. Isabel shudders in my arms but calms after a minute or two. All of pack leadership is silent behind me, absorbing what she's shared.

After a few long, heavy minutes, she leaves us, and I turn to the group. "What the fuck are we going to do with this information?"

Stone rubs his chin as he and Clay exchange a look. "We need a Plan C. We're at a distinct disadvantage numbers-wise, and what she shared makes me more confident than ever that barreling in guns blazing is only likely to get someone killed—probably the omegas."

After we agree to think about it overnight, I return to my cabin, but I'm frustrated and on edge trying to come up with the best way to help my girls.

CHAPTER NINE

cassian

AT FIVE AM, I'm pacing my small cabin, putting the beginnings of Plan C together, when I hear the gentle purr of Cherry's car. Throwing clothes on, I open my front door and step out onto the porch. Cherry parks at the first cabin, the one closest to the street, which makes her my neighbor.

She hops out of the car, shivering at the bitter cold as she pulls her coat tighter. And immediately I smell booze and sweat and men. Growling, I leave my cabin and walk the forty yards to her. She stops on her porch, giving me an anxious wave. When I make it to her, she sighs and opens her front door.

"I can see I'm about to get a pack alpha lecture, so come on inside, and I'll get you a coffee at least."

I'm not this pack's alpha. I shouldn't lecture anyone, but I can't help it.

"Are you doing what I think you're doing, out until five am?" I question as I follow the buxom omega into her cabin. Her bags are still mostly unopened, sitting in the entryway. The cabin looks barely used. No fire has been built, and there's almost nothing in the kitchen.

That makes me fucking mad, because it means her mate isn't taking care of her.

"Cass, you're freaking out; what's going on?" Cherry's throaty voice stops me in my tracks as I turn. She's aware the state of her mating is fragile; I don't want to make that worse.

"You need a fire," I state instead. "Hang on a minute." Jogging out of her cabin, I head quickly to mine and grab as much firewood as I can carry and a box of matches. Back at her cabin, I arrange the firewood and get a small fire going as she joins me with two cups of black coffee.

"I can see you're dying to say something, alpha. Spit it out," she encourages, slumping down into a chair in front of the fire.

"Talk to me about where you're coming back from." I sit across from her, sipping the strong coffee she gave me.

Cherry sighs. "Lord, I don't have time for the snark I'd usually give you right now, so I'll be blunt. I've started stripping at the Moonlight. I need to regain some control in my life, and stripping is the only happy time in my day right now."

Concern rises in my chest. "Does Stone know about this?"

She sighs again, twirling her vibrant cherry-red hair around her finger. "I haven't said it outright, but he knows. He's not pleased about it, but it's not like he's gonna lock me up in the lodge."

My alpha senses ping. "You realize this is a terrible time to be out and about on your own, Cherry. Right? Declan is a raging asshole and getting worse by the second. Why risk yourself like this?"

"To be honest," she drawls, looking down into her coffee, "I don't feel like it can get much worse. I'll probably leave, Cass. I'm saving up money from the nights I strip. And once I have enough to move on, I might go. I love Asher with my entire heart, and it would kill me to leave him behind, but I am so miserable watching him wrestle his demons. I can't fix that for him, and it's my opinion he's not doing enough to fix it for himself."

I agree wholeheartedly with that.

"Don't leave," I encourage her. "Why don't I call Mahikan from the pack up north? I wouldn't say his pack is less civilized, but they're old school, more connected to alpha history. Maybe there's something they can do to help Ash."

"You think so?" Cherry questions, a sudden urgency in her tone.

Shrugging, I take another sip of coffee. "There's no way to know for sure, but why not try?" Looking back up at her, I cross my feet at the ankle. "How'd it go on your walk with Ash?"

Cherry grins at me. "Oh, you mean apart from stumbling across you and Julia making out like a pair of teens at the drive-in?"

God, how old does she think I am that she says drive-in and not movie theater?

Gritting my teeth, I say nothing as Cherry shifts forward in her seat with a spark in her eyes. "You wanna talk about it, alpha?"

"Nothing to say," I hedge. "I can't have her forever, but she's hard to resist."

Cherry sighs and slumps back into her seat. "Knowing in your heart of hearts that you belong to someone, but feeling like all the external forces keep you apart is the fucking worst. We should form a sad sap association. We can drink here every Friday starting at noon."

I hate that I can't fix the issues between her and Ash, but I resolve to talk to Stone about it. Ash is wallowing in self-hatred, and it's time to be done with that bullshit.

Cherry looks over at me. "Hey, the girls all know I'm stripping, but I haven't told Ash outright. Shit, he can probably hear us talking about it right now, that damn seer hearing. But, still, let me have that conversation, okay?"

I nod as I stand and cross the small cabin to dump the coffee in the sink and wash out my cup. When that's done, I return to see Cherry absentmindedly staring into the now roaring fire, a mournful expression on her face.

"Keep this banked while you're here, honey," I murmur, pointing to the wood I stacked next to her fireplace. "It's cold out here, and the heater doesn't seem to keep up."

She gives me a soft nod, but she's lost in the torment of her thoughts right now. And I can't fix it. The list of issues I can't fix is piling up and choking me, and I'm ready to fly into a rage about it.

I leave, grabbing my walkie and radioing Stone despite the time. "I need to spar, alpha. You up?"

"Fuck me, Cass, what time is—goddamn, alpha." There's a rumble, a groan and a slapping sound that must be Erin. "Fine, come up to the lodge."

Normally I'd feel bad about waking him, but we've started sparring early every other day, and it's been a good outlet for my numerous frustrations. We fight like hell and leave battered and bloody, but it feels good. I can beat on another pack alpha like I can't anyone else. Stone knows that, being the good leader he is, so he humors me. I like to think fighting me might help him too, but he's never said as much outright.

Opting to jog up to the main lodge, I set off. When I get there, it's quiet up front except for Isabel from my former pack. She nurses her daughter Abigail as she sits in the front window seat, staring out toward the road I just came up.

"Morning, alpha," she murmurs, stroking Abigail's cheek as the baby suckles at her breast.

God, they're beautiful together. A wave of protectiveness hits me so hard, I barely keep myself from crushing them both to my chest, reminding them how I want to be there for them. Isabel gives me a smile as the baby shifts, but she winces, and I know the injury Declan gave her still bothers her, even after a healer's touch.

Abigail's mouth pops off her mother's swollen nipple and lets out a little sob. Isabel's eyes fill with tears. She's exhausted, and I'm sure asking her to share her history last night didn't make things any easier.

I sit down across from her, grabbing the burp rag off her shoulder before reaching out for the baby. A tear slides down Izzy's cheek as she hands Abigail off to me, sighing and flopping back against the seat.

"God, Cass. Motherhood is so fucking hard. She's constantly hungry, and I'm so tired."

"I'm here for you, Izzy. We all are. You can rely on the people here; it's not like with Declan's pack."

Isabel is immediately on guard, clutching the baby's blanket to her chest. "That fucker. I'll kill him if I ever get the chance to."

Cocking my head to the side, I assess her and think back to the bullshit that went on when I was still part of Declan's pack. I reined him and the rest of leadership in as much as I could, but I was still one alpha in a pack of many. My priority was always protecting the omegas—it's why I stayed in a horrible pack for so long, despite being a pack alpha and craving a family of my own where I could lead.

"He's Abigail's father, isn't he?" I question, keeping my voice low as tears spill down Izzy's face.

She nods, looking utterly miserable, as I lay the baby gently up onto my shoulder and alternate rubbing and patting her back.

"I never want her to know, okay? I don't want her to grow up aware that she was the product of such a violent, horrible asshole. I want her to grow up with love and laughter. Keep it to yourself, okay?"

I dislike the divide between those of us who are newer to Stone's pack and those who were already here. Despite the fact that they've been nothing but supportive, this pack doesn't feel like home yet. Maybe it never will for me, but I'm confident it can be for Izzy and Abigail.

"It's not my secret to tell," I remind her. At my shoulder, Abigail nuzzles against my neck, letting out a tiny burp.

Then a wail starts up, and Izzy groans. "Pass her back, alpha. She needs a new diaper and a nap."

Reluctantly, I hand the baby back over after nuzzling her chubby neck and drinking in that new baby smell. "Smells good." I laugh as Izzy gives me a wry smile.

"Unlike me," she barks back. "Pretty sure I smell like poop and barf and baby milk and like, gross, just a lot of sweat and..."

"Stop," I encourage her, tilting her chin up as I look deep into her eyes. "You've got this, mama. And we are all here. Find me after naptime, and I'll take her between feedings. You can get some rest or take a bath or whatever the hell you want to do."

Izzy nods in agreement, Abigail clutched to her chest. "I'm gonna take you up on that. The omegas here keep offering, but I feel bad, like all I've brought is Declan drama. It's awkward."

"Declan isn't your fault," I reassure her. "Ask for help; the people here are happy to do it. Also, if you don't find me, I'll track you down and kidnap this child for a few hours. Don't test me."

Izzy laughs and leans forward, pressing a gentle kiss to my cheek. "Love you so much, alpha. I'm so glad you're here. Please never leave."

I hold back a retort to that. I don't belong here. Plus, when some alpha shows up who might be James and Julia's third, it'll fucking kill me to see them mate someone. Shit, for all I know, it could be Leandra. The female alpha is obviously attracted to Julia.

But I don't want to give Izzy anything further to worry about. Instead I pass Abigail carefully back and hug them both.

Stone stalks quietly through the lobby and leans over,

smelling the baby just like I did. "Damn, why do babies smell so good?" He beams when he grins at Izzy, and I respect the hell out of him for it. He's a damn good alpha, intuitive and caring and incredibly protective. "You good, honey? You need anything?"

Izzy shrugs. "I'm making it. Cass is gonna babysit for me in a bit."

Stone chuckles. "If there's anything left of him after we spar." There's no aggression in his tone though—it's playful, so I don't bark at him for the jab. He smiles and continues, "Let me get that baby after he has her. I want you to have the rest you need."

Izzy waggles her brows at me. "Sounds good. You two have fun. I'll catch you in a couple hours, okay?"

"Done," I reassure her. "I'm ready for baby snuggles."

She tucks Abigail close to her chest and walks slowly toward the broad staircase leading to the second story.

"She's tired," Stone murmurs, watching Izzy go. "I sense she doesn't want to take us up on our help. I could use your advice on how we can make her feel at home here. Single parenting is hard enough, but she's not alone."

"I'll keep reminding her," I tell him. "Life is fucking complicated, but Izzy's strong as hell."

Stone grunts but gives me a wry, assessing look. "Let's get to the gym; you look like you've got a frustration or two, friend."

Nodding, I turn and pace through the lobby for the stairs to the basement, where the huge, dark gym is located. Stone follows silently, but when the hair on the back of my neck stands on end, I duck without thinking.

A black wolf leaps over my head, landing and spinning almost faster than I can follow.

"Motherfucker," I snap, leaping at the wolf's jaws. I'll never admit it isn't fair for Stone to fight in shift form. If anything, it raises my own ire, angry red taking over my gaze as I lunge for his wolf, gripping him around the neck as I use my larger frame to toss him down.

I'm on his neck fast, but a wolf is a powerful beast, and a pack alpha's shift even more so.

Stone's wolf shoves off the ground hard, tossing and pinning me.

We do that dance for an hour before the strung-out edge of my mind gives way to intense focus, and finally to mellow exhaustion. I circle the big alpha back in his human form. We're both cut and bleeding from dozens of slash wounds. Stone's got a black eye.

I feel fucking good.

"Why are you still here?" Stone questions, catching me off guard.

The moment I pause to consider the question, he bolts across the gym, slamming me into the wall and hitting me with an uppercut so goddamn hard, my head snaps back, hitting the hard concrete.

An angry bellow leaves my mouth as I knee him right in the nuts, shoving him off me as he whines and falls to the ground. I'm on him before he's ready, and we grapple hard for a moment until we're locked together so tight, neither of us ready to give in or tap out.

Finally, Stone gives me a look. "I'm done, asshole. And you haven't answered my question."

I flop off the big alpha and reach a hand out to help him up, ready for him to return the nut kick. But he stands with a wary look and crosses his big arms. "I'm serious, Cass, why are you still here? You could have your own pack. I know we both know that. Why do you stay?"

"We've got shit to do," I rumble. "The omegas, remember? I'm not doing anything until my girls are safe."

"You don't need to be here to do that," Stone reminds me. "I'd wager a guess there's a little omega upstairs who's part of the reason you haven't left."

"Sal's doing just fine here without me," I retort, purposefully misunderstanding him.

Stone snorts out a laugh and shrugs. "You know, it should be fucking awkward to have two pack alphas here. I sense you feel a little weird about it, but to be honest, I prefer having you here. It feels good and right. I feel like I have backup, and I like that."

When I say nothing, he continues, "When Mitchell Bancroft arrived with his pack, we got along. Hell, I fucked his mate right alongside him, and I don't like him half as much as I like you. You should stay."

Well, goddamn. There's news I haven't heard yet. I don't even know what to say.

"I'm not saying I wanna fuck you," Stone barks, clearly worried about the odd look I'm giving him.

"I can only fend off so many people in this damn house," I growl as he laughs, pausing to look at me.

And there it is. That under-the-microscope feeling of a pack alpha picking you apart to understand you. I'd growl, but Stone's partially right. I don't fight with him unless we're sparring, not like I fought with Declan when I lived there.

Plus, now I'm imagining Stone, Mitchell and his mate Alice in bed together, and I've got a fucking hard-on. Because two alphas and an omega in the bedroom is something I've been ruminating on a lot lately.

"Go on," Stone snarks. "Ask me."

"Ask you what?"

Stone takes a step closer, his growl low and soft. "Ask me what it was like to fuck an omega with my dick touching another alpha's. Ask me what it was like to take her from behind while she rode him. Ask me, Cass."

I feel my throat bob, because I've fantasized about everything he's described.

"Whose permission are you even waiting for to take what

you clearly want?" Stone continues. "Not hers, you've got that, and we all know it. James's? Mine maybe? Or are you lost in your head like Ash?"

"Don't mistake my lack of action for indecisiveness, Stone," I warn. "You need all the mated shifters you can get, but if I play with them, I put that in jeopardy. I'm not a healer or a spirit. And if we take it all the way, I'll want to keep her."

"And what about James?" he questions, dark eyes meeting mine.

"What about him?"

Stone grins. "I can't tell you how this story is going to turn out, but the three of you feel natural to me. You feel good. I know you sense that too. So maybe, for the good of everybody, you should just try it and see what happens."

"Bound to end in disaster," I bark back, but I feel my own control slipping, especially after yesterday's tease. I'd love nothing more than to barge into Jules and James's room right now, even if it was just to watch them.

"There's something else," I say, changing the direction of our conversation. "I think we should call Mahikan about Asher. He's wallowing in self-pity, and Mahikan might have a unique take on his situation."

Stone takes a step back. "You think I'm being too easy on him? You didn't see Ash when he arrived, alpha. They had him strapped to a granite block, and we had to lock him in the cooler downstairs for a week before it was safe to let him out. The American Task Force tortured him for years. He's got a long road ahead of him." Stone's tone is sharp with irritation.

"I know I didn't see that," I counter. "But I've seen him since. Mahikan and Leon might have access to power we don't. Those packs are...different. They don't operate like we do."

Stone strokes his chin. "Alright. We'll talk to them about you too, then."

"Meaning what?" I feel myself bristle at the unexpected change in our conversation.

"Chill out, old friend. But if there's ever been a time an alpha mated a healer and spirit and their omega, Mahikan would know."

I don't know how my love life suddenly turned into a decision by committee, but I growl as Stone grins and jogs out of the gym to head back upstairs. I don't want to admit that hope begins burning hot in my chest at his words, but it does. And that worries me, because hope is a dangerous fucking thing.

CHAPTER TEN

julia

IT'S hard to sleep after everything we learned in town. Even with James curled protectively around my back, my mind spins with what Betty shared. I'm certain James will spend a majority of tomorrow locked in Stone's office with the pack leadership group, trying to figure out what to do with the new info. He told me what Isabel shared, and it's harrowing. Our options for saving the omegas seem to be dwindling by the minute.

Eventually, I fall into a fitful sleep. But sweet dreams become nightmares as I relive my accident. I feel the crush of the truck knocking me off my bike. I remember waking up and trying to clear the feeling of fuzz in my brain. My hearing was gone, and my parents' faces were grim as they shared the news that the accident took my hearing, and there was nothing anyone could do.

We were traveling through Ayas then, and they went home to Quebec after I recovered physically. But I stayed. I stayed because I met Stone and Titan at the bar, and they were immediately protective of me. It was like finding two big brothers who always had my back. Shit, I practically lived at Titan's bar, Teddy's, while we all learned sign language together on

YouTube. After a month of trying to learn, Stone flew in a teacher for me, and we never looked back.

There was a lot of texting back and forth on phones to communicate in those early days. But I could never leave Ayas. Truly, I think that experience is a big reason why I love this pack so hard. Stone and Titan were there for me at a time when I experienced something harrowing and soul-crushing. But I came out of it on the other side because they were there for the good days and the bad days and every day in between.

I learned to look at my hearing change not as a loss, but a different way of experiencing and interacting with the world. Are there days I miss hearing a favorite song or a friend's voice? Definitely. But I've also gained a better appreciation for my remaining senses, and my ability to communicate in so many other ways.

The accident itself is on my mind a lot, visiting my dreams to remind me of the pain of that time. Sometimes I sleep well, and sometimes I don't. Tonight is one of the bad nights.

I wake in the morning to find James already gone. Searching our bond, I find him downstairs in Stone's office. He'll be there all day, if the last few days are any indication. I hate that I feel useless to help our pack with security or much of anything other than being a good packmate. I've spent a lot of time helping Betty in her store, Tournesol, but that's done now.

We have self-defense this morning with Titan. I'd love to say I'm picking it up fast, but it's not my strong suit. Especially when I look at Luna, and she's so freaking good. She was already a black belt in karate, and she has handed Titan's ass to him a time or two. Of course, it helps that he's hella distracted by her huge tits.

Sighing, I look down at my own. That'll never be me. But I leave my room resolved, because I want to be as prepared as possible if I have to defend myself or anyone else in this home.

The other omegas are already in the gym with Titan when I

arrive. Titan grins at me, crossing the room to give me a high five. "You're doing great, Jules. You're gonna crush this, okay?"

I love his kind pep talk, but half an hour later, I'm absofuckinglutely not crushing it. I'm flat on my back, Luna hovering above me after body slamming me into the damn ground.

The hair on the back of my neck rises. Darting a look to the left, all the air disappears from the room. Cassian stands there with a hot pink blanket on his shoulder, Abigail straddling one of his tattooed forearms with her arms and legs dangling over either side. She's fast asleep, her fat cheeks flushed.

I'm not sure if it's possible for ovaries to erupt into flames and immediately cause pregnancy, but it's happening to me right now. I'm soaked between the thighs watching the big alpha stand in the doorway with that tiny baby.

Luna snaps her fingers in my face to get my attention, and when I look up, she's grinning so big at me.

Don't you say a fucking word, I shout with my eyeballs. Luckily Luna reads people well, and she gets it. She helps me up before we cross the room to Cass.

Luna, bless her dark soul, signs as she reaches for Abigail. "Hey, want me to hold the baby for a few, and you can help Julia?"

Hope sends my heart racing as Cass transfers Abigail carefully to Luna. Luna grabs the blanket and turns back into the room, pacing as she rocks from side to side with the baby cradled to her giant boobs.

Cass's gray eyes flick to me as he signs, "You look frustrated. Need help?"

He's looking at me with such a tender, longing expression, and I can't help but wonder if he's thinking about yesterday and all the teasing.

"I suck at this, but I'm determined to get it," I reassure him.

"I think you'd respond better to a different training style," he retorts back, his lips drawn into a thin line.

"Oh yeah?" I tease. "You wanna be my teacher and throw me around like Titan does Luna?" I waggle my brows as he laughs, the corners of his mouth tilted upward.

"You need to be pushed. You need to get a little bit angry," he signs. "Anger would help you with where you're struggling."

"I'm not an angry person," I laugh as I respond. "I'm literally never mad. Ask James. I'm mad when people are rude, but that's about it."

Cass ignores my commentary. "Come." He curls his fingers as he gestures for me to follow him. Heat spreads through my chest watching his back muscles pull tight as he rolls his shoulders. God, I want to see him naked again. All those tattoos, that tan skin, the salt-and-pepper chest hair.

Swoon.

When he turns, there's a neutral expression on his face. "Focus, omega," he snaps, signing. "And stop thinking about my dick."

I'm so surprised he just signed that to me, I miss him reaching out and shoving me. My back hits the wall hard enough to knock the breath from my lungs.

"Imagine I'm attacking you," he signs. "You know to go for the nuts, so take me down, little one."

"I don't want to kick your nuts," I sign angrily, gasping for breath.

Cass gets in my face and grips my throat so hard, I struggle to breathe, scratching at his hands. "Angry," he mouths, and that simple word is easy to lip-read.

I shake my head as he drops his grip and steps back. But the moment he does, I attack.

How dare you, I want to shout. *I wasn't ready.* But I'll never be ready to be attacked by an alpha. So I feint and kick out, and my foot barely misses Cass's balls as he leaps back fast. Then he grins at me. "Good. Again."

We practice for a solid half hour before I realize everyone

has vacated the gym except for us. The moment that realization hits me, white-hot need fills my system. I could take him right here on the floor, if he'd let me. Nobody would be any wiser.

James shows up in the doorway moments later. *I felt you, mate,* he whispers into our bond.

Cass turns from me to James. "We were just practicing."

"And it's got me all hot and bothered," James signs, reaching down to stroke his own visible erection. "By all means, continue manhandling her."

I watch Cass's eyes fall to James's hand, my throat going dry as a fucking desert.

When Cass hesitates, James crosses the gym, not looking away from me. He grins, dark lips parting as his fangs appear. *Let's tease the fuck out of him, baby girl. You down?*

Oh God, I'm so down. I'm soaked with slick and sweat, dying of lust as I look at both my alphas in the room together. Cass isn't running yet, so that's a good sign.

James's dark eyes leave mine to focus on Cass. "We're not done teasing you, alpha. Yesterday was just the beginning." James presses himself flat against the wall, taking my hand as I drop to my knees in front of him. James gives Cass a seductive look as I watch from his feet. "Wanna see how good she is with that pretty mouth?"

I groan as I unzip James's pants, his dark erection falling out, thick and hot. God, he's got the perfect dick. Swirling my tongue around the tip, I take him in, breathing through my nostrils as I deepthroat him. James brings one hand to the back of my head as I sense Cass move to my right.

Looking over, I'm presented with a mouthwatering bulge at the front of his pants. He leans up against the wall, watching me suck my mate off with open longing on his elegant, angular features.

James lets his head fall to one side, his mouth dropped open as I suck on him like a lollipop. Cass's pale eyes move from me to James's neck.

My mate's hips rock softly as I watch Cass watching James. I don't miss the way the big alpha's chest rises and falls in rapid, shallow movements. I'd give a million dollars to know what he's thinking right now.

Good girl, James teases into our bond. *He looks ready to bust.*

Moaning, I work both hands along James's cock as he rips his shirt over his head, grabbing Cass's hand. To my surprise, Cass lets James guide it to the back of my head. And then they're both stroking my hair as James's hips start to move faster and faster. He's so hot from this tease.

My surprise deepens when Cassian wraps a fist through my hair and holds me tightly in place so James can fuck my mouth with measured, even strokes. His dominance brings goose-bumps to the surface of my skin as James praises me through our bond.

Gonna come, little omega, he whispers along that golden tether. *I'm gonna come so hard in that sweet mouth of yours.*

Do it. I wanna drink you down, I urge. James explodes, hips bucking as his cock fills my throat, cum dripping from both sides of my mouth as Cass's grip on my hair tightens. I'm caught, so caught, between the two of them. And there's nowhere I'd rather be.

CHAPTER ELEVEN

I GASP and moan as orgasm forces a bellow out of my throat, my stomach clenching as my girl sucks me off. Cass holds her tight as I fuck her, heat from his big frame sending my desire sky high. My eyes don't leave his as I come, and what I see there cements what I know to be true. He's attracted to me, and he desperately wants to take what we started yesterday further.

Thrusting gently into Julia's mouth, I practically sob with need when those pretty pink lips pop off my spurting cock. "God, you're good at that," I sign, slumping against the wall as Cass pulls her upright by the hair.

Steely eyes move from me to her as he tugs her head back and brings his nose down to her neck. He breathes in deeply, possessively. I'd swear he's about to rip her clothes off and yank her onto his dick, but he moves along the column of her neck before dragging her shirt down and scenting along her collarbone. He bites her shoulder hard, fangs sinking into her skin as she yips and leaps in his arm.

But she's caught by him. Too caught to move, absolutely dominated by the big alpha.

I find myself wondering how adding him might change our

dynamic. I'm dominant, but our love is tender, thorough, and scorching hot. I sense he and Jules together would be a hurricane of intoxicating, violent need, and I want it.

Cass lets go of her hair as my breathing returns to normal. They share a heated look for a long moment before he glances over at me. "I need to meet with Stone about changing our plan to rescue my girls, and I don't want to do this with you two on the gym floor. Let's do dinner at my cabin tomorrow. We'll talk."

I love him in pack alpha mode, all plans and demands.

All I can do is nod as he looks at Jules for confirmation. When she signs "yes," he nods at me and leaves the gym. The moment he's gone, Jules sinks into my chest with a needy sigh.

God, that was hot, she moans into the bond. *So fucking hot.*

I want to watch him manhandle you, I admit.

Same. I want my drawings to come to life. I wonder what changed, she muses. *You think we finally wore him down?*

Don't know, I admit, groaning as I look down at my watch. I've got to get back to Stone's office. *But whatever finally broke him, I'm thankful for it. Grabbing what's good in life, when you can, is what matters,* I remind her. *That's why we're chasing this alpha, despite all the other shit going on. Our happiness matters, Jules. And I will always fight for yours, no matter what.*

Half an hour later, Asher finds me in the kitchen, making a snack for Jules.

"So, things are progressing?" His dark eyes flash with mirth as I laugh aloud. I miss this version of Asher, this happy-go-lucky jokester who charms the shit out of everyone. I saw this a lot more when we first came to Bent Fork from New York. I've seen less of it lately than I'd like.

"If getting sucked off by one person while getting eye-fucked by another is your definition of progress, then yeah."

Asher lets out a whistle as he crosses his huge arms and leans up against the doorway. "Jules isn't going to give up, no matter what anyone tells her. Cass hasn't got a chance in hell of denying her."

"Oh, don't I know that," I murmur as I finish a sandwich for Jules. "Stone mentioned he'd like us to be more welcoming to Isabel, to make it super clear we are here for her. I'm gonna bring her a sandwich and steal that baby for a bit. Come with me?"

Ash nips at his lower lips, fangs descending as he runs both hands through his dark hair. It's getting longer, the dark strands falling into his eyes. He messes with it all the time, I've noticed.

"I don't know if that's a good idea," he hedges.

I'm with Stone on this topic—Asher isn't nearly the danger to everyone he seems to think he is. I hand him two plates with sandwiches and grab some waters for the girls, tugging at Julia through our bond. She went to shower, but I know she'll want to hang with us if we're visiting Isabel and Abigail.

I don't bother to give Ash an out as I leave the kitchen and head upstairs for Isabel's room. I knock quietly in case Abigail is asleep, but Isabel opens the door with a bright smile, blue eyes flashing.

"I just got this baby fed and now you're coming to steal her again?"

Giving her my best smile, I gesture to Ash who's a silent, anxious shadow behind me.

"We brought lunch, and I think Jules wants to come visit too. Is now a good time to hold Abigail? Stone says she smells like heaven and I need a hit."

Isabel preens and holds the door open wide, grinning at Asher as we enter her room. If she's worried about my enormous packmate she sure doesn't seem it. I hope he can tell that, but I make a mental note to make it clear later.

Ash hands Isabel a sandwich as I cross the room to the sweet baby in a swinging chair. She's not asleep, fat hands and feet wiggling around as blue eyes look up at me.

"I didn't think babies could focus this quickly," I murmur as Isabel joins me, her mouth full.

"They don't," she confirms. "But I guess alpha babies do. She's been tracking me across the room. It makes me wonder how quickly she'll grow."

My heart feels like it's being squeezed inside my chest. I want this with Jules and Cass so badly I can barely breathe.

Isabel laughs. "You got a little baby fever, James?"

"I have three brothers," I snort. "Endless nieces and nephews. I fucking love babies."

Isabel takes another bite and sits in the chair behind Abigail's rocker. "Feel free," she says.

Goosebumps coat my skin as my mate enters the room, crossing to me as I lift Abigail gently out of the rocker. I tuck her to my neck and purr my heart out, and she lets out a contented burp and nuzzles into the side of my neck.

Julia beams at me as she takes the second sandwich from Ash, and then she sits with Isabel as I pace back and forth across the room with the baby. Stone's right—she smells delicious. She smells like all the best things on the planet, and I can't resist rubbing my cheek along the top of her head as I walk. She begins to drift off as Ash, Isabel and Julia eat.

After a few minutes, there's a soft wail and she vomits all over my shoulder. It sinks right through my shirt as I groan. The baby smells incredible. The barf not so much.

Without thinking, I cross the room to the closest person— Ash—and hand the baby right to him. He lays her gently against his chest, holding her with both hands as Jules darts out of the room to grab me a new shirt. I pull mine over my head, wiping baby puke off my neck as Isabel gives me a baleful look.

"It was bound to happen to someone eventually, I'm so sorry James!"

"Don't give it another thought," I laugh. "No apology needed. Abigail is our pack's first baby. Can you imagine how spoiled she's going to be when she grows up? All of this love in this house for her?"

Isabel smiles again, softer this time, her blue eyes moving to Ash.

He's holding the baby like she's a bomb waiting to go off. He looks fucking terrified. But he purrs deeply, and Abigail's blue eyes flutter closed as we watch.

"You're really good with her," Isabel murmurs, reaching out to rub Asher's shoulder. "I know it's weird holding someone's baby, but you're a pro."

"Someone take her," Ash moans. "I don't want to hurt her."

I know what he means. Not that he'll inadvertently crush her. He's worried he'll have some sort of episode and Abigail will be hurt. But the reality is that I've seen Ash use his power for good. I've seen him use it to protect everyone in this house. There's no doubt in my mind that if Abigail was in danger, he'd give everything to help her.

What Ash needs is confidence in his own power.

"You've got this," I say. Julia comes back in and hands me a new shirt, waggling her pale brows at my half-naked figure.

But Ash's breath is starting to come faster. His dark eyes are wide as he looks from me to Jules to Isabel, who reaches for the baby when he hunches over in her direction. He seems relieved the moment the baby is out of his arms, but Isabel looks up at him with a sad smile.

"For what it's worth, I was never worried for a second, Asher. I trust you." Her words seem to roll right off him though.

He nods, but he leaves the room, ducking out the door as we watch him go.

Julia looks to Isabel with a sad smile. "I've got some work to do for Betty, but can I get you or Abigail anything at all?"

Isabel thanks us but declines, and I follow Jules out into the hallway, wrapping my arms around her as soon as we're out the door.

Never thought I had a breeding kink, I growl into our bond, *but I need you pregnant. I need to see Cass touch you while you're holding our child. God, mate, I need it when we're free of all this insanity.*

Julia turns in my arms with a saucy look. *That can be our step two. Step one is locking down our mate. Make no mistake, I want it too.*

I only wish that step one was a little bit easier.

julia

MY MIND SPINS with that interaction in Isabel's room. Watching my mate and Ash with a tiny baby. It's so damn heartwarming, and it crushes me to think that Ash doesn't trust himself to be careful. In fact, he disappeared after that, even though I spent fifteen minutes looking around the lodge for him.

Eventually I hole myself up in Stone's office and spend all day working on inventory for Tournesol. It's something I can do to help without leaving the property. It honestly feels like a moot point though—Betty closed Tournesol when we left yesterday. While I know it's a temporary move, and the right one, I can't help but feel my usefulness has run out.

Tournesol was a happy place for me, not only because I got to hang out with Betty, but I loved meeting people traveling through Ayas. I love the beauty of the store itself, and it makes me proud to help Betty manage it since she travels often for purchasing.

Good thing I can double down on making Sal and Isabel feel comfortable here. Their time in Declan's pack was terrible, and

Isabel in particular is struggling. Being a new mom looks so hard, but I'm committed to helping her.

Cherry comes into the office, smiling when she sees me. She crosses the room and flops down across from me at Stone's conference table, signing, "Why do you look so grumpy?"

"Betty closed Tournesol. You heard about Declan and the whole protection racket bullshit?"

Cherry rolls her eyes. "I heard. Erin's meeting with the town council today to talk about it, but it sounds like they're encouraging people to leave if possible."

I sit back in my chair and cross my arms. "Are you still going to work at the Moonlight then?"

Cherry's gray eyes, so much like Cass's, flicker with irritation. She nods curtly, and I know I've hit a nerve.

When I don't say anything else, she sighs. "My mental health is the worst it's ever been. Dancing at the Moonlight is for me what your art is for you."

"Leaving the ranch puts you in danger," I continue, although she's so strong and confident, I know she'll do whatever is needed to regain her happiness.

Cherry simply shakes her head. "When Mitchell's pack first came here and brought Asher, tied to a slab of granite, I knew he was mine. And in the beginning, he had good days where he was flirtatious and charming. We bonded right from the get-go, even though we both knew he had demons to battle. How could you not, after being a Task Force prisoner for years?"

I'm silent because she's never shared much about her feelings. We all knew she and Asher connected immediately. She seemed to help him focus when he first arrived, and he improved quickly with her support.

She sighs, pulling her brilliantly red hair into two low buns. "I promise you, there's nothing worse in this world than being at odds like Ash and I are right now. I can't fix him, and I shouldn't have to."

At that precise moment, Asher strides through the open office door with an angry scowl on his handsome face, his fists balled in anger. When he sees me, he tips his head to the side in greeting, but pitch-black eyes flick back to his mate.

"I'm trying to protect you," he growls, speaking and signing. "All of you. You know that."

"That's not your job," Cherry retorts, standing as she points a finger at him. "You're letting the demons win, and I'm sick of it. That's why I moved out, and it's why I'm gonna move on if you don't get your head out of your ass."

"You don't mean that," Ash whispers, barely signing out of shock for what she's just revealed.

"I do," she confirms. "Shit or get off the pot, alpha. I'm done." She leaves the room without looking back.

Ash turns to watch her go, but once she's gone, he looks back at me. There's such tense, anxious longing on his face. He's so clearly torn.

"Ash. What do you need?"

"I don't know," he signs back. "I wish I fucking knew. She doesn't understand. Nobody does."

"Help us understand," I encourage him. "Tell us more about where you're stuck. Is it memories from that time? Or visions of what's ahead of us? Talk to me."

Ash shakes his head and looks up at me.

"I have to fight to keep my emotions in check, Jules. That's why I put Abigail down. When my emotions are high, I struggle for control, and being around Cherry is an emotional roller-coaster. I never feel like I have control around her, and it's terrifying. I don't want to hurt *anyone*."

"You know none of us believe you're capable of hurting someone here, right?"

"I don't know," Ash whispers. "My mind is a battlefield most days, Jules. I try to hide it because nobody needs to go through it. There's so much pain, and so much terror, and I don't know if the things I see are whatever's behind me, or something that's coming."

With that horrific pronouncement, he turns and leaves. I've known him for months now, and I know he'd ever hurt us. But it's clear he thinks he might. It's true he's unpredictable at best. One moment he's happy and charming, and the next he's angry and distant. Asher's emotions are a rollercoaster, and I can't imagine that's fun for him.

I don't even know what to do about that. But I shudder when I think about his demons being a portent for our future.

I push harder against the pedals, racing against the oncoming storm. My mountain bike has great tires, but it's freezing in this part of Western Canada. I've already been out for three hours, and Mom and Dad are expecting me for dinner at a cute little restaurant in the small town of Ayas.

Lightning flashes across the sky as pitch-black clouds roll over the horizon. I fly through the dense pine forest, wishing I'd remembered my helmet cam so I could post this ride to my mountain biking YouTube channel.

A quarter hour passes as I push against the exhaustion in my legs, desperate to get back to the parking lot just off the main highway. It's remote out here in Ayas, but this town has been perfect for a week away with my parents. The world is in a crazy upheaval right now with the virus running rampant, but Ayas is remote enough to feel safe.

I don't realize I'm holding my breath until I see the parking lot up ahead of me, my Jeep parked right alongside the highway itself.

Hopping off my bike, I open the trunk with the key fob, unlatching my helmet when I hear the screech of tires. Looking up, I'm horrified to see a truck barrel around the corner of the highway, the driver veering from one side of the road to the other.

Time slows as lightning cracks across the sky again, distracting the driver and me. I can't see who's behind the wheel, but the truck veers sharply as the driver overcorrects, and before I know it, headlights blind me.

I throw myself to the side, but I'm not nearly fast enough. Next there's the sensation of being thrown down, and then crushing pressure and heat until I mercifully black out.

Two weeks after the accident, I awoke from a coma in Ayas' regional hospital, my hearing gone and my parents sobbing with relief that I was alive. But all I can remember is the ear-splitting noise of lightning streaking across the sky, and the all-consuming heat and pressure of being run over…

I wake with a start, struggling to fill my lungs with air as I reach for James. It's still dark outside, but he's not in bed.

Throwing on my coat, I leave my room, heading down the big staircase for the front of the lodge. I'm looking for James, but my feet pull me to the front door. God knows what time of night it is, but I hop on the nearest ATV and gun it.

Freezing air bites my cheeks and my bare legs, but all I can think of is a pair of big, warm arms to take this pain and banish it back to the darkness. I'm barely awake, thinking about James as I gun it toward Cassian.

Minutes later, I'm banging on Cass's door rapid-fire as cold air snakes up the open bottom of the coat. My chest is being crushed from the inside out as my breath comes in shuddered gasps. Air, I need more air.

The door flies open, and Cassian stands there shirtless, eyes wide and concerned. When he sees me, he yanks me inside and slams the door shut, rubbing both hands up my arms.

He takes a step back. "What's wrong? Where's James?"

"Can't breathe," I sign, bending over at the waist as my hands go to my hips. Suddenly I'm mortified that I came here to fall apart in front of him. I'm trying to seduce this man, not show him how sometimes I still can't sleep because of the nightmares.

I should have gone to find James like I always do. But I was pulled here, pulled to Cass's comfort and security.

Big arms scoop me up, the rumble of a purr vibrating against me as Cass tucks my head under his chin and crosses the room. He deposits me in one of his fireside chairs and drops to one knee in front of me, tilting my chin up. Gray eyes pierce me with their intensity as he draws both hands away. "Talk to me, little one."

"I can't," I sign as my breathing turns choppy. I can still feel the heat from the truck as it ran over me. Oh, God. Tears stream down my face as Cass pulls me up into his arms and flops down in the chair, dragging me on top of him. He tugs my head to the side, and then there's the sharp prick of alpha fangs in my neck.

Peace floods my system as I let out a groan. Cass's fresh, clean scent wraps around me like a warm hug, his bite sending endorphins crashing through my system as the heat of the truck fades away, replaced by an awareness of his hands on my body. Cass's lips move softly against my throat where he bites. Goosebumps cover my skin as I sink into that bite, the rough brush of his lips on my skin producing a new heat deep between my thighs.

Dark thoughts and memories fade until my mind is blissfully blank, Cassian's purr vibrating against my chest. Now I'm unbelievably aware of how different he feels from James. Cass's embrace has a harder edge to it, like at any moment he might flip me over this chair and fuck my worries away. James usually puts me face down in bed and kisses my entire body from head to toe. It's beautiful, and it's so him.

I slump against Cass's warm, hard chest, both hands on his muscular pecs as my head falls further back, bliss relaxing my muscles one by one. One of his hands goes to my hair, and he strokes it lazily as he purrs and bites harder.

I don't know how long he holds me, his teeth buried in my

throat, but I needed this peace. Nothing can hurt me while I'm in his arms. There's a sense of safety and protection and absolute trust that's so beautiful, I could sob at the strength of it. Everything about this big alpha feels right to me, just like James.

When Cass finally breaks the bite, he licks softly at the wound his teeth made, sending heat shooting through my core as I thrust my hips against his. He was wearing nothing but pajamas when I arrived, and his hard cock is nestled right between my thighs.

He freezes, light eyes finding mine as I lean forward, our mouths almost touching.

I need you, I think, wondering if he can feel me at all. He gives no sign he's heard but stands with me in his arms. For one tense moment, I think he's about to kiss me. But he deposits me back in the chair and drops to his knees in front of the fireplace, stacking logs before lighting a starter underneath them.

Big muscles pull and stretch under tan, tattooed skin. I grip the edges of my coat to avoid leaping out of the chair to throw myself on him. Underneath this coat, I'm wearing nothing, a fact I'd love to exploit right now.

I'm shaken from the nightmare but sated from his bite. The rush of endorphins that accompanied it has me horny as hell. Slick wets my thighs as Cass pauses, drawing in a breath as he turns to me, still on his knees.

Gray eyes drop from mine to my legs as I step them out wide and unbutton the coat. I'm naked underneath, and his eyes drink me in greedily as I slide one leg up over the chair arm.

Predatory focus forces goosebumps to the surface of my skin as Cass stands, towering over me. But then he stalks across the cabin and grabs a walkie. He talks angrily into it, signing what he can one-handed, so I don't get it all. The gist is he's calling James, as if I haven't already done that myself.

Mate, I whisper into our bond.

You alright? he questions, stroking me softly through that beautiful tether. *I felt you go to him, but I'm here if you need me.*

I need his touch, I murmur. *And I miss you.*

I love you, he returns. *Enjoy him, and call me if you want me to join.*

Our bond goes quiet as Cass shouts into the walkie some more, finally tossing it onto the countertop and turning to me. An obvious erection strains at the front of his sweatpants as he eyes me like I'm a deadly viper.

"I need you," I sign. "I came here because when I needed help, I thought of you."

He shakes his head. "I asked James to come get you, but he says he's—"

"James is busy," I retort. "I don't need him to come get me, because I'm right where I want to be." I shove the coat all the way off my shoulders, my leg still thrown over the chair arm as I slide my other hand between my thighs and stroke.

I don't say another word because, as I watch, Cass is losing the war against his formidable self-control. I'd laugh, knowing little old me is about to take down a seven-foot pack alpha, but I hold it in as he falls apart.

His big, tattooed chest heaves as his muscles begin to tremble. Eyes the color of storm clouds focus on my hand as I touch my clit, slick wetting my coat and his chair. A moan leaves my mouth as I watch blood appear on his lower lip as he bites it, his fangs piercing the soft skin.

Something seems to snap, and he meets my gaze, a smirk curling his plush lips up into a deviant smile. "I'm at my fucking wits' end trying to deny you," he signs. "And if I taste you, I won't be able to give you up one day if you find your other mate somewhere."

I don't bother to respond to that, because I still know what I always have known—Cassian *is* mine. I know it like I know the sun will rise tomorrow and then set again.

Standing, I cross the room and hop up into his arms, smiling when both hands go to my bare ass, his fingertips teasing at my ass crack. The hint of a smile is still on his face, although I know he's just shared his worst fear with me—that we'll connect, and it'll be perfect, but it won't work out.

Good thing I have zero doubts.

CHAPTER THIRTEEN

cassian

I'M LOSING my goddamn mind. I told James to come get her, that if she stayed here, I was fucking her. Because I have no self-control left. Not when she needs me, not when she showed up wearing nothing but a winter coat. Not when she showed me every bit of that sweet pussy she likes to play with.

I've been dreaming about her for almost a year. I have to get another taste.

James declined to take this beauty out of my arms, knowing full well I'm about to fuck her. It's what he wants—what they want—he told me that yesterday. Why should I bother holding back?

For a long minute, she smiles at me, and it's breathtaking. Eyes the color of the sea, pale skin covered in freckles. Her strawberry scent fills my nostrils, blossoming because she's so worked up for me. All for me.

The dam of my self-control breaks, and need floods my brain as I fist her hair and slant my mouth over hers. Our teeth clash, tongues tangling as I turn us and press her against the wall so I can use my hands. Reaching up to her small breasts, I pinch both nipples as she bucks in my arms, gasping in pleasure when her head flies back. Teeth marks still line her throat from my bite. Goddamn, she looks so good like this, covered in my scent, my mark.

I purr my fucking heart out as I search for any sign of her in my chest, any indication at all that we've got a bond like she and James do. But it's dark and silent. She'll never be mine like that. Bitter reality threatens to drive this temporary happiness away.

But I banish it. She's not mine for good.

But maybe she can be for a time. We both want it desperately.

We part as she moans, her thin hips rocking against my stomach. My dick is hard as a rock for her.

Pulling her away from the wall, I stalk to my bedroom, still kissing her. I toss her onto the mattress as she shifts up onto her elbows.

"I'm not a gentle lover, Jules," I sign. "I'm not great at being tender. Do you know what you're asking for? This is your last chance to walk away from me, little one."

Pink lips curl into a devious fucking smile as she steps her thin thighs wide and gestures for me to come to her.

I hesitate for a moment, drinking in the sight of the gorgeous omega who stole my heart all those months ago. I tasted her then. I can taste her again now. The only thing at risk is my heart, but that was lost to her already. Why shouldn't I enjoy her?

I ignore the voice in the back of my head that reminds me how this is destined to end badly, how it'll kill me if she meets an alpha who is her match. But maybe that'll never happen. Maybe I'll get to enjoy her for a long time.

Sinking down onto the bed on my knees, I grip the backs of her thighs and drag her up against the front of my body. I bury my face into her sweet pussy and lick a stripe from her ass up around her clit.

Julia cries out, hands flying above her head to grip the sheets as I groan. There are no words to describe how it is to taste her again. She's the ripest of summer berries with the cool sweetness of cream. I tried to forget how perfect she was, knowing she belonged to James, but I'm lost now.

"Goddamn," I groan, sucking her clit as I wrap one arm around her to hold her against me. Both legs are over my shoulders as I eat her roughly to the edge of orgasm, then stop. Julia coats my chest in slick as that strawberry scent grows stronger for me, blooming with urgency.

This omega is so needy, and I'm the alpha to fill that need tonight. Maybe for a long while, if I'm lucky.

I bring her to the edge again with my lips before biting the inside of her thigh hard and tossing her down onto the bed. I flip her over and run my hand between her thighs, gathering that beautiful slick and sliding my fingers between her ass cheeks.

I want her here first. I want to show her how an older, more experienced alpha fucks.

Jules presses her ass up to meet my fingers, slick coating the backs of her thighs as I groan.

I press one finger into her ass, then two, using her slick to lubricate her before I shove my pants down. Sweet honey drips onto my cock as I fuck her ass slowly with my fingers. Keeping my thumb in her ass and my fingers across her skin, I slide the tip of my cock along her sweet pussy.

James should be here.

The thought enters my mind so fast, I struggle around the weight of it.

I want him to watch me fuck her. I want to see it turn him on when I get her off on her hands and knees between us. I want to spit-roast this little omega on two alpha cocks until she chokes, maybe even introduce her to breath play if she isn't familiar.

I want all of it.

Removing my thumb, I grip Jules's thin hips and slide the tip of my cock in her ass.

She cries out, the sound ragged as her breath leaves her in a hissing gasp.

"Please," she signs with one hand before bringing her other hand above her head. "I need it, alpha. Give it to me."

I'm just about to slide balls-deep into her when that knowledge hits me again—I want James here for the first time between us. It feels right.

Sliding my cock through her pretty ass cheeks, I groan as I flip her over. I'd almost laugh at the furious look on her face. What might it be like for her to fight me? What might it be like to dominate her through a fight like that? God, I want it so badly.

"Tell James to come," I sign. "I want him here."

Blue eyes go from narrowed and irritated to sly and mischievous as she bites her lip. "Done," she signs a few moments later. She pauses for a beat before sliding up onto her elbows. "What changed, alpha?"

I stare deep into those beautiful blue eyes, knowing I'm stepping through a door I can never close. "I want to watch him with you."

Jules's cheeks flush as she reaches for my hand, pulling me down on top of her. Her kiss is tender, scorching. And I search inside for any indication of a goddamn bond that would allow me to hear her and read her emotion.

There's nothing.

But I roll over anyhow and pull her on top of me, both hands fisted in her hair as I devour her. We kiss until my front door slams open and I hear quiet footsteps.

He's here. Good.

I roll over, laying Julia down gently before standing.

James appears in the doorway, a knowing grin on his face. My eyes meet his, and I realize that somewhere along the way, I did feel like I needed his permission to take this all the way with her. It's his claiming bite on her delicate skin. It's him who'll have to deal with the fallout if this turns out badly. Because if it does, I'm leaving this place for good. I can't watch another alpha have them. It would kill me.

And the reality is, it would be better for the pack to have them mated successfully to the right partner now. It would mean more shifting alphas, more alphas with powers, and a step closer to the omegas developing their own powers, which requires a solid percent of the pack to be happily mated.

All those thoughts flee my mind as James takes a step closer, peering in my bedroom to smile at Julia. "You called?"

"I need to watch you," I command.

"Where do you want me?" His voice falls low and possessive as he licks his lips. Heat spreads across my shoulders as I roll them and look from him to Jules.

"I want to watch you together," I sign. I can't admit any more than that out loud. Thankfully, James seems to understand. He steps past me, reaching out to pick up Jules's foot. He kisses the instep tenderly then places it back down as I cross the room to sit in a chair across from my bed.

And that's when I realize I'm sitting here with my pants half off my hips, my hard dick swinging like a damn baseball bat as another alpha eye fucks me.

Growling, I shove the pants all the way down as they both watch me. James grits his teeth but never looks away. Julia lets out a soft, needy mewl and props herself on all fours, ass presented to me as she looks at James.

His eyes finally leave mine as he grins at her.

"What are you saying?" I question and sign.

"I'm gonna translate every word for you, alpha," he

murmurs. "Every thought, every feeling I get through our bond. I'm gonna share it with you until you feel it yourself."

Dangerous hope threads its way through me as I lean forward, elbows on my knees. I don't want to miss a minute of this show. I want the future he's describing so fucking badly, I'd give almost anything to have it.

James smirks at me before shucking his pants off, his cock hard and leaking already as Julia sinks onto her stomach. Her lips part as he pulls his shirt over his head. James grips his substantial cock at the base and teases her mouth with it.

My balls feel heavy and achy as I watch James stroke Jules's hair away so I can see everything. I watch her take him deep into her mouth and suck before he laughs and steps away. She growls and watches him, but he laughs again and lies on the bed, patting his chest as he winks at her.

When she crawls up his big body, he grips her hips and drags her up onto his face. That strawberry scent fills the room as she hunches over, her body clenched tight. And then the only thing I can focus on is the way she moans and pants and the sloppy sounds of his tongue between her thighs.

She's right on the verge of coming as I fist my cock, not even realizing I'm doing it. But then James shifts sharply and throws her down, covering her with his much larger body. Gently, he settles between her thighs, drawing his dark fingers up her leg to her knee, which he presses up and out.

With a quick punch of his hips, he buries himself inside his mate, and I growl at the heady pleasure that watching them produces in me. He teases her with halfway-there strokes, not giving her all of his long shaft. Julia goes from soft moans to angry demands, scratching at his arms as he takes her pleasure masterfully.

When she comes, she throws her head back and looks at me, and James buries his teeth in her throat. She screams herself hoarse, one arm falling off the edge of the bed as her fingers reach for me.

And God help me, I drop to my knees and take those fingers in my mouth.

Just a little taste, that's all I need. Just a little bit more of her.

I'm already fucked, though, because this will never be enough. I will always want more of them.

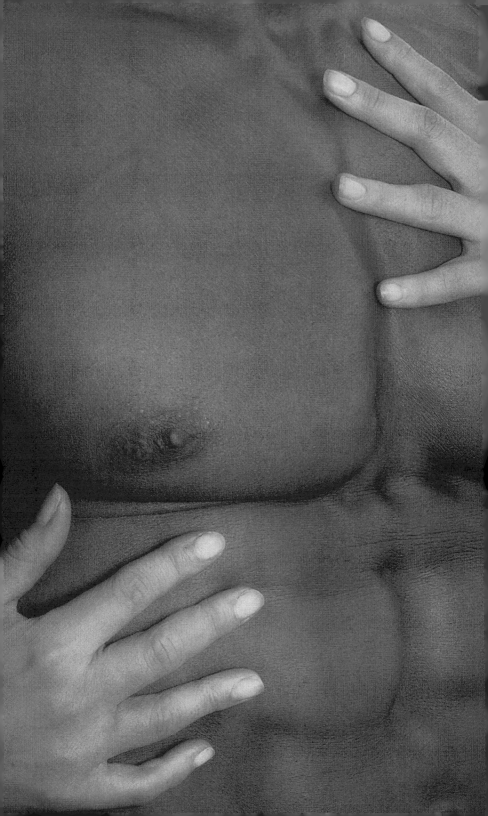

CHAPTER FOURTEEN

cassian

JULES FALLS ASLEEP QUICKLY after multiple orgasms, and I eventually drift off watching them hold one another in my bed. They're so goddamn beautiful together.

I wake in the morning so satisfied, but so needy. Julia's face is buried in my chest, both hands over my heart. Behind her, James's dark eyes are already open.

Memories of our first kiss flood back to me then. How aggressively dominant he was, how confident, how good he felt up against me. My body tightens just thinking about it.

James grins, the hand he has lazily wrapped around Julia's waist snaking over toward mine. Big fingers trace the outline of my hard cock, and it leaps when he touches it. I want to roll over and let him have his way with it, to see what he does when he has my permission. Last night was about her—her pleasure and need and her lust for us.

I want now to be about him and me.

James grips my cock hard and strokes as I let out a groan and shift my hips to give him more access. He unwraps himself from Julia and slides over her body and on top of mine.

My eyes flick to her, but she snores softly, the blankets

pulled up to her chin.

"She's got another hour of sleep in her," James signs, settling himself on top of me. Like this, I'm painfully aware of how handsome he is. He's muscular, just as muscular as I am, his shoulders thickly stacked.

I run a hand up his beautiful dark skin, over his pecs and down impossibly chiseled abs. James shifts his hips, the length of his hard cock brushing along mine as I groan. "Wanna play until she wakes up?"

I give him a look, and he grins. "Shit, alpha. We could play after she wakes up, and she'd love watching every minute of it."

"I want it," I grunt, reaching out to stroke his cock as he thrusts against me again. This time yesterday I had never touched a man, and now I can't keep my hands off him. James's rhythmic movements drive me wild as I watch our dicks together. All I can think about is Stone sharing how hot it was to fuck Alice with Mitchell's dick touching his.

Reaching into my nightstand, I grab a simple pocket pussy, the kind that's open at both ends. James chuckles as I guide it down over my length and then flip us so I straddle him. I grunt when he grips his cock and shoves it up into the toy alongside mine. We're both leaking precum, and the toy is coated already. I groan at the feel of his hardness against mine. I test it out as he holds the toy and I thrust against him.

James grunts and arches his back as he squeezes tighter, and then I'm fucking his hand and the toy so hard the bed shakes. Julia's gonna wake up any second and see us, and knowing that makes me want to scream in pleasure.

I gasp as my balls tighten up, my cock slipping out of the toy. James's chest heaves as he tosses the toy aside and grips us in both of his hands. "I like it hard, alpha," he growls. That demand shatters my restraint, and I grip his hip in one hand and his throat in another, shoving myself into his hands as orgasm builds between my legs.

"I'm gonna come so fucking hard," I grunt out, not wanting to miss a second of his pleasure.

James's face is screwed up tight, his dark lips parted, and all I know is I need to feel them when he comes. Leaning over him, I take his mouth, bruising him with how hard I am, biting and sucking as he cries out.

I can't fucking believe Julia's not awake for this, but when I roar into the cabin, screaming out James's name as I spurt all over his stomach, her blue eyes flutter open and widen. She props herself up on one elbow as James joins me, but then he's pulling her in for a desperate, heated kiss as he bellows into her neck. She eye-fucks me the whole time, sending me into another soul-rending orgasm.

James's abs are coated in release as my thrusts slow and finally stop. He kisses Julia tenderly, shuddering when I slip out of the toy and toss it aside. She smiles into their kiss as he presses her flat on the mattress, looking up at me.

"Wanna see how I wake Jules up?" he signs with a grin, still rubbing me with measured, teasing strokes.

"Yes," I demand. I want to know everything about their routine. I want to be part of it.

James slides down the bed and grips one of Julia's knees, shifting her onto her back as he slings one leg over his shoulder.

Goosebumps pepper my skin as he kisses a trail up her inner thigh, biting gently before closing his mouth over her clit.

He sucks softly, running circles over her skin as she begins to stir in my arms, a soft moan leaving pretty, swollen lips. James gives me a heated look as he sucks harder, her thin hips rocking up to meet his mouth.

Blue eyes flutter open, finding mine as a flush spreads across her pale cheeks.

"Good morning," I sign before stroking strawberry blond waves out of her face.

She moans as she looks up at me, hands moving seductively. "Would be better if you were both down there."

Fuck. Oh fuck. The image she's painting sends a stab of need through me as James's head bobs between her pretty, freckled thighs.

Shifting to her side, I grip her other thigh and press it down, rubbing my beard along her skin. Julia shudders as James begins to purr. The combination of their scents together drives me wild as I bite harder, marking my way up her thigh.

James groans as he shifts to make way for me, and then my mouth closes over her clit as he licks below that. Jules's hips buck as she lets out a guttural cry.

God, she tastes amazing. There's her natural scent, combined with the evidence of what we did last night. She's close, so close as we suck and lick her right to the edge of orgasm.

My eyes meet his, only to find a darkly devious expression on his face. He still wants me, despite the multiple orgasms we just had. It's clear in the way he's looking at me right now, like I'm something he can't wait to sink his teeth into again.

Groaning, I nip softly at Julia's clit as her cries amplify. She comes with a ragged scream, James never taking his eyes from mine, except for the moment she coats him in slick, and his eyes roll back into his head at how good she smells.

We lick her through to the other side of pleasure before she taps me on the shoulder. "My turn, alpha," she signs. "I need you to fall apart before we tackle this day."

I'm so hot with need for them at this point that I couldn't say no even if I wanted to. Reason and logic should probably be doing their jobs right now, but they aren't.

I flop onto the pillows next to Julia and pull her on top of me. Before she can slide down, James covers her from behind, biting his way along her neck and shoulder as her head falls to one side.

I ache to mark that pretty expanse of skin, but James's claiming bite is clearly visible from this angle. I remember how I can't have them forever, how this is just for a time. Gripping Julia's throat, I pull her down to my mouth and slick my tongue over the rough skin where he claimed her.

The effect is instantaneous. Julia bucks in my arms as I groan into her neck. James grips her hips and pulls her down, slick wetting my cock as she grinds on my erection. Between the friction and her hips, I'm almost feral. I squeeze Julia's throat tight as we focus on her pleasure. James grips both of Julia's wrists, guiding her hands to me.

I let out a groan when tiny, delicate fingers wrap around my throbbing cock. He eye-fucks me over her shoulder as she grins, gripping me tight as they stroke me off together. The desperate urge to flip them both over and have my way with them hits me so hard, I can barely breathe around the need for it.

My head falls back as I imagine what it would feel like to sandwich her between us, to do what Stone mentioned—slide into her with my dick rubbing James's.

I fucking want it.

"Fuck her," I growl and sign, my alpha command strengthening my tone. I watch it hit James hard, goosebumps coating his arms as his eyes roll back.

"I love your bark," he snaps back, signing it with both arms still around Julia's waist, his hands visible to her.

Julia winks at me as James pushes her forward, guiding her hands to my chest. He moves his hands between her thighs and coats her with her own slick. Her swollen lips are open, the bottom one puffy from my teeth.

She grunts, fingernails clawing at my chest as James slides into her ass from behind, one hand on her shoulder and the other on her hip. He thrusts slowly, steadily as her thighs quake. Julia coats me in slick, my own dick soaking wet from all that sweet honey. I need to take and take this little omega.

Reaching down, I line my cock up with the entrance to Julia's heat and look up at the grinning omega in my arms. "Sit," I sign, reveling in the way she gasps but follows my command beautifully, sinking down slowly onto me as I belt out a string of curse words. Slick, wet heat wraps around my cock, tighter than her mouth and so perfect.

"Fuuuuuck…" I grab her hips and pull her off me to yank her down again as she cries out. Her head falls back against James as he holds them both upright.

She's so fucking full like this, James taking her from behind, me taking her from below.

James looks down at me as I pause, sliding out and back in with deep, measured strokes. He signs with a devilish grin. "You want her hard, alpha, I can tell."

I hold back a needy whine at his words. I do. I'm a violent lover. I'm being careful with Julia because she's not crafted for me; she's not my mate. I could hurt her. Still, I want to toss both of them around and dominate until they're begging for mercy.

"She'll be fine," James growls. "She's strong as fuck."

I don't doubt that for a moment, but...

Julia leans forward, directing me to look right into those beautiful blue eyes. "Use me up, alpha," she signs. "I've been dreaming of unleashing you since the moment we met. I want it."

For half a moment, I stare at her in wonder, this perfect woman who feels like mine even though she can't be. And then I lose my goddamn mind as need takes over.

Gripping her throat, I bring one hand to her hip and fuck up into her hard and fast. Her pulse throbs under my fingertips as James pauses behind her, letting me lead the pace. But every time I yank her down, he fills her ass with a possessive growl.

Her cries grow louder and louder as that tight pussy stretches around me, clenching as it strokes me. God, I'd give anything to knot her and give her my claiming bite. I'd put it right next to James's so I could suck at them both when we're mid-fuck.

"More, alpha," James commands, grunting when I pick up the pace underneath them. Julia bounces on my cock so hard, I worry she'll bruise. But they asked for this, and I won't deny the need any longer.

Her small breasts sway violently as I fuck harder, sweat breaking out across my neck and shoulders. I'm going to come so damn fast inside her.

When a warm hand grips my balls, tugging softly, my entire core clenches. I bellow into the cabin as release hovers a breath away. Julia pants above me, every muscle trembling as she gets close.

The hand on my balls rolls them, pulling and tugging rhythmically as I grit my teeth. "More," I demand. "I want more."

I don't just mean right now, like this. I mean everything. And I know James knows, because he lets out a dark laugh as he reaches around Julia to sign. "I know you do, alpha. And we're going to give it to you."

"Oh fuck," I grit out as Julia shatters around me. She screams into the cabin as her pussy milks me, and I fall over the edge into a blistering orgasm that sends sparks shooting behind my eyelids, my grip on her neck brutal and punishing. A vein in her neck throbs as I press against it, my gaze pinned to the way her blood pulses underneath my fingertips.

Orgasm batters me as she unleashes, riding me wildly until I can't see or focus on anything but the sweet scent of her.

We come together for a long time, until Julia slumps forward on my chest with a sated groan.

Behind her, James beams and continues to take her ass, his movements unhurried. "I'm thinking we need round two," he murmurs, picking up the pace as my cock pops out of her soaked pussy.

Jules huffs out a pleased sigh in my chest as James takes her.

When he reaches down and grips my cock, stroking it, I jolt. He pauses, looking up at me with a satisfied grin.

And then he strokes again as I rock my hips up to meet his hand, so warm, so rough.

"Harder," I command him as he grips me tight and works my cock over. He's still taking Julia's ass with slow thrusts, the sloppy sounds of him fucking her sending my need over the top. I'm gonna come again like this. And again and again.

James reaches down and lines my cock up so that every time he leaves her ass, his dick brushes mine. I'm feral with need for them by the time he's ready to come, his thrusts taking on a harder, needy edge.

His skin brushes mine, her slick coating us both as he purrs his heart out for our girl. "Come with me," he demands as his chest heaves, dark lips parted as he breathes heavy and fast. "Goddamn, it feels good to touch you."

Julia begins quivering again as I purr, holding her tightly to me so James can come in her ass and fill her with his seed. I want to fill her again. Goddamn, I didn't even realize it until right now, but I wanna fill her so good, she swells with my babies. Visions of a pregnant Julia tip me over the edge as I fantasize about how we could take her like that.

Bellowing my release, I capture her mouth as she comes with James and me, screaming into the kiss as he rails her hard and fast.

When that blinding pleasure finally fades, he and I lavish affection on her before taking her into the shower and doing it again.

And despite how good it feels, how beautiful this connection is, I know it can't last. I'm already making plans B and C in my mind to save my girls.

But an alpha sure could get used to this.

CHAPTER FIFTEEN

TODAY, for the first time, I can envision how a permanent relationship would be between the three of us. It's not like I haven't fantasized about it, but it's easier to see our dynamic after last night and this morning. Cass is so powerful, so over-the-top commanding. I shudder when I think about him unleashing that on us. It was so damn good.

After watching Titan and Luna go through such a struggle to find one another, I know that sort of miscommunication is not my cup of tea. That's why James and I have been brutally clear with Cass—I don't want there to be any doubt in his mind about what James and I want.

I stand in the doorway to Cass's closet and watch him dress, nibbling the tip of my finger because he's so freaking handsome. He grins at me, that beautiful smile growing wider when James joins us and kisses his way up my neck, his rumbly purr vibrating my back.

"It's easy between us, don't you think?" I question Cass as he cocks his head to the side, looking like he's trying to hold in a smile.

James reaches around my waist, signing a quick "yes" as

Cass's gray eyes move to him. When he looks back at me, I know he's going to admit that being with us feels right.

"It is, and that terrifies me. I want what we have to last, but I want James to shift and you to get powers. I'm worried I'm standing in the way of that." His smile falls a little when he shares his fears, but I cross the small space into his closet and rub my cheek on his chest.

Taking a step back, I sign with quick, sure movements, because there is no doubt in my mind that he's meant for me. "It's you for us, and it'll never be anyone else. We want you for you, not for what our gifts to the pack might be. I can't say what's in the future, but I know for sure that future lies with you both."

Cass grips the back of my head and buries his face in the crook of my neck. It's like he finds comfort in my touch, and I wish I could speak into his mind the way I can James's. I'd tell him he's doing this because I'm his, and one day it'll all work out.

James's warm hand slides around my waist, then runs up under Cass's shirt to rest on his pecs. Cass's purr grows faster and more insistent, but I nearly cry when he pulls away, giving us both a sorrowful look. "I've got a few things to do today, so I'm headed up to the lodge. You two want to come?"

"Hell yeah," James signs. "I'm gonna feel you up on the ATV."

Cass's lips tilt up into a smile, but there's still a sad crinkle in the corners of his eyes. It'll take time for him to acknowledge we're meant to be, but I'm alright with that as long as we communicate about it. If there's one thing I know from James's and my conversations about ethical nonmonogamy, it's that being up front and keeping the lines of communication open is critically important.

We manage to make it back up to the lodge despite James teasing Cass the whole way. I'm in the middle of a sexy alpha sandwich, and I'm practically preening by the time we make it up to the house. When we hop off the ATV, I sign to the boys, knowing James needs to check in with pack leadership. "I want to check on Isabel and the baby and see if she needs anything. I'll catch you later?"

"I'm headed that way myself," Cass signs, taking my hand as we head for the door. We split in the lobby, James going to Stone's office as we head upstairs and to the right where Isabel is staying.

I'm unprepared to open the door and find the twins with Isabel, who's resting comfortably in her chair in front of the fire. Rogue sits next to her, Isabel's feet in his lap as he massages them. Isabel looks up when we approach, smiling as she points to the twins. Cass translates for me since she doesn't know ASL yet.

"The twins showed up this morning insisting on watching Abigail and the foot massage. I've never been so relaxed in my life."

"I'm an excellent masseur," Rogue chirps from his spot next to the weary omega, winking at Cass as he rubs Isabel's feet.

Sal comes through the door then, signing something about lunch to River, who looks down at the baby as if to say she's got her hands full. Without thinking, I cross the room and open my arms for Abigail. River hands her to me as Isabel smiles, and all I can do is grin as I turn to Cass.

The look on his face stops me dead in my tracks. His brows are furrowed, his eyes wide and desperate, as if the sight of me holding a child is almost more than he can take. It doesn't take a mate bond to know he wants what he's looking at.

Good. I want him and everything that goes along with that. Someday, in the future, when we're free of Declan's bullshit.

Cass takes over for Rogue so he can help his sister and Sal. They return shortly with food, and then it's like a mini pack meeting as I sit with Abigail on my chest. Cass feeds me as Isabel relaxes. My heart is so full, I can barely stand it.

"It feels so good to have you here," I share, Cass translating my message.

Isabel smiles at me, transforming her face from the usual worry to something confident and beautiful.

"You belong here," I continue. "And we're here to make things easier for you, okay? Please count on us for help with the baby or anything else."

Isabel's smile broadens as Abigail yawns in my arms.

"Not for diapers, though," River snorts. "Fuck all the way off with diapers. I am drawing the line there."

Isabel and I both laugh, but Rogue looks over at me with a gentle smile.

"I'll do the diapers," he signs. "I fucking love babies."

His sister gives him a curious look, and for a long time after that, we sit in companionable silence, and it feels perfectly right.

CHAPTER SIXTEEN

cassian

I SPEND several hours with Rogue and the girls, and it's the closest to having my own pack I've ever felt. As if he can hear my train of thoughts, Rogue looks up from his spot next to Isabel, who's fallen asleep in the chair. Julia still holds Abigail, seated in the window, and I realize even River is quietly watching me.

"What is it?" I question, watching her smile grow wider.

"Feels like we're waiting for you to tell us what to do or something." River's voice is gentle as she looks over at her brother.

A sense of rightness hits me as Julia gives me a knowing look. *You belong here,* she seems to reiterate.

"I need to speak with Stone about a plan for the omegas," I offer instead. River's right. Sitting with this smaller group feels good, like they're mine to protect and cherish. It fucks with my head because I'm not the pack alpha here, no matter how good I'd be at it.

My thoughts turn sour. "Julia, walk me out?"

The twins grin as Julia signs her agreement, passing Abigail to River and following me out of Sal's room into the hallway. She plants a tender kiss on my chest as I press her against the wall. Gripping her hair, I lean down and take her lips. I'm about to go caveman and claim her right here in the hall, because I want everyone to know she's mine after the morning we spent together.

Except she's not. For all I fucking know, Leandra could be a healer or spirit. Julia might wake up tomorrow and want Leandra more than she wants me, a biological need that can't be ignored.

I swear to God I'll kill the female alpha if that happens.

Pulling away from the tender kiss, I look deep into Julia's blue eyes, feeling how right she is. She feels like mine in every way that matters, as if her soul was crafted to fit mine like a puzzle piece.

"Go figure out how to help the girls. But hurry back," she encourages me with a saucy wink before reaching out to stroke my dick with her small hand.

Groaning, I thrust into that touch, even though we're right in the middle of the hallway. Now that I've tasted her and James, I'm addicted. I could no sooner give them up than—

No. I've got to shut that train of thought down fast. This is a temporary solution to scratch that itch.

It's a lie, and I know it as I think it, but she's still stroking my cock through my jeans, and I'm about to lose my mind. There's got to be a record for how many times an alpha can come in one day, and, damnit, I want to know what that number is.

After she kisses my chest again and disappears back into Isabel's room, I marvel at how strong my feelings are for her. Of course, they've been there since the day I tasted her in the hot springs. I just shoved them way down because I didn't think I could have her.

Turning, I head downstairs and across the lobby, through the back halls to Stone's office.

When I arrive there, it's quiet with the exception of Luna pecking away at her computer. She's still working her day job as a toy designer for a sex toy company. She and Titan are working to patent his Omegamatic invention, something that will bring a shitload of money to the pack if she's right about its potential.

Having used the giant sex toy on a stand myself, I know she's right.

Not that it compares to the real thing.

Goddamn, I've got to get my mind out of the gutter.

Dark eyes flick up to mine, and Stone gives me a lazy grin from behind his massive dark desk. "You smell like them," he murmurs, low enough that I hope Luna didn't hear. Because if she did, I'll get questioned within an inch of my life.

"Like who?" I hear in her bubbly, happy voice.

Stone snickers as Luna hops out of her chair, blond waves flying. "Oh my God, you fucked them finally? I'd ask you to tell me everything, but I bet you're the silent type. But that means you're sticking around, right?"

After giving Stone another irritated grimace, I look at Luna and cross my arms. She doesn't wither under the alpha stare like some women would though.

Instead, she grins at me and crosses her arms. "Don't try that pack alpha stare with me. I've been dealing with the US Patent Office all day, and I am in no mood. So...you finally broke under the pressure, huh?"

Stone laughs aloud. "Luna, give the man a break. I'm sure you can get the details from Julia during movie night. I've got to talk about some real-world issues here."

"Ugh, fine." She shakes her head in irritation. "I'm gonna find out everything though, mark my words."

"Fine," I bite back, wondering what Julia and James would tell her. How much detail would they share? I'd love to be a fly on the wall for that conversation.

Turning from her, I sit in a chair facing Stone. I suspect he's not going to love what I have to say. "I've got a Plan C. I'm going to go up and listen to Gabriel give his sermon today. I'm curious why Declan and Gabriel are so insistent on the townspeople joining, and I'd like to lay eyes on the omegas."

Before I think better of it, I barrel on, "There's a likely future where I try to get back into that pack in order to get the girls out, especially with everything we learned from Isabel. It's that or an all-out war, which is obviously a less-than-optimal path."

One of Stone's brows travels up into his hairline as he grits his teeth. He shifts back in his seat and steeples his fingers, then gets on his walkie and radios Clay to join us. "I hate this fucking idea," he barks at me, "but you might not be wrong."

We say nothing, eyeing each other silently until Clay shows up and sits in the chair next to mine. When I look over, there are dark circles under his eyes. "Not sleeping?"

"Hell no, brother. Are you?" Clay's southern drawl is pronounced, showing his Texan origins.

"Did okay last night," I say gruffly as Stone snorts out a laugh.

Clay looks from him to me, then leans in and gives my shoulder a big sniff. "Well, goddamn, it's about time, brother. Tell me everything." His big green eyes sparkle with mischief as he crosses one ankle over his knee. Behind us, Luna snickers but gathers up her stuff and leaves the office.

Rolling my shoulders, I let out a frustrated growl. "I'm not gonna relive the whole thing here in the office. It's probably gonna end in disaster when their real mate shows up. Can we talk about this plan please?"

Both alphas freeze when I mention the temporary status of my current relationship with Julia and James, but Clay perks up a little when I share what I'm thinking about Declan's pack. I pause after I repeat what I told Stone.

Clay sighs. "To be honest, I've been considering this since

you joined us, and I hoped it wouldn't come to this. But Declan's attack on Isabel proves he's willing to hurt anyone, and having a handler isn't stopping him from being violent. Other than an outright war, which we should avoid at all costs, trying to get you back into his pack is our next best option."

Stone gives me a look. "Have you talked about this with Julia and James?"

"No," I counter. "It's something I've been considering, and I'm telling you first. Things with James and Julia are new...and temporary," I remind them.

Stone frowns but doesn't say anything about that comment, moving on instead. "You almost killed Declan a few weeks ago. How are you planning to get back in?"

That's the rub, really. Because it's true—I would have killed Declan when he kidnapped Erin, Luna and Rogue. I had to make a choice to rid Ayas of Declan or save Rogue, and I chose Rogue. If things had gone differently, my girls would all be free from Declan right now. I can't stop thinking about that.

"I'm planning to start attending sermons. I'll tell him the message intrigues me, and I want back in. He'll probably fight me, but I'm hoping I can appeal to Gabriel's religious angle. Maybe I never fit in because Declan had no direction, but this new God's chosen people bullshit is up my alley."

"There's a chance they'll just kill you," Clay gruffs. "How will the rest of leadership feel about you trying to come back?"

"Half and half," I admit. "I mostly got along with JB and Will, but Bek and the rest are throwaways; they're complete assholes. They won't be happy to see me, but since JB is the pack enforcer, he can push the issue if Declan agrees."

"What about the fact that you were Declan's strategist, but he's got Gabriel now?" Clay asks the obvious question, the one I've been mulling over a lot.

"It's a risk," I admit finally. "But short of calling Jacob, Leon and Mahikan from the northern packs to give us more bodies to throw at a war, what are the options?"

"Oh, it's likely to still come to that," Stone murmurs. "But I agree this is a possible intermediary step."

"What would you do?" I question, watching as Stone bristles against another alpha's pack tone.

"Exactly what you're doing," he says finally in a soft, soothing tone. "Still, I want some plans in place in case this goes south, which there is a high likelihood of. It probably makes sense for you to feel this out before we commit to this plan."

"Agreed. We've got to get my girls out, Stone. It's killing me thinking of them living there without anyone to protect them from Declan and leadership."

The three of us fall silent at my words, and it's a harsh reminder for me too. I had the time of my life last night with James and Julia, but there are bigger things at stake here than my temporary fun with a hot alpha and his mate.

Growling my frustration, I stand and nod at them both, leaving the office. Even from here, I can smell that sweet, fresh berry scent. Julia's close by. Despite the thoughts I was just having, I ache to hold her for a moment before I go about my day. I want to bury my nose in that strawberry blond hair and soak her in.

I round the corner into the lobby and freeze, my body bristling. In the front window, Julia sits with her tablet propped on her knees, reading something on a screen. Leandra sits next to her, watching her read, her eyes firmly planted on Julia's tits.

My first instinct is to tear the house down and bury Leandra somewhere in the middle, but then I remember I'm not Julia's mate, no matter how much I want that to be the case. It would be better for this pack if everyone mated who they were meant for. The ability to shift and access powers are on the line.

Deciding to torture myself, I stand in the shadows of the

doorway and watch them. Julia nods at what she sees on the screen, then hands it back to the surly alpha.

"The sign for thank you is this," she signs to Leandra, showing her how to move her hands.

Leandra fucks it up, and Julia reaches out, arranging her fingers so the sign is right. When she gives the female alpha an encouraging smile, I swallow the roar about to force its way out of my throat.

Leandra grabs her phone again and types on it, then hands it to Julia. She doesn't know ASL, but she fucking figured out an easy way to communicate. I hate it, because Leandra cares enough about communicating to do this when she should be resting for her next shift.

Julia reads the screen and laughs, a slight blush turning her cheeks pink. "That's much harder to sign." She chuckles, typing on the phone and handing it back.

For a long moment, Leandra stares at Julia with such open longing, I can barely stand it. But to her credit, Julia gives her a pleasant but not terribly sensual smile.

I'm proud, angry and on edge. Stalking across the lobby, I growl as I get closer.

Leandra frowns up at me and stands. "You need something, alpha?" Her tone is disrespectful. This is a woman with a chip on her shoulder. I dislike her intensely.

"I need you to get your rest so you can do the job you came here to do," I bark back, watching my alpha command hit her square in the chest.

Leandra stands up taller. "It's my free time, Cassian. I can do whatever I want with it."

"No, you can't," I counter. "When you take a job guarding people, they come first. Not what you want. It's the same for me as pack alpha. You—"

"But you're not *this* pack's alpha," she retorts, her tone acidic. "You're just *here*, for some fucking reason. Why is that?"

I don't restrain the angry roar this time.

Leandra steps back and throws both hands up in the air. "I guess we'll pick this up another time," she snorts, glancing at Julia before signing goodbye and leaving through the front door.

When she goes, Julia lets out a little laugh and pats the bench seat in front of her. "Sit with me a second, alpha," she demands.

I drop immediately to the cushion, possessive rage still barreling through my system as I look at her.

"It's cute that you're jealous," she signs with a mischievous grin. "Don't bother trying to deny it. It bothers you that Leandra's a flirt."

"She's not flirty with everybody," I sign angrily.

"She's only been here a day," she retorts. "She might be."

"I don't care who she flirts with as long as it's not you. Unless she's you and James's mate. And then I don't know what I'll do."

Julia puts her tablet down and hops to her knees, scooting across the bench seat and straddling my thighs. She settles herself down in my lap, rocking her hips against me once.

"Leandra's not our mate," she signs with a grin. "You are. James and I both know it, and we'll continue to remind you mercilessly until it sinks in. You're going to claim us, Cass. I'm calling it now."

I groan as I take her lips gently, then suck at her tongue as my need grows. I could fuck her right here in the window and feel nothing but intense pride that she's mine.

"I'm not," I remind her instead. "I'm the wrong designation, remember?" I'm fucking miserable as I say it.

"Doesn't matter." Julia shrugs. "I know it in my heart. And I can't wait until you know it too."

With that, she slides off my lap with a teasing grin. "James is free today. You should take him with you wherever you're going." She turns to leave, and James is there, grinning at us.

I pride myself on being an excellent communicator, but the focus of my day today is something I'm not ready to cover with them just yet. They're going to find out soon enough, and I'm going to get an earful. I'd rather be certain that Plan C has a chance before I share. There's no need to upset them needlessly.

Shit.

CHAPTER SEVENTEEN

CASS FROWNS AT ME. "I've got some things to do alone today, but I can drop you in town."

"That's fine." I wave away his excuse. "Titan needs help in the bar for a bit. Drop me there and then get me on your way back." I find myself wondering if he needs time to sort through what we did last night and this morning. Or maybe he's just worried about the omegas. It's probably a combination of all those things.

It's clear, at the very least, he needs space. I can do that.

For a moment, the big alpha wavers. Then, finally, he runs both hands through that salt-and-pepper hair and nods once at me.

Holding back a grin, I search inward for our mate.

Gonna tease the shit out of him on the way home, sweet girl. I'll send you the play-by-play.

Oh God, tell me everything. I'd kill to watch you touch one another again.

Soon, I promise her. *Soon he'll realize how fucking serious we are.*

Our bond goes quiet but tense with anticipation as I follow

Cassian down the front stairs and toward the vehicles. Normally he takes his Harley, but I can see him debating whether or not he wants me riding behind him or in front.

Finally, he heads toward one of Stone's trucks, hopping in the driver's seat.

"Not gonna open my door for me?" I laugh, sliding into the passenger seat as he looks over and blanches. "I'm kidding, Cassian," I joke. "You look fucking stressed, alpha."

"I just want to get my girls out, James," he gruffs back.

If we were farther along in our relationship, I'd suck him off in the car to take that tension out of his big shoulders. We're not there yet. He's still coming to terms with me and Jules and not believing we're meant to be. But now is not the time to press him on that, despite our beautiful connection last night.

Cassian's quiet all the way to the bar, and when he drops me off without a word, I don't push him. I can't imagine how hard it is to be a dominant pack alpha in a pack with a great alpha already. It's not like he could displace Stone. But he hasn't left yet either.

When he said "my girls" in reference to Declan's omegas, I'll admit there was part of me that wondered if he'd prefer to build his own pack away from ours. We haven't had that conversation, but I'd like to. I'm a big fan of open communication, but given our connection and how new it is for him, I understand if he needs a little space to think.

Heading into the bar, I wave at Titan and his bar manager. It's dead in the bar, so I give him a skeptical look.

"You said you needed help, brother. There are tumbleweeds blowing around in here. What gives?"

Titan grins at me. "Said I needed you to come to the bar, not that I needed help. Four-thirty is the dead zone for most restaurants."

"Okay," I sigh. "Out with it then. This sounds like an enforcer chat. Let me guess. You don't want Ash and River listening in?"

Titan shrugs as he cleans an already immaculate whiskey glass. "It's not enforcing, per se. Tell me about Cass and what's going on between you three. Anything I need to be worried about?"

"Worried? Hell no." I laugh. "We want to fuck him, T, not start a pack war."

Titan laughs and grins. "Point taken. Still, there's the issue of him being the wrong designation. How's that gonna work?"

"I don't know," I admit. "But Julia and I don't care. We want him anyway."

"And what about the pack?" Titan presses, blue eyes locked onto mine.

"What *about* the pack?" I growl back, sitting stiffly on the closest barstool.

"Well, the pack could use a healer and a spirit, and two more shifting wolves. You mate a pack alpha, and we don't get that. Have you considered it?"

Fuck that. I'm not easy to anger. Of our whole pack, I'm probably the most low-key man here. But I won't stand for this line of questioning. "Tell me, Titan. If Luna wasn't an omega at all, would you deny your bond with her? Would you cast her aside for the rest of us?"

He says nothing, but I know I've got him. He loves that girl so hard.

"You're wrapped around her goddamn pinky, brother, so let's not play the *what the pack needs* game, alright? We're all working on instinct—"

"Except that Cassian's instinct is that you're temporary. He's said as much himself," Titan returns, throwing his hands up when I snarl at him. "I'm not saying anything he hasn't already said to you, right?"

I press on. "His instinct is what pulls him to us. It's what he *thinks* is logic that's making things hard. You'll see. It's going to work out fine in the end."

"Okay," Titan says simply, pouring a glass of whiskey and passing it across the bar to me. "Then talk to me about the mill site and the valley's security. You've been busy the last few days, and we haven't done our usual update."

Sighing, I dive into that, talking for a little while. Just because Declan's been quiet for the last week doesn't mean he's not busy.

Titan's scowl is almost etched on his features by the time we're done talking through things.

"What?" I demand. "You look more pissy than usual."

His face falls, and a look of such hopelessness replaces the scowl, I almost jump across the bar to pat him on the back.

"I'm so worried for the omegas, James. We were doing that food drop for them before Declan caught on, and one of them is pregnant. I try to imagine Isabel back there with those religious nutjobs, and I just want to tear something down."

"We're all worried for them," I reassure him. "I know Cass has been talking with Mitchell Bancroft about just going over to get the girls, but I don't know how it's changed since our story didn't get aired on the BBC."

"Mhm," Titan murmurs noncommittally. "Barging over there guns blazing is likely to get one of us or the girls killed. I'm in agreement that it should be a last resort."

"Wholeheartedly agree," I remind him. Titan's been worried about those girls from the very beginning, and I know it's killing him that we can't just go snatch them away from Declan and his goons. "We're going to save them T," I continue on. "Cass will never stop until we get them out of there."

Titan nods, but he's lost in thought as he aggressively cleans a beer glass.

God, I can't wait for Cassian to come back and get me.

CHAPTER EIGHTEEN

cassian

I'M LOST in thought after dropping James off. I'd much rather he come with me for this horse shit, but I have to do this alone. His coming would look even more suspicious than my going alone. Plus, I'm not ready for the conversation about what my endgame is. While it feels wrong to keep this plan from James and Julia—and I won't forever—I do feel compelled to keep it to myself for now. It's dangerous, and I'm not ready to answer the barrage of questions I'll get when they find out.

I pull off the highway exit toward Declan's, praying I'll see the omegas at the sermon. When my packmates came here before, all the girls were there.

Packmates.

I just thought of Titan and Ash and Stone as packmates. A confusing swirl of emotion accompanies that realization. It feels right, but it's surprising. As a pack alpha, I'm wired to be sure of my decisions, to lead so others can follow and thrive. That's how I'm built. I can't help commanding my brothers when I'm at the lodge.

I still wonder if I'm stepping on Stone's toes. Eventually, he'll get tired of having me around, no matter what he said last time we talked.

Grumbling under my breath, I pull into a big empty field where a giant white tent is set up on one side. When Titan came here before, he said there weren't many cars. That's not the case this time. Fifty or sixty cars are parked behind the tent, a good number of people already seated and waiting for the sermon to start. It makes me wonder just how far Declan has taken this protection racket business. And I'm more certain than ever that it'll come to war between our packs unless I can head this off at the pass.

As I hop out of the truck, a big alpha looks over at me. The moment our eyes meet, his go wide, and he stands, exiting the tent. He crosses the field quickly, stepping between me and the path to the tent.

"What are you doing here, Cassian? You're not welcome."

"JB," I deadpan. "I came to hear the sermon."

"Like hell you did," he snaps. "The last time we saw you, you tried to kill our alpha. There's no way you're coming in here."

"Look," I hedge, trying to make it clear I didn't come here for violence. "We both know Declan was losing his way. I've seen Gabriel. I've heard about the sermons. I want to know more about this philosophy. Declan could be a good man with the right direction."

It's a fucking lie, and JB's an asshole, but there's a softer side to him that I don't think he ever showed anybody but me. Of all of Declan's leadership crew, JB is one of the only alphas with the semblance of a conscience.

He licks his lips, eyes darting toward the tent before landing on me again.

"JB," I bark, watching my alpha dominance roll over him.

"What?" His voice is an angry hiss. "You're putting me in a bad spot, strategist."

His use of my former title sends a stab of pain through my

heart. It's a reminder that I fulfilled a role I wasn't meant for in this pack, and it didn't work well. That's how I know it can't work with James, Julia and me. I'm not meant to be anything other than a pack alpha. The only reason I even agreed to that role was I saw how cruel Declan was to his pack's omegas, and I wanted to be a barrier between them and him.

Sighing, I throw my hands up. "I truly just came for the sermon. I'm not here to cause trouble, and I'd be happy to speak with Declan directly, or even Gabriel, if you'd prefer that. I'm interested in what I've been hearing."

JB pauses, and I sense he's calling for backup through the mental bond leadership alphas share, so I lean against the truck with my arms crossed, attempting to look non-confrontational.

Declan himself shows up a moment later with Bek in tow, his healer. "Well, if it isn't yerself," my former alpha purrs with an evil grin. JB steps aside but remains in front of him. Bek brings up the rear, a mini gauntlet of alphas between the tent and me.

"I'm intrigued by the message here," I begin, knowing that of this whole group, Declan will read me best because he's a pack alpha like me.

"Oh, I bet yeh are." He laughs. "Yeh're not welcome, old friend." He says the word "friend" as if it's only got four letters, his voice dripping with disdain as he glares at me.

And this is where I'm gonna have to grovel a little, which makes me want to scratch my skin off. But for the omegas' safety and happiness, I'll do it a hundred times over.

"Listen, you and I disagreed in the past. But things are different now. This new messaging? I think you might be onto something." When he says nothing, I continue, "Tell me you couldn't benefit from a strategist."

"Got Gabriel for that," he snarks, his body tense as if he's waiting for an attack.

"Gabriel's not an alpha; it's not the same. Imagine if you had both."

I say nothing else, waiting for Declan to toss me out or let me in.

Finally, he gives me an evil grin. "I'd like Gabriel himself to speak with yeh, and if he wants to give yeh a chance, I'll be the bigger man and allow it."

That's an interesting answer, because it tells me precisely how much of a hold Gabriel has over Declan in a short time. The DPM ostensibly sent Gabriel to handle Declan, to keep him from wreaking havoc on our valley. But that's clearly not the true motive here, because the violence hasn't ceased. If anything, Gabriel has made Declan far more dangerous, because now he has a goddamn cause.

I gesture for Declan to lead the way, but he shakes his head. "Yeh know I won't have yeh at my back, alpha. You first. Pick a seat up front. Yeh can hear the sermon and speak with Gabriel afterward."

I head to the front, trying not to look around too much. But at the rear of the tent, the omegas sit. Cara is visibly pregnant, sitting alone in the back seat with a dark bruise along her cheekbone. The rest of my girls sit several rows ahead of her, heads down as they sit in silence.

It's so fucking wrong. These girls are brave and strong and kind. Sitting there cowed is just... I want to rip the goddamn tent down.

Instead, I use that anger to fuel my resolve. This is a long game, and I'm probably going to have to do plenty of shit I don't like to get the omegas out. If I can avoid an outright war between our packs, that would be ideal until the girls are out. Once they're safe from him, all bets are off.

My former pack leadership group eyes me like I'm a viper, glaring as I take a seat toward the front of the stage. I can practically feel the girls' eyes on me, and I hope they know why I'm here, that it's all for them. I don't risk a glance over.

Sitting in front, I watch as Gabriel Velos walks up onstage, his footsteps oddly loud, although he's a diminutive man. Pale skin, pale hair, a large slash of a scar crossing his face.

Declan and JB sit, and Bek drops down next to me, leaning into my space. "Try a fucking thing, and I'll drop you where you sit, asshole."

I don't bother responding as he lays one hand over the back of my chair, his palm close to my shoulder. Normally I'd fight over him getting this close to me, but I remind myself of the long game.

For the next forty minutes, I listen to a series of horrifying proclamations about alphas being "God's chosen people." How they existed for a time, until the trappings of modern society emasculated men in general, forcing alpha genetics into hiding. But thank God for the virus! Because the virus unleashed alpha potential once more. Alpha future is bright, and Gabriel is confident God will lead alphas to supremacy.

I hold back the urge to scoff the entire time, noticing how Gabriel never mentions the omegas at all. Everything is about alphas, how they'll rebuild society stronger and better, how we were made to do that by God himself. And the rise of alphas means the subjugation of regular humans, as the natural order of things demands.

It's surprising to see just how many humans are in this tent tonight, but I recognize it for what it is—Gabriel's converting followers through force. Regardless of what the DPM told us when he sent Gabriel out here, his ultimate intention is to wreak havoc. That's clear based on the bullshit spewing out of Gabriel's mouth.

When the sermon ends, Gabriel hops off the stage and shakes Declan's hand.

"Wonderful sermon, as usual," Declan purrs as Gabriel

beams. Pale eyes travel toward me before he looks at Declan expectantly.

"New friend?" His voice is low and respectful to Declan, yet still commanding. This is a man accustomed to guiding others.

"Former strategist," Declan says with a meaningful rise of his brows.

Gabriel smiles and turns to me. "Cassian. I've heard about you, naturally."

"It's probably all true," I say with a laugh, trying to appear non-threatening. Bek's hand comes to the middle of my back, a warning of the damage he can do with his healer power, if he chooses to use it that way.

"What brings you here, then? Certainly not camaraderie with my pack." Gabriel's voice is a simpering purr, but there's a strength in him that rankles. Surrounded by a pack of enormous alphas, he exudes a confident, righteous air.

"We had that before," I admit. "I was a good strategist. Declan and I fought, it's true. We didn't have something to bind us like this message. I hoped things might be different now."

"Are you a believer, then? What do you think about what you heard?" Gabriel's tone is light, but I sense he's wary of me, and now all of my former leadership group is hovering in a circle, ready to take over if I try something.

Which I wouldn't. I was the only unmated member of the group before. I can't shift. I'm at a disadvantage.

"I'd like to know more," is all I can really agree to. "I've definitely felt alphas lacked a unifying message of any sort, given how the outbreak started and how geographically scattered we are. The call to community is wildly appealing."

Gabriel eyes me for a long moment before folding his hands back and smiling. "There's another sermon in a few days, alpha. We'll talk about any future involvement once you've got a better understanding of our philosophy. We could use an alpha of your presence, a natural leader. But I am not totally sold, based on your personal history with my alpha."

"Understandable," I murmur, not looking away from Gabriel. It's a chance, and I'll take it. "I'll see you in a few days, then."

Gabriel nods and steps aside, gesturing for me to go. I walk through the small group, taking care not to focus on the omegas. My presence alone is a message to them—I'm here to get them out, however long it takes.

My heart breaks as I leave, knowing my girls probably saw me and watched me walk away.

I'll never let you go, I think, wishing they could all hear me. *I'm here for you. I'm coming for you.*

CHAPTER NINETEEN

I'M desperate to know where Cass went, and I'm worried Jules and I took things too far with him. He's convinced we are a temporary situation, and I hate that. When he stalks through the bar doors, my heart leaps into my throat.

"Thank fuck." I smile as he crosses the bar. For a tense moment, I think he's about to pull me into his arms and bury his face in my neck, like how he connects with Julia. But he stops in front of me, a drawn, weary expression on his face.

"You want to go home? Or stay at the bar?" His voice is tight and tense.

Titan looks up from the table where we're playing pool. "Stone wants a leadership meeting tonight to discuss the plan for rescuing the omegas and Asher."

"What happened with Asher?" I bark out.

Titan sighs. "Nothing specific. He's spiraling. We need him whole and mated, for both of their sanity. Stone's got a few ideas about how to push him toward that."

"Do pack alphas ever just stay out of people's business?" I gripe as Cassian shakes his head.

"Hell no," he confirms. "Being in everybody's business is

literally our job. Stone can't help it, and he won't stop until Asher is well and mated."

Mated. That word sends a flash of heat through my chest as I look up to see Cassian staring at me. Titan mumbles something under his breath but turns back toward the bar.

"Ready to go?" Cassian's voice is low and commanding, pulling goosebumps to the surface of my skin.

"Yes, alpha," I tease, trying to make a tense situation feel a little lighter for us both.

A blush spreads across his cheeks as he gestures toward the door. From behind the bar, Titan grins at me but says nothing as I follow Cassian out the door. The knowing look on his face tells me he knows what I do—I'm Cassian and Julia's. It's happening.

When we get to the truck, Cass surprises me by coming around to my side and opening the door.

I stop in front of him, noticing how tense and tight he is, how his muscles quiver slightly. "What do you need, alpha? Did we take things too far? I'm sorry if we did…"

Cassian takes a step closer, close enough that our bodies are almost touching. His gray eyes are full of anguish when he looks at me. "It's not that, at least not completely. I need to control something, because our world is a fucking mess, James."

Taking another step closer, so my chest brushes against his, I slide one hand up under the front of his shirt, stroking along his waistband. "I've got a few ideas about how to channel that concern, alpha. Shall we?"

Pale eyes find mine again as Cass nods, grabbing my hand and dragging it behind my back as he leans in, his lips tickling at my neck. His voice is gruff against my skin. "I tried to be gentle for Jules, but it's not natural for me. She's so tiny. I don't know if I can hold back with you."

"Good." I laugh, pinned to his chest. "You don't need to do

anything other than be yourself with us. When she finds out you held back, she's going to be mad as hell."

Cassian chuckles, fangs scraping my neck as I sigh. "You smell so damn good," he growls. "Different from her."

"If you said I smelled like strawberries, I'd laugh," I whisper back, cocking my head to the side as his fangs travel up my neck. He places a hard bite under my ear, chuckling when I groan.

When he takes a step back, our eyes meet. I'm not prepared for the look of pure need there. It's the same strength Stone exudes, but with Cass, there's a seductive, intense threat underpinning the way he stares.

"Let's go," he commands, nodding toward the interior of the truck. When I hop in, he shuts the door for me as I grin like a fool. It's so sweetly romantic, and I wouldn't have expected it. But it cements what I already sense about him—he's the dominant alpha between the two of us. It doesn't mean I can't fight, but, at the end of the day, I'm going to take that big alpha dick like a champ.

Sounds perfect to me.

Cassian rounds the truck and climbs in, a bulge visible at the front of his jeans. He looks over at me with a smile. "You ready to get home to your girl?"

"Our girl," I correct. "I'm ready to get home to *our* girl."

Cassian shakes his head but grins. "If I thought that could be true forever, there's nothing I wouldn't do for it."

"What about me?" I ask, not realizing how badly I need to know the answer. We played around last night, but we haven't had more than a cursory conversation about who we are to one another.

Cassian looks over at me, leaning back against the window of the truck. He smiles, and it's so seductive, I barely hold myself back from flinging myself into his arms.

"This is new, what's between us," Cassian admits. "And I'm

still certain it'll end poorly when you find an alpha with the right designation to have you both." He pauses for a moment, looking out into the dense winter forest before he glances back, gray eyes flashing. "But I can't keep away from you either."

It warms my heart to know he's coming around to the idea of us, even though he's still convinced this will end badly.

I know better.

So I smile. "You wanna learn something, alpha?"

Cassian's nostrils flare as his tongue peeks out to lick at his lips. "What did you have in mind?"

"I want you to learn how to swallow my cum." I give him my best grin, the same one I used to hook Jules that first day we met.

He hisses in a deep breath as those piercing eyes travel to my lap.

Reaching down, I stroke my already hard cock and look around. "Nobody here but us and the darkness. Whaddya say?"

"Take your pants off, James," he commands, rolling his flannel sleeves up to the elbow. I'm presented with the mouth-watering view of forearms covered in intricate scrolled tattoos. Cassian grins and points at his crotch. "Show me first, and then it'll be your turn."

My entire body clenches at the command in his voice, my shoulders rolling under the weight of it. I want to flop down on the seat and beg him to have his way with me. But I'm equally dying to get my mouth on him, and I've got an open fucking invitation.

If he spent today pondering what he did with Julia and me, he seems to have moved past the reservations.

Grinning, I fall forward onto my elbows and reach for his fly, sliding it down as Cassian shifts in the seat. I keep my eyes on his as I slide the zipper all the way down, his erection visible through tight briefs.

Reaching out, I stroke my way along that gorgeous thickness

as he groans and pumps his hips up to meet my hand. I grip his cock through the fabric and tease him, watching him watch me, pale eyes intense with desire.

"Lift your hips," I command, my tone hitting him as he growls against it but shifts for me so I can slide his jeans down to the floorboard. "Don't like an alpha barking at you?" I tease as I slide my hand through the leg of his boxers to stroke him again.

"Harder," he grunts, big hips rising to meet my touch as I grip him and stroke hard. Precum leaks steadily from him, and I gather it with my fingers, teasing his head as he growls. "Feels different from her, so different."

"She's tiny." I laugh, gripping him hard as I drag my fingers down his rock-hard length. "My hand is far larger, far rougher."

The sounds filling the cabin grow sloppier as he wets my palm with precum.

"You ready for more, alpha?" When our eyes meet, Cassian nods, one hand coming to rest on my upper back as I lean over his lap. When I open my mouth wide and suck at the tip of his cock, he bellows into the cab.

"Fuuuuck, James. Goddamn, alpha."

His outburst fuels my need as I slide him down my throat, taking him all the way as he pants and claws at my shoulder, gripping the steering wheel with his other hand.

My tongue swirls at the thick head of his cock before I bite it gently, dragging my teeth along the sensitive flesh as Cassian grunts, his head falling back against the window as it fogs up.

I suck him all the way down again, keeping my touch slow and steady but hard as his chest heaves faster and shallower. Then I pop my lips off his cock and slide back to my seat, pointing at my lap. "Your turn, alpha." I'm teasing him because I want to go home and have Julia between us. Gray eyes flash as I grin at him, so I press on. "You wanna fight about it?"

"Fight?" His salt-and-pepper brows knit together in the middle, as if he's surprised by my offer.

"Not uncommon for alphas to fight a little before they fuck." I shrug as my grin deepens.

"You've fucked other alphas?" There's an angry hint to his tone, but I don't want to keep anything about my past a secret.

"I was unmated when I lived with Mitchell's pack, not celibate. I had a few gay and bi packmates. We enjoyed one another from time to time."

Cass lets out an angry growl as he reaches out and pulls me into his arms, flopping down onto the seat. "Take the goddamn pants off."

Oh fuck. Sliding my jeans off, I straddle his big chest, my hard dick sticking up between us. Cass props himself partially up against the door and grabs my ass, hauling me up toward his neck. Before I know it, he's sliding my cock between those lips, taking it deep as I groan.

Fangs drag down my length as I gasp out in the growing heat of the truck. Of course he'd be good at this. He's mine, and I'm his. He's meant to take me.

Cassian's tongue swirls around the tip before he bites his way along the underside, nipping at my skin as my cock throbs. When he starts purring, the reverberation sends a pleasant tingle through the backs of my thighs.

I'm not gonna last like this, Cassian's mouth stretched wide around my dick. Heat streaks along my spine as he goes wild. I can't do anything but moan and gasp and fuck his face as he eats me like a champion in a hot dog contest.

"I'm close," I cry out as Cassian shoves me off his chest and back into my seat, a cry of distress leaving my mouth.

"Not yet, alpha." Cass grins, giving me a devious wink. "I'm going to take everything from you, but I want us all together. I want to watch the way you look at her when you come on my cock."

"Okay," I gasp out, my dick still hard and leaking as it spears the air. Groaning, I tuck it back into my jeans, my skin a livewire of need. "Oh, fuck, please don't make me wait." I'm about to beg.

"You happen to bring lube with you?" Cass laughs. "Because even for alphas, I'm guessing spit isn't an ideal lubricant. And we don't have our omega here to coat us in slick."

"Goddamnit," I hiss, throwing my head back. "Then when we get home, we're going right to your cabin to have her."

"Deal," Cass laughs. "Let's go home and get our girl."

CHAPTER TWENTY

JAMES DIDN'T MEAN to send me damn visions of him and Cass, but our bond was awash with pleasure, and I'm dying from an overdose of it. Flying to my room, I grab my biggest ribbed battery-operated boyfriend.

We're coming home, James purrs suddenly into the bond. *He brought me to the damn edge and stopped. We need you. Be ready, baby girl.*

Oh fuck, yes!

I hop out of bed, throwing on warm jeans and a big puffy coat. Heading out of my room, I run right into Erin, my pack omega, who smiles and pulls me in for a big hug.

"Where are you off to in such a hurry?" she signs when we part.

"Going to find my mates," I reply with a big grin. "Things are progressing nicely." I waggle my brows at her as she laughs.

"I knew you were never gonna give Cass a chance to escape your clutches."

"Hell no," I sign furiously. "You've seen him. Why wouldn't I lock that down immediately?"

Erin laughs again and reaches out to stroke my hair back

over my shoulder. "Just be careful honey, okay? The designation thing is a real issue, something to consider. I know you want him, but he's right to be worried about that."

Frustration makes me let out an angry harrumph. "I don't know why everybody can't just believe me when I say he's mine and I know it. James feels the same. Whatever happened to just believing in me?"

Erin's smile turns a little sad as she nods. "I get it. I swear I do, and I'm not trying to give you a hard time. But I'll use Leandra as a great example. She's been here two days, and she's clearly interested in you. What if she's a healer or spirit?"

"She's not my type," I sign back, frowning. "I don't want her like that."

"And that's fine," Erin presses on, "but not everything works out, honey. Look at Asher and Cherry. He can see their bond, and it's still a shitshow between them."

"That's gonna work out fine though," I counter with confidence. "It'll probably blow up first, but I have faith."

"I do too," Erin signs with a smile. "But still. I don't want to see your heart get crushed, or Cassian's, or James's."

"Appreciate the pep talk," I sign bitterly, "but I've got to go find them. Catch you later?"

"Okay, I'm sorry, honey. I just love you all so much," Erin signs, but she steps aside to let me go. Even so, as I leave, her warning echoes in my head. I know she's not right, but what if it means something that even Cassian doesn't believe we'll ever be a long-term thing?

Thankfully I don't see any of my other packmates on the way out, which is good because I'm in a bad mood after that chat. Hopping onto the nearest available ATV, I drive past the researchers' trailer, giving Leandra a friendly wave as I go by. She grins at me, giving me a sly wink as I head up the road toward the aspen grove and past the remains of our former general store.

Damn, is everybody hitting on me all of a sudden? Am I giving off super available vibes? What in the hell is going on? I'll admit, it does make me wonder about what Erin said. Especially given Leandra's addition to our pack. I don't feel called to the female alpha at all, but what if one day she walks in, and it's just...her. I recognize her as mine, and I have to have her?

Scrunching up my nose, I grit my teeth against the bite of the freezing air, finally passing through the aspen grove until Cassian's cabin comes into view. Cherry's occupying the cabin next to his, and when I pull up, she's out on her porch drinking something out of a steaming cup.

Pulling the ATV up in front of her place, I hop off and join her on the porch, leaning up against the support. "What's going on, honey?" I question as she sets her cup down.

"Just the usual," she hedges.

"No trouble with your late-night trips?"

"None at all," she quips back. Which makes me wonder right away if she's lying. We used to have such an open, tight friendship, but the fighting with Asher has turned her into our pack's most secretive person. It's the total opposite of her usual state of being. She's always been cheerful and plucky, but these days she's a husk of her former self.

I lift my hands to say something, but Cherry shakes her head and lifts her own quickly. "Please don't tell me it's all going to be fine, Jules. I can't stand to hear that bullshit one more time. I've almost got enough saved to leave, and once I do, I'm out of here."

Tears fill my eyes as I throw myself into her arms and squeeze her neck tight. Tears fall from my eyes, and when I look up, she's crying too. I cling tightly to her, willing her to know how much I love her even though I can't fix any of this. We sob together for a while until a truck pulls off the main road.

Cherry scoots me off her lap with a wry grin. "Your mates

are back, honey. Go get your happiness, because someone should have it."

My earlier sensual mood has faded though, and after talking with Erin and sobbing with Cherry, I'm feeling far less sexy. That's exacerbated when Cassian parks in front of Cherry's cabin and hops out, a drawn expression on his handsome face. "Stone wants us up at the lodge, needs to talk to us and you two."

"Oh fuck," Cherry signs. "What now?"

"Oh, I've got an inkling," Cassian signs, declining to say anything more.

Cherry stands and looks at me in concern, but hops down the porch and gets into the truck's back seat. Cassian crosses the small yard to me and reaches out, pulling me close to him.

"Missed the hell out of you today," he signs. "James and I had fun plans for you this evening, but something tells me that's not gonna work out."

"We've got time," I reassure him. "Stone wouldn't call us if it wasn't important."

Cassian nods, guiding me to the truck and lifting me up into the lifted truck's back seat, his big hands warm on my waist.

Five minutes later, I'm back in the lodge I just came from, staring at a tense table. All of pack leadership is here, along with Erin, Cherry and me.

"Do we need to call the twins in for a little bit of comedic relief?" I question the table when nobody speaks.

Stone smiles at me but picks right up. "Cassian, I'm sending you, James and Julia up to see Mahikan from the northern packs. We need to sort out the state of your mating, and, unfortunately, given our security threat, I'd rather know sooner than later if your bond is real or not."

"What the fuck?" I sign, my jaw dropped open. "How is this your concern?"

"Because it is," Stone replies with short, measured signs. "We need every shifting, mated alpha we can get. If that's what your alphas are, we need to know. Not only for their own good, but the good of the pack."

He turns to Cherry. "You and Ash are going for the same reason. The northern packs don't work like we do. Mahikan seems to think they might have more information than a usual alpha seer. It's a chance we have to take."

Cherry slumps in her chair with a miserable expression, Asher stone-faced next to her.

Stone turns back to Cassian. "Aside from the mating bonds, I'd like to understand how much help we can expect from the northern packs if it comes to war, which it's likely to. If the security footage we've seen is accurate, Declan's pack is about twenty alphas bigger than ours and Mitchell Bancroft's combined, and Mitchell isn't reliably in town.

"We don't know if any of Declan's omegas have powers, so that could be in our favor. But if I'm going to start a war to save those trapped women, I want to be sure I'm going to win."

Erin sits silently next to him, her jaw gritted tightly. It's clear we all hate having this horribly direct conversation. But he's right. She looks up, making eye contact with the table.

"I've spoken with the town council, and they agreed to encourage the humans to leave if they can. Everyone seems to believe this will come to war at some point. We have to be ready for any eventuality."

It's a somber admission, and everyone looks miserable when she says it.

"We'll go immediately," I sign before anyone else responds. "You're right. We need to know, so we'll leave tomorrow."

Both my mates turn to look at me, but Erin and Stone are right—we have to have every bit of info we can to ensure we rescue the omegas and keep this town safe.

For the next quarter hour, we work out the details of a plan to leave in the morning.

As we split apart to leave, I see Stone ask Cass to stay behind in the office for a minute. James and I respect their need to speak alpha to alpha, and we go. I can't help but wonder what conversation they're having that we're not privy to.

Hours later, dinner is somber as Stone shares the details of our plan with the wider pack. Leandra scowls when I mention we're leaving for a short trip but purses her lips when Cassian gives her a withering look.

After dinner, River finds me and taps me on the shoulder. "Movie night? It's going to be so boring if you and Cherry leave." She misses a sign or two, but I still get the gist. I was planning to spend the evening with Cassian and James, but I decide I'll drag them to movie night too.

"Hell yes," I reply. "What's Rogue up to?"

"Date night with Sal," she quips with an angry expression. "I mean, obviously they can't go anywhere, but he's got a whole setup on the back porch for her, and I'm not allowed out there."

I know she's happy for her brother to have found connection, but it's hard for her at the same time.

"Why don't you come with us?" I sign, the idea coming to me. "You've got freaky seer hearing. Why not come and see if there's more to that? Maybe the northern packs know something."

River's face lights up. "You think it's okay if I come? I'll have to like, sit in your lap or something unless we take two trucks. And I need to check with Daddy Stone."

I laugh aloud at the ridiculous nickname Clay and the twins have started using for our pack alpha. "We'll squish," I sign. "Come with us. It'll be a party."

It is not, in fact, going to be a party. Because she'll needle the shit out of Cassian and Ash the whole time, but I find it kind of cute how much she likes to ruffle the alphas. She's stinking adorable.

PRETTY LITTLE SINNER 179

An hour later, River's on one end of the sofa under a pile of blankets. Luna and Titan snuggle next to her. James and I are on either side of Cassian, tucked into a corner of the giant pit sofa. We're watching *Practical Magic* for the thousandth time, but by the time Gillian encourages her sister to pour belladonna in the tequila, Titan's already carried Luna upstairs over his shoulder. River is asleep on the sofa, snoring loudly with her mouth open, and Cassian is staring at the screen with a vacant expression. It doesn't take a mind reader to know he's worried for the omegas, even though we'll just be gone overnight.

I can't change what we're doing tomorrow, but I can make tonight a little more fun. I can remove the crease lining Cassian's face as he frowns. Looking over at James, I give him a grin I'm certain he'll decipher, and then I lie on my side, one leg threaded through Cassian's, my body shielding him from River, God forbid she wakes up during what I'm about to do.

I slide one hand under the blankets and rub him with slow, sure strokes. Cass turns to look at me, possessive desire clear on his angular features.

One sprinkled brow curls up. *What do you think you're doing?* he seems to ask.

Hopefully my answering smile makes it clear. I know it does when he steps his feet wide. James chuckles and slides his hand under the blanket to meet mine, unzipping Cass's pants. The moment his hard cock springs free, we grip it and stroke, James's hand around mine as Cass clenches his jaw tight, looking over at James.

God, I'd give a million dollars to know what he's thinking now. Is he remembering what he did with James earlier? Wanting more?

I can't wait until we hear him in our bond, James sighs into our own. *It's going to be amazing.*

If we hear him, I think bitterly. Erin's earlier warning is still fresh in my mind.

I have faith, James returns. *No matter what anyone thinks.*

Cass's mouth falls open as he struggles not to groan around the pleasure our hands bring him. Watching his cheeks turn pink, his head falling back on the sofa as he rocks his hips slowly to meet us, I could die from how good this feels. This is what I've wanted every moment since that day in the hot springs.

James's hand releases mine, and he slides lower, stroking Cassian's balls as the big alpha clenches.

Suddenly, Cass flings the blanket aside and growls, staring down to where James and I are pleasuring him. He's on the edge; I can sense it. Snarling at me, he moves our hands and zips himself back into his jeans. Then he tosses me over his shoulder and reaches for James, leading us both around a snoring River and up the big staircase to James's and my room.

When we get there, he throws me into the bed and looks at James. "Get on her, I want to watch you."

James grins and pulls his shirt over his head, depositing it on the floor as he gazes seductively at me. My nipples pebble in my shirt as he crawls on top of me, taking my mouth with practiced ease.

His soft tongue slides along mine, his kiss demanding but tender, the kiss of a lover who knows me almost better than I know myself. *Love you,* he murmurs into the bond as I pant into his beautiful dark lips.

It occurs to me then that while speaking in our bond is easy for us, it leaves Cass out, because he doesn't hear us. So I look over at him. "What do you want to see, alpha?"

James grabs the front of my sweater and rips it straight down the front, buttons popping off as Cass snarls, fangs descending from his lips.

"Kiss him," he commands with sure movements of his hands.

Turning, I capture James's lips with mine as Cassian moves behind us, yanking my jeans off before laying a hard slap on my ass. I yip, but then his big fingers stroke my clit with even, measured teases. God, he feels so good.

Under me, James bites at my neck as he fists my hair. I feel a rustling, and Cass pulls James's pants off as well.

Big hands grip my ass and shove me forward before Cass's tongue is on me, licking from my clit all the way along my pussy, which leaks profusely for him. James's bites grow harder and needier until he sinks his fangs deep, groaning into my neck, the vibrating of that noise evident against my skin.

Rocking my hips back, I feel Cass's head bobbing between James's thighs. God, I'd give anything to turn around and watch this show. But then his tongue turns to my clit again, and I gasp out, my forehead falling to James.

Suddenly, Cass grips my hips and yanks me down onto James's cock, a soundless scream leaving my throat as he licks my ass, even as James begins to fuck up into me with a relentless, teasing rhythm.

Every time James jolts, I imagine what Cass is doing to him, what pleasure he's learning to wring from our big mate's body.

Then orgasm hits me, and I explode all over Cass's tongue and James's dick, covering my mouth with my hand so I don't wake up the entire lodge. Pleasure rolls over me until I think I'll pass out, and when I fall forward onto James's chest, he strokes me through the bond, grunting as Cassian continues playing with him.

I climb off him and turn around, presenting James with a perfect view of my very used, very soaked pussy. And then I watch the show: Cass biting, sucking and licking on James's huge cock. Leaning forward, I gently tug James's balls with one hand, grinning at Cass when our eyes meet.

James's hips leap underneath me as I lean in and lick along his cock the same time Cass sucks at the tip of it. I bite my way up the length before capturing Cass's mouth. He tastes like James and my slick. I've got to have more.

Together we bite our way down his dick as it swings in the air. Cass takes over massaging James's balls as I work my hand around the base of his cock where his knot is. He loves to have his knot massaged. So, I work my hands in a steady circle as the base swells, Cassian going wild on the tip, biting and sucking and playing.

James explodes under our attention, filling Cass's mouth with sticky white cum as my big alpha swallows it, both hands on James's thighs. The rhythm of my mate's hips slows as the aftershocks of orgasm hit him, and when they do, I throw myself into Cass's arms and take his mouth. It feels so fucking dirty to slide my tongue along his and taste the proof of James's pleasure. But I suck the tip between my lips and growl as he falls into the bed with me in his arms.

"Your turn, alpha," James signs, but Cass shakes his head.

"We need rest. You're both sated, and that makes me happy."

"It'll never be enough," I reassure him. "We will always want more of you, every fucking thing you have to give."

The tips of Cass's lips turn up in a smile, but he pulls me close and reaches for James. We thread our legs together, and even though I don't mean to fall asleep so quickly, I can't help it when both my alphas purr for me. The lovely rumble pulls me under.

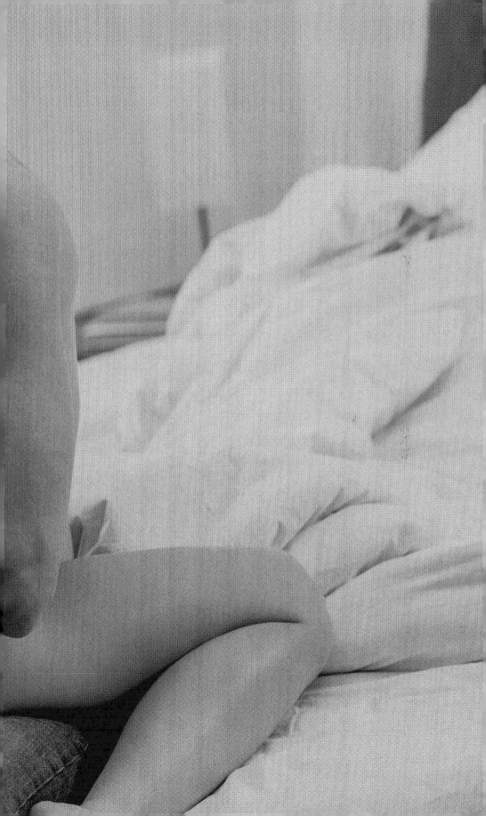

CHAPTER TWENTY-ONE

cassian

I SLEEP LIKE SHIT, knowing in the morning we're leaving to find answers—I suspect I won't like what they are. Last night, we connected so beautifully. Every time I touch James and Julia, I can't shake off the soul-deep knowledge that they're mine, both of them, no matter what alpha biology says.

But the biology is fucking important, and that brings me back to the cruel reminder that, at any moment, an alpha could show up who's meant to partner with them. Threats to my happiness abound, and I remind myself that this is fun, and I'm fucking attached, but I'm riding the train to heartbreak city, and I need to be ready for the fallout.

In the morning, I wake to find James and Julia intertwined together, their legs across mine possessively. I roll out of their bed to go to my cabin and get ready for today. I'm aware that River wants to come too, which means we need a damn minivan to get all of us there.

Stone radios me as I'm packing. "Got a minute, alpha?"

"Always," I reply evenly, knowing I'm still the extra alpha in this pack.

"I hope you don't feel I pushed you toward something you wouldn't choose for yourself." Stone's words surprise me.

"You're the alpha here," is all I can think of to say.

"But I'm not," Stone replies gently. "I may have started as this pack's alpha, but you don't want to leave. Let's call it what it is. I like having you here. When you get back, we need to talk through the logistics of this."

"I've never heard of two alphas in a pack, not successfully," I counter. "Have you?"

"No, but if I've learned anything about being an alpha, this time around isn't like alpha history. Things work a little differently now. I mean have you ever seen an alpha channel an omega's power like Asher did Hale's? Well, you weren't there that day, but it was fucking terrifying. He took her power and threw it back at her. It was insane."

There's a momentary pause as I absorb that information. I've heard about it, of course, but forgot until now.

Stone presses on, dark eyes boring into mine, "All I'm saying is that we can't assume the way things worked in the past is how it has to happen now. I want your happiness, Cass. I want James and Jules to be fucking happy, and all they've ever wanted is you. That means something."

"I'd love to believe that," I huff, my voice falling off when I can't think of anything else to say.

"I'll just keep repeating it, I suppose," Stone growls, irritation evident in his tone. "As long as you come back in time for Gabriel's next sermon, our plan should not change. Call me tonight after you talk to Mahikan. I want to know every detail, no matter how small."

"Done," I agree, clicking off the radio as I consider his words.

Could there be a future where we co-lead an unusual pack of misfits? Maybe...but given all the external forces pushing us toward war right now, I'm inclined to think it's not a great idea.

I wish I had a fucking strategist of my own to talk this through. Lost in thought, I pull the truck up to the lodge to pick up a cavalcade of packmates for this adventure. When I get there, Rogue and River stand on the front steps, two suitcases at Rogue's feet.

The teen gives me a big, toothy grin as he slaps his twin on the back of the head. "Riv tells me you're going on an adventure, and there's no fucking way I'm staying home. I should go with you."

It's on the tip of my tongue to ask him about Sal, since they're connecting, but he shakes his head. "She encouraged me to come, so I don't wanna hear it, alpha."

"We're not gonna fit in the goddamn car," I gripe as James and Asher come through the door, Cherry right behind them. Trailing the group, Asher's dark eyes meet mine, and I see a broken man. I know, for a time, Stone felt Ash was improving, that he was healing from whatever bullshit the American Task Force put him through, but that's no longer the case.

"We'll get answers, alpha," I reassure him as I clap his shoulder. He nods once, disbelieving, as he follows Cherry down the stairs to the minivan.

Once everyone is loaded in, I look at the grocery getter and sigh. Never thought I'd be driving a minivan full of alphas and omegas to find out about our love lives. We sound like a fucking reality show from hell.

Two hours later, James and I exchange matching groans in the front seat as the twins and Cherry sing off-key from the middle and back seats. Asher is way in the back, eyes on the road as we pass through dark Canadian forest.

Time passes at the speed of molasses, but after six hours of speeding as fast as I safely can, we pass the sign for Vass, the small town where Mahikan, Leon and Jacob's packs live. When I was first exiled from Declan's pack, I spent a very short time here before bouncing around in Ayas, determined to stay close enough to help the omegas where I could.

"How hopeful are we that we'll learn anything useful here?" Ash's voice is dejected.

"Don't be dense," River barks back, reaching behind to slap his knee. "Why would we come here if we didn't think we'd get answers? Some days, I swear..." her voice trails off as she winks at me in the rearview mirror. I know she and Ash have a kinship of sorts. Both having such incredible, seer-level hearing. She looks up to him, a fact I'm feeling compelled to remind him of.

Grabbing my cell, I toss it over to James. "Let Mahikan know we're almost there, would you?"

James picks up the cell and dials Mahikan's number to let the reclusive alpha know we're almost to his home. The minivan falls silent as we pass through familiar streets, finally turning off onto a dirt road to begin a ten-mile climb back into the mountains.

The road is harrowing, as River reminds us every ten seconds. "Oh fuck, alpha, it's like a two-mile drop on this side, gah!" she shouts from the middle seat, signing as much as she knows how to. "I'm fucking terrified of heights; are we almost there?"

"It's ten miles like this," I bark back. "Chill out, River!"

"You chill out!" she shouts back. "I'm going to have a nervous breakdown! Oh God! Oh fuck, we're so closeahhhhhh!!!!!"

I'm half tempted to pull the van over and bark, but Asher saves me from the back seat. He drops to the floor between the middle seats and takes River's hand, putting it on his chest just inside his shirt. Despite myself, I can't help but watch them. It's such a seer move to do this.

"Breathe, Riv," he croons. "Breathe with me, friend."

Riv sucks in gasping breaths as Ash starts purring, that sound deeper from him than I've heard it from any other alpha. The moment he does, Cherry claps her thighs together in the back seat, looking incredibly miserable.

Still, Ash focuses on River until we make it up all ten miles of the fucking insane road, finally rounding a bend into a small valley filled with tiny houses, geodesic domes, and one big lodge in the middle marking the packs' meeting place.

The road evens out, and we make our way into the valley, arriving at the edge of the village. I drive through until we come to the large middle lodge, the meeting place. Mahikan stands there already, thumbs looped into his belt as he looks at us.

Every time I see him, I'm surprised how big the pack alpha is —it's one of many ways the northern packs are different from others I've encountered. Every alpha is enormous. I've often wondered if they come from completely separate bloodlines than the rest of the alpha world, but they're cagey about their history. That he, Leon and Jacob even allowed us here is a miracle.

I put the minivan in park and hop out, striding forward to shake his hand.

"Wouldn't peg you for the minivan type." Mahikan laughs, looking at the horrible vehicle behind me.

"I've brought an entire motley crew with me," I grumble as his dark eyes travel behind me. He watches the twins roll out, followed by James, Julia, Cherry and Ash.

"Cherry, ohmyfuckinggod!" a woman shouts as our group turns toward the noise. A beautiful young omega runs from a nearby doorway and flings herself into Cherry's arms. "Oh my God, I never thought I'd see your gorgeous face again. It's so good to see you."

Cherry swings the omega around before setting her down. She makes the rounds of hugging James, Julia and Asher, but stops at the twins and me.

Cherry's smile is bigger than I've seen it in a long while. "Cassian, you remember Nita; she was formerly part of our pack but moved up here recently. Nita, honey, this is Rogue and River. Titan brought them into the pack, and we haven't let them leave."

Nita shakes hands with them both as River cocks her head to the side, a frown on her face. "Somebody's arguing about us being here..." she says in a soft tone. Next to me, Mahikan stiffens but takes a step forward, towering over the teen.

"You can hear that?"

"Dude," she harrumphs. "I fucking hear everything. It's soooo annoying. I'm told you're all magical and shit, so are there any kind of alpha earbuds I could use to just shut out the noise?"

Mahikan lets out a disbelieving laugh and turns to me. "There's a lot for us to discuss; let's head into the meeting hall. Leon and Jacob will join us shortly."

I step aside, watching my people as they follow Mahikan.

Julia links her arm through Nita's, holding her hands up to sign. "Tell me everything about him. You look pretty pleased with yourself."

Nita laughs and signs to Julia as they follow the rest of the group.

Asher and I bring up the rear as he leans in. "Riv is right. Someone named Jacob doesn't agree with our presence here. We need to keep an eye on him."

"Noted," I mutter under my breath. "Tell me if anything else comes up, seer." I've met Jacob several times, and he's a surly motherfucker.

Ash nods and ducks through a doorway into the giant wooden dome. Inside, the dome ceiling is full of skylights, bringing natural sun into the large open hall. There are multiple entrances off to the side, including one I know leads to the kitchen.

Mahikan sits at the nearest table, Nita to his right as we all take our places. We wait just moments before Jacob and Leon come through the opposite doorway, Leon smiling and Jacob with his signature frown. He's the most unfriendly alpha I've ever met, something I'm sure would be remedied if he got re-mated. But as it is, he's so fucking ornery, and this community is so remote and small, if he hasn't found someone here now, I don't know that he ever will.

Leon crosses the room and reaches out to shake my hand, clapping me on the shoulder. I get just a scowl from Jacob as they pull up seats next to Mahikan. Like this, they're all seated at the head of the table, and it reminds me how Stone said these packs don't do things like the rest of us. It's true, from what little I could tell when I stayed here before.

I'm certain they hid a lot about how their pack worked from me, but maybe after we helped them save their kidnapped omegas, things will be different.

Mahikan speaks first, dark eyes intensely focused on me. "Stone has questions about your mating bonds and that fucking asshole who took our omegas."

I appreciate that he's straight to the point.

Nodding, I gesture to Cherry and Asher first. "Ash, you or Cherry want to talk about your bond?"

The look on his face screams "not particularly," but he looks at Cherry and then nods, turning in his seat toward the three pack alphas. If I thought being under another pack alpha's scru-tiny was bad enough, three is far worse.

Asher rolls his shoulders and slumps back in his chair. "I was the first alpha. My sister created the Awaken virus, and a lab accident turned me. Or, rather, it activated dormant alpha genes, and here I am. I was in custody immediately, and the Task Force experimented on me for years.

"I was doped up the entire time. I have memories I'm not even sure are mine, and while I do hear voices in my head, they're hurtful, not helpful. I'm in love with my mate; I have been since we met. But I know deep in my heart that I could hurt her, and so I push her away."

Cherry shifts uncomfortably in her seat, but all three alphas turn to her. Jacob gives her a gentle smile. "Omega, what is your take on this issue?"

"That he needs to get the fuck over it," she barks, crossing her arms. "But we've had that discussion many times. Even the day he channeled Hale's power, we connected afterward but—"

"Wait, what?" Jacob barks, looking from Cherry to Asher. "You channeled an omega's power?"

Asher waves his hand as if to say "yeah, I suppose," but Jacob turns toward the other alphas and glares. "All the more reason not to let them remain here."

"Stop, Jacob," Mahikan growls, and it's the growl of an irritated pack alpha. It makes me want to scratch at my skin, although Jacob sits back in his seat, frowning but saying nothing else.

Interesting.

"We will revisit the channeling later with our omegas. Several of them have come into their powers, and I'd like to see if you can replicate what you did. I'd like more information on that before we continue to discuss your bond."

Asher and Cherry both fall silent, the look on Cherry's face unimpressed.

Mahikan turns to me next. "And what of you, old friend?" His dark eyes spark with mischief.

James and Julia turn to look at me, and I hate that I have to share an answer they'll disagree with. Lifting my hands, I sign as I share aloud, "I have a deep connection with both James and Julia. By all indications, James is the pack's healer or spirit, and I am definitely a pack alpha. I don't have the right designation to claim them. Stone thought, given how your packs do things a little differently, you might know if an alternative pairing has ever happened."

Mahikan turns to James and Julia. "You realize this is not likely?"

James bristles but translates for Julia as all three alphas stare at her, just realizing she's the one who can't hear the conversation.

Julia scowls as James translates but turns all her fury back to the three alphas. "Cassian is ours, no matter what you say here today. But if you can find a way to make him believe me, it would be much appreciated."

That tears my heart into shreds, because I do want to believe her. With every ounce of my fucking body, I want to believe there's a future where our bond is possible, but I don't know how it could be.

When I look away from her, Mahikan's dark eyes are on mine. "This is highly unusual, but…" he pauses, looking to Jacob and Leon. Jacob shakes his head even as Leon nods.

Mahikan continues, "I'm not going to share all the secrets of our pack today, but because our community is remote and small, we aren't always able to find every designation. There is a process to open an alpha's mind to the concept of another designation. It is tricky and painful. Are you willing to do that, Cassian?"

Jesus Christ, that's news to me. Changing a designation? Dangerous hope fills my chest at the very idea.

"I'm willing," I murmur, looking over at James and Julia, wondering how they're absorbing this info. What he's just shared has given me more hope than I've had this whole time. If they could be mine, if I could claim them? I've got to try. It would give us two more shifting alphas and get us a step closer to omega powers.

"Good," Mahikan says in a sobering tone. "It'll just about kill you to do, but if it takes, there's a chance you'll be able to mate as you choose. We'll try later." He points to Asher. "Come with me, alpha, I want to see what you can do." His dark eyes flick over to Cherry. "You too, come on."

"Not without me there," I remind him. This pack is my responsibility, and there's no way I'll leave Cherry and Asher to three other alphas' mercy, even if they're technically friends.

CHAPTER TWENTY-TWO

AS EXCITED as I was to get up here and figure out if the northern packs could help us, the idea of them doing something painful to Cassian does not sit well with me. Not at all.

It sits badly enough that I plan to discuss it with him as soon as we're done chatting with the alphas. I'm going to have to wait, though, because they want to see Asher's power now. Cherry walks next to me as we leave the giant center hut, following Mahikan through a field full of small houses and up into the forest.

Cherry vibrates with tension as we enter a clearing of sorts, and three omegas stand there. All the hair on my nape stands as I look at them. They're all striking with beautiful olive-toned skin and varying shades of chocolate hair. One of the girls gives me a friendly wink before settling her gaze on Mahikan.

Nita stands across from me so I can easily see her hands when she translates. God, it's so good to see her again. We've visited on the phone a few times, but there's so much I'd like to know about how she's getting along here.

And Mahikan. I want to know all the things about Mahikan, because there's clearly something between them.

I'm broken out of those thoughts when Mahikan turns to Cherry. "No matter what you see us do to him, do not intervene, omega."

Cherry bristles as she glares at him and points to Asher. "If you hurt him, you will absolutely deal with me. He's been through enough."

Mahikan grins as Asher comes to stand in front of Cherry, moving her behind his big body. My heart breaks for him, because it's so clear to me that his instinct is to protect her, and I wish he had more confidence in that instinct.

Even now, Cherry's hands are on his lower back as she rests her forehead against him. Despite her assertion that she's leaving us soon, it's obvious she loves him. I watch a single tear fall down her cheek as his big muscles begin to tremble in anticipation.

Mahikan's command cuts through the heavy tension of our group as Nita continues to translate for me. "Asher, Laura stands to my left. Her power is like your friend Alice's—she can command the elements. I am going to have her call rain, and I'd like you to attempt to push it back."

Nita gives me a soft smile as Laura steps forward and raises her hands. On cue, the sky explodes as lightning streaks across it. I don't hear the thunder that comes next, but it rumbles the ground under my feet. James pulls me into his embrace as Cass stands at our side, arms crossed as he watches Asher.

Asher focuses on Laura, his lips curling into a snarl. She takes a step forward, a dark cloud rolling over top of us. Raindrops begin to fall lightly, and she sneers at Ash, "Push my rain away, alpha."

James rests his cheek on top of my head. I sense he's worried for our packmate and hoping desperately this unlocks something for Asher and Cherry, something that will help them heal the rift in their bond.

Asher's mouth opens, and he roars. Suddenly raindrops

press outward from our group, pushing off into the trees in a wave. The rain begins to pour down harder, but nothing hits our circle. Then Ash's concentration seems to break, and rain begins to pepper us again, going from gentle mist to stinging bullets.

I watch Asher's fists ball, the concentration on his face becoming desperation, and finally sorrow, when he's unable to move the rain. It continues to pellet us as James covers me the best he can. We're all soaked, and I hate this for Ash, because I can see him giving up right in front of me. I push my way out of James's arms and cross to my packmates.

"You can do this," I sign. Then I place a hand on his side. River comes to join me, placing her hand over mine, and a look of resolve passes over Ash's handsome angular features. He turns to Laura and focuses. Underneath my palm, his muscles quiver violently, but the hail becomes rain again, and then the clouds above us part, and a ray of sunshine bursts through, highlighting the clearing and all of us.

I feel absolutely victorious for him, and when I look at Cherry, she's staring at her mate in wonder.

Laura snarls, and the sky opens on us, dumping buckets of rain down as Asher bellows, his body vibrating under my palm. Next to Laura, one of the other omegas steps forward and looks dead in Asher's eyes.

"Careful," Cass cautions. His signs are clipped; he's worried for Ash. Whatever this second omega is doing isn't a visible power, and I have to wonder if she's like Carmen and can touch the bond between an alpha and his wolf.

Asher falls back a step, both hands coming to his head as Cherry pushes me to the side. She goes back to him immediately, wrapping an arm around his waist as he snarls, drool dripping from his mouth. His eyes are wild, but I can see he's trying to focus on both women. The rain disappears then returns then disappears again.

"More," Mahikan tells the omegas. The third steps forward and shifts quickly into a large black wolf. Her equally black eyes move from Asher to Cherry, and she snaps her teeth. Her threat is clear—she's a predator, and Cherry is the prey.

Asher's roar shakes the ground, his hands balled into fists as he yanks Cherry behind him. His eyes roll back into his head until all I can see are the whites.

"Keep going," Cass commands when the omegas shoot Mahikan a concerned look.

He agrees, and the second woman steps closer to Cass, her eyes glowing with intent as Ash backs Cherry into a tree, still behind his larger frame. Ash snarls and snaps, and then shakes his head.

A percussive explosion bursts out from him, knocking everyone to the ground. All the trees lining the clearing are blown outward away from us. It's so impossibly powerful, all I can do is cling to James as Ash's power licks over my skin like flames.

Cass is the first one up, sprinting to Asher as I struggle to sit upright. Mahikan is up fast too, standing in front of his omegas as they struggle to get upright. They hover behind him as Cass shakes Asher's shoulders.

"Alpha! Alpha, are you with me?"

Asher's eyes are still rolled back into his head. He snarls at Cass once, and it's like the time he channeled Hale's power—he's unresponsive, his eyes wild as he looks for the one thing that centers him. He shrugs Cass off and turns to Cherry, picking her up and cradling her to his chest.

"Asher," Cass signs.

"Mine!" Asher shouts back. He doesn't sign, but it's so forceful, I'm able to lipread it. He skates around the edge of the clearing, and Mahikan keeps himself between his omegas and Ash. Ash roars at them, but then takes off into the trees with Cherry in his arms.

"Are you going after him?" Mahikan turns to Cass, and Nita continues to sign for me, even though she's visibly shaken.

"They need this," Cass retorts. "They'll be back in a bit."

Mahikan runs both hands through his dark hair. "I've never seen anything like that; I've never even heard of it." He turns to the women. "What do you sense about him?"

Laura speaks first, but it's clear from the way she trembles that she's unsettled about what just happened. Shit, I'm unsettled myself. Even the twins are silent as they look in the direction Asher and Cherry went.

"It's...his power feels broken to me," Laura admits. "When he channeled it, it was like he was taking the power from me, and I didn't know if it would come back. For a moment, when everything exploded, I thought my power was gone."

Mahikan shoots Cass a heated look. "Who have you brought to us, Cassian?" He's clearly angry that things could have been much worse.

"We don't know," Cass admits. "The American Task Force experimented on Asher for almost three years before he was rescued by his sister's pack. It's been a long road for him."

"I won't risk my pack again," Mahikan barks as Cass bristles.

"We came here hoping you could help him, that you might know something that would get him past his demons."

"I don't know if that's possible," Laura continues. "Maybe if he came and lived here, and we could practice often? But, to be frank, I'm not sure he *couldn't* steal our power, and I'm not willing to risk that."

"We won't ask that of you," Cass reassures her. "But if you think of anything that might help him, if a seer has any insight, we'd appreciate it."

Mahikan remains skeptical, gathering the omegas and gesturing back toward camp. "We will have our seer speak with him later, but I will not attempt this again. When he returns, have them come to the dining hall. They can speak with our seer before dinner."

I recognize it for the olive branch it is. Despite how Asher's power surprised them, they're willing to try and help if it doesn't put them at risk. I respect it, even though I'm shaken by the display. Still, while it surprised everyone, he didn't hurt us, and I know he could have.

Cass turns to James and me, pulling me into his arms as if he's got to touch me. I give him a quick hug as the twins join us. Rogue gives me an apologetic look before speaking and signing what he can. James translates the rest.

"Ash could have hurt us but didn't. It feels like we're just missing one little key to unlock his control."

River barks out a laugh. "Yeah I'd like to not get knocked on my ass again. He nearly blew out my eardrums. How did he even do that, by the way? What kind of power is it? Is he like Alice?"

Cass shakes his head. "I don't know, but, Rogue, I think you're right. How we figure out the key when there's never been anyone like Asher is another story. Still, I'd rather not leave here without some answers for him, or at least light at the end of the tunnel."

We stand somberly as I reflect on that, my brain spinning back to our own situation. Because I'm desperate to see the light at the end of our tunnel too.

An hour later, Cass, James and I are in a small hut, waiting for Asher to return. Dinner's not for an hour. Cass stands in the doorway, looking out into the forest. I know he's hoping Asher returns soon.

"I want to speak with you both about tonight," I begin, pressing a hand to his back. He turns in the doorway and pulls me into his arms, leaning way down to bury his face in my neck. Warm lips come to the hollow of my throat, and he plants a tender kiss there. His breath is warm on my skin as James joins us, leaning into Cass's warmth. We stand silently for a moment, but I push my way out of his arms.

"I don't want you to do this process. They said it was dangerous."

"I want you, and I can't have you," Cass retorts, signing with clipped, frustrated movements. "If there's a chance this could work, that it could make me what you both need, I have to take it."

James rubs at Cass's chest. "I agree with Julia. We don't need you to do this. You've always been ours. We've always known it."

I give him a look as if to say "see?!"

Cass shakes his head before responding, "You know I want you, and I've shared many times how I worry that another alpha will show up who is a healer or spirit, and they'll take you from me. It's not that I don't believe you; I simply worry that biology has another plan for you two. Please don't ask me to live under the weight of that worry. It's already eating me alive because I want you two so goddamn much."

I slump back against the doorframe. I don't have a good answer for that, because he's right. He's communicated his worries to us over and over again, and we've heard them but cast them aside. His worries aren't the same as mine, but I shouldn't discount them. It's a very real issue to him, even though I'm confident it'll work out.

An idea comes to me. "Maybe we should stay another day and speak to the seer again? And maybe that'll help Asher too?"

A shadow passes over Cass's handsome face. "I can't delay here; I've got to get back to Bent Fork. There's something I need to tell you both."

CHAPTER TWENTY-THREE

A CHILL SNAKES down my back at Cassian's words. "What is it?" I question him more harshly than I mean to, but whatever he's about to share is bad, based on the sheepish look he's wearing.

He crosses his arms and leans into the doorway, looking out at the forest again. It's almost like he's willing Asher and Cherry to show back up so he doesn't have to have this conversation. I pull Jules into my arms to steel her and myself for whatever he's about to say.

Cassian's pale eyes flash. "Based on everything we've learned about what Declan's doing, we know we need to avoid an all-out war. We're at a disadvantage on so many levels. The only way I can think of to help my girls is by trying to get back into Declan's pack. I'm already laying the groundwork for it."

"What?!" I shout at the same time Jules sinks back into my chest, her hand flying up to her mouth before she signs in angry, rapid-fire.

"You can't! They'll kill you! How could that plan possibly work?!"

I scowl as he looks from her to me and back again. "It's a

long shot, but I told Declan and Gabriel that I was intrigued by their message, and they're expecting me at a sermon tomorrow. I can't delay here because I need to be back for that."

"How long have you planned this?" My voice is sullen and irritated.

Cassian has the gall to give me another sorrowful look. "I've been thinking about it for a while, but I hoped it wouldn't come to that. The day you rode into town with me, I went up to the sermon to get a sense of whether it was even possible."

Anger stabs me in the gut at the way he connected with me after that. He was wild and needy, and I realize now he was frustrated because of what he'd just gone to do.

But he still didn't bother to fucking tell me about it.

"You're angry," he states softly, reaching out to grip the back of my neck. He pulls Jules and me close, wrapping one arm around us both as he forces me to look at him. "You have every right to be angry, but I'm telling you now because I don't want secrets between us. I needed a day to come to terms with what I'm going to do, but you deserve to know. I have to get them out." His voice is barely a whisper by the time he finishes his pronouncement, but all I feel is an unsettling mix of anger and sorrow.

I'm mad he wasn't more forthcoming, but I understand at the same time. And it's not like he didn't tell us; he just didn't tell us the moment he thought it.

In our bond, Julia is frustrated, not speaking, but her emotions mirror my own wild rollercoaster. She's irritated and angry and sorrowful for him all at once.

"None of us want to stand in the way of you helping them," I respond when I can find my voice, "but it would have been nice to talk this through with you, rather than you making this decision without us."

Cass nods, reaching down to tip Jules's face up to his. "To be honest, I think I'm guarding my own heart. If I don't share everything with you, if I don't include you like I would my true mates, then maybe I won't be heartbroken when someone shows up and takes you both from me. It's an ass-backward way of trying to protect myself."

"How's it working out?" I grumble as he sighs. He doesn't respond, because there's really nothing else to say.

"I'm glad you told us, but I'm terrified and angry," Jules admits.

Cass reaches down and pulls her up into my arms, pressing us both into the doorway. He plants a tender kiss on her lips, humming as she wraps her arms around his neck. He turns to me next, his kiss hungrier, even though a tangible thread of sorrow lies between us.

We part when we hear footsteps—Cherry and Asher are returning.

Julia squeezes out from between us and takes off for them, running up to Cherry and throwing herself into her arms. Cherry smiles softly as she swings Jules from side to side. Her hair is mussed, and the scent of pheromones slaps me.

"They connected at least; that's probably good," I grumble as Cass takes my hand, leading me out of the hut.

We join our packmates, and our focus turns to them, which is a good thing. I'm frazzled and grumpy from what Cassian shared. There's a deeply innate need to protect Julia's happiness and emotions, but an equally harsh need to protect my own.

Ash looks embarrassed when Cass and I join him. "I'm—shit, I'm sorry. I didn't hurt anyone, did I?" It's clear Ash doesn't have a full recollection of what happened.

"You didn't; you protected us," Cass reminds him. "And then you needed your mate."

"That happened before," I muse aloud, watching a blush stain Cherry's cheeks bright red. "Sorry, honey," I press on. "I don't mean to be all in your business, but when Ash channeled Hale's power, it was the same. Him channeling the power is obviously connected to your bond somehow."

Asher looks at his mate like she's the center of his universe, reaching out to stroke her red hair over her shoulder. "I needed you," is all he says, and I feel like an intruder in their conversation.

For a long, tender moment, we watch in silence as something unspoken passes between them, and then Ash's dark eyes flick to Cassian. "You were waiting for us. What happened?"

"Mahikan wants you both to speak with his seer. I'd like River to go as well," Cass shares.

We're all quiet as we follow Cass. Julia and I are upset, and Ash and Cherry are disconcerted from what happened in the woods. All in all, we're a somber fucking group.

Mahikan meets us in the dining hall with Jacob, Leon, and a younger alpha I haven't met yet.

Jacob glares daggers at us as Leon points to the new male. "This is Ven; he's our primary seer. We'd like him to speak with Cherry, Asher and then River."

He looks crazy young, like Rogue and River young, maybe seventeen or eighteen.

Light brown eyes sparkle as he reaches out and shakes our hands. "I'm told you scared the shit out of the omegas; can't wait to learn all about it."

Asher blanches but shakes the male's hand.

Ven turns to Cassian. "I'll be handling your session after dinner as well; nice to meet you."

Cass grunts, and I can tell he's wary, but we came here for help. I learned long ago not to underestimate someone because of their age, and this is no different.

"You're mated?" River asks the question skeptically, I'm assuming because Ven looks so young.

"Mhm," he laughs. "Laura is my mate. Asher knocked her on her ass earlier, if you remember."

"Oh yeah, she went flying. We all did." River laughs. Asher sinks back into Cherry's arms as if he's dying of embarrassment.

"How do you need to proceed?" Cass questions Ven.

Ven shrugs. "I just need to sit with everyone individually, then I'll go process what I've learned for a bit. If I find out anything helpful, I'll let you know."

Cass grunts but gestures to Asher first.

A long, quiet hour passes as Ven sits with Asher, then Cherry, then River. He's silent as he places a hand on each person's chest. Every now and again, his brows furrow, eyes darting side to side behind closed lids. When he's done with River, he takes a step away from us, looking confused. He glances up at Mahikan.

"I need to process this. I'm going to check on Laura, but I'll be back for Cass's thing. Have someone bring us dinner?"

Mahikan nods, and we all watch as Ven strides away without another word. The big alpha turns to us with a somber look. "Ven is the most powerful seer I've ever met. If anyone can find answers for your people, it will be him."

Cass nods, but the rest of us are silent, because what can we even say to that? We came here hoping to leave with answers, but there's no certainty of that even happening.

CHAPTER TWENTY-FOUR

cassian

MY PACK ALPHA senses are on overload here with Mahikan's people. Asher and Cherry are quiet after today's events. Rogue and River are equally somber. James and Julia are distant, and I can't blame them.

I shared my plan for getting back into Declan's pack. It didn't feel right to keep it from them any longer, but I know it hurt them that I wasn't more forthcoming. The thing about leading a pack is that sometimes I have to make decisions without consulting everyone.

Would having mates change that? I have to assume so.

I don't know with certainty, but if there's any chance Ven can switch my designation, I have to take it. The longer I spend around James and Julia, the more sure I am that I want to keep them forever.

Dinner is a quieter affair than usual, and I find myself missing Bent Fork. I miss River's normal hysterics and Sal's quiet laughter as she talks with Rogue. I miss Luna's barking laugh and Titan's constant scowl. I miss Clay's guidance and sparring with Stone. I miss feeling like there's another alpha in my corner who understands packs like I do.

Suddenly, dinner is over, and Ven appears in the doorway, pulling a chair up to my end of the table. He looks sideways at me. "Better to try and get this over with, and then we'll talk about your packmates, okay?"

"Take care of them first," I grumble, but he shakes his head.

"That was more me telling you what order this is gonna go in. You first, then them."

He gives me a meaningful look, as if he's saying that a pack alpha taking care of himself so he can care for his pack is priority number one. It's not lost on me that Mitchell and Stone have both shared that concept with me in the past.

I shake that aside, nerves beginning to bundle low in my stomach. Very little makes me anxious, but Mahikan made this process sound dangerous.

"If this is going to work, it'll work quickly," Ven shares. "If it doesn't work quickly, then it's not possible for me to do this for you."

"How often does it not work?" I question as he leans on his forearms and grimaces.

"Eh, about half the time. It doesn't work on everybody. It depends on how open the alpha is to it, and how strong they are to withstand the pain, honestly. Some alphas are just meant to be what they are."

Julia and James are stiff as boards next to me. "Please, you don't have to do this," Julia pleads one last time.

I pull her into my lap, kissing my way up her neck. "I have to know if this can work, omega. Please, let me try."

She lifts her hands to continue, but I grab them with a stern look and place them back in her lap. "Enough, little one," I warn. "I've made my decision."

I can see she wants to sign that she doesn't agree with any of this, not after Mahikan's earlier commentary, but I've settled on this path forward. James's expression is worried, but I give him a look he reads well. He pulls Julia into his lap and wraps both arms around her.

Ven claps his hands together. The dining hall is nearly empty. Only my pack and the northern alphas remain.

"I'm going to place my arms around your neck, over your heart. You'll feel heat and discomfort, but that's how it goes. If it doesn't work, I'll stop quickly."

I give him a thankful look and drag my chair out into the room a little. Ven stands behind me, sliding both hands through the neckline of my shirt to cover my heart. James watches me with a neutral expression, but the look on Julia's face is so heartbroken and possessive, I ache to comfort her.

But I equally ache for the bond they have. I want to taunt and tease and stroke them through it. I crave the level of connection they have with each other. If there's a chance I can have that, I have to take it. And if it doesn't work? Well, then I'll have my answer, and so will they.

"Close your eyes, alpha," Ven instructs. "What we're trying to do is to unlock your mind's ability to channel latent power. Long ago in alpha history, alphas became what the pack needed because the communities were so much smaller. In more recent history, as in the last three thousand years, biology picked the designation each alpha was strongest as. But there is a little of every power in each alpha, even an alpha who's not part of a leadership group to begin with."

Our group is fascinated as Ven teaches us, his hands still on my chest. He continues, "We want to focus on your latent power. I'm going to push a scenario into your mind and try to coax a second power out. I'll stop speaking aloud, but you will hear me anyhow. Be ready, Cassian."

That's the last thing Ven says as his palms begin to warm on my skin. There's a slight discomfort in my mind, as if something's trying to worm its way through my brain. I don't sense anything negative, though, so I will myself to relax as the heat of Ven's hands becomes uncomfortably warm.

A whisper comes next: *Think of them; imagine running with them under the moonlight.* I grunt as the heat morphs into a stabbing sensation. The whisper in my mind repeats as my muscles begin to tremble.

I'm tense, my body recognizing that something is wrong, preparing to fight. Somehow, I know I need to relax to let this happen, but my mind and body are at war with one another. Without meaning to, I press against the consciousness in my mind, snarling at it to get out.

Power trails along the edges of my mind as I force my imagination to picture James and Julia, to wonder what their wolves would look like. I imagine the soft pad of their pawprints through the forest, the way Julia would run between us—always protected, always cherished.

A knife cuts deeply across my stomach as I bellow into the room. It slashes again and again, and I struggle to focus on the vision around the horrific pain of whatever Ven's doing.

My eyes flick open to find the room spinning in slow motion. All I see is Julia struggling to get to me, clawing at James as he holds her back. Tears stream down her face as she reaches for me, arms outstretched. He's equally devastated, and somehow, I know whatever Ven's power is doing, it's not working.

Deep in my mind, walls snap up as my alpha nature unleashes itself on the intruder. I scream as my mind shreds itself. Vaguely, I'm aware of Ven screaming too, and then everything goes mercifully black.

Consciousness returns eventually, the soothing tendrils of a healer's power making their way through my mind, putting back together what Ven nearly broke.

I struggle to sit upright, and James is there immediately, hoisting me up against his chest as Julia sinks into my lap, her arms tightly wrapped around my neck. She sobs into my skin, her grief tangible as I manage to get an arm around her waist and groan.

"I almost killed you," Ven mutters, seated in a chair across from me. "I've never felt such dominant power. It resisted the change every step of the way." His dark lashes flutter. "I'm sorry, alpha. You are what you are, and I can't change that."

He's not saying anything I didn't already suspect, but when I look around at my pack, it's clear everyone is devastated. Julia sobs in my arms as I let my head fall back onto James's shoulder. His body behind mine is a comforting, warm presence. I had hoped, after Ven's touch, I'd feel James and Julia in my chest.

I'll never have them that way. I knew that was the case, but having it confirmed is goddamn devastating.

Kissing the top of Julia's head, I shift her off my lap, distraught as she wraps herself immediately around James, needing connection and reassurance.

Every bone in my body aches; every muscle, every sinew screams in agony. It lingers even though Ven's hands aren't on my body any longer. What he attempted has taken its toll, and I'm ready to find a place to crawl away and lick my wounds. My heart thuds slowly in my chest as if it, too, is struggling to find the will to keep going.

I turn to Ven with a wry look. "Thank you for trying, alpha. I hope I didn't hurt you. Please share what you learned with my packmates about their circumstances. We need to get home."

It turns out there's really not much news there either. Ven and the other seers have never heard of an alpha with power like Asher's.

"There's a spot of good news, though," Ven shares as our group deflates. "River's definitely a seer. It's not unheard of in alpha history; it's just very uncommon."

Next to her brother, River lights up. Rogue shoots me a knowing, triumphant look. He's proud of her, and I'm happy for them both.

Ven addresses the happy teen directly, "Like all seers, you won't access your full power until you take a mate. But when you do, you can serve that function for a pack."

River's eyes flick to mine. "I'd be honored to serve like that."

I smile at her. She'll make some pack a worthy seer when she grows into her power. I hope I'm there to watch her fill that role, but I'm barely able to think past tonight. My head throbs, and my entire body feels like it's falling apart.

Remembering my final task from Stone, I turn to the other pack's alphas. "War is coming between our pack and Declan's. We need you to help us. We're outmatched."

Jacob shakes his head no as Leon and Mahikan nod. They're obviously not in agreement, so I press on, "We found your omegas when Declan kidnapped them. We fought to return them to you. He's getting more violent by the minute, and I need to save my girls. I need your commitment."

I'll force the issue if I have to, but I can't leave here without their verbal consent to be at our side for the war to come.

"We will be there if your plan does not work," Mahikan counters.

Julia and James look over at me at the same time.

Mahikan continues, "I called Stone when you passed out. He shared your plan, although, Stone and I suspect the other pack will just kill you. If they do not, we will be at the ready."

Julia comes to stand in front of me with a furious look. "Stone is in on this plan too? You planned this together?"

Fuuuuuck.

CHAPTER TWENTY-FIVE

TO SAY I feel betrayed is an understatement. It's not that Cassian wants to help the omegas so badly that he'd work to get back into Declan's pack. It was bad enough that he didn't trust Julia and me enough to share that plan with us early on. But, apparently, my own goddamn alpha was aware of this plan and didn't tell me either. I have to wonder if the rest of leadership is aware, and if they are, why they didn't bother to fucking mention it?

"Does everybody know?" Julia's signs are slow, belying how shocked she is. "These alphas know, Stone knows. Does everybody know about this plan except James and me?"

Mahikan shifts in his seat, clearly unaware that what he just said was news to us.

Cass shakes his head. "I discussed this with Stone and Clay right before we left, and right after I attended the sermon. I wasn't set on it; I shared that with you already."

"But Stone and Clay know," Julia presses on. "All of you decided to make this plan without speaking to us, your mates."

Cass opens his mouth to speak but slumps against a table leg.

He's exhausted by the attempt to switch designations. Even though I'm hurt and angry, he's not in a position to talk this through with us right now.

Looking into my bond with Jules, I stroke her softly. *He needs to heal, baby girl. Let's get him back to the hut. This is a conversation for later.*

For a long, terrible minute, she and Cass hold a visual stand-off, but then Mahikan and Leon hoist him up off the ground. He's so weak, he can't even walk back to the temporary hut by himself. In my mate bond, I read Julia's anger and frustration and worry. We watch the alphas lay Cass down, and he passes out almost immediately.

Rogue, River, Cherry and Asher show up in the doorway, and we sit together with Cass for a while, watching over him. He doesn't wake for hours and hours.

"I thought they killed him," River whispers. "And my heart just about stopped in my chest."

Rogue puts an arm around her shoulders and pulls her close. Worry lines mark the middle of his forehead as he watches Cass's chest rise and fall softly.

Cherry drops to both knees by Cass's bedside and feels his pulse before examining his hands and feet and listening to his chest. She falls into nurse mode naturally, and it reminds me of how she did the same for Asher when we first arrived at Bent Fork, all those long months ago.

"His vitals are good. I think he just needs rest," she whispers, turning to look at Jules and me. "What do you two need?"

Jules shrugs, but Cherry crosses the small space between them to face her. "I'm gonna tell you what you've told me so many times, sweet friend. Everything is going to be just fine, okay? You're meant to be together; it's written in the stars, and I don't care what this pack has to say about it."

Julia's eyes fill with tears, but Cherry squeezes her tighter.

Eventually she, Asher and the twins leave, and I'm left with a distraught mate whose emotions mirror my own.

I pull her close, sliding her tee over her head. Peppering kisses along her shoulders, I undo her bra and toss it aside. I'd bury my tongue between her thighs and get her off if I thought it'd distract her, but I read her well enough to know that's not what she needs.

Dropping to one knee, I slide her jeans down her thin legs, kissing her lower belly before I rise and pull her into bed with me. We pretzel our legs together, and I infuse all my love into our bond as she presses her back to my front.

Even though we're devastated at tonight's events, we're still drawn to him. And even though I'm upset at the way things happened, I'm reasonable enough to understand why Cassian has done some things the way he has.

Stone is going to hear it from me when I get home, though.

Hours later, Jules is asleep in my arms as I watch Cass's chest move gently. I fall into a fitful sleep and wake early.

By then I've made the leap from shocked and horrified to really fucking mad.

The following morning, Cass sits on the opposite bed, leaning forward with his forearms on his knees. Pale eyes are focused on me as I wake. He's dressed, his bags packed for our return trip this morning.

There's a sorrowful look on his face, but it's resigned too. It's a look I know well, because I've seen the same look on Mitchell Bancroft's face when I was with his pack. I've seen it on Stone's. It's the look of a man who made a decision he didn't ever want to make and is living with the consequences.

"Do you want to talk about it?" Cass's deep baritone sends a rumble through my belly, settling deep in my balls. I want him, and I'm so fucking mad at him, all at the same time.

"No," Jules signs from my chest, having awoken just after me. "I'm furious that you and my alpha and my fucking strategist made plans about your life without talking to us. It should always be us first, and everyone else second."

Cass opens his mouth to say something but thinks better of it.

Jules shifts out of my arms and grabs her dirty clothes, throwing them haphazardly in a bag before she strides out of the hut.

Cass watches her go, a mournful look on his face, but I steel my heart against feeling sorry for him.

I grab my own bag and toss everything into it before turning to him as I sling it over my shoulder. "You talked a big talk about communication, and I thought we were on the same wavelength, but I won't stand for this. Your mates should never be the last ones in on something so important."

"You're not my mates, though," Cass whispers softly, standing to pull me close to him by the belt. "I'd give any fucking thing under the sun to change that, but how can you be when I'm the wrong goddamn designation? You saw what happened last night. Ven said it—I am what I am. My power fought him, James."

I shove out of Cass's embrace, because if I continue to touch him, I'm going to want to fall into bed with him, and I can't do that.

Instead, I walk to the door before turning. "I don't give a fuck what Ven or Mahikan or anyone here has to say. It should be enough for you that *we* say you're ours." For a long moment, he looks at me with open longing, a muscle ticking in his jaw. But he says nothing, and I go.

We meet Asher, Cherry and the twins and say a quick goodbye to the northern packs.

My mind is awash with angry thoughts the entire car ride home, with Julia equally lost in thought next to me. Ash sits silently up front, so the only sound at all comes from Cherry and the twins. They play games and chatter on the way back, but the rest of us say not a fucking word.

When we get back home, my focus turns to Julia. It's unlike her to be so silent, but knowing Cassian is making these plans without even talking to us cut her deeply. She's my priority, as ever. If he can't shit or get off the fucking pot when it comes to us, I'm done. Because now he's hurt her. So no matter how strong that draw is between us, I won't pursue it.

When Cassian parks the minivan, Julia gets out immediately and heads up the front steps. I trail her, sensing Cassian at my back. I'd revel in the protective vibe rolling off him if I wasn't so fucking irritated.

She heads straight for Stone's office, pushing the doors open. Piano notes ring out, but our alpha stops playing as he turns with a smile. It falls the moment he sees us, but he sighs and gestures for us to approach.

"What happened?"

"Was there ever a point where you planned to let James and me know that Cassian's trying to get back into Declan's pack?" Julia's question is abrupt, and it shocks Stone, who slumps back against the piano.

"You didn't even tell me?" I question as I stand next to Jules. Cass comes to stand beside us.

"It came up right before you left," Stone hedges. "I planned to speak with all of you together pending what happened at Mahikan's."

Julia stomps closer to Stone and grips his chin, turning his face so he can't look away from her as she drops her hold to sign. "I'm going to make this clear one final time, and I want you to hear me good, alpha. Cassian and James are both my mates. But if the two of you make decisions without involving me, then you're acting like assholes. Frankly, I'm disappointed—disappointed enough that I want you to leave me alone. I'm pissed that neither of you will just believe me when I tell you something important. And I'm furious you thought to make a plan about my mate without including me in the conversation."

Stone opens his mouth to speak, but Julia cuts him off with a palm held up as Cassian crosses the room and reaches for her. She shakes her head and continues, "I'm upset with you both, and I'd like you to give me space. We said we'd be good at communicating, but this was a terrible breach of trust. Do you understand?"

Cassian nods but looks miserable, and Stone just looks angry—at his fucking self, I hope. Jules hasn't said anything I want to expand on, so I glare at Cass. "I trust you can update him on the trip?"

The big alpha nods, gray eyes mournful as I grip Julia's hand and lead her out of the room. By the time we get to the stairs, I sense her overwhelm. Scooping her up into my arms, I trot up to our room and lay her gently in the bed.

Beautiful blue eyes are filled with tears as her emotions begin to unravel. Mine mirror hers, our bond tense and loose at the same time, as if we're untethered from something so important, we're no longer grounded without it.

Reaching down, I kiss her stomach and then undo her jeans, sliding them down her slender legs. When I get to her boots, I pull those off too. Her sweater goes next along with the delicate cotton bra she picked for our adventure.

What a disaster, she moans into the bond. *I'm so fucking frustrated.*

I'll admit, I expected things to go differently, I growl into our tether. *I hoped he'd see what you and I have always known. But this is something he needs to figure out for himself, mate. We can't force him to love us, not when he's his own biggest roadblock.*

I know, she sobs into our bond. *Make me forget, alpha. Come here.*

Pulling my own clothes off, I fall into bed and roll gently on top of her, showering her with my love as our bond burns bright. But there's still something missing. We both know it.

And I can't fix it.

CHAPTER TWENTY-SIX

cassian

I WATCH James and Julia go, knowing I've fucked up. I tell myself it's better that we don't continue carrying on our relationship. But I don't believe it. My heart is already tattered and sore. Everything in me tells me to go to them, to claim them and make them mine—designations be damned. But that's not the way this works. We aren't the northern packs. We tried and it didn't work.

Stone watches them go in silence, then crosses his arms as he turns back to me. "What the hell happened up there?"

I fill him in on the whole sordid tale, his gaze softening when I mention how Ven nearly killed me, and I'm still just me.

"Are you sure it didn't work?" Stone's voice is soft but distraught as I shake my head.

"Ven said it didn't. There's no reason to believe he'd lie about it. I am what I am. Maybe I'm not meant to have who I want. So, the best thing for me to do is proceed with the plan to get the omegas out."

"I'm not inclined that way anymore," Stone replies after my assertion. "Clay and I have been talking it through, and I don't think we'll avoid an all-out war with Declan and Gabriel."

"And if it comes to war, he'll hurt those girls first, Stone. I know he will. That's just the kind of asshole Declan is."

Stone nods but seems lost in thought.

"I've got to try," I press. "What am I going to do otherwise? Sit around and keep making James and Julia miserable? I've got to do something. You know, from one pack alpha to another, waiting is not our strong suit."

"Not at all," he agrees. "Which is why I'm giving them the night like Jules requested. I'll be apologizing first thing in the morning. She was right; we should have shared the plan. It would have angered her, but at least we would have been up front."

I'm so miserable I can't even agree, but I continue on, updating him about Cherry and Asher and the unhelpful information we got on that front. All in all, the trip felt like a bust, with the exception of the twins, who burst in moments later, talking over one another so much that I can't get another word in.

I leave Stone to deal with the hooligans and go to my cabin, sorrow sinking all the way into my very bones. I'm surprised when Rogue follows me out into the lobby, his steps quiet behind mine. When I turn, he's got his hands in his pockets, looking at me with such an assessing expression that he appears far older than his seventeen years.

"You don't have to leave this place to be who you are," he says with uncharacteristic seriousness. "You belong here just like Riv and I do; I feel it in here, especially after our trip to Mahikan's." He brings one hand up to rub at his chest, eyes not leaving mine.

When I say nothing, he continues, "I've been having weird feelings, weird intuitions lately. And I thought maybe it meant I didn't belong here. But I think it just means our pack needs to be like Mahikan's, a mishmash of multiples—stronger together."

Cocking my head to the side, I take a step closer. "Where is this coming from, alpha? Wishes don't make reality. Believe me, I fucking know."

God, do I know.

"Just a sense of knowing." He smiles before his dark eyes find me again. "How would you feel about having a teenage strategist, Cassian?" There's a confident smile on his face, but his words shock me.

A fucking teenage strategist? I blink rapidly, trying to digest the information. But there, deep in my chest, there's a certainty now that he's said it. Have I got my head so far up my own ass that I'm not even following my own intuition any longer? I think back, and it's true Rogue has been around a lot lately. Helping with Sal and Isabel and Abigail. It seems like he's there every time I turn around.

"I know it's shocking," Rogue continues. "I've been thinking about it since the railroad tracks, but something snapped into place for me that day. If you left this pack, I'd follow you even though it would kill me to leave the ranch; I love it here. That means something, alpha."

I'm rooted in place, staring at the seventeen-year-old, whom I realize now has trailed me around quite a bit since I came here.

Can you hear me? I question, looking for a hint of the bond I should have with a strategist.

Loud and clear, Rogue sends back with a toothy grin before he continues speaking into my mind. *You look a little shell-shocked; it's been a long forty-eight hours. I'm going to go spend some time with Sal, but let's talk more tomorrow?*

I nod as he turns to go, but watching him makes one thing painfully clear to me. If I've got a strategist, then there's no doubt I'm a pack alpha. And if I'm collecting leadership, then that means a pack alpha is what I'm supposed to be.

And I'll never be anything else.

The afternoon passes in a blur. I attend Gabriel's sermon, but it's low key, and like before, Declan insists I sit up front. I leave more frustrated than ever because I expected something—anything—to happen. But it's clear I won't get back into his pack quickly at all.

As soon as I get back, I trail through the lodge to find Rogue. I've always thought of him as half of a pair of goofy twins, but he's far more serious than his sister. He's been protecting her for years, so it makes sense. Somehow, the idea that I've got a seventeen-year-old strategist doesn't scare me half as much as it should.

I share what I heard at today's sermon, but there's not much he hasn't heard at this point. He and I spar for a few hours in the gym before dinner. When James and Julia don't come down-stairs for it, Rogue claps me on the back and suggests I chat with Stone.

After dinner, I find the pack alpha in his office. "Got a minute, alpha?" I'd like his perspective before I go give the apology of a century.

He smiles at me but settles back into his big chair, waving for me to go on.

I'm too on edge without James and Julia's comforting pres-ence to deliver my news with much tact. "Rogue is my strategist."

Stone's lips curl up into a big grin as he sits forward in his seat. "Oh? Do fucking tell."

I fill him in on what Rogue told me, and by the time I'm done, Stone is gobsmacked but thoughtful.

"Say something," I bark as he looks out the back windows of the lodge.

"Maybe River's your seer," he says finally, as if he's speaking to himself. "Wouldn't it be fucking great to have two here?"

Shocked, I look over at him. "You've got nothing to say about them being seventeen?"

"Why the hell should that matter?" he barks back. "They've been on their own since they were fourteen. They've had enough reality to last them a lifetime. I've been teaching Rogue piano, and, honestly, we've had some really good conversations. He's very mature."

I don't know why hearing that opinion of Rogue makes me smile, but I've learned the same thing about the young alpha.

"If you find your leadership group, what will you do?" Stone questions, dark eyes sparking. "Will you move on?"

"I don't know," I admit. "Can you imagine two packs living here? Not being the only alpha? I don't know how that would work. This is your house, your ranch, your valley."

"So let's build another fucking house," Stone barks gruffly. "Whatever we need to do. Why couldn't we lead like Mahikan, Jacob and Leon do? I talked to Mahikan this afternoon, by the way."

"And?"

"And he agrees with me that you're meant to be an alpha, to lead like I do."

Hatred for my designation settles in my gut at those words, because I've always known they were right. But that means—

"He also thinks James and Julia are yours."

"What?" I look up at my friend. I hate that hope immediately fills my chest, but it does, because I'd give anything to have them.

"He says he knows they couldn't switch your designation, but your relationship felt natural to him. It's the same way it always felt right to me, and the way it feels right to you. Cass, what if we just don't do things like other packs? I'm more and more inclined to believe that following our instinct makes a lot more sense than preconceived ideas of how packs should work."

Slumping down across from him, I run both hands through my hair. "I need to run," I growl. "Go with me?"

Stone grins and hops up out of his seat, opening the doors to the back balcony. "It's a twenty-foot drop. Think you can do it, old man?"

Snarling, I cross the office and bump him with my chest as he laughs and steps out of the way. Then I leap over the balcony and land down below, pushing into a run as Stone jumps and catches up with me.

"Race you to the far end of the valley," he shouts into the blistering winter cold. I push my arms and my legs hard, relishing the burn and the freezing bite of the air as we sprint up the scrabbly valley floor toward the rocky far end.

"You run like an old man!" shouts Stone as he shoves me, sending me tumbling into the dirt with an angry bellow. Picking myself up, I dash after him and leap on top of him, shoving his face into the dirt before I take off again. We needle one another the entire way to the far end of the ranch, not stopping until we get to the giant rock formation that gives us a great view of the entire valley.

The lodge sits in the middle, the store up at the far end close to the highway. It's so fucking beautiful here.

"You don't want to leave, do you?" Stone questions, giving me a knowing look.

"No," I admit. "I want James and Julia, and I never want to go anywhere."

"We could put a lodge at this end of the valley, you know," Stone suggests. "You'd have a gorgeous view up toward the middle. And a better view of the stars."

I let his words sink in as I imagine a big house for James and Julia and myself. Add in the twins, and it's starting to sound pretty fucking good.

Stone chuckles. "River would die of boredom without me to

needle twenty-four-seven, but I suppose she can start irritating you instead."

"I'll send her to you on an ATV," I grumble. I look over at Stone, and he smiles at me as I suck at my teeth and look away. "I'm a little surprised how natural it feels to talk about this. You think that means something?"

Stone looks toward the lodge. "I do, Cass, and Erin agrees. She loves having you here—everyone does. I think we should decide on a path forward and fucking stick to it. I want you here to finish rebuilding the store. I want you here to help me deal with the researchers and Bianca's wild-ass sister."

"Jesus," I grumble. "What's going on with her?" I imagine she's plotting ways to steal Julia from me as we speak.

"She's a handful," Stone mutters. "She threw a fit while you were gone. Bianca shared that she's being required by the research program to formally register our pack for something called the Transitioned Database. Apparently it's legislation put forth by the DPM, although I don't remember hearing that tidbit on the news."

"You're fucking kidding," I growl.

Stone shakes his head. "Bianca's not feeling good about the new tests she's receiving from headquarters. She can't put a finger on it, but she and the team have all decided not to send any more of our info until they get some clarity from Devraj Eller, who runs the program."

I growl under my breath. "This is all Declan. And Gabriel and the fucking DPM. This is all tied together somehow. But why?" I look over at him. "I'm more convinced than ever that I need to get in there and see what the fuck Declan is doing. We're missing something here, Stone."

"If you're insistent on trying, I'll do everything in my power to keep you safe. But Mahikan is on standby if we need him."

We fall silent after that, watching lights twinkle at the lodge. After a long time, Stone turns to me with a wink. "You know,

James and Julia are probably in their room right now, stewing about how we weren't forthcoming. I'm going to issue a heartfelt apology tomorrow, but it seems to me that you've got an opportunity to make it up to them. And tell them about Rogue."

For a long moment, I look toward the beautiful home nestled right there in the valley. I was devastated when Ven's attempts didn't change anything for me, but maybe they're not meant to. Maybe if I throw myself headfirst into something with them, it'll work out.

It's that moment where I come to a realization. Maybe I wasn't meant to have James and Julia, but I've never been a man to let the world dictate my actions until this. They want me. I want them. Maybe that's all we need.

"Let's go, alpha." Stone laughs, bumping my shoulder with his. "I need my mate, and you need yours."

He sprints up the trail toward the valley floor, but I watch for another long minute, wondering what they're doing now, my mates. Testing that word out in my mind feels good; it feels natural.

Goddamn, it's perfect to think of them that way. Maybe this is a terrible idea, but I don't have it in me to care anymore. One afternoon of their ire is longer than I ever want to experience it again.

Taking off after Stone, I sprint through the valley until we reach the lodge. He waves and jogs around the side of the house toward his wing, and I veer around the right side, sprinting all the way around to the front where our room is.

Our room.

Snarling, I leap up onto the side of the lodge, using my claws to dig into the wood, and then I pull myself up until I get to the second story, landing on the balcony quietly. Leaning against the window, I peer in from the shadows of the porch. Julia's in front of the fire, drawing on her tablet.

God, I wonder if she's drawing James and me again. I've got to know.

James comes out of the shower with a towel wrapped around his waist, but dark eyes flick up toward the porch. He senses me out here. He frowns and crosses the room to tap on Julia's shoulder. She looks up at me with such disdain, I can't fucking stand it.

Gripping the door handle, I slide it open and let myself into the room. "I'm sorry," I begin, crossing until I'm right in front of them both.

"Sorry's not enough," James signs, stepping in front of Julia. "It was a breach of trust."

That's the moment I realize that holding back from being who I am around them has gotten us to this point. No more.

Darting forward, I grip his throat with my claws out, yanking him to my chest. Then I knock his legs out from under him, guiding him fast down onto the floor between Julia's thighs. His back is up against her legs as his big chest heaves, dark eyes flashing with anger.

Straddling him, I smile at her before returning my attention to my alpha mate. "Mine," I growl, and then I lean in to bite his lower lip, tugging on it as he returns my angry rumble.

"Not yours—you made that very clear at Mahikan's," he manages as I squeeze harder, making him buck in my arms.

"Mine," I repeat again, looking up at Julia to find her biting her lip as she watches us.

When I return my mouth to James's, his dark lips part for me. But I don't want to be gentle and tender; that's not the sort of lover I usually am.

Slicking my mouth over his, I go wild on him, my lips bruising as I demand a return of my attention. James kisses me back in between desperate pants. When we finally break, I use my thumb to guide his head back between Julia's knees, and then I bite my way hard down his beautiful dark skin, all the way to that seductive place where his neck and shoulder meet.

I sink my fangs into the muscle and purr as his hips thrust against mine, the towel falling open as he flails. He roars into the bite as he scrambles to undo the buttons on my shirt, sliding it down my shoulders as my gaze connects with Julia's.

The scent of her slick drives me on as I release the bite, blood dripping from my fangs. Leaning over James, I nip at her knee, then her inner thigh, then a little higher up as she wriggles in the chair.

Rocking back, I grin at them both. "On your knees in front of me, alpha," I command as James sits up.

"I'm still mad," he signs, glaring at me.

"I'm going to fuck that anger away," I assure him. "I won't tell you to get on your knees again." Dominance rolls off me in waves, hitting James as he hesitates. But then he turns and cages Julia in, presenting me with a mouthwatering view of stacked back muscles and toned, dark thighs.

Reaching between James's muscular thighs, I slide my hand up Julia's inner thigh, finding her already slick for me. Laughing, I bite James's back over and over as I stroke her. He groans as she shifts to meet my hands, and then I use that beautiful slick to coat his cock with it, marking my way down his back before I bury my face in his ass and lick.

James grunts out a string of expletives, head falling forward into Julia's lap as one hand comes down to stroke his own dick. Slapping it away, I shove his legs wider apart and rip my shirt off. My jeans go next, and then I reach around him, gathering slick from between Julia's legs. She's so wet, she's soaking the chair, her thighs shaking with anticipation.

"You next," I sign with a grin as she looks at me, face flushed, her red lips parted. "I feel your need, omega."

"Then do something about it," she signs back haughtily.

I reach down and coat my own dick with all that wetness,

and then I line it up with James's ass. With one thrust, I fill him as he bucks against the intrusion, flying upright as I reach around to use my hand on him. He's so caught like this, so stuck, and I fucking relish it.

Growling, I put one hand on the back of his neck and shove him down to hover over Julia. I slide out and back in with a possessive roar, waves of pleasure washing through my core.

"So fucking good," I groan. "You thought you'd teach me something about how men fuck, alpha. But you don't know how much I've fantasized about taking you."

James's answering groan is muffled, his face pressed to Julia's chest, which heaves as she watches us. Her blue eyes never leave mine, even as she reaches out to rest one hand on James's tense back.

"Mine," I tell them again, reaching out to grip James's shoulder as I slide in and out slowly, reveling in the feel of his body taking me in. Possessive need hits me so hard as I look at them, ready and willing to set aside that anger.

"I'm yours," I sign to Julia. "And yours," I repeat aloud as I thrust back into James's tight ass. He cries out as I pick up the pace, unleashing for the first time with him. I fuck him so hard, he crushes Julia back into the chair, her gaze firmly cemented on me.

She's so strong, so goddamn strong.

"James," I growl as heat sends hot daggers down the backs of my thighs. The rhythm of my thrusts picks up pace until I've lost all sense of time. I'm so hot from the feel of him, from watching him hold on to her like a life raft, sobbing with the pleasure I wring from his body.

I slide one hand around his hip and fist his cock with both of my hands. The combined pressure of my dick and my hands is too much for him, and he explodes with an ear-shattering bellow, ropes of cum coating my fingers as I bite his shoulder hard, sending a fresh wave of orgasm over him.

Laughing as he comes down, I slow my pace and kiss my way along his broad back. "Well done, mate," I murmur into his skin. "My sweet, good boy. I need you again in a few minutes."

James grunts and slides off Julia's lap, falling to his back on the floor, chest heaving as he looks at me. "I imagined myself playing more of a professor role in your bi-awakening, to be honest." His tone is curt, but I read him as utterly sated. He flops onto his back as I reach for Julia and pull her up out of the chair.

We step over James as I look down and laugh. "Sort yourself and join us when you're ready, alpha."

James gives me an exhausted thumbs-up as I lead my omega into the bathroom.

This feels right. So goddamn right. And I'm done waiting for the other shoe to drop.

CHAPTER TWENTY-SEVEN

julia

"I HOPE you're prepared to grovel," I sign to Cassian as we enter the bathroom. He laughs and leans around me to cut the water on. When he turns, there's pure dominant fire in the way he looks at me.

"If by grovel you mean apologize as I fuck you into the wall, then, yeah, I'm ready for that." Steely gray eyes narrow as he licks his lips.

Goosebumps cover the surface of my skin as he leans forward and rips my shirt right down the middle. My pants go next, and then I'm naked in front of him.

He's never been like this with us, unleashed in this way. This is how I thought he'd be, how I wanted him to be.

"What's changed?" I demand. "I love hard, and I demand honesty and respect. You can't come in here and fuck us and then have secrets the next day. I won't stand for it."

"No more secrets," he signs as he takes another step forward, pushing against my chest so I step into the shower. Leaning forward, he picks me up into his arms and presses me to the tile, water spilling down over our bodies.

"I need your word on that," I reiterate, signing then gripping his chin to ensure he's looking.

"I give it. I give you everything," he responds then reaches down to soap up his dick. He brings his hands to my breasts and pinches my nipples gently. My body responds immediately, even though my mind is at war with my desire. Will he feel this way tomorrow when Declan pulls some new bullshit?

I have to believe Cass will, and take him at his word.

Growling, I rock my hips along his hard cock, coating him with slick as he captures my mouth expertly. This kiss is different from any of the previous ones. It's demanding and needy, forcing me to give as good as he does. Our lips and teeth clash together so hard, I know I'll be bruised tomorrow.

When Cassian lifts my hips up and pulls me down onto his dick, I let out a desperate scream, my head falling back to the tiles. Just like with James, there's no waiting for me to adjust, no asking if I can take it. This is a pack alpha in all his beautiful, virile glory.

Cassian rails me into the wall, his teeth nipping along my shoulder as I struggle around the unbelievable pleasure. I come hard and fast, shouting, orgasm prolonged when James steps into the doorway, eyes hooded with lust as he watches us.

You look so good like this, James purrs into our bond. *Caught in his arms, fucked within an inch of your life.*

Cassian picks up the pace, bringing me to another blistering orgasm, my body locked tight around him as I shatter. James joins us in the shower, leaning against the tile to watch as I gasp for breath. Cassian laughs into my lips, his beard tickling my chin as he licks my swollen skin. He lifts me off himself, but James meets us and picks me right back up, spreading my thighs wide around his muscular torso. He pushes until Cassian's back is to the glass, mine pressed against his chest.

Pinning me with his hips, he grins at me, then over my shoulder. "You take her back there. I want her here."

James reaches between my thighs and strokes me, then reaches farther back to touch Cass. The rumbly vibration of Cassian's purr warms me from the back as he lines his cock up with my ass and slides in gently.

I squeak and jerk. God, oh god, I'm so fucking full. My head falls back against Cassian's shoulder as he licks and sucks gently at the side of my neck.

"Easy, my love," James signs. "Relax and enjoy that big dick. You ready to take two?"

I'm panting so hard, I can't even respond as James steps forward and slides into me slowly, pleasure streaking through our bond as he throws his head back and snarls. For a long minute, all I can do is throb around the intense fullness of my mates, but then I feel Cass say something, and James's dark eyes snap open before he looks at me.

Move, he whispers into our bond.

"Gladly, alpha," he signs before bringing his hands to the backs of my thighs and pushing them up and back. The angle hits differently, my head falling back as James picks up a steady, deep pace. Behind me, Cassian remains still, but his dick jumps in my ass every time James thrusts inside.

God, I wish I could read him in a bond right now. Is he losing his mind like I am? James's pace loses its steady rhythm as he moves faster and faster, his mouth opening as he gasps in pleasure. I'm about to come just watching how good this feels for him. Our bond is tight with tension and overwhelm and need.

Orgasm hits me so hard and fast, all I can do is scream as my mates come with me, filling me with their seed until it drips out —there's so damn much of it. James keeps fucking me slowly, even after I come down. And when I do, they drop me gently to the tile floor. Cassian lathers my hair with strong, confident touches, and James washes my body.

When we get out, James wraps me in a towel and carries me

to bed. Cassian follows us, sinking into the mattress. He unwraps me like a present, and we start the whole thing over again. For hours, my alphas lavish me with attention.

This is everything. This is what I've needed and been dreaming about.

They are my gifts.

In the morning, James moans softly in my ear. When I turn to look at him, he's still waking up. But hovering over his thighs is Cassian with James's hard dick in his mouth as he sucks slowly, reverently.

"Changing up the morning routine I see," I sign as I crawl down toward him and kiss his big shoulder.

He licks his way up James's cock before pulling me close, capturing my lips, his tongue intertwining with mine. It's a possessive touch, but I wriggle away to suck on James's beautiful cock myself. Cassian grins and parts James's big thighs, reaching his hand between them to play with his heavy balls, kneading and rolling them in his hand.

James's warm hand sneaks up my back. *Good morning, mate. Goddam—* his greeting breaks off as Cassian begins sliding his fingers farther back.

"Let us please you," I sign as I straddle him, sliding myself down onto that beautiful cock one torturous inch at a time. James bucks, but behind me, Cassian pushes James's thighs wider apart. He presses me slightly forward, and then I get to watch James's face morph from shock to pleasure to ecstasy as Cassian takes him. Inside me, James's dick leaps and pulses.

Cassian reaches both arms around me, his warm chest to my back. "Ride him," he commands. "Fuck him while I do. I want him to fall apart before we do anything else today."

Grinning at James, I lean forward and slide myself off him

and back down, slow and steady. But I feel Cassian with a steady rhythm behind me, James lost to pleasure, his hands on my hips. His fingers grip my skin hard as he arches up into me. Dark lips fall open as his brows scrunch together.

You're so fucking beautiful like this, about to come, I whisper into our bond.

James cries out, reaching one hand up to cup my breast, pinching my nipple as we chase pleasure together. James comes hard and fast, trying desperately to rock his hips to meet mine, but he's caught by Cassian. I ride that wave of his pleasure before falling over the edge myself, Cassian joining me, kissing his way along my back as he wrings ecstasy from James.

When that blinding emotion fades, I fall forward onto James's chest, and Cassian rolls off us onto his side, stroking my back as he grins.

CHAPTER TWENTY-EIGHT
cassian

MINE. The word repeats itself over and over in my brain as I watch James and Julia get ready for the day. Last night and this morning? They were perfect, and I have no regrets.

I watch Julia pull a bulky sweater over her tiny frame and gesture for her to come to me. She obeys beautifully, giving me a huge smile as she sinks gracefully down onto my lap.

"Something happened yesterday," I share with a smile. "Rogue is my strategist."

"What?" Julia's shocked as James drops to a knee next to us.

"How'd you find out?" He looks a little surprised and suspicious, as if I kept another secret. I want to dispel that right away.

"He came up and told me, shocked the hell out of me, to be honest. But he's right. I can hear him. We have a bond."

Their faces fall at the mention of a bond.

"It doesn't change how I feel about you both," I reassure them. "But it happened, so…"

Julia smiles up at me before I press on. "I'm going to go see Declan again today," I sign.

My beautiful omega's smile falls, her strawberry blond brows pulling into a scowl as she crosses her arms. She wants to help the other girls as much as I do, but I read her as frustrated and worried. She's not totally over the fact I didn't include her the first time this plan came to me.

"I want to include you now." My lips brush along hers. "I still need to help the omegas, little one," I remind her.

She presses her forehead to mine. "Of course, but you're going to see him alone?"

"I am. I'm doing it to protect everyone, you and James included."

James stands, giving Julia a gentle smile. "After considering it, he could be right, Jules. If we can avoid a war, we should."

Julia scoffs and turns back to me. "I don't believe there's any scenario where this will turn out well."

"If it goes poorly, call Mitchell and tell him to bring the omegas." I laugh. I'm only half kidding. If my plan to get my girls out goes to shit, someone will have to move heaven and earth to help me.

Julia crosses her arms, sliding off my lap. When she turns from me, I slide an arm around her waist and yank her back to my chest, between my legs as I sit on the edge of the bed. The breath whooshes from her as she grunts, but all I can think of is the sizzling, anxious need I have to take her and fuck that worry away. I need to sink into her heat and prove the depth of my devotion.

James comes to stand in front of us, tilting her face up to his with a finger under her chin. His dark eyes flick to mine as he grins. He wants to tease our girl.

Growling, I fist my left hand in her hair and yank her neck to the side, baring it for us both. His mark is there, that pale scar that identifies her as taken. My growl intensifies as I bring my lips to his mark and suck at it.

Julia bucks in my arms, gasping as she arches into my chest.

"She needs your mark right next to mine, alpha," James

reminds me. "Think how good she'll look with two bites on that beautiful, soft skin."

An overwhelming wave of possession hits me so hard, I can't hold back. I sink my teeth lightly into James's bite, reveling in the way she squeals in my arms. Goddamn, it feels good to have my fangs in her skin. The rich scent of her slick fills my nostrils, which flare as I breathe her in deeply.

I bite harder, groaning as James steps between Julia's thighs to stroke the side of my neck. "You look like you're about to lose your fucking mind, Cass. Let's have her before we do anything else today."

A whine leaves my throat, because there's a lot on my to-do list today, and I need to get going. But maybe there's time to fuck her quickly.

I banish the thought as soon as I have it. I don't want a quick fuck before I leave them. I want long, languorous hours in bed. I want to be all over them both, getting them off time and time again before I let myself come.

Julia grabs my right hand and brings it to James's chest. I grip his shirt and pull him closer, releasing my bite to take his mouth. His dark lips part for me, so responsive to my need. She turns when I let go of her hair, sliding onto my knee as I kiss James.

I want to put on a show for her, and I want hours to do it. Frustration builds in my system when she strokes James's cock and he grunts into the kiss, panting from the pleasure of her touch.

"Fuck, I need more time," I snarl.

"Please, Cassian," he moans into my lips. "Get us off once before you go."

I grunt around the need as my muscles tremble. I always want them, but this is even deeper than usual, even more powerful. Somehow, I know if I fall into bed with them now, I won't come out all day.

"I can't," I snarl. "Play with one another, and when I get home, we'll do it again. I've got to get a few things done, and if I start up with you two, I'll never get out of the bed."

James snaps his teeth at me, lips curled into a sneer as he collars my throat. His emotions run so high, dark claws tip each finger. I can feel them poking into my skin as I rise from the bed, Julia slipping off my lap.

She watches us as I bump James with my chest. If he wants to play at a game of dominance, he will not win. I am the alpha in this trio.

His dark lashes flutter, and I know what he's doing. He's teasing me, trying to get me to break and fall back into the sheets with them.

Jesus, I want it. But then I think of my girls, and I know I have to keep pushing forward to help them—no matter what I have to set aside to do that.

James sees the moment my brain goes elsewhere, and his hand falls to his side. For a long, tender moment, he looks at me with deep understanding on his elegant features.

He takes Julia by the hand with a smirk. "Let's go, omega. We've got things to do."

A whine bursts from my lips as I watch them go. Pack alphas are so possessive, so over-the-top lustful, but I swear it's amped up since I came to their room last night. Opening the floodgates to what's between us tore something free in me. I'm dying to mark them both as mine, even though part of me knows I need to hold back on that.

Despite what Mahikan said, there's still lingering doubt in my mind, and I hate that.

I follow James and Julia out of the room and down to the lobby.

Leandra is there, speaking with Clay and Stone just outside the doorway to the dining hall. I grab Julia's hand as we join them. I don't miss the way Leandra's dark eyes fall to my fingers threaded through Julia's, but I give the female a possessive grin.

Mine, my glare is saying. *Always mine.*

Stone looks over at us and smiles, but it's tense and tight.

"Everything okay?" I question.

"This is an issue for the pack alpha," Leandra snaps, bristling.

Stone stands up taller and glares at her. "Cassian is the pack alpha, one of two we have on this property. If I'm not around, consider him the boss. Shit, even if I am around, you could come to either of us. That's how *this* pack works."

My heart warms in my chest. While we've talked about this pack functioning as a mix of multiples, I didn't realize he was ready to present that publicly. I hadn't even covered it with James and Julia. But by my side, I read them as thrilled.

A thread of empathy for Leandra niggles at the forefront of my consciousness. It's not her fault Julia's taken.

"What's going on, Leandra?" I repeat in a more encouraging tone. "I'll help if I can."

The female alpha sighs and crosses her arms. "I came out of my tent first thing this morning to find your seer standing outside the research trailer, staring at the door, muttering to himself."

That's...odd.

"Did you say anything to him?" I ask.

"No, I just stood there with my coffee and watched him like a fucking idiot," Leandra counters. She bristles when I do, standing up straighter as I growl in warning.

"And?" I question, relishing the way my dominance hits her square in the chest. She sinks back a step and nods.

"I called his name, but he never turned or acknowledged me at all. Just cocked his head to the side as if he was trying to figure out something. When I approached him, his eyes were rolled all the way into the back of his head, just the whites showing. It was something out of a fucking horror movie, to be frank."

"What happened next?" Stone questions, concern evident in his tone.

Leandra shakes her head. "I touched his shoulder, tried to shake him out of it a little bit. One minute his eyes were white, and the next they were back to normal, and he was surprised to see me, surprised to be outside. He seemed confused and asked me how he got there. When I told him I didn't know, he took off into the woods. He's fucking fast."

Looking over at Stone, I give him a meaningful look.

"We can look at the security footage to see when he came out and if he did anything."

"We should talk to him about that though," Clay warns. "He's our packmate, and he needs our help."

"Absolutely," I agree. "Leandra, do you need anything for the researchers?"

She shakes her head. "Everybody's fine. He didn't do anything. But I couldn't shake the feeling that he might, or that he was just about to."

My alpha intuition picks up, that need to check on people and lead. I'd like to find Asher and talk with him about what Leandra just shared, but I've also got a pressing need to move forward with my plan to help the girls.

"I've got this, alpha," Stone murmurs, reading me like a book. He turns to James and Julia. "While Cass heads into town, I'd like to speak with you both. I owe you an apology."

Julia gives him a soft smile, sliding both hands up my shirt as she kisses my chest tenderly. She has to lift up onto her tiptoes to do it, and despite us having an audience, I want to pull her into my arms and devour her.

God, I'm unhinged this morning.

James kisses me next. It's tentative, as if he's still not sure if I'm alright kissing him in front of other people. So I take his lips tenderly, making it clear that he's as much mine as she is. When we part, Stone watches with a crooked grin. Leandra stands there with her lips pursed but says nothing.

"Come on, you two," Stone encourages my mates. I watch them trail him through the lobby before I turn to go.

"You're a lucky son-of-a-bitch," Leandra growls as she follows me to the front door, sailing through when I open it for her.

CHAPTER TWENTY-NINE

cassian

LEANDRA and I walk in silence to the research trailer. Remembering I have a strategist now, I call for him through our bond. Already, there's a deep-seated need to include Rogue whenever I have a decision to make.

I'm compelled to check on the researchers even though Leandra said everything was fine. Stone has primarily dealt with their team, and I know they're in a holding pattern right now because Bianca feels uncomfortable with what they're being asked to do.

Rogue jogs down the front steps and joins us, giving me a big grin. Leandra opens the door, holding it for me as I step up into the brand-new trailer. Inside, the team sits hunched around one screen. Asher is there too, much to my surprise. His big shoulders are hunched over, and he's got a remorseful, ashamed look on his face. When we enter, he looks at me and then away, as if he can't bear to see a look of disappointment.

"I came to apologize," he says gruffly. "I scared everyone this morning, and I didn't mean to."

"Damn straight you did," Leandra barks, crossing her arms.

I give her a look, but she rolls her shoulders and stands defiantly. "It was fucking weird, alpha."

Remorse rolls off Asher, and I know nothing about this situation is helpful to him. I turn to Leandra and her team. "You're in a holding pattern with the research, right?"

Bianca frowns. "Yeah, some of the directives coming down make me uncomfortable. They want us to officially register packs and powers, and I just won't do it. There's probably a near future where I get fired, but there are lines I'm not willing to cross."

I glance at the other members of her team, wondering how they feel, but they both stand and nod. They seem to be in agreement with her.

Rogue clears his throat. I know he and River have spent some time with the researchers. They're actually on a more friendly level with the group than the rest of us. "Can you do a deep dive into Asher's health? Maybe spend time with him to sort out what's real and what's not?"

Asher stands quickly and shakes his head. "I don't want to hurt anyone."

"It's a shitty idea," Leandra spits.

But the research team is already lighting up about the idea; I can see it on their faces.

"It's a solid idea," I say, just as much to Ash as the research team. "We'd be grateful if you learned anything medically that might help."

I don't want Asher pulled apart like a research specimen, so I clarify. "Ash can share as much or as little of his history as he wants, but I won't have you bully him into sharing. I'd like to know which of his visions are seer visions and which are memories. Maybe you've got equipment here that could help with that?"

The physician gives Asher a reassuring look. "We do. I'm not a psychologist, but we can get a start on that, as long as Asher is willing? It might help!"

Leandra scoffs at all of us. "Okay so we're going to take the crazy person and keep him right here? In the goddamn trailer?"

"Aww, what's wrong, alpha?" Rogue teases her. "You don't think you can take him?"

She scoffs again and rolls her eyes. "Let's not get into a dick-and-tit measuring contest over here. He's big as a goddamn house."

"Well, you'll have to be really fucking fast then," Rogue laughs.

There's a look on Ash's face that tells me this is the right thing—even if it doesn't work out, there's something he can try to get more information. This might not be a fix, but it's already giving him hope.

Next to me, Rogue beams with pride. I give him a look, and he follows me outside.

"You're going somewhere today. Do you need me?"

I shake my head. "I can't take you with me, strategist."

He breaks into a huge smile when I use his official title, but it feels good to say.

"How can I help?" His tone is soft as he presses on.

My lips curl into a snarl. "Call Mitchell and Mahikan if it goes poorly. I may need all the help I can get."

Rogue purses his lips and nods, but through our new bond, I can sense he hates this as much as I do.

Welcome to the club, brother, I think to myself.

I pick up my cell and dial JB, unsurprised when he picks up with a growl. "What do you want?"

"I need to talk with you at Vee's place. You free?"

There's a momentary scuffle, and I hear JB's mate hiss something at him, but he comes back on with a sigh. "Meet me there in fifteen minutes." He clicks off without saying anything else as I hop back into the truck, navigating out of town and toward the remote homestead where his mate Vee's parents live.

Of everyone on my former leadership team, JB is the only one I'm remotely close to. He's an unkind asshole, but when it was just him and me alone, I saw a softer side of him. I can never forgive him for being a dick to the omegas, but if there's anyone who can help me get back into the pack faster, it'll be him.

When I pull up in front of the modest one-story ranch, Vee comes out with JB by her side. The curvy omega smiles at me, although it's sad and weary. Even though she's mated to Declan's enforcer, I can't imagine life is much easier for her than the rest of the girls.

JB steps in front of Vee as I put my hands up. "I meant what I said at the sermon, JB. I want back in."

JB cocks his head to the side as he assesses me. "You want back in to what?"

"Alphas aren't meant to be alone," I hedge, knowing he'll push back.

"Plenty of other packs in this valley for a castoff. Shit, you could just go elsewhere. Move on. I would, if I could."

And there it is—what I already know. While JB would protect Declan with his life, there's no love lost between the two. There's a pack bond, and I'm counting on that to be my in.

"I started with Declan," I remind JB gently. "I'm his strategist, unless he's replaced me."

JB frowns, but Vee rubs his forearm tenderly. How the fiery omega puts up with him, I'll never know. But somehow, they're a good match. She tempers his angry nature into something more controlled—usually.

"I need your help," I press on. "I'm not meant to be on my own. I'm meant to help lead and guide. We both know Declan was a wild card before. He did a lot of things I didn't agree with. Things you didn't agree with," I remind him as Vee clears her throat and crosses her arms.

"Encourage him to let me back soon," I press, knowing my alpha command hits JB the same way Declan's does.

He rolls his shoulders and snarls, but nods. "As long as you promise you're not there to stir up shit, I'll press the issue."

"I'm not there to stir anything," I reassure him. "The only thing I've ever wanted was to be useful and help the pack be successful. The sermon struck a chord with me. I want to know more."

JB purses his lips. If he doesn't buy my bullshit about the sermon, he's not going to question it. I fall silent, waiting for what he'll say next.

"Come to the sermon again tomorrow and then swing by the neighborhood after. I'll tell Declan I asked you for dinner. You can see how things are these days, decide if you really want to come back or not. It's not the same, you know."

I obviously fucking know, I want to shout. I had to hold my guts in with my hands last time we squared off. I held Isabel's hand as she gave birth to a twelve-pound baby sired by Declan himself while she was still recovering from a wound *he* gave her.

Still, I hold back the anger, shoving it down and burning it as fuel for my resolve.

"You should go," JB says finally.

"It was good to see you though," Vee whispers. "We've missed you around the neighborhood for sure, the girls especially."

I can't think of a suitable response that won't give away my intention, so I nod.

"Give me tonight to talk it through with leadership, then come to tomorrow's sermon," JB instructs.

I thank him and turn to go, still wary and worried for my girls, but hopeful to have made some progress.

CHAPTER THIRTY

JULES and I follow Stone all the way to his office, and when we arrive, Clay and Erin are already there. Clay's green eyes are sorrowful as he looks from Erin to us.

Stone leaves the doors open and sits on the edge of his desk, gesturing for us to sit in the small area in front of him. Jules perches herself on my knee, folding both hands over her legs like a goddamn queen. In our bond I can tell she's not even mad anymore, but she is expecting our alpha to make a heartfelt apology.

I'm gonna need a little more than that, though, because while I understand pack alphas sometimes have to make quick decisions, the purpose of pack leadership is to make decisions with multiple viewpoints in mind.

"I'm so sorry," Stone begins. "Cass shared his idea with Clay and me, and it really felt like it was in more of a stage of ideation, so I didn't call a leadership meeting about it. That was a mistake, though, because it left you both, Titan and Asher out of the loop. I'll be apologizing to each of you individually."

Jules gestures for him to go on, and I stifle a laugh. I'm mad; really, I am.

Stone's lips snap shut, but fangs slide down from his upper lip. His emotions are high. Erin clears her throat, and I watch his dark eyes flick to her and back to Jules and me. He and his mate have obviously discussed this.

"I'm sorry we've operated under the assumption you might not be mates with him. I'll admit, the lack of a visible bond and his pack alpha designation make it seem unlikely. But I don't want to undermine your own beliefs, especially considering how vehement you've been, Jules, from the very beginning."

"That goes for me too," Erin presses on. "I suggested maybe you were wrong the last time we talked about Cass, and I feel like an asshole for that. I'd never want you to think we don't believe you, because we love you both so fucking much. We want you to be mated, however that works out."

Julia stands and crosses the room, pulling our tall pack omega in for a hug. It warms my heart as I watch them.

Stone turns from the omegas, continuing, "You heard me call Cass this pack's alpha this morning, and it's another thing I need to cover with you both." He goes on to share how Mahikan called after we returned, and how he ran with Cass and that led to Cass coming to our room last night.

By the time Stone is done, I'm surprised how right it feels to me.

Once Stone finishes, I give him a look. "Anything else I need to know as part of pack leadership?"

Stone shakes his head. "To quote Mitchell Bancroft, I don't want to lead in a vacuum. I'm sorry again that I let an idea take hold without consulting you, most especially about your mate."

Julia signs a quick thank you, and then there's a sharp rap at the door.

Betty comes in and smiles at us. "Julia, Arnaud and I are going to spend some time with the twins and omegas. Would you like to join us?"

Jules grins at her and crosses the room to lean over and give me a quick peck on the cheek.

Once Jules goes, Stone turns to me. "Come with me to the research trailer? They need tech help with something."

Intrigued, I agree and follow him to the front of the lodge. The research trailer sits just outside.

Stone slips his hands into his pockets as we descend the front steps. "The research team is holding off on any further research because Bianca isn't comfortable with what she's being asked to do. You know that already."

Our involvement with the research team is sketchy as fuck to begin with, but we've never been able to figure out how we got looped into the government program. We've always assumed Declan had something to do with it, but we have no certainty.

When I remain silent, Stone continues, "Bianca wants you to dive into their tech and see if you can use their access to find out anything about the new mandates. It would be harder for you to do that from the outside, but she's linked to their servers. It's a long shot, but it might lead us to proof of something weird going on."

"If it's there, I'll find it," I huff out. After his apology, I'm mollified but still irritated. He and Cass withheld information from us, and that hurt my mate. I can't stand for that, and I'm not going to get over it quickly.

"I'm sorry, James," Stone says again as we come to a stop in front of the trailer. "I value every member of this pack, and I undermined that when I wasn't up front with you. I'll never do that again. I need your guidance, alright?"

I nod. It's nice to hear, even though I can sense how apologetic he is. Stone had a rough go of it with his prior pack, and ours is tightly knit.

Which made his not telling us feel even worse, because he's always so up front about everything.

My pack alpha opens the door to the trailer and gestures for me to go in. "After you, brother."

CHAPTER THIRTY-ONE

julia

JAMES WILL BE busy with the rest of leadership for a while, so I follow Betty and Arnaud through the halls and into the lobby. We round a corner to the seating area where we tend to congregate for movie night.

Sal and the twins, plus Cherry, Luna and Isabel are already there. Rogue paces slowly back and forth, Abigail pressed to his chest as he purrs deep and low. Isabel sits in a chair, watching him with a grateful smile.

Now that I know he's Cass's strategist, I look at Rogue in a different way. Are we building a new pack right here in this very house? Are we building a combined pack like Mahikan, Leon and Jacob? I don't know, but I am certain that the way we are feels perfect to me.

Betty sits gracefully on the sofa next to Isabel, Arnaud at her side. The chatty Frenchman leans over Betty, who translates for me as Arnaud talks to Isabel. "My dear, can I get you a drink? A nice tea, perhaps?"

Isabel agrees and thanks him as Arnaud reaches her to pat her arm. "You are doing a wonderful job, sweet Isabel. Motherhood is difficult, is it not?"

Isabel laughs and nods, and Betty beams at Arnaud as he stands to head for the kitchen.

Isabel's pale eyes flick over to me. "How'd it go with the northern packs? I haven't asked Cass, but I saw him earlier, and he looked frustrated."

Betty signs the question and I share the majority of the story. It takes me the better part of twenty minutes to get through my emotions, but the group is silent as they listen. Every now and again, Rogue pitches in with a helpful detail, and between the two of us, we get all the way to the end.

I'm still tender about everything, honestly.

"I'm super intrigued by the mish-mashed pack concept," Sal muses. "Granted, I've only ever been in Declan's shit-ass pack and now this amazing one, but it's an interesting thought."

River shoots Sal a victorious look. "Okay, girl, hear me out. You mate my brother…" she makes a fake puking face before barreling on, "and then he can be something in the pack. And I'll be the seer, obviously, because of my wild hearing. Julia can be the pack mama bear, and then maybe we can just like, pick and choose who does what?"

I have to laugh a little at the simplified version of what she's sharing. Rogue joins me and flops down on the sofa, the baby still cradled to his chest.

"I don't care what I am as long as I get regular baby snuggles," he says. "Because this baby smells better than anything in the world."

Sal must make a noise, because his eyes flick up to her, and he grins and blows her a kiss. "Not better than you, omega. I'm joking."

The shy omega crosses over to us and slides onto the sofa next to Rogue, rubbing Abigail's back. It's perfect like this, this amazing squished-together pack.

After a few hours of chatting, I leave the group, ascending the steps toward my room. It's been a wild couple of days, and I miss my tablet, so I think I'll draw a little before dinner. I nearly run into Cherry at the top of the stairs as she leaves Asher's room with a scowl on her face.

"What's up?" I question when she sees me and smiles.

She shakes her head, so I grab her by the hand and drag her into my room, pointing to one of my chairs. "Sit, girl. Be my muse and tell me what's going on. Why were you leaving Asher's room looking so pissed?"

Cherry sighs as she flops in the chair. "I went to ask him if he remembers leaving the lodge to go stare at the researchers' trailer, but he shut down as soon as I asked the question."

Frowning, I grab my tablet and start sketching the outline of Cherry in the chair. I fiddle with it for a minute as I consider her words. "Have you tried throwing yourself into his arms?"

Cherry scoffs but agrees.

"And how's it going at the Moonlight?"

That's when her frown morphs into something happier. "It's great; I love it there. I feel sexy and confident. I feel like me, Jules," she admits. "It's my happy place right now."

Nodding, I start to shade in her hair, that vibrant red that's become her namesake. I work on her pale skin next, and then, instead of drawing her with clothes, I draw her luscious, full frame in sexy lingerie.

"Mahikan said he'd come down with Ven to work with Ash some more," she signs slowly when I look up. "What are you drawing, anyhow?"

Grinning, I flip the tablet around and show her. Her plump lips part before a huge smile splits her face. "It's fucking gorgeous, Jules. This is how you see me?"

"Yeah," I sign, handing her the tablet. "I see a stunning, smart, caring, incredible person who deserves only the best. And I know those are all reasons Ash thinks he can't have you. So how do we prove to him that he's perfect as he is, that his past is just that?"

"It's not though," she counters, passing the tablet back with a quick sign of thanks. "He truly thinks it's a matter of time before he hurts someone. Jules, it wouldn't surprise me if we woke up one day, and he was gone."

Gone? I stiffen in my seat, but Cherry's eyes flick over my shoulder.

Turning, I find my mates both entering the room. I'm sure they saw what we were talking about. Even if they didn't, it doesn't take a genius to guess we're talking about Asher.

Cherry shuts down when they come in, even when Cassian drops to one knee next to her chair and strokes his knuckles along her jawline. "You wanna talk about it, Cherry Bomb?" I watch him sign the nickname we gave the fiery American when she showed up two years ago.

"There's nothing new to tell," she admits with a miserable wave of her hands. Standing up, she gives James a quick squeeze and then tugs gently on my hair. "You did good, Jules; I love it. Will you email it to me?"

"Of course," I respond, watching as she leaves, her shoulders slumped as she pulls the door shut behind her.

Cass and James both watch her go, and I sense Cass's need to help her, to do something. The mood in our room is somber for a moment, but James pulls me into his arms and flops back down in the chair. "Nothing new to report with Declan or the mill site. No new alphas coming off the train either."

"That's good, right?" I question, looking from him to Cassian.

Cass shakes his head. "We don't know for sure. Clay thinks it means he's done gathering forces so he can move on to whatever comes next. I'm inclined to agree."

"'What's next' meaning what, exactly?" I question. "We still don't really know his end game. He trafficked omegas and drugs, but was that just a side hustle?"

"Still unclear," James says.

"I'm going back for the sermon tomorrow," Cassian shares.

I lift my hands to say something, but Cassian drops to both knees and takes them, running them up his shirt to rest on his heart.

"I love you," he signs, "both of you. And I will do everything in my power to protect and cherish you for the rest of my life. But I can't leave my girls there at the mercy of that fucking asshole."

"We know, alpha," James signs, reaching around me to place his hand over mine on Cass's heart. We're still for a long moment, the heartbeat under my palm strong and steady as I stare at my big alpha mate while wrapped in my other mate's arms.

There's no place I'd rather be than right here with them.

After a quiet minute, James shifts his hips, tapping my thigh. Cassian pulls me up out of James's lap with a grin, turning toward the bed as he pulls me toward it.

"Lie down," Cassian signs as James rummages around in his dresser.

"What are you up to?" I retort as Cassian grins, watching James join us. James opens his palm to reveal a small butt plug.

Cassian grins at James, and then grips the backs of my knees and flips me gently before sliding my jeans down over my ass. I'm face down on our bed, but I swear I feel the weight of my alphas' stares. My skin is covered in goosebumps. I want to know what they're doing. Are they touching as they look at me?

I startle when warm hands come to my ass and spread my cheeks wide, and then a tongue licks from the seam of my pussy upward. Groaning into the bed, I fist the sheets as that warm tongue probes gently before being replaced with a finger, then two.

A second set of hands runs up my back as the fingers gently stretch and tease me. I'm soaking my alpha's hands in slick by the time one of them drags the butt plug through my swollen folds, coating it. Growling into the sheets, I push backward. I need more connection than this. I need more touch. I want to come, but they're just not touching me quite enough to get me there.

"Fucking teases," I sign, earning myself a slap on the ass in response. That would be Cassian. James isn't a spanker, but I love that about them both.

One of my alphas spreads me wide again, and the other slides the butt plug inside as I grunt and arch my back. Cassian reaches around and grips my throat, his thumb running along my lower lip as he kisses his way from my shoulder to my neck. His fangs tease at my skin, hinting at the incredible pleasure he can bring with them.

I'm so damn full of the plug. But then I leap in Cass's arms when the fucking plug starts vibrating, sending shockwaves of warmth through me as slick floods my thighs.

Cassian groans into my neck, releasing my throat to sign. "You smell like strawberry shortcake, little one. We're gonna eat you alive after dinner, but until then, we're gonna tease the shit out of you."

A whine leaves my mouth as both alphas step away from me. James slides my pants back up over my ass as I turn. "You don't mean you're leaving this in during dinner?"

"How scandalous," James agrees, handing a cell phone to Cassian. "The app is ready, alpha. Have fun."

My nostrils flare as I look from one alpha to the other. Cassian gives me a devilish grin and unlocks the screen. When he draws a swirl on the phone's face, the plug zings in a rising pattern in my ass, my knees buckling at the pleasure.

Oh fuck. I grab for the phone, but Cass laughs and locks it, putting it in his back pocket before pulling me into his arms.

"We're gonna play with you, sweet girl," James signs, joining our embrace as Cassian leans over, capturing James's dark lips with his own. They deepen the kiss as I watch, fangs clashing as their dominance plays back and forth. I whine at how perfect they are together, how beautiful.

Mine. They're mine.

If I don't die of pleasure at dinner.

CHAPTER THIRTY-TWO

cassian

JULIA AND JAMES walk in front of me as we head downstairs and across the lobby to the dining hall. I can already smell Clay's grandmother's chicken parm, and that makes me grin—it's a pack favorite.

I watch James guide Julia to her usual seat, taking the one next to her but leaving one open for me. It seems like everyone's eyes are on us as I sit next to Jules, laying my big arm over the back of her chair possessively.

Stone grins but says nothing, and the rest of leadership give me knowing looks.

At the end of the table, River sits smugly in her chair, grinning at me.

Little shit.

With her insane hearing, there's a solid chance she heard what we were doing in our room earlier. Well, she's about to get the surprise of her life if she keeps snooping after I pull James's phone out of my pocket.

There's something about knowing everybody here will be able to hear it when I tease our girl that gets me hard. I want them all to know. I want to throw her on the table and have her in front of them, to stake my claim so thoroughly and completely, no one can deny us—not even the missing bond.

Possessive desire hits me so hard, I grip the back of Julia's chair as I watch a vein in her neck pulse gently with her heartbeat. The steady whomp of her heart fills me with a deep sense of knowing. That heart beats for James and me. Every inch of her delicate figure, right down to those ten perfect tiny toes, all crafted for us.

Wild need builds in my stomach before I realize Asher is staring at me, brows furrowed as if he's cataloging my every move. Cocking my head to the side, I look back at him, watching his nostrils flare. Eventually, he looks away.

Rogue shoots me a look. *You okay?*

You keep asking, and I'm fine, I bark back, realizing I'm being too brusque. But there's a wild, crazy buildup happening in my body, like I'm about to burst if I don't do something soon about my lust.

Dinner begins, but I'm too hyped on the pheromones coming off Julia and James to eat. I pick at the food, but my girl is so ready, so hot, just waiting for me to do something. James feeds her with his fingers, teasing me when her pink tongue sucks at his thumb.

Jesus, I'm about to explode in my pants like an untried teenager.

I make it all of ten minutes before I take the cell out of my pocket. When James told me he wanted to do this tonight, he gave me a little primer on the app. It's primarily designed to work for folks in long-distance relationships, but damn if it isn't perfect like this.

Swiping into the app, I look at the screen. When I draw on it, the plug will vibrate in her ass. I can't wait to make her a sweaty, sticky mess. Grinning, I trace a slow circle on the screen. Next to me, Jules jumps in her seat and grips her napkin tight under the table.

When I look up over her head, James is grinning at me like the cat who got the cream.

"More," he signs.

So I give her more, dragging my finger in a rectangle, testing all the various options as Julia squirms in her seat, her chest heaving slightly as she lifts a bite of chicken to her mouth, but she can't manage to focus.

"Whatcha doin' over there?" River's voice rings from the opposite head of the table, a position she's started taking in recent weeks. I love that she sits there like a queen and stares at Stone. Wouldn't surprise me if she started barking orders—she's bossy as hell, and I love it.

I wonder where she'd sit if she and Rogue moved with me to a house at the end of the valley. I want to know...

"Eating dinner," I bark back as she curls a brow upward.

"I mean with your phone, alpha," she croons, teasing me.

"Sexting my girlfriend," I purr, sitting back in my seat as her grin vanishes, replaced by a scowl.

"Oh, gross, I was just messing with you. You didn't have to go there."

"Where'd you think it was gonna go, Riv?" Rogue laughs from his place next to his sister.

River scoffs and looks at her brother, who's watching me with a sly smile, his arm around Sal at his side. *Just cater to her,* Rogue whispers into my mind. *She appreciates it.* He leans down to kiss Sal's forehead, purring softly as she smiles at me and nuzzles against him. When his attention shifts back to me, I realize my chest is heaving, my breath coming in short, heavy pants.

Something's not right, he murmurs into our bond before standing to come around the table and look at me. *You feel off to me, alpha.*

Do I? Blinking away my surprise, I sit back and focus, trying to push all the other voices out of my consciousness. He's right;

I am on edge. I'm extra needy, which I attributed to the hotness of what James and I are doing to Julia right now. But it's something more than that, something threading its way through my consciousness.

I'm ready to flip the table over and fuck James and Julia right here, so ready, in fact, that I grip the edge of the chair to try to hold back as a slight tremor begins to take over my body.

Growling, I stand and hand James my phone, giving Stone a look. His eyes go wide, and he hops up, gesturing for me to follow him into his office. As a pack alpha, he reads people well. Something is wrong, something's happening.

I sense my mates and Rogue behind us as we enter Stone's office. I'd close the door, but River and Asher are going to hear this whole conversation anyhow.

"I think I'm going into a rut," I mutter. "Right fucking now. We've got a few hours maybe."

Jesus, Rogue growls into our bond. *Is that what this is? This is why you've been edgy since you returned from Mahikan's?*

I think so, I murmur back, a soft whine leaving my throat as everyone turns to inspect me.

James and Julia round on me at the same time, James looking into my eyes for confirmation. I can't resist that dark gaze, or the way his throat bobs as he swallows. God, I want to fuck that pretty mouth. Reaching out, I drag him to me and bury my face in his neck, moaning at his comforting, woodsy scent.

"You smell so goddamn good," I groan as Stone clears his throat.

James turns from me as I growl, dragging him back. He pushes against me with a scowl. "Give me a second, alpha."

"I'm gonna give you a lot more than that," I snarl, baring my fangs as his eyebrows curl upward, the corners of his mouth tilting into a smile. I've never been this forward with him in front of the pack, but I'm losing my goddamn mind.

A cry leaves my lips as Julia takes James's place. "Eyes on me, alpha," she signs, stroking my chest as Stone pulls James aside, grabbing his wrist.

"Hands off," I snap, and both alphas turn to look at me as I growl at Stone. "Hands off my fucking mate."

Stone scowls as Julia rubs at my chest. Anger churns in my gut as I watch the other alpha look at James again.

"We need to separate you all long enough to get the heat cabin ready. Good news is I figured we'd need it at some point, so it's stocked; it just needs a quick clean. James, you come help me with that. Julia and Rogue can stay with Cassian."

"No," I moan. "James, don't you dare leave." I'm commanding and begging at the same time. In the span of ten minutes, I've gone from having control to hanging on by a bare thread.

James crosses the room, lifting Julia up into my arms and pressing himself to her back, dark eyes on me. "I'm only leaving long enough to prepare a safe space for us. When I come back and get you, you can have me any way you want. But we need privacy, alpha."

"This is such bad fucking timing," I roar. "The omegas, my goddamn plan." I'm angry and horny, and my ire is running high with James about to leave.

Stone turns to me. "You can't help them in a rut, alpha. Your best bet is to fuck your way through it fast. We'll hold down the fort here. I'll call the northern packs and ask for their help again. By the time you're through your rut, they'll be here."

"I'm supposed to go to a sermon tomorrow," I shout, my fists balled as Julia strokes my chest.

"I'll figure out an alternate plan while you're out," Stone counters. "I promise I've got this, alpha." He gestures to James to go, and they leave as I whine.

Titan and Asher appear in the doorway, Ash with his arms crossed. "Ah, that's what I sensed. I couldn't tell; you just seemed off."

"Aura's pitch black too," Titan offers helpfully. "Very needy-looking."

"You two done?" I bark, relishing the way it hits them hard.

"Probably not," Titan smiles. "What can we get you, alpha? Do you need anything from your cabin?"

I can't think of anything. And that's when I remember the plug in Julia's ass. She's still in my arms, still rubbing softly at my chest. Fisting her hair, I drag her head to the side so I can smell her skin.

Strawberries. Sunlight. Fresh cream. She's a fucking dessert, and I want to lick every inch of her. Sighing, I drag my fangs up her neck, letting that scent soak into my skin. I want hers to combine with mine and James's until we smell like a goddamn picnic in the woods. A whine leaves my throat again as that vein in her neck throbs in time with her pulse.

My senses go into overdrive, focusing on the steady beat of her heart and the way she's already slick for us. My attention is fully on her as I cross the room and flop down into a chair with her straddling me.

"Don't start this here, alpha," Titan warns. "Or we won't get you out to the cabin without a fight."

"Don't start a fucking fight then," I snarl, nostrils flaring as our pack enforcer curls his fingers into fists.

Alpha, Rogue warns in my head. *We're trying to help. Hold back just a few more minutes. I know you're ready for your mates, but we need your patience.*

Trying, I growl back as he grins at me.

Asher turns to look at Rogue. "You're already talking through the strategist bond?" Titan turns to Asher and then Rogue, a shocked expression on his face.

"Mhm," Rogue confirms, not taking his eyes off me. "We can chat about it another time." He's already growing more centered and confident by having a designation, losing some of that teenager looseness with his emotions.

Titan looks at me. "Have you been through a rut before?"

I shake my head. I know instinctively I'm going into one because I've barely got ahold of myself, but I haven't had one before.

"Okay, Rutting 101." He laughs. "It'll last a couple of days max, and it could spark Jules's heat. Since you haven't formally claimed her, that's unlikely though. It'll just be nonstop sex until your dick feels like it's falling off, and when it starts to hurt a little, you're nearly through it."

"Why this, why now?" I question, slumping into the wall as my muscles quiver with anticipation.

"Oh, probably all the stress and longing," he laughs. "For alphas, it's a control and dominance thing. Once you're mated, it gets worse for a while, but I'm told eventually it evens out."

I have thoughts about that, but James sails back through the door with a big grin. "Let's go."

When Stone turns to follow us, I growl, stopping him in his tracks.

"I know where the cabin is," James offers, clapping Stone on the shoulder.

"Yeah, but are you gonna make it there, or are you three going to fuck on the front steps? Because I'd rather not see that."

I open my mouth to snap something else, but Julia presses her lips to mine, and when we part, she grins.

"Let's go, alpha. We're ready."

CHAPTER THIRTY-THREE

WE BARELY MAKE it out to a waiting ATV before Cass is all over Julia, devouring her as if he's starving. From two steps ahead of them, the scent of her slick slams into me. That, combined with the scent of Cassian so ready for her, is enough to make me lose my mind. I wonder, briefly, if him being in a rut might throw me into one.

God, could our little omega survive two of us like that?

I know she could, and I'm half wishing for it.

I haven't seen a rut before, but I'm painfully aware of what terrible timing this is for our pack. Cassian is fast losing awareness as he sets Julia down on an ATV in front of him, growling at me to seat myself in front of her. It's up to me to keep us focused, maybe to push us through his rut a little faster than we'd normally go.

I don't know if that's even possible, but I know I have to try.

I'd give anything to simply enjoy them during this, but a lot of things depend on Cassian being mentally present. Lives are at stake. The only way out is through, and I trust Stone to take care of an alternate plan in the meantime.

Throwing the ATV into gear, I barrel away from the lodge

and into the forest, but I don't make it a half mile before Cassian is reaching around me, dragging my jeans open to grip my cock. His touch is far from tender as he fists me roughly. Through my bond with Julia, I sense how overwhelmed she is by him like this, how he's already got her on the edge of orgasm.

Wondering what they're doing behind me has me rock hard as he squeezes the tip of my cock, forcing precum out. He swipes it up, and his hand disappears as I mutter and pray for some fucking focus.

Moments later, I hear Jules sucking his fingers, and I whine at the filthy vision she sends me of what he's doing to her. Fingers in her mouth, his hand between her thighs, his teeth teasing her neck. They groan and pant behind me as the fucking heat cabin blessedly comes into view.

I slam to a stop in front of it. Cassian leaps off with Jules in his arms and kicks the front door open, striding across the sparse cabin and tossing her into the bed. She squeals as he reaches down and rips her sweater right down the middle. The jeans come off next, her body jerking in his rush to get at her.

For half a moment, I worry he'll hurt her, because she's so delicate, and he's never let himself go like this. But then she yowls at him, clawing at his belt buckle, and I find myself wondering if I'm about to see a side of my pretty little omega that I've never seen before.

Cassian growls and pushes her backward with his big body, dropping to both knees as he presses her thighs up to touch her belly. Julia tries to shift her hips, but she's caught like this, bared open for us. Our big alpha looks at her, that pretty pink mouth dropped open as she watches him bend forward, pressing his lips to her clit.

When he growls low and deep into her pussy, she screams in pleasure, and my dick leaps. I kick my pants off and shuck my shirt over my head. But what I failed to realize was that Cassian's tease of Jules was just that. By the time I get my shirt off, he's standing and turning to face me. His pants are open, hanging low on his big hips. His erection bobs as he cocks his head to the side the way a predator would, assessing.

There's nothing left of the cool, calculating alpha I'm falling in love with. What's there now is a feral, dominating energy that's heavy enough to bring me to my knees.

Fangs descend from his upper jaw as his pupils widen, his lips parted as his chest rises and falls. Goosebumps cover my skin, my own dominance rising to meet his. I don't run from a fight. I don't back down from shit. And it's obvious to me in the way Cassian rolls his shoulders that he's gearing up to be rough.

My eyes flick to Julia behind him, but she's propped against the cabin's wall, both hands between her thighs as she soaks the sheets and touches herself. She gives me a little wink, but before I can respond, Cass shoots across the space between us and grips my jaw hard, my mouth popping open as he drags me toward him.

I break the hold with a snarl, and he butts up against my chest, snapping long canines in my face as we growl at each other. I'm so hot from the violence of it, so amped up on adrenaline and pheromones. Reaching out, I let my claws slip from my fingertips and drag them down his chest, down those gorgeous, stacked abs, and then back up his thigh. He shudders, storm-cloud eyes never leaving mine, his lips pulled back into a snarl.

A laugh, low and wicked, rumbles from his chest as he kicks one leg out, knocking me to the side. I snarl as he flips me, shoving me face down onto the bed right between Julia's thighs.

No place I'd rather be, although my alpha ire rises as he kicks my legs wide and settles himself between them possessively.

Claws rake down my back as he pushes his hips forward, nudging my face toward Julia's sweet pussy. "Eat," he growls.

"Lick, suck, taste. I want to see how long you can concentrate on her while I fuck you."

Heat rushes down my core, my cock jumping at his filthy words. But when I look up at Julia, she's watching me with pure heat in her eyes. She slides down slightly, rocking her hips toward my mouth as she eye-fucks me.

Cassian's cock slips through my thighs, rubbing the underneath of my balls as he reaches around and drags me backward, far enough to give himself room to jack me off. And, God, he does it well, tugging and yanking slow but hard, his grip firm and practiced. He teases the head as I groan and drip cum onto the floor, already failing to pay attention to my mate's sweet pussy. I'm lost to this violent version of Cassian, this version where he's everything alpha and none of the tender, conscientious gentleman I know he can be.

His hand slides over my shoulder so he can stroke her heat, her thighs trembling with need as I watch his fingers slide gently inside her. When he removes them, his hand comes to my mouth.

"Spit."

I shudder as I obey his direction, and then there's nothing but the sloppy, filthy noise of him coating his own cock in our combined wetness. Julia shoots me a pained, needy expression as Cassian grips my hips and slides into my ass with a choked roar.

A grunt leaves my mouth as he goes wild behind me, fucking so hard my hips bang against the edge of the bed, rocking the entire frame into the wall. Heat builds deep between my thighs, my balls tight as he grips my shoulders for leverage.

"Jules. Fucking. Sorry," I gasp out. I can't concentrate on a goddamn thing as Cassian pistons his thick length over and over at a punishing, brutal pace. Sudden realization comes over me as her chest heaves. He's going to knot me like this. I'm going to take a goddamn alpha knot while I scream into my omega's pussy.

No.

I can't have it like that.

Growling, I grip Jules's thighs and drag her to me, moaning even as I dive into her heat and lick my way up to her clit, tugging it gently between my lips. She and Cass moan at the same time as he picks up the pace until it's frantic and crazed.

"James," she signs. "Oh fuck, I'm so close watching you both."

That knowledge is enough to throw me over as I come with a roar, nipping and tugging at her clit as she joins me, screaming my name into the cabin. When she falls, Cassian's hips take on a ragged, harrowed pace until he bellows so loud, the walls shake. Immediately, the base of his cock begins to swell, filling my ass until I'm biting my teeth against a combination of pain and the most intense fucking pleasure I've ever known.

I'm unmoored, rocked by the strength of this connection, so fucking out of my mind that all I can do is lash out. Gripping Julia's thigh, I sink my teeth into it, a claiming bite so bright and hot that she comes, slick gushing out of her, soaking the sheets as she screams again.

Cassian reaches for Julia's foot and bites his way along her instep as he hovers over my back, his knot locking us firmly in place as my dick throbs, cum still dripping steadily from me as orgasm prolongs.

I don't know how long I come for, or when it truly stops, but when his knot deflates and he slides out of my ass with a grunt, I slump to the floor and fall onto my back.

Cassian laughs and steps over me, nudging my shoulder with his foot. "I'm not nearly finished with you, mate. Get on the bed and be ready for more. Unless you wanna fight a little first."

Groaning, I slap his thigh as high up as I can reach, then manage to roll myself over and flop up onto the bed next to Julia. Her chest heaves as she reaches for me, pulling me in for a kiss. Her own need still runs high, her kiss demanding as she rolls me on top of her.

Need you, she whispers into our bond. *Need every inch of you, alpha.*

I don't know if I can survive days of this, I laugh into the bond.

I have literally fantasized about this since the day I met you both, she laughs back.

Groaning, I slip the tip of my still-hard cock inside her, pulsing gently as she snarls.

Across the room, Cassian's quickly washing up, but he turns to watch us, his cock hard and leaking as he strokes it. "Let's have her together," he signs. "She's still wearing the goddamn plug."

Oh, holy shit. In the craziness, I'd forgotten. But Cassian grins and crosses the room, digging the cell out of my pants. He opens the screen and presses his finger to the phone with a devious grin, and the plug starts vibrating in Julia's ass. It's vibrating hard and loud, and her body jerks.

"Goddamn," I grunt, "I can feel that every time I slip inside her."

"That's not where I want it." Cass grins, gently reaching between us to remove the plug from Julia's ass.

She whines as he grins, tucking the plug under his arm to sign, "I'm gonna give you something better, my sweet girl. Something bigger."

She grins at him, so fucking ready for everything he has to dish out.

"You're perfect," I tease, still slipping gently in and out of my omega.

CHAPTER THIRTY-FOUR

SOMETHING BIGGER AND BETTER? Hell yes. I've been trying to get all over his bigger and better for months now.

Cassian crosses the room with the plug and washes it, then joins us in the bed. He pushes James roughly back into the sheets, and I'm fascinated by the dynamic between them like this. James is a dominant but tender lover. Cassian is something else entirely. Rough and commanding and more domineering than anything else. It's fucking perfect.

Domineering seems to be the theme of the day when he lifts me up and sets me on James's lap. "Ride," he commands, pushing me forward as he grabs a nearby bottle of lube and coats the plug. I feel him push James's thighs wide as James's mouth splits into a grin.

Days of this, Jules. Imagine it, he teases. That tease falls into a groan when Cass slides the butt plug into James's ass. Immediately, I feel the vibrations all the way through my pussy. The damn thing is turned on the highest setting, I'm sure of it, but it's making James's dick throb and vibrate inside me. It's such an otherworldly feeling, I'm almost ready to come again.

Cassian shoves James's thighs wider and reaches around the front of me, stroking my clit with measured, even touches as my head falls back against his shoulder. His beard scratches at my skin as he bites and nips, slick coating his fingers as I ride James.

"I'm about to lose my mind," James signs. Half a moment passes where his eyes roll into his head, and then his hips buck as he comes hard, rocking up into me as Cassian growls in my ear, the vibration traveling along my skin as I clench around James's orgasm.

We watch him together, Cass's chin on my shoulder as James screams and gasps, overwhelmed by the heat.

I need more, though, more touch, more of that delicious vibration.

"Need you," I sign, lifting my hands so Cassian can see. He grabs them both and draws them behind my back, holding them in one of his big hands as the other lines his cock up with my ass. He slides in slowly, giving me a moment to adjust as I squeal around the fullness.

James still throbs in my pussy, and now Cassian fills me from behind.

And then he starts goddamn moving, and I think I'll lose my mind. He starts with slow but hard thrusts, my ass shaking every time his hips meet my skin. But the thrusts take on a needy edge as he fucks me harder, deeper. The hand on my hip moves up to my breast, fingertips pinching my nipples one after the other as I clench around James.

My mate leans forward and sucks my nipple into his mouth as Cassian rolls the other between his fingertips. I'm so shocked at this violent side of him, so overwhelmed by the attention on every sensitive part of my body.

Orgasm hits me hard as Cassian's teeth sink into my shoulder. Not a claiming bite, but no less full of need or love. Even though the bond doesn't burn bright in my chest, I imagine for a few moments that it does, and that he can feel how much I want him through it.

We ride that wave until it crests and crashes, obliterating any conscious thought from my mind. There is just Cass and James and the wild clash of our bodies as we take our pleasure from one another.

———

Time passes, days I'm sure, but it's hard to tell. We're a constant tangle of limbs and mouths and tongues. I watch Cass and James fuck dozens of times. They watch me with one another. We lose our minds together. It's perfect, and by the time I feel Cass's intensity begin to slow down, I know what I want.

We're lying in bed, James snoring softly next to us, one arm thrown over his head. I stroke his stomach softly from my place on top of Cassian.

Sitting up, I grin down at him. He looks well used, something I'm fucking proud of as his lips curl into a grin. He pinches my side as I lift my hands.

"Now that you're not a wild animal, I have a request," I begin.

He shifts upright in the pillows, bringing us eye to eye as he smirks at me. "What's that, little one?"

"I want your bite," I sign.

His gaze turns into a scowl as he strokes my neck. "I've bitten you plenty over the last few days."

"You're deliberately misunderstanding me," I chide, reaching out to slap him on the chest. "You know what I mean."

"If the bond hasn't magically appeared yet, I don't think that'll make a bit of difference." His expression is wry and weary, but this is the hill I'm ready to die on.

"I don't care if it never appears," I remind him. "You're mine, and I want that mark, alpha. We've known it was coming to this, haven't we?"

"You are fucking relentless," he signs, pulling me forward to bury his face in my neck. The soft rumble of his purr sets my body on fire, even though I'm so damn sore from being so thoroughly used.

Cassian reaches between us and guides me down onto his cock. He's gentler now, more tender, although the first thrust of his hips sends heat coursing down my spine as I groan. Throwing my head back, I relish the feel of his hands in my hair.

And then James is awake, lying there watching us with a pleased look on his face. *Me next,* he murmurs into our bond.

Cassian picks up the pace, his thrusts taking on a teasing edge as he nips at my neck, playfully biting until he settles on a spot right next to James's mark.

My body is tense in anticipation of the pleasure his bite will bring. When he pours that intention into the bite, I'm going to explode all around him.

My big alpha opens his mouth wide and sinks his fangs into my shoulder as orgasm builds between my thighs. But instead of the blistering pleasure that should accompany this, blinding pain hits me so hard, all I can do is scream as my body clenches. The pain is so unbearable, I'm taken right back to my accident, to the way the truck drove right over me. I feel the heat from the undercarriage. I'm right fucking there again.

I scratch at his chest, trying desperately to push him from me, to get away from the searing pain as my soul rips in two.

Cass releases the bite immediately, tipping my chin to his as he taps my arm. I'm trembling like a leaf as James shifts me off him and they examine me.

My shoulder hurts like a bitch, and when I look down, my skin is torn with deep puncture wounds that send shooting pain through my entire upper body. I squint against how fucking horrible it is even as I watch Cassian bark at James.

James flies across the room for a first aid kit, and I watch as a singular sentence falls repeatedly from Cassian's lips.

I'm sorry, I'm sorry, I'm sorry.

I know his bite was a claiming bite, full of intention and love, so why the fuck didn't it work?

CHAPTER THIRTY-FIVE

cassian

I'M FUCKING HORRIFIED as I watch Julia grit her teeth against the pain of my bite. What should have brought us both intense pleasure only felt good for me. Her shoulder looks like hamburger meat, and it reminds me of every time Declan bit his first omega and hurt her. She wasn't truly his; she was forced to be with him, just like the omega he's taken now.

Just like this beautiful omega trying to hold back tears in front of me.

It shouldn't have hurt her, and the only reason it would is if she was never meant to be mine in the first place.

James and I clean her wound without saying a goddamn word, because what is there to say? We want each other, but it was foolish to think I could treat either of them like they're really mine. So what we have, while it's fucking beautiful, isn't designed to last, no matter how many times we intentionally choose one another.

James gets Julia cleaned up while I radio Stone to call Mitchell's healer. Ten minutes later, the heat cabin is full of people getting Julia taken care of. She watches me like a hawk as Stone gestures for me to step outside.

I'm about to get the grilling of my life, I suspect, and I can't help the snarl that rises from my throat in anticipation of a standoff with the big alpha.

"You okay?"

Shocked, I look sideways at him, my eyes narrowing. Finally, heartbreak settles in well and good, crushing me as I slump against the side of the cabin, shaking my head. I don't have to be strong all the time in front of Stone. He's a leader just like I'm supposed to be. Of everyone here, he understands the burden a pack alpha carries.

"I'm not okay in the slightest," I murmur. "I hurt her, Stone. She asked for it, yeah, but I hurt her."

His gaze softens as he looks out into the trees, sighing before he turns back to me. When he opens his mouth to say something, I shake my head. "You can't fix this, alpha. You can't make this any better. It is what it is."

"I know," he murmurs, reaching out to clap me on the shoulder. "I'd offer you a hug, but I hear Asher coming, and if I hug you, it'll be jokes for days."

"No offense taken," I grumble as we turn together, watching Asher sprint through the woods toward us.

He slides to a stop, eyes bright and focused for the first time in a long time, although the look on his face sends my heart sinking in my chest.

"What's wrong?" Stone and I bark at the same time.

Ash cocks his head to the side. "I got a vision, a real vision, I think. It was clear for the first time."

Stone steps toward the seer.

"Of what?" I bark.

Asher turns as he reaches out for my hand, placing it on his chest. "I don't know if this will work. Can you see anything?"

Closing my eyes, I wait to see if his vision is visible to me through touch like it would be a mated seer. I'm disappointed when nothing happens. Shaking my head, I remove my hand.

Asher grumbles, "It was the omegas at Declan's. He's doing something with them soon. I don't know if he's hurting them or sending them away, but I see women fading into darkness. It feels...urgent."

My girls. Oh fuck.

I glance over my shoulder as Stone crosses his arms. "I can see exactly what you're thinking, and if you think you can leave right now without telling them, you're out of your mind. They deserve to know if you're going."

Sucking in a breath, I nod. He's right. It's not James and Julia's fault everything went sideways. I should be grateful for the beautiful days we had together, the best days of my goddamn life, if I'm honest.

Opening the door, I head back in to find them both scowling at me.

"I heard," James snaps and signs. Julia's arms are crossed as the healer works on her.

"How are you feeling, little one?" I question as I drop to a knee and reach out to rub the side of her foot tenderly.

"I'm fine," she reassures me. But she doesn't look fine. Her face is drawn and pinched in pain, and James is visibly anxious for her.

"I'm so fucking sorry," I repeat for the millionth time. "I didn't foresee that, but it won't happen again."

"Cass," she starts, but I hold up a hand to stop her.

"These days with you both were perfect," I tell them. "But my girls are in trouble, and I'm out of the rut. You understand I have to do this, right?"

They don't nod their agreement, but they don't outright disagree either. Finally, I stand and leave, feeling the heartbreak behind me. It mirrors my own as I leave them in the cabin and hop on the closest ATV, heading back for the house with Asher in tow. He repeats every detail he can remember of his vision, and I catalog it away.

I'm sure I've missed the sermon I was supposed to attend, and I need to get back to that right fucking now.

An hour later, I meet JB at the bar to explain where I've been after I asked for his help but disappeared like an asshole.

"A fucking rut?" He looks disbelieving. "And you got through that how?"

"Painfully," I grunt, thankful when he doesn't question me any further about it.

I spent half an hour scrubbing every sign of James and Julia off my skin in preparation for this moment. "Imagine going through that without a mate, JB."

He winces as he looks around the bar. "Can I talk you outta this?"

"No" I counter. "What have I missed?"

"Gabriel, mostly," JB continues. "That weirdo is a piece of fucking work. He's the only one Dec listens to anymore. It's unnatural; he's not even an alpha. But he's turned Declan into a sycophant."

I'm unsurprised to hear this. Declan has always been an unhinged asshole, but JB tries to see a better man in there somewhere. I don't think that better man exists.

"Are you gonna help me or not?" I growl finally.

JB sighs, relenting. "I floated the idea a few days ago, and while I don't think the leadership crew is anxious to have you back, they won't stand in your way. Gabriel is forcing a divide between us, and we hate it."

"Why would he do that?" I question aloud, more to myself than anything.

"He thinks of us as foot soldiers, if I'm honest," JB growls, standing and gesturing to my bag. "He and Declan are the generals, and the rest of us are just grunts to be used until he's done with us. I've been thinking about leaving. Vee wants to."

That's news to me. He's stuck with Declan through so much bullshit.

"Why now?" I bark, sending a wave of dominance over JB as he turns and sighs.

"I'd rather follow no alpha than continue on with him. I've put up with a lot; we all have. We've hurt people, good people. It was easy to get caught up in things when I watched him drag people back when they tried to go. I'm an asshole, but it wasn't worth it to me until this week."

"What happened this week?" I demand.

"Declan's so fucking focused on the omegas getting powers to have the most powerful pack. He cornered Vee, said if she didn't come into her power, he'd get rid of her. Those are the words he used, Cass. Get rid of her. I've ignored a lot of horrible shit he did—it was easy to set it aside when it wasn't happening to me. I know that makes me an asshole, and I'll have to live with that. But he threatened what's mine, and it's the one thing I can't stand for."

It's on the tip of my tongue to rip JB a new one for all the hurt he let happen that didn't affect him, but I need to remember the long game.

"Let's just get back, and I'll see if I can help," I mutter, looking around the bar to see if Titan happens to be behind it, but it's just his bar manager, a nice enough human guy.

There is no help coming for me, so I give him a nod and follow JB out into the brisk afternoon air.

CHAPTER THIRTY-SIX

AFTER CASS LEAVES, I sit with Stone in his office. Julia paces from side to side, unable to sit still for more than a minute. She winces every time she turns, and I know, despite Brady's healing, the wound is bugging her. I search every day for any hint of the powers that usually come with being mated. But even after our connection with Cass during his heat—there's nothing.

Stone has Mahikan and Leon on his speakerphone as I translate for Jules. "It'd be best for you to come down now. I don't see how we can avoid an all-out war. Cassian returned to Declan's pack this afternoon."

I bristle when he says it, but my pack alpha gives me a baleful glance. He knows Cass leaving is ripping Julia and me to shreds, but we're all committed to saving the women stuck in Declan's shitty pack.

"We need to prepare for a few eventualities, but we can be there tomorrow," Mahikan agrees evenly.

"Good," Stone continues. "Cassian would like to avoid war, but I'm not convinced we can. I've already spoken with Mitchell Bancroft. He's in the States, but part of his pack is ready."

Anxious energy builds in my system as I think about Cassian being in the middle of that fucking pack of psychopaths. I can't change his decision, and I wouldn't. He's dedicated to those girls, just like we all are. But it doesn't make the pill of him leaving any easier to swallow.

Clay speaks up from his spot at Stone's side, "Our seers have agreed to help us eavesdrop as much as we can. If we think things are going badly for Cassian, we'll fight to pull him out— we need you here for that."

The plan is simple. Between Asher and River's insane hearing, we're posting lookouts near Declan's neighborhood. There's a chance they'll hear us, of course, but it's a chance we have to take.

"Seers?" Mahikan questions.

Stone grimaces at that. "Asher received a vision of Declan hurting the omegas. It's what prompted Cassian to go back today. River may not have official powers, but she's taken to calling herself our other seer after talking with you, so now I've got two seers."

"Ah yes," Mahikan muses. "Tough little shit, isn't she?"

"That she is," Stone laughs.

Julia tugs at the arm of my chair, indicating I should slide back. When I do, she flops down into my lap and buries her face in my neck.

I know, my love, I murmur into our fraught bond. *I promise we'll figure this out, okay?*

And I mean everything. Not just the omegas and this immediate threat to our pack, but our bond with Cassian. I don't know why it's not working like other bonds have, but I'm just as certain of him as she is. Despite the roadblocks we face. Despite what happened during Cassian's rut.

Once Stone hangs up with Mahikan, he turns to look at us. All of pack leadership is gathered here. Clay looks over at Stone. "At some point, I think it'd be a good idea to pull the town council into this, maybe even hold a town hall. Not while Cass and the omegas are still there, but once they get out. This is likely to spill into a war, and I'd rather the normal humans be aware it's coming. Some people are probably aware that Declan is doing the protection racket, but the average citizen might not be."

"What's the downside to that?" Titan growls from across the table.

"There's really not one," Clay muses. "Other than Declan finding out we're gearing up for war. But if he can't tell that by now, then he really is a fucking idiot. What other reason would he be trucking alphas in from other places if he wasn't doing the same damn thing himself?"

Everyone turns to me, and I'm glad I prepped before this meeting. "Nothing new on that front," I report. "No new arrivals in the last five days…just that dozen right after the fight at the mill. Whatever he's doing, he's got the army he's working with."

Clay nods, shrugging as if to indicate what he previously said still stands.

I stroke Julia's back as the attention slowly turns to us. It's like the pack can see we're broken from what happened at the heat cabin and Cassian's subsequent departure. And I'd be a damned liar if I didn't acknowledge it's true. My heart is crushed that he tried to share a claiming bite with Julia and it didn't work. And it's further crushed that he left afterward. I can't imagine how he feels right now, and I ache to comfort them both.

Growling, I close my eyes and rest my cheek on top of her head, stroking long strawberry blond waves. I wrap them around my fingers as she grips my shirt. After a few moments, she sits up in my lap. "I want to sit with you during the first shift. It's time to go, right?"

I turn to Stone, who nods and radios River. "Riv, honey? You ready for your first shift eavesdropping?"

"Fuck yes!" she shouts into the receiver. Stone gives us a soft smile as I nod at Jules.

Don't worry, mate, I assure her. *We will get him back in one piece, I promise you that.*

I don't know how I'll keep that promise if shit goes south, but I will.

CHAPTER THIRTY-SEVEN

cassian

IT'S a surreal experience riding my Harley behind JB's truck and entering my old neighborhood. I'm certain JB let leadership know I'm coming, because most of the houses we pass have people peering out the windows at me. I recognize familiar faces, but they're expressionless and closed off.

By the time I get to the end of the cul de sac, Declan stands in the street with Gabriel at his side, hands folded primly in front of his belt. "JB tells me yeh want back in. Yet yeh've missed the sermons for days. Hardly seems like commitment." He sneers at me as Gabriel nods, pale eyes not leaving my face.

I opt for a version of the truth, because that seems safest. "I went into a rut, had to ride it out alone in a cabin. I was in no state to help anyone."

"Oof," Declan grins, brows furrowing as he pretends to sympathize with me. "Sounds like yeh got real acquainted with yer hand then."

I don't know how he manages to make everything sound so fucking coarse, but he does. He lacks the sophistication and social intelligence of every other pack alpha I've ever met. It's odd.

"I did," is all I say, because he's clearly expecting a response to that idiotic, childish statement. It opens a doorway, though, so I grin like an asshole. "Makes being in a pack all that much more appealing. I'm sure I wouldn't have had any trouble finding some pretty omegas here to help me ride out the need."

Declan laughs with me, nodding. "While that's true, it would surprise me. Yeh didn't take to the omegas when yeh were here before, did yeh?"

I shrug, not offering an excuse. I never touched a single one of the girls in this pack. Never felt the desire to. One pretty little girl had me wrapped firmly around her finger already. I push thoughts of Julia and then James out of my head, focusing.

Declan continues with a sneer, "I'll allow yeh back in for now, but not at the leadership level. Yeh'll have to earn your way back up the ranks, just like anyone. I don't trust yeh."

While I'm relieved at part of his statement, I'm irked too. "I was a good strategist," I growl. "I can be more helpful in that role."

Declan crosses the space between us, bumping my chest with his as he brings his mouth close to my ear. "I allowed yeh back only because Gabriel felt we could sway yeh to our message, that yeh'd be a powerful ally in the coming months. But I'm not so sure, alpha. So steer clear o' me fer now. Yeh'll start in the barracks with the other newbies."

Behind Declan, Gabriel continues to smile like a maniac, sending a trill of alarm down my spine. A growl leaves my lips as I push my chest back against Declan's, but when he snarls, fangs descending, I take a step back and bow my head. Every instinct I possess screams at how unnatural it is to deign to this alpha, but I'm not here for him. I'm here for the omegas.

"That's it," Declan purrs. "Keep yer fookin' head down and feck off to the barracks. JB!"

JB trots over and gives me a look. "Come on, Cassian. Let's go."

Nodding, I turn to follow him, unballing my fists. I do my best to look around the neighborhood without making it look like I'm on a scouting trip. By the time we get to the end of the street, I'm relieved to see us heading for a little white bungalow that's right across the street from the omegas' home.

Unfortunately, we pass the house and head into the woods behind it, hiking for a solid ten minutes before we approach a goddamn tent camp. There are ten or fifteen tents, alphas milling around in small groups. Some are cooking over a fire. A few spar in a clearing between the tents.

"Welcome to the barracks, as Declan calls it." JB looks at me with a neutral expression. "If you can find an empty tent, it's all yours. No visiting the omegas without permission. We'll radio you if we need anything." Without another word, he turns to go.

Growling, I reach out and put my hand on his shoulder. "I can't help like this."

JB whirls around with a snarl. "We don't need your help. I encouraged them to let you back, but do me a favor and don't cause me any trouble, Cassian. Steer clear of leadership and the omegas." That's what he says aloud, but the look on his face is obvious—he can't encourage me to help them out loud, but he knows why I'm here.

I should be thankful there's a fucking shred of kindness left in him. Although, for all I know, he's hoping I'll cause drama, and he can just take off with his mate and never look back.

I hold back a snarl and nod, watching him leave. Steering clear of leadership doesn't bother me. The less interaction I have with them, the better. But not being able to approach the omegas, that's a whole other issue. I'll figure it out, but in the meantime, I need to learn everything I can about what's going on in this fucking neighborhood. Declan is gearing up for war, but it's always felt like we've only gotten half of his story.

Turning toward the sparring alphas, I let out a growl that stops them in their tracks. "Is there a free tent around here?"

The taller of the two alphas smiles good-naturedly. "Farthest back toward the road is mine, but I'm the only one in it. You can share if you want."

"You're such a pussy, Cam," the other alpha growls. "You don't even know this motherfucker."

"I know we need all the good alphas we can get if we're gonna fight that other pack," Cam snarls.

My ears perk up at that. "Fight the other pack?"

"Yeah," Cam continues. "I guess there's some sort of territory dispute, so Alpha Declan brought us here to help with that. We'll be able to settle here in peace after he finishes." The kid says this with a straight face, although he looks a little skeptical.

"Don't forget the pussy he promised us," the other alpha joins in. "Pussy for days. All the pussy you could want. That's why I'm here."

Cam rolls his eyes and shoves the other alpha's shoulder. "I'm done, man. Catch up later." He looks over at me and gestures toward his tent. "Follow me, alpha. I'm Cam; you probably heard Jim call me that. What's your name?"

"Cassian," I reply, reaching out to shake his hand. His grip is firm and sure as he flashes another kind smile, green eyes mirthful. Seems like a nice kid. I follow him to his tent, surprised to see the inside is orderly.

He watches my gaze and grins. "I served a few years in the Army; they couldn't beat tidiness out of me at this point."

"Were you discharged?"

His emerald eyes cloud over. "I transitioned during a drill and had to run. Barely escaped with my life, but I've been managing ever since." He looks toward the center of the tent camp. "Lots of us have been roaming around together since we transitioned, so a couple of years at least. We're a rough group, but we're not total assholes."

"I hope not," I mutter as I drop my backpack in the tent. I brought nothing with me that would connect me to Stone's pack, not being sure if they'd search me. I've got no phone, no radio.

"Why'd you join?" Cam asks, holding the tent flap open as I step back out.

I sense it's better not to hash out ancient history, so I shrug. "Pretty much the same as you. I've been in this valley for a while. I know these alphas, and I lived here for a time. I left, but it's hard being on your own without anyone to watch your back."

"The fucking worst," Cam agrees. "Well, we're glad to have you, man." He claps me on the back and grins again. And that's the moment I decide that, when I leave, if I can, I'm bringing Cam out with me.

CHAPTER THIRTY-EIGHT

I'M a bundle of nerves as James and leadership finalize plans for how to help Cass if things go south—which I'm certain they will. My heart aches deep in my chest as I will tears not to stream down my cheeks.

I have to keep it together so I can help protect Cass if the moment comes. Stone has a gigantic hidden vault in his closet, and Cherry and I are grabbing guns and ammo to put in a slew of trucks out front. I trail her through Stone's room, grabbing another gun bag and shoving several handguns and boxes of bullets inside, as much as I can carry.

Cherry's hand comes to my back, where she strums her fingers. When I turn, her face is pinched and worried.

"We're going to do everything we can to keep him safe, honey. I'm there every step of the way for you. Do you need anything?"

I close my eyes as tears threaten to fall. "I'm terrified for my mate."

Cherry's eyes—eyes the color of Cass's—move to the angry wound at my neck. She doesn't say anything, but I know what she's wondering anyhow.

"He's still mine," I begin angrily, but she takes my hands and pulls them to her heart, simply nodding at me. No matter what the biology says, no matter what happened during his rut, he belongs to me. If six women's lives hadn't been on the line, I never would have let him leave the ranch.

Luna and Erin join us, squeezing in for a giant hug. These women's love is an almost tangible force to me, as if I can feel it soaking into my body from theirs. We stand for a long minute before Luna extricates herself and starts filling more bags with guns and ammo. When she's done with that, she turns to me. "We're gonna kick ass, Jules. We're here for you and your mates, okay?"

"I'm so proud you're my friends," is all I can say before I finally burst into tears.

Luna holds me for another long minute, rubbing my back before we drag the guns and ammo out front.

My bond with James is tense and tight, and for the millionth time, I wish I could feel Cass. I'd give anything to know how he is right now, even if only to send him my love and support. I want him to know how proud I am of him, that he's putting his life on the line to protect others. But I'd expect no less from the big, hulking pack alpha.

I hold it more or less together until I get out front and see James tucking a shotgun under the back seat of one of Stone's trucks. He turns when he senses me, and the distressed look on his handsome features rips my heart to shreds.

James opens his arms, and I fly into them, feeling his love wrap tightly around the bond. He radiates comfort and warmth as he pours that emotion into our connection. But I feel every level of his attention, and something about him is different. Not just the emotion but how he feels to me: grounded, depthless, soothing.

I look up at James, who grits his jaw tightly, dark eyes flicking over my head. When I turn, Asher strides down the stairs with an odd look on his face. He comes right up to James and presses his big hand to my mate's chest. There's a look on James's face that I can't quite place, as if he's looking for reassurance himself.

Asher removes his hand and smiles at us both, signing the symbol for "power."

My eyes fly up to my mate's as my hands move in a flurry of ASL. "Power? You're getting power? What happened? How do you feel?"

James shakes his head as Stone and Clay join us. Ash smiles at the alphas as I wind an arm around James, feeling along our bond to try to ascertain what's different.

"James's power is coming," Asher tells them simply. "Not fully here, but developing."

My mate's question is soft and unsure when he signs to Ash, "What power is it?"

Ash smiles back, and in that moment, I truly see him for the powerful seer he'll be when his own power has completely developed. He looks at James and me. "What can you both sense? Look deep inside and tell me how you feel."

I close my eyes and press my forehead to James's chest, feeling his heart thrum steadily under his skin. I smile into our bond as I pay attention and try to figure out what I read. There's a deep, peaceful aura that's even stronger than it's always been, like he's a still lake on a cool day. If I dove into him, I'd come up refreshed and rejuvenated.

"Healer," I sign as I press myself out of his arms and look at my pack alpha, strategist and seer. "He's our healer." With a huge smile, I turn and fling myself into James's big arms, loving the way he burrows his face in my neck with a low, loving growl.

I feel his hands move behind my back, and his chest rumbles. He's speaking with the rest of leadership, but all I can think of is how we're missing someone—the other most important person in my world. The only person I want to share this news with.

And then what comes next is a sense of worry and grief—if James is our healer, our pack will never have a spirit, because I'll never take anyone else but Cass.

———

There's a flurry of activity as news spreads quickly about James's developing power. He accepts the attention gracefully, although he's anxious to get going.

Stone can sense our anxiety, and he checks on me multiple times before gathering everyone around. Sal and Isabel stand on the front steps, although they're not coming with us.

"Let's go over the plan once more," Stone addresses our crowd. "We'll park outside Declan's neighborhood in shifts with a seer in each shift. There's a solid chance they'll hear us, but it's a chance we have to take. I'm almost completely sure this is going to go poorly, so we have to be ready with Plans B and C."

I nod. We know this part already, and I'm in the first group to camp out. I refuse to wait on the sidelines while my mate is risking his life to save six others.

Stone continues, "Mitchell's out of the country, unfortunately, so only half his pack is here, but they're on their way over now to be at the ready. Mahikan left this morning, so they'll be here soon too. With all the packs together, we're still slightly outnumbered, but we've got more shifting males and omegas with powers. It's our best advantage."

"What about Hale?" someone asks. James translates for me as I look around.

Asher steps forward, his thumbs tucked into his waistband as Cherry stands by his side, staring up at him in awe. After his most recent vision and declaration about James's power, it's clear he's riding the high of his power. "Let me handle Hale if she tries anything," he states simply.

"We should try to capture her if we can," Clay signs. "She's a dangerous asset for him if she manages to figure out what the fuck she's doing."

Asher shakes his head. "I didn't think we wanted to steal anyone who wants to remain there."

Clay grits his jaw. He doesn't fully agree, and I get it. I've seen her power up close, and it was fucking terrifying. She's like Alice, commanding the elements, but on steroids and mean as hell.

Stone looks around. "We'll be ready with the trucks when Cassian makes a run with the girls. If it comes to a fight, we'll have those who can shift be the first wave. Remember, we don't want an all-out war if we can avoid it."

My packmates rustle around, but all I feel in that moment is steely resolve. We're gathered together as a family, and we'll get through this as a family. We have to, because I won't accept anything else.

CHAPTER THIRTY-NINE

cassian

DINNER IS A LOW-KEY AFFAIR. Someone trapped and caught a slew of rabbits in the woods, and they're now cooking over a fire. All I can think of is how the fucking pack alpha should be providing for these men. But to be honest, most of them are absolute shit, the worst of the worst type of alpha— dumb and mean. They're Declan's foot soldiers, and that's pretty much it.

There's not a single one I'd want in a pack with me outside of Cam. They pick on him relentlessly for being kind, although he lets the hurled insults roll off his back. He checks in with me a couple of times, eyes meeting mine now and again. As a pack alpha, I read him as kind and smart, maybe even a man to have on my side when shit goes down.

Good. Because the moment I get a chance to spring my girls free, I'm taking it. Tonight, if I can. That was our initial plan, anyhow.

After dinner, the young alphas start drinking, and I slip off toward the main part of the neighborhood. Isabel told me Gabriel required Cara, the pregnant omega, to be sequestered away from the rest of the women. I'm hopeful I can get access to her now. Cara's the key to this entire operation because she can get a message to the other omegas without speaking aloud.

Moving slowly and quietly, I peek in the windows of the white bungalow we passed. Sitting in the living room is Cara, the other pregnant omega. I lift my hand to rap on the window when I hear footsteps. Peeking around the edge of the house, I see Declan, Gabriel and Hale coming up the street. Declan stomps in front, his hand around his omega's forearm as he drags her, snarling.

Shit, shit, shit. I duck around the back of the house toward an open window, hiding in the shadows but still able to hear. I'm fucked if his seer, Mark, joins them. He'll hear me out here for sure, but I can't slink away at this point. I settle for keeping myself as quiet and hidden as I can in the shadows, sliding onto my belly and rolling under the window, which juts out of the home's side.

I hear a bang at Cara's door, and then the trio barges in on the pregnant omega, who says nothing.

Gabriel is the first to speak. "Hello again, omega."

"Hello," Cara's voice gives a soft response, so unlike the strong omega who was my first friend in this pack.

Gabriel continues, "We're here for one last attempt at bringing out your power, Cara, and if this doesn't work, you'll be moving on tomorrow."

I hear footsteps as Cara's voice grows louder, full of concern. "Moving on? To where?"

"There are other camps like this one," Gabriel replies in an even tone, although there's a thrilled edge to it. He loves delivering this terrifying news. "You did not bond with anyone here despite carrying an offspring, so we will move you around until the bond does snap into place. Our army will need powerful omegas in the future."

Even from under the house, I can practically feel Cara's ire when she snaps back at the cult leader, "Odd, then, that you consider us such throwaway people when we're pregnant, but we're the future of your stupid cult? Little weird, don't you think?"

She always had a hot temper. I blanch and throw a hand over my mouth when the sound of a slap rings out and a body hits the wall, sending dust down onto my face as I turn to avoid getting it in my nose and mouth. There's nothing I'd like better than to rip Declan and Gabriel to shreds, but I'm outnumbered, and I can't save the others if I act now.

Still, it takes every ounce of my formidable control not to throw myself through the window and kill Declan right now.

Gritting my teeth, I listen to Cara lumber upright. She's nine fucking months pregnant. When I do get her and the girls out of here, I'll come back and raze this entire camp to the ground for hurting them. Anyone who touched them, anyone who didn't help, is going on my personal shit list.

"Let's just try again," comes Hale's voice, harsh and insensitive. "Maybe it'll work this time."

"Oh, you think the hundredth time's the charm, huh?" Cara's still sarcastic and pissed, and I will her to be silent, to tamp down that fiery temper for a few more hours until I can get her out.

"We've got to try, so shut the fuck up about it," Hale barks. Cara says nothing else, and there's silence as I struggle not to move from my spot under the house.

For long minutes, nothing happens, and then the house starts to shake, and Cara whimpers, but when she gasps and slumps against the wall, I know they must have attempted something.

"Jesus fooking Christ, Hale," Declan barks. "You came hard as fuck on my big cock and nearly brought the house down when yer power came in. Why can't yeh do this?"

I've only met this omega a few times, but the fury that rolls off her is tangible even to me. She hates Declan's unkind words.

Gabriel speaks next, his voice soft, although his tone brooks no argument. "That's unfortunate. It seems Cara will not be staying with us. Hale, get dinner for the unclean omega, and then you are free to go."

"Make it quick, yeh bitch," Declan snarls.

There's a sigh, a slamming door, and I hear Gabriel again. "This changes nothing, alpha. Our plan remains the same. Keep cycling through the alphas and omegas, find bonds where we can, and get rid of those who don't fit this pack. Another location has several omegas that did not work there. We'll bring them here and continue the process."

There's an angry growl, which I recognize as Declan being frustrated.

"This is a long game, Declan," Gabriel responds. "My vision for you, for your pack, remains unchanged. You will rule, alpha. I will see to it."

"I'd better," comes Declan's gruff response.

This whole time, Cara is still stuck there with them, and I'm still resisting the urge to rip someone to shreds.

The door opens again, and I let my head fall back as I watch Declan and Gabriel head back up the street toward his home, which sits at the very far end of the cul de sac. As soon as they're too far to hear my movements, I stand up and shove the window open, throwing myself through it.

To her credit, Cara flings herself against the wall, eyes wide, but makes no sound at all. The moment she sees it's me, she throws herself into my arms. I crush her to me, still careful of her protruding belly, and I will every second of comfort and love I can. For a long minute, I hold her before she presses away and looks out her front window. She turns to me, lifting her hands to sign.

When I first met Julia and learned she was deaf, Cara taught me ASL. She taught the other omegas too on the sly, so she can get them a message without even having to get close to them.

It's a beautiful fucking advantage, pretty much the only one we've got.

"When are we leaving?" she questions. She doesn't bother with catching up.

"Three a.m.," I respond. "Can you let the other girls know? I assume everyone wants out?"

"Yeah," Cara agrees. "Still six of us."

"What about Hale?" I sense the omega is miserable here, but she's not my primary concern.

Cara looks torn for a second, then shakes her head. "Mean as a snake. Watch her come back here and spit in my fucking food before she gives it to me."

It matches my assessment of the few times I've met her.

"Let the other girls know to gather here at three, and we're out of here," I press on. "My pack will be waiting, and if shit goes south, they're coming for us, guns blazing. Either way, it's over tonight."

"Thank fuck," Cara signs, her hands trembling. She rests them over her belly before pulling dark eyes up to me. "I'll tell the girls immediately. We knew you'd come back as soon as you could."

I blanch at that, guilt eating at me. "I'm sorry I wasn't here sooner," I admit. "It took us a while to figure out the best plan."

Cara gives me a sly smile. "Maybe a pretty little omega has something to do with your delay?"

I narrowly avoid huffing out a laugh at that. But then my heart pounds in my chest when I think about Julia and James. Jesus Christ, I hope I get more time with them, even if my claiming bite didn't work. I'd give anything to—

A slamming door pulls me right out of my reverie, and Hale stands there with a furious look on her face. In my excitement to get to Cara, I forgot she was coming back.

She steps inside and closes the door as she crosses her arms, glaring cruelly at me. "You're not supposed to be here." Her tone is cold and cruel.

"He's an old friend. He just came by to say hi," Cara counters, keeping her voice low.

"Is that so?" Hale keeps her tone loud as fuck as I resist the urge to slink toward the back door. "I think he's here to help you escape," she presses on. "And you can't. You don't even know half of what Gabriel is capable of."

"Keep your fucking voice down," snaps Cara in a soft tone. "Stay if you want, or come the fuck with us if you want out. But stay out of my way, or so help me—"

"You'll what?" the omega snarls, stalking across the room as I pull Cara behind my much larger frame.

"If you do something to hurt my child's chances at a happy life, I'll kill you myself," Cara whisper-hisses from around me.

A moment of hurt flashes across Hale's face so fast, I suspect I imagined it. It's gone and replaced with irritated boredom. "I'll tell you this one time, since you're clearly too fucking stupid to have realized this yourself. There is no way out of this hellhole. None at all. They watch more than you think they do."

"It's a chance I'll be taking," Cara snaps back as I turn to her.

"Enough, omega." We can't keep talking about this out loud, and I urge her with a stern look to remember that. "I just came by for a quick visit, but I'm on my way to see your alpha, if you'd like to walk with me."

Hale scoffs and rolls her eyes before looking back at Cara. "I came to ask you something about dinner, but I think you'd do better to just miss it tonight."

"Bitch," Cara huffs under her breath, but I open the door for Hale and usher her through. When she goes, I give Cara a meaningful look.

"Three," she signs.

"Three," I agree before closing the door and following Hale up the street.

Hale is silent the entire awkward walk from Cara's cottage up the long street. When we pass by the houses, I watch doors and windows close, curtains pulled in front of them. Not a single person here trusts her, obviously.

"How'd you end up here, Hale?" I ask. "I knew Declan's previous mate." The anger and hurt rolling off her is nearly enough to choke my pack alpha power. She's miserable, and my power aches to fix that, despite how mean I've seen her be.

"He took what he wanted," she snaps, eyes flashing at me before she stalks a few steps ahead, arms crossed. I guess that conversation is done, but a part of me feels bad for her. She's awful and cruel, but, in a way, she's a victim too.

When we arrive at the end of the cul de sac, I see a bonfire in the yard behind Declan's cottage home. There are already alphas milling all around, and I'm horrified to see how large his group has grown—far larger than we thought based on keeping an eye on the comings and goings at the mill.

"What're yeh doin' here, Cassian?" Declan's voice booms as the crowd turns to look at me. JB stands from Declan's side to give me a warning look, his omega hovering just behind him. I remember what he told me about Declan threatening her, and I wonder if push comes to shove, if I might be able to appeal to JB's love for her.

"Do you want me to do anything with the kids in the barracks while I'm there? They don't necessarily seem to be here for the message itself, if I'm honest."

Gabriel shrugs, leaving the crowd to join me. He gestures for the rest of the pack to head toward the fire before he speaks. "In the beginning, we attract brothers by offering what they can't achieve for themselves—power, safety, companionship. But they will stay as they see us thrive and take power. For now, I care less about their believing fully in the message than I do their ability to follow orders."

"I see. My question still stands though." I don't mean to push back on Gabriel, but they sent me to the barracks for a reason.

"You're a natural leader, Cassian," Gabriel agrees as Declan snarls. "Alpha Declan cannot be expected to lead such a large pack without delegating responsibilities. For now, your responsibility is the barracks. Keep the men in line and following our orders, and perhaps you will move up through the ranks as they do."

"Got it. And what are our orders?"

"Be at the ready, Cassian. That is all for now." Gabriel smiles at me, but it's so cruel and wicked, I have to hold back from punching him in the fucking face. The pack alpha instinct in me is screaming at how horribly wrong this whole thing is. This pack and its dynamics are fucked beyond belief.

The alpha isn't caring for anyone but himself, and the younger men have no one as an example. I think of Rogue, and I search inward to see if I can feel my strategist from here.

I can't. I'm too fucking far from him, and my lack of a mate bond means I can't feel Julia and James either. It's an unnerving feeling, even though I know they're camped out, waiting to help me get the girls out if possible.

"Since you're here, join us for the nightly bonfire," Gabriel encourages. "You can learn a little more about our mission."

I grunt my acceptance as Gabriel and Declan turn toward the bonfire. Mark and JB both shoot me warning looks as I trail behind them, ensuring I stay far away enough to not seem like a threat.

The bonfire roars up into the night as the large group mills around. There's a small stage off to one side. Gabriel ascends the steps and stops at the top, a hush falling over the crowd. This must be a regular occurrence by the way everyone turns to face him, ready for a speech.

"Good evening, alphas," he calls out, his voice carrying over the crowd. "Tonight, I call upon you to be vigilant. You know what lies at stake for us, what future we are building. Our path will not be an easy one, but I ask you, are you here for it?"

Rousing answering cries echo around me as I resist the urge to shudder. Vigilance? It's a warning for me; I'm certain of it. Still, I can't allow those inner emotions to be readable to the alphas I know here. I lift my chin high and keep watching Gabriel as he continues.

"There is a near future where we function as the alpha nation, and this group here is the genesis of that. You are the future of our great country, the alphas who will lead their own packs all across Canada, and eventually, the world. You are here to learn from Alpha Declan, to find your mates and come into your own powers, to take over. It is your God-given birthright!"

His voice rises to a feral crescendo as Cam joins me with his friend from the earlier sparring.

With Declan now at his side, Gabriel continues, "As always, mingle with pack leadership, ask questions. Learn, absorb how a real pack works. Take that knowledge to bolster your own natural abilities. And then visit the omegas, my brothers. I relish the day each of you meets your mate and comes into your power. New women are joining us soon."

Catcalls and rough barks ring out as I growl, unable to stop myself. Cam darts a glance over at me, looking uncomfortable as the crowd begins to dissipate.

His friend claps him on his shoulder. "Cam, you pussy, can I finally convince you to come taste these fucking omegas? So good, brother. So compliant."

"You know I'm not into that," Cam growls back. "Not today, and not any other day."

The other alpha rolls his eyes. "Fucking fine then, you idiot. Guess you'll be single forever."

We watch him jog off to join the other alphas as they head

up the street toward the end of the road, where two houses hold most of the omegas. I quiver with rage as I think about this huge group of men forcing themselves on my girls over and over.

"Every night," Cam whispers. "It's like this every night. I wish I had never transitioned, so I didn't know alphas are like this."

I resist the urge to tell him it doesn't have to be this way. Declan and Gabriel remain standing on the stage, their eyes boring into mine. I know what I read there: a challenge. Swallowing my pride, I nudge Cam in the chest and follow the rest of the alphas up the street.

CHAPTER FORTY

POWER. I can't believe my power is coming in. I started to feel it at the end of Cassian's rut, but it got so crazy with Jules's bite that I didn't even realize it. Still, there's no time to focus on that now. I'll think about my power and what it means for our pack later.

Julia is tense in my arms as we drive to the exit Declan's neighborhood is off of. We're taking the first watch, and I'm trying to be strong for my girl, but I'm terrified. I can't shake the horrible feeling that something's going to happen to Cass. He just left this morning, but I'm a bundle of nerves.

The only saving grace is having seers here who can tell us what's happening.

Samson and River are both with us. Asher stayed at the lodge to rest for his shift. Jules and I haven't gone back yet. To be honest, I don't think I could pry her from this spot if my life depended on it.

River gives us the play-by-play of Declan, Gabriel and Hale hassling one of the women. I want to die knowing Declan's fucking omega knows our plan, but all I can hope for is that she won't tell Declan. There doesn't seem to be much love lost between them.

The truck is quiet. We can't risk Declan's seer hearing us if he's listening.

My cell vibrates, and I look down to see a text from Stone.

Mahikan and pack are here. Half of Mitchell's pack is here. We're on standby.

I send back a thumbs-up and show Julia, Samson and River. Worst comes to worst, we've opted to have Samson and Pen sit shifts with us, because if Declan manages to hear and find us, Samson or Pen could shift into their birds and fly us out fast.

Samson looks over at River with a sly grin. "Any questions regarding what I showed you last time we met?" He signs the words since we've agreed to be silent.

He's referencing the time he allowed River into his mind to investigate her incredible hearing. Whatever he showed her that day, she hasn't shared it with the rest of us.

River honest-to-fucking-God blushes and shakes her head. "It was pretty clear, alpha. So I don't know what I would ask."

Samson gives her a slow smile and lifts his hands, making the signs for "You might ask when it will happen?"

River squirms uncomfortably in her seat, looking at Jules and me before turning her attention back to the big blond seer. When she says nothing, he grins and looks back out the window. But then he makes the sign for "soon," and she lets out a strangled gasp, slumping in her seat.

"Spill the deets, girl," I sign, slapping her on the head. "You're always the one needling us, so tell me every single thing."

It's not that I can even focus much in this moment, but I'd give nearly anything to focus on something other than the silence. I can tell River's dying to question Samson but doesn't want to do it in front of us. Reaching around to the front, I grab my cell and type in a note because she doesn't know enough ASL for this yet.

It's time for Pen and Asher to replace you guys. Why don't you head back, and you can grill Samson on the way?

Samson looks at the screen and nods, rubbing at his chest as he smiles. A shadow passes over the truck, and then something lands on the roof, crushing the truck under its weight.

River looks up at the roof and rolls her eyes. "Show off," she signs before hopping out and swatting at the huge bird that's perched on our truck.

Asher drops off the top of the truck, and Samson steps out of the driver's seat, reaching up to lift his mate off the truck as soon as she shifts back into human form. She's naked, so I avert my eyes. Samson hands Pen clothing, which she dons before he pulls her in for a sensual kiss.

They're giving up so much to help us, Jules purrs into our bond. *I'm so fucking terrified and grateful.*

Kissing her forehead, I pull her into my arms as Pen waves goodbye to Samson and hops into the driver's seat. We watch her mate fly away with River tucked in his huge claws. I'm dying to pepper Pen about what Samson alluded to, but now isn't the time.

Asher folds himself into the front seat and turns around to smile at us in the back.

"You seem oddly settled," I sign.

He smiles and shrugs. "Settled isn't the right word. Helpful, maybe? I've been helpful this week for the first time in months. And it feels really nice."

Pen rolls her eyes and reaches out to slap the back of his head playfully before slumping into her seat. "I don't need to continue to harp about the similarities between your journey and Samson's, so this is me, *not* harping about the similarities between your fucking journeys."

She gives him a knowing look as Julia and I hold back a laugh from the back seat. Asher smiles at Pen, but it's a little forced. There are just enough differences in his experience that he doesn't see it the way Pen does. I, for one, am holding out hope that it'll work out just as well for Ash as it did for Pen and Samson. I was present for their journey too, and it was a hell of a rollercoaster to watch.

"Your power will come," I reassure Asher, "but we're grateful for you every day no matter what."

He smiles a little bigger at that before sticking his tongue out at Pen, who sticks hers out back. She turns in her seat just like he does and produces a deck of cards from her pocket.

"Strip poker anyone?"

I hold in a groan as Julia tosses her half-full water bottle at Pen. They silently laugh together as we settle in for a long night of listening. Three a.m. can't come soon enough.

CHAPTER FORTY-ONE

cassian

CAM IS quiet all the way back to the tent camp. I hold back a roar as we pass the last two houses on the street. Lines of alphas wait out front. Shit, this might put a pretty big chink in my plan.

"How long are they out there waiting for omegas?"

Cam frowns. "They've usually gone through everybody by midnight." He looks mortified as he shares, and I resist the urge to do something. Not for the first time, I wish like fuck I could shift or had any sort of power. I'd love nothing better than to take a flamethrower to the line of men waiting to fuck women who don't want them.

Cam says nothing until we get to our tent, and then he turns to me with a baleful look. "You're here for the girls, aren't you?"

I hiss out an angry bark and gesture for him to be quiet. His brows knit together as he shrugs, clearly not understanding.

I look around for a piece of paper, but he hands me his cell and opens it to an empty note, handing it to me.

The fucking seer's gonna hear us. Yes—here for the omegas.

Cam gives me a confused expression. "Seer?" he mouths the word, but doesn't say it aloud.

I type fast into the phone note. *You don't know what a seer is?*

He shakes his head, nibbling at his lower lip, green eyes on me as dimples appear at the sides of his mouth.

Fuck. I run my hands through my hair as I shake my head, then write again. I've already decided I trust Cam, and when I leave tonight, I'm taking him with me if he wants to go.

The omegas are in danger. I'm getting them out tonight.

Cam gives me a look, cocking his head to the side again before he grabs the phone.

Why do I feel like I should listen to you even though I don't know you? It means something, right?

I give him a thumbs-up and point to myself. "Pack alpha," I mouth.

He scribbles hastily on the page: *And the omegas?*

Not safe. Declan wants to trade them to other camps, I reiterate. *I'm leaving tonight.*

Cam looks around the tent camp, but I shake my head. "Only you," I mouth. He shoots me a sorrowful look but nods. The rest of these assholes are just that; they have no place coming with us.

I type a few more details to Cam, and then he packs his things quietly, filling one small bag as I watch sadly. I mourn for my girls, and I mourn for my mates.

And I mourn for the young alpha in front of me whose entire life fits in a small rucksack.

CHAPTER FORTY-TWO

cassian

BY THE TIME three a.m. rolls around, I'm pacing the tent, so goddamn ready to go. I shake Cam's shoulder, and he sits up in his cot, grabbing his backpack and slinging it on.

The camp is quiet. Everyone's asleep, and the fire's burnt down. Around us I hear only snoring, although we wait a couple long minutes before we creep out of the barracks and toward the end of the neighborhood.

Cam follows silently behind me, and when we get to Cara's, I open the back door. We enter the small bungalow, and Cara rounds a corner, her eyes widening when she sees Cam. He gives her the briefest of nods, his eyes going over her shoulder.

In the living room stand five other omegas. Tear-filled eyes find me, and I rush to them, so fucking happy to see them here. They surround me as I try to hug everybody at once, relief flooding my system at being reunited with them all in one place.

Cara holds a finger to her lips as she crosses the room and looks out the front door. "All good," she mouths as I turn to the silent room.

I gesture the omegas toward the back door, pausing to listen for anything. Hearing nothing, I sneak out the back, heading for the woods toward the highway. It's a solid two miles, but my pack is there waiting. And as soon as we're closer to them than Declan, we'll pick up the pace. I think of James and Julia and Rogue and how desperate I am to be near them again, and dangerous hope fills my chest.

Cam grabs Cara's bag, slinging it on top of his as the girls eye him thankfully.

Looking around at my girls, I give them a reassuring smile. "Just a short walk, omegas. Sal and Isabel can't wait to see you." One of the girls bursts into tears at the mention of our friends but wipes them away quickly.

The omegas are as silent as they can be, Cam bringing up the rear behind our group. I'm thankful that, despite him not knowing me well, he knows this is the right thing to do.

I peek around the back door, but the forest is silent. We're fucked if Mark, the seer, is up and paying attention. But I have to hope he's buried balls-deep in his own mate right now. Or better yet, asleep.

We creep quietly out of the house and into the woods, angling away from the camp and toward the road. For ten minutes, everything is quiet. There's not a sneeze, not a single cough. There's nothing but the soft sound of footfalls.

We come to the edge of a small field, the last open space we need to cross. There's no tree line here, but once we cross the field, we'll be halfway to the highway, and my pack is there and waiting. Plan A was to get to the truck quietly. I hope I don't need my Plan B.

That's when I hear the roar of an ATV.

From the back of the group, Cam hisses out, "Run!"

"Straight ahead!" I bark, pointing toward the highway. Cara sprints past me as Cam takes off with the bags, running alongside me. When one of the girls slows, Cam slings her up onto his back with the bags and keeps up a shockingly fast pace.

The roar of multiple ATVs echoes from behind me as I bellow for the girls to move faster. They fly across the field, but the ATVs are barreling down on us.

"Lead them, Cam!" I roar, stopping in place as I throw my bag from my shoulder. They need a distraction; there's only another mile to my pack. If I can fuck with these assholes long enough, my girls will get out.

My heart shreds in my chest for James and Julia and the pack I never got to build as lights show in the distance, four ATVs barreling my direction as footsteps fade behind me. The girls are across the field, still fleeing toward the highway. I toss my pack aside and sprint toward the line of ATVs. Bek is on the first one, fucking asshole. I clothesline him as I leap through the air, knocking us both to the ground.

He shifts into his wolf in a heartbeat, snapping his teeth around my torso as I pummel his head, his wolf yipping as he drops me to the ground. Two ATVs fly past us as I bellow for my girls.

Then something metal hits me on the back of the head, and, as I fall to the ground, snarling, I see Gabriel's face.

"How very foolish to assume we didn't see this coming, alpha," he sneers. He smiles, and everything goes dark.

I blink my eyes open what feels like moments later, but it can't be. Fluttering my lashes, I groan as I shake blood out of my eyes. I reach up to feel the wound on the back of my head, but I can't move my goddamn arms.

Groaning as I come to, I struggle as I realize I'm tied to a cross. Both arms are strapped out to my sides, my legs pinned together at the feet. In front of me, Cam and the omegas sit huddled in a miserable group.

I hear an alarm, and then the clearing where they had the bonfire earlier fills with alphas. It's a rallying cry, men flooding out of every house to join us. They look up at me with angry jeers.

From somewhere, a rock flies and hits me in the eye as I snap and snarl, fangs elongated as I jerk against bindings that don't give. One of the omegas sobs, and Cam puts his arm around her. The moment he does, Declan grabs him by the scruff and tosses him out of the group and toward the younger alphas from the barracks.

"Take care o'that one, men. He betrayed us."

I watch his pack alpha command hit them hard, but Cam was with these men before they came here. There's a moment of hesitation before Declan bellows, and when he does, the alphas fall on top of Cam and begin to pummel him.

The girls scream as Gabriel watches the frenzy, turning while they beat Cam senseless. He lifts his arms, pale eyes focused on the remaining gathered alphas. "Do you see? I cautioned vigilance just tonight. And it is because of the vigilance of one of our own—Alpha Declan's own omega—we knew Cassian attempted to infiltrate our home. He came to steal our women, to steal what's yours. It will not stand!"

Gabriel screams the last sentence as the group parts from Cam, who is bloody and unrecognizable on the ground.

I look around for that fucking omega, but Hale is notably absent. Declan doesn't even bother to look for her, his green eyes focused on me as he watches the hope leave mine.

"This alpha came to take," Gabriel shrieks, pointing at me. "He is not a believer, and he will never be. We will make an example of him!"

For the love of God, please, I beg anyone up in the sky who

might be listening. Please let my people come and get the girls and Cam, if he's still alive.

Just then, there's a rustle at my feet, and I look down as much as I can to see Mark and Bek stacking piles of wood under the cross I'm lashed to.

Jesus fucking Christ.

I bellow and struggle against the ropes as I realize what they're doing.

They're going to fucking burn me alive.

CHAPTER FORTY-THREE

I DON'T KNOW how I managed to drift off, but Asher shakes me awake. Jolting upright, I look at the clock. It's 3:25. Fuck, Cass must be on his way with the girls.

Ash is on the phone. "Now," he growls into the receiver. In the driver's seat, Pen is already awake and hopping out of the truck with urgency.

Julia is snoring in my arms, but when I shake her, her eyes open instantly. She's up and out of the car fast. Hopping up onto the truck tire, she uncovers the bed full of guns we've placed for this precise moment.

Oh God, she moans into our bond. *What happened? Are they hurting him?*

"What's going on, Ash?" Pen demands, grabbing guns and knives and arming herself to the teeth. We can't go in without our pack for backup, but they'll be here in twenty minutes, some of them even faster.

Ash speaks as I translate, "Cass's running toward us with a small group, but ATVs are following them. They won't make it." He looks at me as I look at Pen. "Don't even think about it. We won't make it either if we try to help them right now."

"Bullshit," Pen snarls. "They don't have anybody who can shift. I'll swoop in and grab whoever I can. They're only a mile from us!"

Julia surprises me when she grabs Pen's arm. "We have to give this the best chance for success, and if you get caught, it's another person we have to rescue. They'll know we're coming if you go now."

Asher hisses in a breath, clutching at his chest. "If they're listening, they'll hear us anyhow. Shit, he's caught. They're being dragged back to the neighborhood. Fuck!"

He picks up the phone and yells into it, "Alpha, faster! You don't have much time!"

My bond with Jules hums with urgency. We're desperate to do something, anything to save Cassian.

Seventeen fucking minutes pass, during which Asher gives us the play-by-play as Declan and his fucking crew drag Cassian back. Gabriel gives a horrific speech about Cassian's infiltration, and they beat someone, another alpha.

When Asher hears our people coming, he roars at us to get in the truck. We do, taking off at breakneck speed up the offramp. Behind us, more than a dozen trucks fly up the ramp —our pack, some of Mitchell Bancroft's and the northern alphas too. Mahikan veers off into the woods as the rest of us head straight for the front of the neighborhood like we planned.

"God, I hope this doesn't turn into an all-out war," I pray aloud, my hand on Julia's thigh as she taps her foot anxiously.

Pen grins from the front seat. "I, for one, am ready to rip Declan's head from his shoulders if the opportunity presents itself."

"Faster," Asher growls. "They're doing something to him!"

Julia screams in our bond, shoving a fist in her mouth as she struggles not to lose it.

Ash speaks up, his voice grim but steady, "They're ready for a fight, but remember the plan. We avoid an actual brawl at all costs."

To be honest, I had no doubt it would come to this. It was foolish to think Cass could escape with the omegas. It was always going to be a fight. The downside is now they've got Cass, and they'll hurt him—or worse.

We fill the end of Declan's street with trucks and hop out. The asshole himself stands in front of his home in the cul de sac with all of his leadership and fifty alphas beside them. Behind him, in his front yard, stands a giant wooden cross. Cassian's strapped to it, both arms lashed to the crossbeam. There's a pile of wood all the way to his feet, a small flame already smoldering underneath him.

He's bleeding profusely from cuts all over his face and torso. I can't see the omegas, but I hear soft crying and the pained grunt of another alpha. And blood. So much blood.

Parking the trucks and grabbing guns, we exit until our pack and half of Mitchell's stands in a protective line, facing off with Declan's group. We don't have the numbers advantage, and I'm horrified to see Declan's group is even larger than we estimated based on activity from the mill site.

Declan looks around at his pack and grins. "It's like I told yeh, brothers. They were gatherin' an army just as we were. This is our foe, gentlemen, standin' right in front of yeh. This is the pack who came to take from us. Not only that, but they've brought the fight to us, right to our very home."

Rousing shouts bolster Declan as I grip my rifle, ready to haul Jules behind me if bullets start flying. Gabriel steps forward, arms wide as a maniacal grin lights his face up. Julia growls from her spot next to me.

"You sent an alpha to infiltrate our home, to take women from us, women who don't want to leave," Gabriel shouts. "You cannot have what is ours. We will fight if we have to!" It's an odd speech from him, given everything that's happened between our packs. Discomfort eats at the edges of my consciousness. Something about this isn't right.

Asher looks up into the sky, squinting as if he's focusing on something.

Stone steps forward, fists balled. "We're here for Cassian and the omegas, and anyone else who wants to get out of your pack."

"Yeh want to take the women, do yeh?" Declan roars. There are murmurs from the crowd, as if it's exactly what they were expecting.

Julia steps forward, signing with confidence as I translate for her, my voice carrying across the distance between our packs. "Before you fight over the lives of six women who don't want to be here, you should know what sort of alpha you're following. I'm sure he's promised you everything you could ever want if you just let him lead, but at the end of the day, he cares about no one but himself."

Good job, baby girl, I praise her in our bond. *Keep him focused on you.*

Declan grins at Julia with an evil look in his eye, balling his fists as the smile grows wider. "Yeh're that little bitch I hit with my truck, then. The one who can't hear?" He looks at Jules as horror sinks in my gut, realizing what Declan's just admitted to.

Gabriel folds both hands in front of his belt as if his alpha hasn't just admitted to a hit and run that nearly killed someone. Murmurs fill the crowd, the younger, newer alphas looking at Declan in surprise.

Behind Declan on the pole, Cassian goes crazy, roaring into the cul de sac as he struggles against the chains. "I'll kill you. I'll fucking kill you!" He rages over and over as I repeat what Declan said in my bond with Julia.

My entire pack leadership simmers with rage. This fucking asshole ran her over with a truck and left her for dead. He stole her hearing and hurt her.

Stone and I grab for Jules at the same time as she darts forward. Our bond is a shredded mess of wild fury and terror.

Easy, baby girl, I urge her through the bond. I can't imagine what the fallout from today is going to look like, but I'll be there every step of the goddamn way. Jules quivers in my arms as Declan laughs. His leadership crew is on high alert, and for a moment, everything is silent.

Stone snarls at Declan, "Give us Cassian and the omegas, and we'll leave here without a fight. We don't want to hurt anyone— I'm making that clear now. But we'll fight if we have to."

Declan roars a challenge and looks around at his men. "We're not scared of a fight, are we?"

A chorus of no's and snarls reaches my ears as Griz, Mitchell's strategist, laughs from his place next to Stone. "If you're foolish enough to fight two packs with fully bonded leadership crews and omegas with powers, be our guest." He glances over his shoulder. "Samson, Pen, if you will."

We're counting on surprising most of the new men with the power of our shifts and omegas, knowing Declan has been trying to achieve this for himself.

Samson and Pen step in front of us, clothes shredding, shifting in a slip of smoke. Moments later, two enormous, predatory black birds stand where Pen and Samson were. There are murmurs of shock among Declan's pack, but he nods and turns to his men.

"And this is the beauty of a mate bond. The power that lies ahead of you. This is what I've been teaching yeh, what Gabriel's been teaching yeh. This is what lies in store for each of yeh once we find the woman meant to take you."

Griz's mate, Jude, steps forward next, rubbing Jules's arm as she passes. She stands next to her mate. "Nothing lies in store for you if you continue on like this. You can't force power; you can only accept it."

"Worked just fine for my woman when I took her," Declan

roars. Behind him, the other men join in his laughter, although it's easy to see that some are uneasy about what he shared and what they're seeing now. Declan's eyes narrow when he realizes that Hale hasn't stepped forward next to him. She's nowhere to be seen, and with a flick of his eyes, he sends one of his crew off somewhere.

"This is growing tiresome," Declan rumbles, the force of a pack alpha's anger hitting me. Unlike Cass, it's a painful need to roll over and show him my stomach, despite everything he's done. It's a good reminder of the innate strength in a male like Declan, even though he's a total asshole.

Declan lifts a revolver he's holding in one hand, looking at us with an evil grin. He turns and points it straight at Cass, and time slows as I watch him depress the trigger. Declan's enforcer, JB, throws himself against his pack alpha, knocking his aim wide.

The rest of his leadership crew throw themselves on JB, but at the same time, a huge bird darts out of the sky, one of Mahikan's, landing on top of the pile. Declan's seer screams out a warning as the gunshot reverberates off the pavement below our feet.

Behind Declan, the rest of the alphas sprint toward the pile, but the bird pushes off the pavement with a wolf in its claws, taking off up into the sky. There's a momentary pause as he swoops up over the neighborhood, and everybody realizes Declan was the one who got snatched.

Gabriel throws a hand up as the alphas advance behind him, guns trained on our group. But we're ready for this fucking fight. We just needed them to focus on us for a moment.

Declan's wolf snarls and snaps as the bird lands on our side, the wolf under his enormous foot. The predatory bird looks over at Stone and nods once.

Gabriel gives us an evil smile.

"A distraction," he murmurs, not bothering to look at the

fallen pack alpha. "What will it take for you to leave our home without further violence?"

"Cassian and the omegas," Stone snaps. "Right the fuck now."

"And my alpha?" Gabriel questions, pointing to where Declan's wolf still struggles under the foot of the giant bird. "If we do not agree, what will you do to him? Hurt him? Perhaps kill him?"

"I'll send him your way as soon as I've got my people," Stone returns. "All six omegas and Cassian. I won't ask again, Gabriel."

Behind the group, the flames are licking up the pole Cassian is strapped to. They've reached his feet as he bellows and struggles against the bindings. We don't have much time. Rogue is a livewire of anxiety next to me.

Gabriel folds his hands over his waist and pauses, giving us a long, curious look before he turns to the pack's leadership. "Mark, please cut Cassian down."

Mark sputters indignantly, his hand around the back of JB's neck. JB is cut and bloodied, and the whole pack is silent as he drops his hold on JB and stalks through the omegas, whom I now see are handcuffed together in a group behind most of the alphas. We just couldn't see them before.

Hope wars with a terrible sense of impending doom, and my bond with Julia is fraught with terror as she watches Mark slice at the ropes binding Cass. We watch Cass fall unceremoniously to the ground in a heap, and it's quickly apparent that he won't walk out of here on his own two feet.

"Ash," I bark at our seer. "Help me."

Jules joins us as we trot wide around Gabriel, reaching for Cassian who's snarling softly through the pain he must be in. He opens his arms for Jules, who flings herself into them.

"Not the time," Asher barks, hauling Jules up out of Cass's arms and pulling the big alpha up. I sling one arm around his waist as he slumps into me.

"Get that alpha," Cass mumbles, jerking his head to a

bloodied body lying on the ground next to his cross. "Helped me." That's all he says before his head falls forward, his teeth grinding.

I watch Samson take off in the air to join us, picking up the body and returning to our group.

We make it past them, terror eating at me the whole way. There was a part of me, a large part, that worried Gabriel would decide Declan's life wasn't worth it, and they'd fight us anyway.

The bird lets his foot up, and Declan's wolf slides out from underneath him. He turns and snarls, and the bird snaps his beak at Declan's eye.

Almost there. We're almost to the line of my packmates and the waiting cars. Power roils under my skin, desperate to help Cassian.

"Hold on, mate," I whisper, knowing he can hear the low tone.

The whole street is silent as Asher, Julia and I drag Cassian back. The omegas huddle together in front of us, moving with purpose toward our waiting trucks. Rogue stands protectively, ready to leap into action for Cass.

Declan passes us with a snap of his teeth, returning toward his pack as we face off.

I hold in a sigh of relief when we're nearly to the trucks.

That's when I hear the cocking of a gun.

CHAPTER FORTY-FOUR

julia

I FEEL James tense in our bond, and that's how I realize something's happening. Even though he and Asher are carrying Cass behind me, I whip around to figure out what's going on. A desperate need to scream in terror claws up my throat. James throws his body in front of me as the reverberation from a gunshot tickles the bottoms of my feet. It's tangible across my skin as time slows, my lashes fluttering as I watch smoke exit the barrel of Declan's gun.

There's a victorious look on the alpha's face as the bullet hits his enforcer, JB, in the chest, exiting out the back. Blood spurts from JB's mouth as my alphas form a tight, protective barrier in front of me. All our guns are trained on Declan and the confused circle of alphas behind him.

Rogue rips the truck door open, not pulling his eyes from Cass's bloody figure.

Asher manhandles Cass into the car as I look around James to watch JB sink to his knees. His eyes flick to Stone, and then he falls forward into the street, dead. A woman runs from somewhere, throwing herself across his prone figure as she visibly sobs, shaking the dead male.

Even though he was an asshole, he helped us at the very end. My heart aches for the woman as she points at Declan and appears to shout. I turn because I can't watch, all my focus moving to Cass and James.

I watch my pack shuttle the rescued omegas and the bloody alpha into two trucks as I climb in beside Cass. Dropping to the floorboard, I run my hands over his bloody midsection. James climbs in next to me.

We're not out of the woods yet. This could go south the moment we turn to leave, but all I can focus on is my big, strong mate. His shirt is ripped to shreds, his skin a bloody mess for the second time in less than a month. The bottoms of his feet are a charred, burnt mess of blackened skin.

I look up, my eyes meeting James's. If I had the power to tear Declan limb from limb, I'd do it. But first my mate needs safety and healing, and the omegas need to be taken care of. It's what Cass would want us to do.

Then one big arm slides toward me, and Cass pulls me up on top of himself even as he grunts in pain. I don't want to hurt him, but I don't want to move and make it worse. So I nuzzle into his neck as he lets out a sigh of relief, stroking the back of my head gently. I pepper his neck, chin and cheek with kisses.

I'm going to try to help him, James murmurs into our bond.

Cass stiffens and moans as my bond with James fills with power. He hasn't had time to learn how to be a healer yet, so all I can hope is that it feels natural and obvious to him.

The truck is tense as Asher climbs in the front and drives away. I peek up out of the back window to see a line of the dark birds, standing guard as we pull away. Mahikan came through.

Beyond them, Gabriel and Declan stand shoulder to shoulder. Declan is clearly fuming, fists balled as he watches us. But Gabriel has a soft smile on his face that sends fear straight to my core. Something isn't right about this whole thing, but I don't know what, and I can't think about that now.

When we get home, I need to see to the security immediately, James whispers into our bond, pulling me out of the fear. *I'll heal what I can now.*

It's almost like Asher can hear what we're saying. He taps on my shoulder from the front seat and signs, "You both take care of Cass. When we get home, I'll handle security with Mahikan and his people. Mitchell's pack is staying on-site for a few days too. It's going to be just fine."

The twenty-minute ride home feels like forever as Cass clings tight to me, his lips buried in the hollow of my throat as he breathes rapidly. Every now and again he moans as if in pain, but I hold him tighter, willing him to know we're here. I'll never allow anyone to hurt him again.

When we pull onto Bent Fork land finally, relief floods my bond with James. The truck is quiet as we finally pull to a stop in front of the lodge. I gently press up off Cass's chest. James helps shift him upright, and I hop out of the truck as Cass gingerly slides out after me. Pale eyes find mine, so full of relief as I press myself to his chest and hug him again.

Still, I sense his worry for his girls, even now.

Brady and Connor, Mitchell's healer and spirit, jog over to us. Brady sighs. "I'm stitching you up more than I'd like, alpha. Let's get you taken care of."

"The omegas," Cass signs gruffly, gesturing to the trucks with the girls as they exit.

"We're fine," one of them signs back before looking at me with a shy smile. "I taught him ASL; I'm Cara."

Grinning, I thank her as I approach. "Cass would want me to help you get settled. We've been worried sick about all of you."

She smiles back and shares with the other omegas. Just then, Sal and Isabel come flying down the steps, throwing their arms around the girls. I break through just long enough to take Abigail from Isabel, and the girls are crying and hugging as they reunite.

After a tender minute, they turn to Cass, and it all starts over again. The omegas crowd around him, and while I can't hear what they're saying, it's clear they're thankful and shell-shocked and overwhelmed.

Someone hugs him, and I watch his lips fall open in pain. The omegas press backward, and I gesture them up the steps. There's a sudden flurry of activity around us as James and Asher haul Cass up the stairs. Stone, Mahikan and Leon are talking at the top with Griz, Mitchell Bancroft's strategist. A dozen alphas stand guard, watching in every direction for a follow-up attack from Declan.

I know James and leadership prepared for all of this ahead of time, but I'm still grateful to see my pack alpha. Titan shows up to my right, one arm slung around the waist of the alpha Cass demanded we bring. He glances up, and I can see he's younger than us by a bit, maybe a little older than the twins. My heart breaks for what he went through today, and in the near future, I suspect I'll owe him some thanks for helping Cass.

When we get there, Stone speaks and signs to the omegas, "You're safe and welcome here. We'll get you settled, but for anybody who wants a tour, any alpha here can give you that. You're free to come and go, and anything in the house is yours."

"Except the ramen!" River shouts. "He gets touchy about those!"

Stone gives her a heated look, but she bumps his hip with hers before leaning in for a hug. River's eyes flick down to the young alpha next to me, and there's a hint of confusion.

He looks up the stairs, his dark eyes falling on River before he looks at Stone. "I'm Cam. I met Cass, and..." He seems to lose his train of thought as River lets out a gasp.

"What did you say your name was?" There's a shocked expression on her face before she steps forward.

"Cam?" he says it again like he's not sure how she misunderstood.

River pales, wrapping her arms around herself as she takes a step back. "It can't be. You're here. You're... What is happening right now?"

Cam looks at her like she's got ten heads, and I'm just about to question her myself when Samson steps forward, back in human form and fully clothed. "River, shall we chat about this?"

She shuts her mouth and looks over at him with a nod, following him to the opposite end of the porch.

Cam scoffs and looks up at Stone. "That was weird. I've never met her."

Stone gives Cam a soft smile. "Doesn't mean she's never met you, brother."

Cam's eyes widen, and he looks over at Cass before glancing back to Stone. He says nothing else as we're ushered inside.

I'm getting to the bottom of that as soon as I get these girls settled and Cass taken care of. Leading the omegas inside, I point out the dining hall and kitchen. Knowing this was coming, we've got water and snacks on hand. Pen and Cherry are already there, ready to check anyone who needs medical help that's not serious enough for Brady's attention.

The omegas let us get them through that gauntlet, and then I lead them upstairs, heading to the right, the empty end of the hallway. "This whole end is free. You can pick rooms, and they're yours until you decide you want something else."

Cara translates for me before reaching in and pulling me in for a big hug. When we part, there are tears in her eyes. "I know Cass is yours, so we have to thank you for letting him come for us. If we didn't know he would never leave us there, we couldn't have possibly held out hope. He's the best alpha in the entire world."

I nod, tears springing to my eyes when I think about how dedicated he's been to getting them out. Smiling, I lift my hands. "You'll find all the alphas here are fucking amazing. There are three packs here right now, and there's not a single bad apple among them. Please, feel free to come and go as you wish."

I help the girls find rooms, reminding them they don't have to share here. Eventually, they're settled in. Some opt to go downstairs and check in, and a few need peace and quiet. Once I know they're feeling alright, I turn for my room and my mates.

Opening the door, I'm greeted by the sight of Brady and Connor hovering over a half-naked Cassian, James by his side in the bed with his computer open. I know he's poring over our security system, worried Declan will come for retribution.

"I think we're safe for a bit," I reassure him as I join them on the bed. Cass looks over and sighs, reaching for my hand so he can pull me into his arms.

Connor grins at me. "So…a threesome situation, huh?"

Cass answers first. "I wish," he growls. His gray eyes fall on me as I wrap an arm across his broad chest.

Connor cocks his head to the side. "I thought I heard Mahikan could work to switch that."

"Didn't work, but it doesn't matter," I remind him. "We belong to one another, and that's all that I care about."

"The bite didn't work," Cass reminds me. His voice is so low, so sad. He's still heartbroken over it.

"But I got powers while you were gone," James presses. Connor and Brady are silent as they watch us have this conversation.

Cass's eyes spring wide open as he pulls James on top of his chest. I slide to the side, watching as Cass grips James's throat. "It was you who healed me in the car? I was in so much pain, I was half out of it."

James gives Cass an apologetic look. "Tried to, but I still don't have total con—"

Cass silences James's words with a quick press of his lips. My core heats even as I sense Brady and Connor leave the room. The love between my men is so tangible, I could almost reach out and wrap my hand around it. I want to hold it close to my chest and infuse it with a little bit of me too.

"You'll be better in a day or two," James continues when Cass parts from him.

"As long as the omegas are safe, I'm good," Cass signs. "I've got everything I need right here."

"They're settled into their rooms," I offer. "Some wanted to rest, and some are downstairs. I know they don't feel totally relaxed because of how everything went down, but I'm sure you want to check in with them yourself."

Cass nods and sits up with James's help. "I need to see them for myself, make sure they know I'm here. And then I want you two and our cabin and some privacy. I need to hear more about this power."

I ask what I've been wondering since James mentioned his power. "You don't feel anything? No seer power? No bond?"

Cass's eyes come to mine, and he shakes his head morosely. "No," he growls, "but it's not going to stop me from having you until the day someone shows up and fits you better."

"Never happening." James laughs. "Maybe I'll develop the other power and get lucky enough to have both."

Cass chuckles at that but reaches for James so he can shift up off the mattress. James slings his arm around Cass's waist and helps him to the door. When we get there, two of the rescued omegas stand there, about to knock on the door.

A minute later, Cass is surrounded by all six of the girls. James leans up against the wall, pulling me into his arms as we watch our mate check in with each girl. There are so many hugs, so many tears, but eventually they're cried out.

After a few minutes of tearful, joyous reunion, Sal and Isabel join us. Cara, the one who taught Cass ASL, gives the other girls a meaningful look.

"Let's give Cass some privacy, alright?" she signs as she talks to the girls, and I'm so thankful for her. I can't wait to get to know each of these women. I'm sure I'll love them if Cass does. Sal takes Abigail, and Isabel herds the girls up the hallway, and then I'm alone with James and Cass.

Gray eyes find mine as my big alpha reaches for us. "Come, mates," he purrs. We follow him down the front steps and to a waiting ATV.

Ten minutes later, we arrive at Cass's cabin. Stone's already made a fuss because we're close to the street, but there's so much security on property at this point, I'm not worried about it.

We pulled off a miracle today, and all I want to do now is enjoy it.

CHAPTER FORTY-FIVE

cassian

I SHOULD BE TIRED. I should be impossibly exhausted. And I suppose there's a part of me that is. But my girls are safe and integrating. They've got everything they need right now.

Being tied to that goddamn cross, watching Declan terrorize everyone I love. It cemented what I know in my heart. Despite the lack of a bond between James, Julia and me—they're mine. I can't give them claiming bites because we know that didn't work. But they're mine in every other way, and that's enough for me.

Julia opens the door to my cabin as James helps me in. It's only then I hear the ATV that followed us. I'm not ready for more visitors today, so I turn and snarl. I'm surprised to see Cherry and Asher arrive and park in front of the cabin.

Ash smiles at me as he helps his mate off the ATV. For once, they're both smiling.

"I want to try to help you with your bond." His words are simple, but I sag against the doorway when he says them. My goddamn feet are killing me, despite the healing from both Brady and my mate.

My mate. I love calling James that in my mind.

Shaking my head, I look at Julia and stroke the side of her neck. It's still red from my bite. "It hurt her, Ash; it's not worth trying again."

Ash hesitates, but Cherry nudges his side. "Tell them."

James stands calmly next to me as Asher comes closer, running both hands through his hair. "I don't know why my power seems to have stabilized slightly, or why I can channel Declan's omega's power but not Alice's. I don't have a lot of answers. But I have the sense that I should try to help you. I don't fucking know if it will work, but I watched Ven when we went to Mahikan's. What's the worst that can happen?"

"You could kill me," I bark. "It almost happened before."

James reaches out and puts a hand on my forearm. "I trust Asher with your life, alpha. What if it works?" Next to James, Julia grins at me, waggling her brows. I can almost imagine that she's teasing me with how much sexy shit we could share in the bond.

Glancing over my mate's heads, I nod at Ash. "You wanna do this now?"

"No time like the present," Cherry chirps before looking up at Ash. "You need anything from me?"

He smiles and reaches out to stroke her cheek. "Just be with me while I do it?"

"You've got it." She grins, rubbing Asher's lower back as he gestures to my dining room table.

I don't know what happened between them. But right now, they seem to be on the same page.

Asher gestures us inside. "Sit there, alpha. James, Julia, sit next to him and touch him. Hold hands, just something that connects you all physically."

I flop down into the chair, wincing at how tender my ribs are. Pulling Jules into my lap, I drag a chair right next to me, putting my hand on James's upper thigh as he lays his arm over the back of my chair. Perfect. It's perfect having them both like this. Looking over Jules's strawberry blond hair, I smile at James. He is worth this, whatever pain it is. They're both worth it.

Resting my chin on top of Jules's head, I soak in her comforting scent. She's like a delicious fucking dessert perched in my lap, and I want everybody to leave so James and I can taste her. There's nothing like dying to make you want to lose yourself in your mates one last time.

I feel a presence behind me, and Ash's hand comes to the back of my neck, gripping it hard. There's an immediate pinch as warmth spreads through my body, traveling through my core until it tingles all the way to the ends of my fingertips.

"Should I be doing something?" I growl out as the hair on my arms rises.

"Be silent," Ash commands. Normally I'd snap at him for commanding a pack alpha, but there's a whispering in my mind, someone trying to tell me something.

Closing my eyes, I focus on chasing that voice, and I recognize it finally as Ash. But he's not speaking to me, not to my consciousness. He's whispering in low tones as the heat in my body intensifies. I begin to squirm in the chair as it becomes uncomfortable, a low whine leaving my throat when I remember how much pain this previously caused me.

But this is Ash, and he's asking me to trust him. I do, and I push that pack alpha sense of knowing back at him, that sense that if my life is in his hands, I know he'll be a good guardian of it.

There's a rush of searing heat as I let out a bellow and Ash removes his hand from my neck. "Okay," he laughs, "all done."

"All done?" I turn in my seat and look at him. "Where's the agony? Where's the—"

Oh God, I hope this worked, I hear in a throaty, seductive voice.

Don't worry, mate, James chuckles.

My eyes meet his gaze as I reach out and place a hand on his chest, my own heaving as I look back toward Jules.

Say something, I command her, wondering if she can hear it.

She gasps aloud, both hands coming to my face as she leans in close. *You can hear me?* Her voice is full of wonder and disbelief as she scans my face, a big grin finally splitting her cheeks.

I hear you, I murmur. *I hear you both.*

I look from Jules to James as he leans in and kisses my lips tenderly.

Fucking finally, he groans into a bond that now gleams bright and golden between us. I can see it so clearly, so beautifully. As if it were there all along and just not activated.

We look over at Asher in wonder. He wears a pleased expression as he grabs Cherry's hand and heads for the front door. "Don't ask me how I knew it would work, because, unfortunately, I don't know. I'm just glad it did. I'll let everybody know to give you space. Come up to the lodge to celebrate when you're...done."

Cherry slaps him on the chest with a giggle, and then they turn to go.

How'd he do that? James questions, pulling Julia out of my lap and up onto the edge of the table. He straddles me in my chair, bringing his lips to mine for a tender, teasing kiss. *How the fuck did he do that?*

Julia wraps both her arms around James's waist and gives me a waggle of her pale brows. *I don't know how, but if that worked, I want to try the bite again.*

Your voice, I murmur into the bond, still signing out of habit. *Your voice is different than I imagined.*

Did you think I'd sound like a man? she deadpans as I laugh and stand with James still wrapped around me.

Come. I tug at her through the bond as I capture James's lips in a hungry kiss. I toss him into the bed, wincing when a pang shoots through my ribs. Even so, I grab Julia next and pull her sweater over her thin shoulders. I shred the bra and push her down into James's arms.

I'm still covered in blood and sweat, but I can't be bothered to change a thing right now. I'm so desperate to touch them, I feel like I'll combust. I'm overwhelmed by the strength of the bond between us. A bond that's not firmly cemented just yet.

James reaches around to play with Julia's pretty pink nipples as I slide her jeans off. His pants come off next as he lifts his hips to help me. Julia turns, presenting me with a mouthwatering view of her naked ass. She rips James's shirt open and starts kissing her way down his chest, waggling her ass at me.

See something you like, alpha? She teases me as she swirls her pink tongue around his dark nipple.

Groaning, I pull my shirt off and slide my jeans down. I lean forward and grab her ass, licking and nipping my way up the back of one pretty thigh before biting the back of it. Julia shudders and sits upright, her back to my chest as I bite my way along her neck and shoulder, reaching down between us to play with James's cock.

He grunts as he props himself up on his elbows. *I could watch you two all day,* he purrs into the bond.

You want to watch us? I tease as he bites his lip and nods.

I like it when you unleash on her. I want to see you claim her. And then I want you to take me and do it again.

Heat floods my system as I look for her in the bond. *Do you want that again? Even though last time was so—*

"Of course," Julia signs with an angry scowl.

Grinning, I flop onto the pillows and pull her on top of me, lining her hips up with my cock. It strains between her thighs as she reaches down and runs both hands along my length. I growl into the bond, *Harder, mate.*

Julia shudders and grips me hard with both hands, pumping as slick coats my cock and drips down my balls.

Pulling her forward, I bring her arms over my head as I kiss her. It's raw and hungry, my teeth clashing against hers as I devour her. I thought I lost them both today, and my emotions and need for control are taking over. Combined with the sudden maelstrom of feeling and sensation in our three-way bond, and I'm ready to possess them completely.

I wrap her gorgeous hair around my fist and hold her tight as I rock my hips against her, coating myself in the honey that drips between her thighs. Julia's blue eyes fly open as she watches me devour her, before I slide down and pull her on top of my face.

A desperate groan leaves my throat when James wraps his soft lips around my cock, sucking on me like a lollipop as I bury my tongue deep inside our omega. She throws her head back with a cry, rocking thin hips to search for more friction. Gripping her hips tight, I eat her hard and rough until she comes all over my face, flooding my lips and neck with her sweet honey. I nip and kiss her clit as she comes down, James still working me deep into his throat.

With a growl I sit up and bark at him. He rocks back onto his heels and catches her when I push her back.

I'm on her fast, shoving her thighs wide as I slide home, deep inside the omega I'm keeping for the rest of my days. There's nothing to hold me back, nothing to make me worry about someone else suiting them better. It's just them and me for the rest of our lives.

Jules screams and clenches around me, shouting curse after curse into our bond as I fuck her hard and fast.

You didn't want gentle, did you, little one? I growl, relishing this newfound way to tease her.

Never, she taunts, thrusting her hips hard against mine as I turn her onto her side, watching James guide his cock into her mouth. She whines in our bond as I slide her leg upward and slip back into her at a punishing pace.

She comes again around my cock, screaming as James gasps

at the pleasure in our bond. When she's practically boneless, I rock back onto my heels and pull her up into my arms, onto my cock again. And I start all over, biting, kissing, nipping. Time loses all meaning as James presses his chest to her back.

Jules's head falls backward, lolling against his chest as I take her hard and fast. And when she's about to come for the third goddamn time, I surge forward, licking my way up her neck. I sink my teeth in deep, and where before she tensed in pain, this time I feel her body tighten and explode. Orgasm overtakes us both as I roar into the bite, our golden bond snapping in place and locking as I send all my love into the claiming.

Ecstasy rolls over us in beautiful waves until I'm so lost, I can barely breathe. There is only her and James, and our bond isn't complete until I have him. Jules groans as I gently turn and lay her on her back. I kiss my way down her soft belly, down her thighs, and then I growl at James.

He grins and crawls on top of her, sliding her thighs out so he can settle himself between them.

Tease her with that fat cock, I command as he groans and rolls his hips rhythmically. His dick slips along her clit as Jules hisses and grips the sheets.

I'm going to fuck you while you tease her, and then I'm making you mine, I snarl, gripping his hips as I slide two fingers into his ass. He's coated with Jules's sweet honey already, and he whines as I take him roughly. I should prepare him longer, tease him more, but our shiny new bond is tight with desperation.

There will be time later for making love to my mates. Right now, they need a good, hard fucking.

Grabbing James's hip with one hand, I guide the tip of my cock between his ass cheeks with the other. I marvel at how obscenely sensual it is watching myself disappear inside him. He's so fucking tight, so hot as he groans and snarls at Jules, teasing her with the tip of his thick length.

"Fuuuuck," he exhales as I slip inside him with a snap of my hips. I relish the way his back muscles bunch up as he rolls his shoulders, cocking his head to the side.

So needy for my bite, hmm? I stroke him in the bond as I slide out of his ass and back in with a hard thrust, watching the tortured look on Jules's face as he teases her. *Fuck her,* I command as I reach around front, guiding him to her sweet pussy. Our mate screams as I pound into him, directing him inside her with the force of my thrusts.

"Hold still," I snarl as I reach for his hip and shoulder as leverage. I hunch over him and let my mind go wild, my body utterly focused on the way he clenches around me and how hot it makes her to experience us like this. He's caught between us, and every punch of my hips drives him deeper inside our needy little omega.

Jules tugs on our bond, sending pleasure soaring through my body as I throw my head back and gasp.

I never knew, I groan into that tether. It's so tight, so strong, a permanent connection from her spirit to mine. *I never knew it would be like this.*

I did, she reminds me. *I always knew, and I never doubted.*

There will never be enough words for me to say in apology. They always knew, and they never doubted us, even when I did.

I cry out as the pleasure builds, reaching out to pull James up into my arms, gripping his throat in one hand. With the other, I yank on his cock as Jules sits up and crawls to him on all fours, taking him into her mouth.

Desperate pleas for release fall from James's lips like a prayer as we take him together, building and pushing that pleasure. I'm out of my mind, somewhere between ecstasy and obliteration when orgasm hits him. He bellows into the cabin as I work his cock, release coating Jules's face as he spurts all over her.

I'm right there on the edge, ready to fall with him as he screams. Rubbing my jaw along his shoulder, I groan as I find the perfect spot. Opening my jaws wide, I sink my fangs into the side of his neck, biting hard.

All my intention and love pours into that bite as James shatters around me, orgasm prolonged as that tether between us explodes and reforms stronger, deeper. I'm aware of him on every possible level—his hopes, his emotions, his need, his endless love for Jules and me. He wraps his hands in her hair and fists it, holding her captive as she sucks on him loudly.

I slow my frantic pace, my cock slipping easily in, watching with pride as my cum leaks out, coating us both.

Need you again. Right now, I command into our bond, relishing the way Jules chuckles and James groans. She sits back on her heels, absolutely covered in his cum, and grins at me.

James pulls her into his arms and strokes her hair as I continue to fuck him slowly, until delicious heat builds again.

I can't wait for the shower, I admit into our bond. *I need you at least once more.*

James growls and elbows me in the ribs. *She's covered in my seed, alpha. Let's wash her first.*

Jules gives me a devious grin and scoots to the side, gesturing for James to lie down. He sighs, but she straddles him and seats herself on his cock before looking over her shoulder at me.

An invitation.

Chuckling, I bring my chest to her back, groaning at how good she feels against me. Bringing my hands around front, I sign, "I love you both so goddamn much. I thought I lost you today."

"Never," Jules responds as James grins up at us.

Never, I agree into the bond as I part James's thighs and slide back into his ass.

I take them over and over until an odd sensation hits me, and I fall to the ground with a thud.

CHAPTER FORTY-SIX

OH FUCK, the shift. With all the fucking pleasure of the last two hours, I forgot Cass and I would shift after he claimed us. The fact that I never shifted after I claimed Jules was my proof I was our healer or spirit. I'll be curious to see if Cass gets spirit powers after what Asher did to us. Not that it matters to me if he doesn't. Our pack is forging a new path, doing things in the way that suits us best, not the way biology dictates. Who knows what else might be different?

Cass falls off the bed with a pained grunt as I look at Jules and grip her chin, kissing her gently. "We'll be fine, my love. Just sit with us?"

Her eyes are wide, but she grits her jaw and hops off the bed, running to the bathroom for a pile of towels. Pain stabs my core as I cry out and slip off the bed next to Cass. His eyes are squeezed tightly shut as he curls in on himself. I'm only moments behind him, so I grab under his shoulders and pull him between my legs, his back to my chest. Wrapping my arms around him, I bury my face in his neck and tell him how in love I am, how in awe I am of who he is and who we are together.

But then the ability to even think escapes me as daggers stab me from the inside out. My eyes roll back into my head, and the only thing I have any awareness of is Jules's comforting presence by our side and in our bond.

I don't know how much time passes before I hear the soft pad of feet in my mind. A cold nose touches mine, and when I look up, a gigantic white wolf stands in front of me. He has Cassian's icy gray eyes, filled with a hint of humor as he looks at me. Realization slowly returns, and I pull to a stand, realizing I'm in wolf form somewhere in the depths of my mind.

Cass turns and lopes off into the darkness, and I follow.

Moments later, I'm aware of his wolf in the shadow of our cabin. Jules already stands in front of him, stroking her way down his forehead as he leans into her gentle touch.

I stand on shaky legs and stretch this new form, reveling in the dark charcoal of my fur. Butting Jules with my nose, I whine for attention as she turns, eyes going wide at the sight of me.

"Beautiful," she signs. "My perfect mate."

Cass joins us, rubbing his cheek along mine as I look for the bond and find it stronger than ever.

Let's run, Cass urges us. *A quick run, and then I want to celebrate you both with our pack. I want to check on my girls.*

Jules claps her hands and grabs her clothes, throwing them on before she finds her coat and hat.

Me first! I laugh into the bond as Cass and I shove each other to get at her first.

No fighting, Jules chuckles, reaching out to stroke us both, *but I'm definitely riding James first. He didn't give me near as hard of a time about being mated as you did.*

Cass whines and snarls as I give him a victorious look. He pushes past us both and shifts long enough to grab the door and sail through it. As soon as he exits the cabin, he's back in wolf form. I marvel at how quick it was the second time.

"Oh!" Jules signs and runs to the bedroom, returning with a small backpack as she stuffs clothes into it. *Can't have you two hanging out naked at dinner. I'll have to beat the omegas off with a stick, and as scrappy as I am, I don't want to fight.*

I laugh inwardly at the vision of her fighting for us, because I have zero doubt she would. She's gentle and fucking trusts everybody, but she's fierce as hell and the most confident person I know.

Lowering myself to my belly, I wait patiently for her to clamber up onto my back, gripping my fur tight. She shifts forward and wraps her arms around my neck, and then I follow Cass out into the bleak chill of the wintry night.

He takes off without waiting, and we follow. We run from the front of the valley to the back, and when we get there, Cass returns to his human form with a smile.

He points to the valley floor below us. "Stone thinks this might be a good spot for a second lodge, if we decide we need a separate space."

Julia scrunches her nose immediately as I laugh.

I love that we're all together, she sighs into the bond. *I don't want to be away from everyone.*

That settles that. Cass laughs. *Let's get back, I need to check in with Rogue and the rest of our pack.*

Our pack. Damn that sounds good, and it feels so right. Our pack has two alphas, and I'm happy as hell about it.

Smiling, I shift again as Jules climbs up onto Cass's back. I don't know what the future holds, or what might change now that Cass is bonded to us, but I can't wait to find out.

Half an hour later, we're back at the lodge. We shift and change on the front porch, and when we enter the lobby, a rousing cheer goes up from everybody there.

Dinner is just about to start, and when we enter the dining hall, Rogue, Stone and Erin come over immediately, wrapping us in hugs.

"Fucking finally," Stone growls, shaking Cass's hand and then mine. He pulls Jules in for a big hug, signing when he puts her down. "Knew you'd set him straight. Good job, little one."

My gorgeous mate winks at him and tucks her hair over one shoulder. Cass can't resist her; I feel it in the bond. He leans over her back and kisses where he claimed her. His bite is right next to mine, just like it should be. I grin when I look at them.

Rogue shakes Cass's big hand, and Cass pulls the teen in for a hug. They head off into a corner of the room, and I know he needs a minute with his strategist to sort out what, if anything, has changed for them.

The rescued omegas show up with Sal and Isabel, and the pack is quick to greet them and help them find seats.

Turning into the room, I look at my found family and the packs that showed up to help us. We're headed for all-out war with Declan; that much is clear. But right now? Right now all I feel is kinship and love.

And that love is worth every moment of heartbreak we've endured.

CHAPTER FORTY-SEVEN

cassian

ROGUE FOLLOWS me into the corner with a grin, big arms crossed as he leans into the wall. "So, it all worked out in the end?"

I grin at my strategist. *Thank you for being there for me today.*

You are my priority, he reminds me through our bond. Then aloud, "We're doing something new here, Cass. This pack? This merge of multiples? It feels right to me. What about you, now that you're fully mated?" Bright eyes come to mine as his grin grows wider. He doesn't really need to ask the question, not when he senses my emotion as easily as his own.

I'm fully mated. It's everything I ever hoped for and wanted, and everything I didn't think I could have.

"I think I need to talk to Stone, but I don't want to leave. I don't want a different house. I want to watch our family grow right here."

"Me too," Rogue agrees, looking around the room. I watch his eyes fall on Sal, and then Cam, who's playfully needling a flustered River about something on her plate. They move to the researchers, who've joined the room even though they still don't look entirely at home here.

My vision blurs for a moment, heat filling my chest as I reach out and put one hand on the wall.

You okay, alpha? Rogue questions me but doesn't seem all that concerned, that big smile still on his face.

When I say nothing else, my breath falling into quick pants as my vision blurs again, Rogue reaches out to clap one hand on my shoulder.

You're getting power, he murmurs into our bond. *I think. You feel like you're changing somehow.*

I slump against the wall as my mates' focus turns to me, but when I look at my strategist, there's a figure layered over his face. A wolf. The wolf is pitch black with eyes that match Rogue's. As I look at him, the wolf's eyes meet mine. He's happy, and my own wolf feels joyous in my chest. In awe, I look from Rogue to my mates and gasp at the vision I see.

When I focus on them, James's charcoal wolf looks at me, happy for my attention. But next to him, Julia's white wolf turns and yips playfully. She can't shift yet. She won't be able to until enough omegas here are mated. But goddamn, she's so *fucking* beautiful.

I share everything I'm seeing with them through our bond, and they turn to me with big, happy smiles.

How did I get this lucky? I murmur the thought into my connection with Rogue, but he claps me on the back.

"You deserve every bit of this, alpha." He leaves me to my thoughts as I stare around the room. There's so much gratitude in my heart for this motley crew. Three packs are represented here tonight, and Rogue's right—Bent Fork Pack is doing things differently than other packs have. We're forging a new path.

My eyes fall on Leandra. When I concentrate on her, I see a black wolf, but my pack alpha power reads her as unhappy. She longs for something, something she's never had and only seen others obtain. She wants a mate so badly. Her eyes are on Julia and James, but there's no real longing for them in her gaze. It's not that she'd take Jules if she could. It's what Julia represents.

I cross the room and sit down next to her, clearing my throat to pull her gaze to me.

"It'll happen for you one day, alpha," I murmur.

She shrugs, but where normally she'd fight me, it seems the wind has gone out of her sails.

"I was the most unlikely candidate," I remind her. "And it worked out in the end."

Leandra turns in her chair, shooting me a haughty look. "Like I once said, you're a lucky bastard."

Stone joins us, and even though he doesn't say it, I know he senses my power and he's following my train of thought. I can't speak to him in my mind like Rogue, but somehow, Stone and I are on the same page. It's a good feeling. Then again, he's always understood me. He's always been my partner in service of this pack.

His dark eyes flick to the researchers. "You've officially defied orders with the Research Group. What's next?"

Leandra stiffens, but I grab her hand and squeeze it. I want her to know I'm here for her and the researchers, just like Stone is.

Bianca smiles, but it's a little forced. "Well, Devraj is freaking out that we won't complete the tasks we've been assigned. But we agreed as a group we didn't feel comfortable registering your pack or anyone's powers. There's a difference between gathering anonymous data and actually tying it to you as individuals. I'm not okay with the second path. None of us are."

"They might come for you," I muse.

"We'll be ready if they do," Stone reassures the human researchers. "We'll protect all of you. You're part of our pack now, if you want to be."

Leandra's dark eyes come to mine as if she's asking the question. She's been so focused on protecting her sister and the other researchers, she hasn't bothered trying to integrate with the rest of us. I get it. I was a lone wolf like that at one time.

I give her a look I hope she reads the way I mean it. *You're ours, if you want to be.*

Bianca smiles as she picks her fork back up. "In any case, Asher has already agreed to be our guinea pig to learn more about seers. So, we're all excited to learn from him. Off the record of course. And if James can use any of our equipment to try to figure out what's going on with the research group, that's a good next step too."

My eyes move to Stone's, his gaze as focused and determined as mine is. Whatever comes next, we're tackling this as a team. He's in my corner, and I'm in his. He gives me a little nod.

Stone stands and clears his throat, and the room falls silent. He looks around at everyone, and raises his glass.

"I couldn't be more thankful for the packs in this room. You risked everything today to help us, and lives were saved as a result of that effort."

At the other end of the table, one of the rescued omegas lays her head on Cara's shoulder, their arms threaded together. Cara and Isabel both look over at me, and I swear my heart bursts at the seams with love and that innate pack alpha need to protect. My girls are here. They're safe, and I have the people in this room to thank.

Julia strokes gently at my bond with her and James. She sends immense pride and love down it as I close my eyes to bask in them.

Stone continues on. "I've always been the pack alpha here at Bent Fork. It's a role I take pride in, something I'm grateful to do alongside my beautiful mate." Erin beams up at him as she stands and wraps herself around his waist, kissing his chest. His eyes drift over to me. "But I'm not the only pack alpha here. Cassian and I are a team, and I want everyone to know that's my official stance on the topic. This is *our* pack, and together we'll protect and cherish you all for as long as we can."

I stand, overcome with emotion as Stone reaches out his hand to shake mine.

"So grateful for you, brother." His voice is clear as a bell when Sal lets out a happy whooping cheer. The other omegas follow her, and then my mates, and even Leandra joins in with a hearty clap and a soft smile.

The room shares in our combined joy as I look at Stone and know with absolute certainty—whatever Declan has planned for us, we'll tackle it together. Saving the omegas was a shit-show, but getting back into his pack was easier than it should have been. There's a long game here that we're missing. I'm just not sure yet how it can bite us in the ass.

Looking over at my mates, I smile. Whatever it is, we'll figure it out together.

I love you both so goddamn much, I growl into our bond.

"I know," Julia signs with a self-satisfied look. "I've been telling you all of this for a while, you know."

"You were right, little one," I agree, grinning at her as James watches her with unabashed adoration in his dark eyes.

Jules preens under the weight of our combined attention. They're perfect, they're mine, and I'm the luckiest motherfucker there's ever been.

CHAPTER FORTY-EIGHT

asher

I RIDE a powerful high as I watch the packs mingle and enjoy a well-deserved dinner. Cass's, James's and Julia's bond is clear and golden to me now, a far cry from the sickly green it's been since I met them. That lucky bastard is coming into his power too. Being healer and spirit makes them so important to our pack. They'll need guidance as their power grows, so it's lucky we've got two other packs on site right now who can help.

As for me? I don't know how I did what I did to their bond, but after tonight's rescue, I just knew I could do it.

It's the second time in a week that I've had any damn certainty about my power.

Risking a glance at my mate, I'm surprised to find her in the window by herself, looking out of the lodge into the distance. I grit my teeth as I realize that seeing yet another of our pack-mates happily mated is like throwing it in her face that she and I aren't, despite the happy face she put on earlier.

I can't formally mate her. Not with my mind in the state it's in.

As if on cue, a vision rises to the forefront of my awareness, and everything in the room fades. I'm strapped to a table as a man depresses a needle into a vein in my arm. The moment the drug hits, all I know is a horrible, desperate craving to fight, to fuck, to maim. I don't even want to kill; I want to drag out the pain.

And I think I do... The vision shifts to dismembered limbs and pools of blood, and I don't even know if I'm myself or seeing someone else's actions.

But then whoever I'm looking through, their eyes close, and I feel myself fall to the ground.

With a snap, I'm back in the dining room, my chest heaving as my eyes dart from side to side. Everybody's still carrying on about our newly mated family, but when I look across the room, Stone and Clay stand side by side, staring at me.

Fuck. I don't think I did or said anything, but when visions come to me, I don't know what I do during them. Sometimes I wake up fucking my pillows. Sometimes I wake up, and I'm staring out the window. Occasionally I wake up, and I've taken myself somewhere else entirely, like with the researchers.

I turn from the curious gazes of my pack alpha and strategist and look toward the window where Cherry stood. She's not there though.

My brows furrow as I scan the room.

She's gone.

Growling, I resist the urge to look for her in our bond. She asked me to shut it off months ago, and I did because I respect her wishes, but I'm about ready to turn it back on, if only to feel her fucking joy again. But I'd also feel her devastation at being pushed away.

Nobody should have to experience what I do all the time; it's not fair to her. It's my burden to bear, and with no real end in sight, I can't ask her to shoulder the burden.

Still, I can't resist being around her because she's destined for me, which sucks for her.

I follow her scent through the lobby and out the front door, where I see her back as she descends the stairs. "Cherry," I call out.

She freezes on the step and turns. The wind whips her bright red hair around her face, and she's so goddamn beautiful, I have to clench my hands tight to avoid stalking down the stairs and sweeping her off her feet.

When I say nothing, she rolls her eyes and turns, continuing down the steps without looking back.

Irritated at my own indecision, I follow her until she gets to the little truck she purchased recently. I fucking hate this truck because she bought it with money she's making at the Moonlight stripping. She doesn't know I know, but she's preparing to leave Ayas. And when she goes, she'll take my fucking heart with her.

She opens the door and hops into the truck, sighing when I lean in, one arm on the door and one on top of the cab. "Ash, I've got shit to do. Please let me close the door."

"Where are you going? You don't want to celebrate with our friends?"

She looks back at the lodge with a guilty expression, then shakes her head. "I've already congratulated them. I really don't want to stay and celebrate, and you fucking know why."

She's right, and I'm hedging because I don't want her to go.

"It's not safe." I try that tack next, even though I know it won't stop her. She's losing her mind being so close to me and not having me. I'm right there with her.

"I don't care," she retorts. "I have to go."

"Don't leave," I press. I mean don't leave tonight, and don't leave ever.

Cherry sighs and pinches the bridge of her nose before looking at me, surprising gray eyes full of anger and a heaping dose of sadness. "I'm going to ask you one more time," she snaps.

Standing upright, I step back and close the door gently, pressing to make sure it shuts all the way. And then I watch her grit her jaw and drive off into the dark, quiet night.

Forty minutes later, I watch from the shadows of the road as Cherry pulls into the parking lot of the Moonlight, a titty bar on the outskirts of town. I drove like a bat out of hell to get here before her and make sure she arrived alright.

I've argued with Cherry till I'm blue in the face about how fucking dangerous it is to come out here given what's going on with Declan. But my fierce mate doesn't care. She wants to reclaim this hobby she loves, and she's planning to leave anyhow.

According to her, the Moonlight remains neutral territory because the big alpha who owns this place is a force to be reckoned with, and he doesn't put up with bullshit.

I hope that's true, but I find it hard to believe. Titan's bar, Teddy's, was Switzerland once upon a time too, and we see how well that worked out.

Pulling my truck into the other side of the parking lot, I listen for Cherry as she approaches the back door and heads into the bar. I'm thankful my hearing is so damn good, because every footstep reaches my ears, along with every damn person in the bar and their conversation.

I head to the front door, not bothering to try to make myself appear smaller. I'm seven and a half feet tall at this point. There's no hiding my being an alpha.

As I approach, I notice a big alpha out front. He's older, maybe early fifties with dark hair slicked back as he smokes a cigar out front. Ah. This must be the owner I've overheard Cherry talk about.

He eyes me as I stop in front of the door, dark eyes looking me up and down as he pulls to a stand. I've got a whole head of height on him, but he's powerful. I can sense that in the way he stands easily and looks at me.

"What pack are you from?" he asks in a gruff, smoky voice.

"The one that doesn't suck," I bark back.

He chuckles and points to the bar. "I'm not shitting you when I tell you the bar is a neutral place. Don't bring your bullshit here. We're all here to have a good time. You'll find alphas and normals mixing here, and that's fine with me too. I won't hesitate to throw you out."

I grin. I'd love to see him try.

He gives me a wry look and whistles once, and a second alpha ducks out of the bar to stand in front of the door. He's so fucking big, I can't even see the doorway behind him. He's not as tall as me, but twice as goddamn wide.

The owner looks at me with a grin. "This is Marv. Marv's an asshole with a temper. I've seen him beat pack alphas to a pulp. You don't want to piss Marv off."

I nod and look at him. "Don't piss Marv off. Got it. And who are you then?"

"Name's Hart. We're the only two who matter here. Hart and Marv. Don't piss *either* of us off, and you'll be fine."

Grinning, I look around Marv and point toward the inside of the bar. "Any other rules I need to know about?"

Marv grins. "Don't touch the girls unless they invite it. Don't forget to tip. Be a goddamn gentleman. That about sums it up."

Don't touch the girls unless they invite it. I bristle when I think about Cherry asking someone to touch her. Holding back a growl, I nod, ducking through the front door when Marv steps aside for me.

It's surprisingly clean and well organized inside the bar. In my mind, I've been thinking of the Moonlight as a titty bar, and it is, but it's nicer than I imagined. There's a stage along the back wall with three offshoots that stick out into the room. Disco balls along the ceiling scatter fragments of color over the dancers and the crowd. It's predominantly men, but there are a few normal women here too.

For a moment, a sense of normalcy hits me. None of these people are aware of the bullshit we went through earlier to save lives. We narrowly missed a fight, but deep in my chest, I know it's coming. There's a deep sense that what happened with Declan was easy—too easy—and I'm waiting for the other shoe to drop.

Heading for the bar, I order a beer and sit in the backmost corner, waiting. I haven't decided yet if I want Cherry to see me, but I hear her getting ready in the back. She's on in two songs.

It's hard for me to tune out the deep, throbbing beats of the seductive music the girls dance to. Two thin women slide up and down poles suggestively, waggling their asses for the leering crowd.

I'm not interested in any of that. Heat builds in my core when I think about my mate wrapping her thick thighs around the pole, gyrating her hips, unleashing her enormous breasts and letting them sway.

Goddamn, I'm hard as a rock thinking about her stripping. I always knew she stripped in college and took pole dancing classes for years. Still, I have no frame of reference. I don't know what Cherry's capable of. Something about that has anticipation writhing in my stomach like a pit of snakes.

Fuck. Kill. Hurt.

The voices in my head decide to chime in, something I've noticed they do when my emotions run high, like when I held Abigail. I've got to hold it together long enough to watch Cherry dance, and then I'll head off into the woods for an hour to rip some trees down. Violence is the only thing that calms the voices temporarily. Trees are a safe bet. Being far away from everyone is a safe bet too.

A new song comes on, the beats slower, deeper as smoke spills out onto the stage. A curtain opens in the back, and a red light comes on, illuminating a figure from behind.

It's her.

I shove myself as far back into the shadows of the bar as I can, watching as the beats pick up the pace. A pink disco ball descends from the ceiling, lights flashing as the beams play across her beautiful figure.

A spotlight lands on her face, and she smirks seductively at the crowd, sending my dick leaping in my pants. My throat goes dry as she eye-fucks every goddamn person in the room, sauntering on stage as the disco ball sends flashes of color across her curves.

Huge breasts practically spill out over a red lace bra. Her thick thighs are so goddamn luscious like this, highlighted by the refracted color from the ball.

She approaches the pole at the end of the walkway and hops nimbly up onto it, gripping it with her legs as she shifts backward, arms stretched wide. The pole begins to spin, and she hovers out over the audience, her hips undulating to the beat of the music as the viewers stuff dollar bills in her panties and the belt around one thigh.

My mate is in her element; that much is clear.

She works the pole like a goddamn expert, sultry and seductive, and not a soul in the room is immune to her.

I barely notice the shadow hovering at my side until Hart claps me on the shoulder. "I've seen that look on other alphas' faces before. Remember not to touch when you ask for a private show."

Private show?

"What the fuck are you talking about?" I bark out as I whirl on the barstool to face him.

Hart grins at me. "You were gonna find me and ask for a private show with her. I can tell. Marv and I made a bet; looks like I'm about to win it. Tell me I'm wrong."

A private. Fucking. Show.

"I want it," I blurt out as his grin broadens.

"Knew you would. It's $300, but she'll dance for you for a solid fifteen minutes."

Fuck me, I didn't bring a credit card, and I don't have $300 in cash on me. My eyes flick over to my mate again as she swirls around the bar. I get a sudden vision of asking Stone for $300 for a lap dance.

"I'll come back tomorrow," I growl, standing as Hart laughs.

"See you later, brother." His gravelly baritone follows me out into the night.

My emotions are as scattered as the light reflecting off the disco balls. The idea of Cherry giving $300 private dances to anyone else makes me want to scream.

Kill. Fuck. Maim. Kill Again.

The voices in my head begin to speak over one another, so fucking loud I put both hands on my temples and hunch just inside the door, begging them to quiet. The desperate need to do something, to hurt someone, fills me so fucking fast, I throw myself out into the darkness. Sprinting around the side of the building, I take off into the woods behind the Moonlight.

I don't know these woods, but I can't focus on anything but dispelling the fury that rockets through my veins.

Kill. Kill. Kill.

I roar into the night as I head into the hills alone.

Always alone. It's better that way...

+++

I bet you thought Julia was getting spit-roasted in that final scene, huh? Well if you want to read that absolute filth, please Sign up for my newsletter at www.annafury.com to access the spicy bonus epilogue where all that (and more) transpires.

Ready to see how Cherry and Asher sexily drive his demons to distraction? Dive into their book, Salvaged Psycho!

books by anna fury

DARK FANTASY SHIFTER OMEGAVERSE

Temple Maze Series

NOIRE | JET | TENEBRIS

DYSTOPIAN OMEGAVERSE

Alpha Compound Series

THE ALPHA AWAKENS | WAKE UP, ALPHA | WIDE AWAKE | SLEEPWALK | AWAKE AT LAST

Northern Rejects Series

ROCK HARD REJECT | HEARTLESS HEATHEN | PRETTY LITTLE SINNER | SALVAGED PSYCHO | BEAUTIFUL BEAST

Scan the QR code or visit www.annafury.com to access all my books, socials, current deals and more!

@annafuryauthor
liinks.co/annafuryauthor

salvaged psycho - synopsis

UNEDITED DRAFT

I'm too broken, too dangerous, too untamed. If I have to push my mate away to save her life, I will, even if it kills me.

ASHER

Finding my fated omega is the best and worst thing that's ever happened to me. The best because she's perfection in every way. The worst because I can't have her no matter how much I want her. I push her away because the demons inside my head claw their way out harder every day. If Cherry stays by my side, she'll pay with her life.

CHERRY

It's bullshit that Asher doesn't trust himself enough to lean into our mating, but I'm done trying to convince him that my trust is enough for both of us. When we decide to give our love a second chance, he picks up a job stripping at the Moonlight with me, making him my newest, sexiest coworker.

We've got bigger problems. War is coming to Ayas and our lives are on the line. Asher's near-limitless power is the key to us winning, if he can figure out how to reliably access it.

Can we banish Asher's demons in time to save not only our pack mates, but our own love as well?

SALVAGED PSYCHO is the fourth book in the Northern Rejects series and features an estranged couple trying desperately to pick up the pieces of their broken mating. There is ALWAYS a HEA in my books...

chapter one

PROLOGUE - CHERRY

My pack alpha, Stone, lays a hand on my shoulder. Concerned chocolate eyes flick down to me before returning to the meat locker door.

"It's not your job to fix him, Cherry Bomb," he reminds me, using the nickname despite the heavy weight of our current situation. I tip up onto my toes to look in the meat locker's circular window.

On the floor inside, a massive alpha sits chained, his teeth gnashing as he looks around the empty room. Asher Chen is the most beautiful man I've ever seen—high, elegant cheekbones frame nearly-black eyes. Dark, long lashes flutter over there as he scowls at the chain connecting him to a drain in the floor. Those eyes dart up when I press closer to the door, watching my breath fog up the glass.

"I'm going in, Stone," I whisper.

"Terrible fucking idea." My pack alpha shakes his head. "The

Alpha Task Force experimented on him for years, Cherry. He's coming off whatever drugs his sister had to use to sedate him. He'll try to hurt you if you go in."

"He won't," I attempt to reassure Stone. One of his perfectly manicured brows travels straight up.

"He *won't*," I press. "I just know it. Plus, I'm a medical professional, and that man is in need."

"Let me call the rest of leadership to be there in case he goes nuts," Stone counters, picking up his walkie and heading out of the basement for signal. He gives me a sharp look. "Do not go in there, Cherry Bomb. I'm serious."

I throw one hand up. "Scout's promise," I lie. The minute Stone disappears around the corner, I open the door quietly and step in.

My whole body heats to a nearly painful point when the alpha on the floor rocks back onto his heels, black eyes meeting mine as his lips part in a lazy, sensual grin. He licks them, fangs appearing at both sides of his mouth, a sure sign his emotions are running high.

"Come closer, little omega," he commands, my body lighting up with fiery need. I work hard to shove it down though. I'm a nurse by trade, until the Awaken virus blew the world up and I got stuck here in Canada where I'm not licensed. These days I work to keep my pack safe and healthy, and I'm actually alright with that.

"Your alpha thinks I'll hurt you," he murmurs, cocking his head to the side. All alphas have incredible senses, but the way he's concentrating makes me wonder just how far away he can hear anyone else.

Steeling my resolve, I cross the room and pop down in front of him, our knees touching. I rest my hands gently on my thighs and look up at him. The lazy smile stills and falls as he leans forward. He tries to bring his hands up to touch me, but the handcuffs prevent that. A soft whine leaves his throat before it morphs into a deep growl.

Slick wets my thighs as his growl increases in intensity. He pushes into my space, and when I let my head fall to the side, inviting him closer, he lets out a chuckle that sends a trill of alarm and want through my system. They're warring sensations that make me feel like a prey being hunted by a predator I desperately want to eat me.

"You're gonna be just fine, sugar," I whisper as he drags his nose up my neck. There's a quick rake of teeth as he moves back down my oversensitized skin, pulling a soft moan from my throat.

"I'm not a puzzle you can just put back together in the correct order," he growls.

"That's true," I confirm when he sits back and stares at me again. "But whatever you do need, I'm here for it, Asher. Any time, anywhere. I'm here."

PROLOGUE - ASHER

My mind fills with visions of chasing someone through a forest, a woman. I hurt her, pulling her to my chest, laughing with a female alpha while we toyed with the unfortunate omega. I watch the omega show surprising power, killing the alpha. Somehow, I don't care that she's dead, though. Or do I?

Is this a memory? Or a vision? Is this my life, or someone else's? I can never tell anymore. My entire existence is coated in a syrupy haze so thick I don't even know what year it is.

Except that now, that fog is lifting little by little, and reality is crashing down on me like a mack truck.

I snarl as I glance around the meat locker, reliving that particular vision again. Who is that woman we hurt? Who is the alpha who died when the omega protected herself? Was I there? Is it a horrible fucking daydream?

Voices outside bring me out of that train of thought. This entire lodge is filled with voices, and I wish I had a trick to make them stop. The unfortunate thing about having incredible hearing like mine is having incredible hearing like mine.

A scent hits me so hard, I resist the urge to double over and thrust my hips against the floor. This scent breaks through the crush in my brain, calling for my teeth. Do I know her? Is she someone I've met at some point?

Have I hurt her, too?

God, I fucking hope not.

It's been a long time since that asshole, Kleiner, brought a woman anywhere near me. I don't hear Kleiner now, though, or any of the other soldiers and scientists who've been my daily existence for—well, I don't know how long it's been. Just that I'm never escaping this place.

I'll never see my sister, Jude again. I'll never hear her laugh or see her eclipse our father's career with her own. God, I'd literally kill to see that.

A deeply masculine voice warns the woman not to come in here, but the moment his footsteps recede, she disobeys and enters the room, shutting the door carefully behind her.

I'm struck dumb at the sheer beauty and sensuality of this omega. The first thing I notice is her shocking red hair; it's the shade of a damn candy apple. It falls in heavy waves around her shoulders. Breasts big enough to spill out of my hands are what I notice next. Thick waist, thick thighs. The only word I could use to describe her is fucking *luscious*.

My mouth waters as I struggle against the chains. Goddamn, I want to touch her.

When I command her to come closer, she does, and even when I remind her that the other voice thinks I'll hurt her, she never gives off that fear scent I'm so accustomed to smelling. I don't know why, though. Why is everyone afraid of me? What have I done?

The omega—because that's certainly what she is, the heady scent of her slick proves it—drops to her knees before me and bares her neck.

Jesus Fucking Christ. I search desperately through my memory banks, wondering if there's ever been a time a woman presented herself to me like this. I lift my hands to stroke that shocking red hair over her shoulder, but I'm chained to the floor. A whine leaves my lips as I lean forward instead, dragging the tip of my nose up her soft, pale skin.

The omega sighs, radiating need and surety.

She's not afraid of me.

It's intoxicating. For some reason, her not being afraid of me is a new sensation.

Everyone is always afraid of me.

But why? Why?

I don't know. Have I hurt people? Are the memories mine?

I drag my lips and tongue back down her neck as goosebumps follow my touch. She's so responsive, so ready to be bedded and taken. She wants me, too.

"I'm not a puzzle you can simply put back together in the correct order," I growl, searching desperately for something to say to this surprising woman on her knees in front of me.

"That's true," she murmurs in a throaty, seductive tone. "But whatever you do need, I'm here for it, Asher. Any time, anywhere. I'm here."

Snarling and footsteps reach my ears as I nip her shoulder, pulling blood to the surface as she huffs out a pant, a small groan my reward.

"They're coming for you, the alpha's pissed," I murmur, my dark eyes meeting hers. They're the color of storm clouds, and I want to get lost in them. Whatever tumultuous insanity rages behind that gaze, I want to dive headfirst and let it batter me until we're sated.

She pulls her shirt up to cover the small bite I gave her. Our eyes meet again.

"Mine," I snarl, irritated at the men who now barrel through the door to drag her away from me.

I'm not dangerous, I want to scream at them as they pile together into the room, pausing when they see her within reach of my fangs and claws. I say nothing though.

Because I am dangerous; I can surmise that much from the way they've got me chained to a meat locker floor. Or they *think* I am, at least.

The omega reaches out and brushes her fingers along my jawline, her pale eyes never leaving mine.

"Remember what I said, alpha," she murmurs low. Behind her, a wall of muscular alphas stand ready to beat me senseless if I hurt her.

But all I can focus on is the stunning, confident omega who rises in front of me. Our eyes meet as she turns.

"Don't give him your back Cherry, for fuck's sake," snarls the alpha, reaching out to grab her by the hand and yank her to him fast.

She squeaks and I roar, pulling up with all my might on the drain in the floor. Metal creaks and breaks as I leap to a stand, snarling at the way he put his hands on her.

"Don't fucking touch her!" I bellow as alphas line up to keep her from me.

She peeks around a big chest and smiles at me, and it's so fucking beautiful I stop to bask in it.

"I'm okay, sugar. We've got a lot of things to catch up on, but I'm going to grab you some dinner, and then I'll be back, alright?"

Dinner, and then she'll return.

I give her a clipped nod before snarling at the line of men standing between me and that fucking scent, that smile, that goddamn body.

They exit the room behind her, ensuring I can't get close to her again, until only one remains—this pack's alpha—Stone.

Dark eyes meet mine as he gives me a cool, assessing gaze.

"Your sister's pack says you've been through hell, alpha, and I don't doubt it, looking at you." He stalks closer until our chests touch, the dominance of a pack alpha slapping me in the face as his fangs descend to mirror mine. "Hear me on this, though," he growls. "If you hurt Cherry in any fucking way at all, I'll put you down myself."

For a long, tense moment, we snarl at one another, but I back down first under the weight of a pack alpha's dominance. Nodding, I turn from him and slump back onto the floor.

I don't want to hurt anybody, and I'm so goddamn tired.

But she said she'd come back, so I sit patiently as the pack alpha leaves.

I'll wait for her.

I'll always wait for her.

about the author

Anna Fury is a North Carolina native, fluent in snark and sarcasm, tiki decor, and an aficionado of phallic plants. Visit her on Instagram for a glimpse of the sexiest wiener wallpaper you've ever seen. #ifyouknowyouknow

She writes any time she has a free minute—walking the dog, in the shower, ON THE TOILET. The voices in her head wait for no one. When she's not furiously hen-pecking at her computer, she loves to hike and bike and get out in nature.

She currently lives in Raleigh, North Carolina, with her Mr. Right, a tiny tornado, and a lovely old dog. Anna LOVES to connect with readers, so visit her on social or email her at author@annafury.com.

Made in the USA
Columbia, SC
08 April 2023

14724880R10239